The Death Bond Conspiracy

By P.A. Gillis

This is a work of fiction. All the characters and events portrayed in this novel are either fictitious or used fictitiously.

THE DEATH BOND CONSPIRACY

Copyright © 2009 by P.A. Gillis
Cover Art Copyright © 2009 by P.A. Gillis

All rights reserved, including the right to reproduce this book, or portions thereof, in any form.

PACorkyGillis.com

Library of Congress Cataloging-in-Publication Data

Gillis, P.A.

First Edition: January 2009

Printed in the United States of America

ISBN: 978-0-9821415-1-9

Acknowledgments

The idea for *The Death Bond Conspiracy* came to me five years before I began writing. I shared the idea with my long-time friend and confidant, Kerry Pulliam, Chartered Financial Consultant, who said, "You've got to write this story." He then forgot about our discussion until it resurfaced in the form of a complete outline four years later. Kerry, thanks for all that natural brainwork and continued friendship.

Elaine and Hubert McGaughey, thanks for the Singer Island retreat to focus on the work.

Dave Williams, instructor and friend, thanks for keeping me in the air, a safe and humble pilot.

Tom Lett and Don Ball for the generous tours of Donamire Farm.

Jimmy Nash, my best buddy, your optimism in people and life is unmatched.

Thanks to My Family:

My late brother-in-law, James Price, for the cover art. Your talent lives on.

My son, Nick, for technical and art support, and the heartfelt attitude that I am a great dad.

My daughter, Taylor, soon to be Taylor Gillis Clement...you are simply the best! I love you.

And my beautiful bride, Nancy. Your faith, love and friendship are cherished beyond words.

My most sincere thanks to
Elizabeth Atkins.
Your tireless efforts and optimism are amazing.
There is no book without you.

Dedicated to my parents

Betty and Bob Gillis

1. Diamond Lagoon, Florida

I'm in danger. The thought flashed like a neon sign in her mind as Lainey Gay sunk into the plush cocoon of Egyptian cotton sheets and pillows on her queen-sized bed. Even the sunset looked ominous. Framed by the enormous picture window at the foot of her bed, the sky glowed with fiery shades of red and orange as the sunset danced like tiny flames on the dark Atlantic. She shivered. The hairs on the back of her neck bristled against the fluffy pillow.

"Are you alright, Mrs. Gay?" asked the maid, Bianca. Concern glowed in the girl's dark eyes as she bent to place the serving tray over Lainey's lap. "Are you cold?"

Lainey shook her head. "Bad feeling, that's all. You know, Harold died six months ago today."

"You are sad," Bianca said, lifting a silver teapot to pour her nighttime ritual of aromatic cinnamon brew into a china cup. "Your cookies," she said, lifting a doily to reveal a plate of warm gingersnaps, "and sleep, will make you feel better for your birthday party."

The eerie feeling intensified as Lainey watched the girl's long dark ponytail sway against her white uniform. Bianca dropped two sugar cubes into the tea.

"Seventy-eight," Lainey said. Her body trembled as if she'd just had a bad dream and was trying to decipher what it meant. But all that came to mind was a nameless, faceless feeling of bad. Evil. Like a ghost. Or that gut feeling she'd had years ago that said *don't turn down that street*, and she later learned that a storm had washed out a bridge on that street, drowning a whole family in their car.

But right now, Lainey was in the safest place—her home—on some of the world's most exclusive real estate. Inside this gated golf community called the Diamond Lagoon Club, her mansion had a high-tech security system. And the Club conducted extensive background checks on the staff, including landscaping crews and maids like Bianca, who had worked here for five years.

I have nothing to worry about. Yes, she missed Harold. But in two days the kids would be here for their February break from work and school back in New Jersey. And Lainey never had more fun than when the three grandkids were romping through this 10,000-square-foot house or splashing out back in the pool. What did she have to worry about? Spending the winter season here in South Florida, the rest of the year back home near the kids...

My life is a dream by any standard. But this feeling...

Bianca reached to the nightstand and handed over a novel. "This will cheer you up. Romance."

Harold's face appeared in her mind. Sadness intensified the eerie sensation. "I can only dream. I'm too old—"

"More healthy than me!" Bianca said. "I don't have the energy to play tennis every morning like you. And golf, all the parties. No medications! You are amazing, Mrs. Gay. I want to be like you someday."

The carefree glow on Bianca's dewy face made Lainey feel a little better.

"I would kill to live in a house like this," Bianca said. "My whole apartment is smaller than this bedroom."

"Marry well," Lainey said, wishing Harold was here to hold her until this feeling subsided. "Every woman needs a good marriage. With a man who's smart with money."

"I like to make my own money," Bianca said. "Remember, you're baking cookies tomorrow for the grandchildren."

"The special chocolate," Lainey said, "Did you get it?"

Bianca smiled. "Of course, Mrs. Gay. Just relax. The tea has chamomile. Very soothing. You'll sleep better than ever."

The maid adjusted the pillows, then left the room, closing the door behind her. Alone, Lainey shivered with that inexplicably creepy feeling. She sipped the tea, savoring the flavor, as she opened the novel. But with every sip, the words blurred on the pages and the sky darkened.

With the lamps still on, she sunk into the pillows and closed her eyes. Sleep would soothe her. Yes, in the morning, she'd be back to her usual happy mood.

But Lainey would never wake up. And no one would ever question why. Her death certificate would read "Death from Unexplained Natural Causes."

Exactly as they wanted.

2. Indianapolis Metropolitan Airport, Indiana KUMP

Hunter Knightly strode faster across the wind-whipped tarmac, hoping to shake off the vague sense of angst that lately had become his constant companion. For now, he had only one remedy: that blue and white beauty straight ahead. That first glimpse of his airplane always set his heart to beating a little faster, whether he'd been away for an hour or a week. Now, he breathed harder, too. The February chill and afternoon sunshine conspired to show the evidence of his excitement—silvery vapors billowing from his mouth.

But as he bounded toward his sleek personal jet, a pang of dread slithered through his gut. Going home to face Meredith's onslaught of attitude made him wish that time could just stand still, as soon as he was up there in the sky.

Plus, the run-of-the-mill claim that had brought him here to Indianapolis was yet another reminder that his work was getting boring. Stale. Mind-numbing.

How had he gone from stalking bad guys in exotic jungles around the world, to sitting in a Midwestern family's living room, seeking clues about who was at fault for their insurance claim for an auto accident?

All horses can run fast, Son, but the question is whether they want to. His father's thick Kentucky accent boomed in his head, followed by Hunter's own life-long fear: "I can never be good enough to please him."

The deafening roar of a plane taking off made Hunter break into a jog. He didn't feel his brown Timberlands hitting the asphalt. Didn't feel the wind bite into his clean-shaven face. Didn't care that this navy blue pea coat was not buttoned.

Because he couldn't climb on and ride his plane soon enough. In just a few minutes, his whole body would tingle with the euphoria of being up in the air, free as a bird. Yeah, up there in the clear blue sky, where nothin' mattered but the incomparable thrill of the moment. Plus, the tremendous focus required by the multitude of aviation tasks required to maintain flight focused every synapse in his brain on the euphoria of flying.

Sweat slicked his palms. His body surged with the kind of subtle anxiety that kept every pilot on his game. His heartbeat pounded in his ears. As he thought about the luscious pressure against his body during take-off, he had to stop himself from grinning. He didn't want to look like a damn fool in front of a half-dozen pilots as they walked to and from the small planes parked this side of his little rocket. A chuckle, however, did escape Hunter's mouth.

Before his quick trip this morning, he swam laps at the health club for a full 40 minutes, barely raising his heart rate. It still beat just 47 times per minute—as slow and strong as a quarter-century ago when he was a Navy SEAL. But now it was racing with excitement.

"You are one lucky guy," said a silver-haired man, jogging to catch up beside Hunter. "Saw 'ya land this mornin'. Had to check my eyes. A Very Light Jet here at Indi Metro? Thought they were the stuff of fancy magazines and flashy websites."

Despite the man's friendly demeanor and Kentucky accent, Hunter kept jogging. In the pocket of his navy blue pea coat, he fingered the cold, hard promise of protection. Never knew when some hot-head with an ancient grudge might come back with a vengeance. Even in broad daylight in the Hoosier state.

"Can I take a look inside?" the man asked eagerly. He wore khaki pants, Rockports and a bomber jacket. Mid-60s, clean-cut, wholesome face. Probably a semi-retired suburban grandfather who owned a business and flew his own plane. Or at least posing as such.

The man pointed toward a 1977 white twin engine Piper Seneca with turquoise and red stripes. "There's mine. I'll be like you in my next life." The guy smiled and gave off the fellowship kind of vibe that flowed naturally between pilots. "I'd love to look at your plane."

Hunter walked faster. "I usually don't let other men get inside my Baby Doll."

The man laughed, wheezing a little as he jogged to keep up. "You don't remember me, Hunter, but I bought a racehorse from your daddy years ago. You were so busy pullin' your little sister's pigtails—" the man chuckled "—your nanny tackled the both of you in a stall."

Hunter cast a *who-the-hell-are-you?* look at this guy.

"I'm tellin' you, your momma was fit to be tied when she came back from ridin' and saw you two covered in hay. I'll never forget. She climbed down off that beautiful chestnut mare a' hers, Chessie Belle—"

Hunter stopped. "You're gettin' too close for comfort."

"Bradley Williams. Went to school with your dad at the University of Kentucky." He stopped moving, but kept laughing. "'Silkie!' your momma scolded. 'You mess with your sister one more time, I'll have your little hide!'"

Hunter pulled his BlackBerry Storm from its leather pouch on his belt. He pushed a single button.

"You back from Indi already, Son?" His father's gruff voice shot into the frigid air.

"Dad, do you know a guy from UK, Bradley Williams?"

"'Course ah do. Sold him a winner. BlackJack, remember? Left every other horse in the dust at the Dreamer's Cup? Oh, you were just a boy. Why? You run into that rascal?"

"Give me a test question," Hunter said. "Something only you would know."

"Son, this ain't no Navy SEAL mission. That's mah buddy."

"Test question." Hunter activated the speakerphone.

"Okay," his father said, "ask him what the hell color a' panties his future bride was wearin' when we raided the girls dormitory freshman year."

The man bellowed with laughter. "None!"

"Well shit the bed! Son, let me talk to that rascal!"

Hunter handed his phone to the man. Over the speakerphone, the older men caught up about wives, kids, and Mr. Williams' career in luxury real estate. The man laughed until he wheezed, then wrote down Dad's phone number. "Ah promise to come down there for a visit," he said.

Hunter took the phone and silenced the speaker. His father barked, "Now son, don't you give mah friend the Goddamned third degree. He ain't an undercover spy stalkin' you in Indiana on your insurance investigation. If you're walkin' around lookin' for that kinda deception an' intrigue, it's time you call up your friends at the Navy."

His father's disapproving tone reminded Hunter why he'd become a SEAL in the first place: rebellion. He'd become a soldier instead of attending college, where most of his classmates at Episcopal High School had gone to top off their nearly $100,000 boarding school educations for ninth through twelfth grade.

"You wouldn't be going through your little season of discontent," his father scolded, "if you'd had the sense to go straight to college, then take the reins here at Knightly Farms. Hell, in my day, we had to enlist. Korea, Japan, Germany. All hell was breakin' loose. Wasn't a choice. So I give you every opportunity in the world, a lifestyle that some guys would kill for, and you run off on your little Navy adventure with—"

"Dad, I need to fly on home," Hunter said, reducing the volume so that Mr. Williams could not hear Dad's weekly rant.

"Go home? Why? To get bitched out? Ya chose a wife who gives you the blues. Ya chose insurance over one of the best horse farms in Kentucky. Ya chose that cracker box house over the palace I built for 'ya. Why the hell wouldn't you sing the blues—"

Dad's words seemed to shoot through the phone and slap Hunter's cheeks.

"I worked my whole life to provide a future for you and your family." There, a jab about no grandkids. Why couldn't Dad just be happy that Heather had given him a grandson and a granddaughter? Hunter's sister and her family even lived on Knightly Farms, and her horse-loving husband helped with the business. "I'll tell you one thing, Son. When they said 'Unbridled Spirit' for the state of Kentucky, somebody had you in mind. Where you get the gumption—"

"Dad—"

"One day you'll wake up, Son, and realize I was right."

"Gotta go, Dad." The truth was, Hunter loved being his own boss. His job gave him freedom. Sure, he needed some excitement. Some adventure. He'd find it.

And I'll live my life however the hell I want to.

3. Miami, Florida

"My wife is gonna kill me," Lukas Witherspoon griped to the valet who pulled his Mercedes sedan in front of the Club. "Late to my own anniversary party."

The 80-year-old had lost track of time, celebrating with 18 holes of golf and a round of drinks at the Club. Now, he was off to the cruise that Lois had spent a whole year planning. The problem was, it was almost sunset. And Lukas hated driving at dusk. It was so hard to see. Why had he been such an idiot, paying no attention to time in there?

His tires screeched as he pulled away from the Club. Luckily, the marina was just a short drive away.

"It's party time!" a rap singer blasted through the speakers. "It's party time!" Lukas chuckled. That young valet had put the stereo on a hip-hop station, like his grandkids listened to back up on Long Island. He turned it down, veering onto the main road. It was so dark already—

Lukas accelerated. As he followed the curving boulevard near the beach, the headlights from oncoming traffic were so bright. Blinding. Until all Lukas saw was black.

Sirens blared in the distance. Far, far away. Then, silence.

4. Indianapolis, Indiana KUMP

Hunter couldn't wait to get on his airplane and fly away. It was almost dark, and he wanted to get home to watch his former classmate—now the Vice President—give her first speech tonight on television. But he'd promised Mr. Williams a look at his plane.

"I'll show you my airplane if you promise one thing."

"What's that?" the man asked, still smiling from his trip down memory lane with Hunter's dad.

"Don't tell anybody my momma calls me Silkie," Hunter said playfully. "My tough guy image doesn't need that. When I was a baby, she wrapped me in the Knightly Farms silks before the Derby, for good luck. The horse that wore that particular silk kicked ass and took more pictures in the winner's circle than Big Brown."

"Your secret's safe with me," Mr. Willams said.

"Deal," Hunter said, as they stopped at the perfect curve of the plane's nose. The older man whistled.

Hunter's heart raced.

"It looks seamless," Mr. Williams said, admiring the sleekness of the body, wings and tail. Dusky sunlight glowed on the windshield, windows on the two pilots' doors and passenger area. An oval tube stretched over the pilot's side wing, providing air for the single jet engine intake.

"Love your custom paint job," Mr. Williams said, admiring the cobalt blue body with white stripes and the face of the school's Wildcat mascot painted near the tail number 137HJ. "UK Wildcats rule the sky!"

"You're lookin' at my Christmas present to myself," Hunter said. "I love her to death, but this Baby Doll delivered the Motherlode of Matrimonial Discord at my house."

The man laughed. "Mah wife's still jealous, an' I been flyin' for long as you been breathin', what, 40 years?"

"I'm 44," Hunter said.

"Old enough to know that nothin'," Mr. Williams said, absolutely nothin', can compare to the thrill of flyin'. Nothin' that you can do by yourself, anyway."

Hunter smiled as he opened the pilot's door. A small stairwell unfolded; he climbed up and in. The plush leather seat fit his body like a glove; he inhaled the scent of new carpet and leather, mixed with the slightest hint of Jet A fuel in the airport air.

"You should know, Mr. Williams, if I'm my father's son, then I don't do anything half-way," Hunter said. "So if I'm gonna show you my airplane, I'm gonna show you my airplane. Get in, sir." Hunter pushed a button that opened the co-pilot's door.

"I can do everything with the touch of a button," Hunter said as the doors closed and the engine hummed. "This avionics suite is custom-built with absolutely the latest in avionic technology. Got some bells and whistles that you wouldn't b'lieve." He pushed a button that made the three flat-screen glass panels across the front of the cockpit light up like Christmas.

A sultry female voice said, "Welcome Hunter Knightly. Checking all systems for flight."

"Sweet mother of God," Mr. Williams exclaimed as the plane vibrated. "I have truly died and gone to heaven."

"She talks to me when I fly. Tells me everything I need to know." Hunter pointed to the roof. "Even got a whole airplane ballistic parachute system."

"I saw that on the news," the man said, "A glider pull cord wrapped around that French pilot's propeller above some mountains. He pulled that lever and the parachute made the whole plane float to safety. Smartest thing they ever invented. As long as you don't pull that lever too soon!"

"You should get one," Hunter said, pointing to the flatscreen panels across the front of the cockpit. "This here's my instrument approach panel, overlayed with glide slope guidance, GPS information, GPS with weather and TCAS Traffic Avoidance and back-up co-pilot MFD."

"You use your plane for work?" the man asked.

"My excuse to fly," Hunter said, typing into a keypad that sat on top of a black keyboard between the co-pilot seats. "And my FADEC sure takes all the work out of it."

Mr. Williams chuckled. "First time I heard that term, FAY-deck, I didn't know what it meant."

"Full Authority Digital Engine Control," Hunter said. "It means I don't have to do a thing to fly this baby, except push a couple buttons. Just like those big commercial planes, with their 'auto land.' Hard to believe, but it actually navigates and can land the plane for them!"

"I was just readin' an article about how UPS does all its shippin' that way, no matter that Mother Nature's got on her mind that day," Mr. Williams said. "Flip on the FADEC, it controls your direction, altitude, speed, flaps, engine power; all the way to a full stop on the runway. Whether you got zero visibility or skies clear as crystal."

Hunter typed in the four-letter codes—KUMP and KLEX—for the airports in Indianapolis and Lexington. "Just type in my trip data, and it programs the plane to fly to my destination. Don't really have to do much after that."

Hunter laughed. "I heard a guy say we've all become 'system operators,' not pilots, with all this technology. But not me. I keep an eye on everything, all the time, since this baby's really still near experimental."

Then, on the 20-inch square center screen that was his Garmin G1000 navigation system, there flashed the map of Indiana, Ohio and Kentucky, glowing neon green against black. A thick magenta line extended from

Indianapolis to Lexington, and a tiny gray airplane hovered at the starting point.

"I thought I was onto somethin' when I got a GPS in my car," Mr. Williams said. "But this takes all the guesswork outta flyin'. Just follow the line."

"Still have to learn to trust your instruments," Hunter said. "Everything becomes a series of cross-hairs on a satellite grid of the Earth. Nothin' short of amazing. Unless the U.S. military switches off those GPS satellites for government security."

"Feels like a rocket, almost a Lear jet type feel," Mr. Williams said.

"If it takes you an hour to fly somewhere," Hunter said, "it takes me 10 minutes. That's why some folks call this baby 'The Rocket.' Fastest personal jet in the world."

"Single engine, Pratt & Whitney JT-15-5," Hunter said. "Listen to her purr. Got 3,190 pounds of thrust fires. Can cruise at 472 kts, or as I like to say, mach .7."

The man's face lit up. "Don't tell me this is that sucker I read about, that can climb at almost 8,000 feet a minute?"

"You're sittin' in her," Hunter said. "In all her 36-foot-wingspan glory."

The man turned around and looked back at the plush beige leather seats in the passenger area.

"Seats five," Hunter said. "Club seating makes her look roomier than she really is."

"You got a son to share all this with?" Mr. Williams asked.

"No, sir. *The Life and Times of Hunter Knightly* skips the chapters with childbirth, baby bottles and little league. Speaking of, I'd better get home, Mr. Williams."

Hunter pushed a button, opening the doors. Mr. Williams handed him a business card. "I mostly do real estate consulting these days. Remember, it's all about location, location, location! If I can ever return a favor, just call."

"Will do, sir."

A few minutes later, Hunter snapped his seatbelt and donned his headset. He flipped the master switch and reignited the burner. He ran up the turbine engines, then scanned the electronic monitors. He had 1,895 pounds of Jet A fuel in his tank.

"Checking all systems," the computerized female voice said. "Activating de-icing mechanisms. All systems go."

Hunter announced his type of plane, then his tail number, which was his SEAL recruit number 137 and his initials, H.K., which he said as "Hotel Kilo." In pilot lingo, just like in law enforcement, every letter had a corresponding word — such as C for Charlie — to guarantee comprehension over the airwaves between the cockpit and the control tower.

"Maverick 1-3-7 Hotel Kilo preparing for take-off," Hunter said into the tiny black microphone attached to his headset. His voice was muffled by the ANR padded headset that cupped his ears with soft leather. Nothing like Active Noise Reduction headsets, although his cockpit was pretty quiet compared to other planes.

"This is Indianapolis clearance, Maverick 1-3-7 Hotel Kilo," the control tower operator said. "You're clear, runway three frequency change approved."

Hunter went through his flight checklist, which was attached to the small keyboard between the seats. After checking it twice, he taxied to the end of the runway. There, he ran another check of all the systems.

Hunter relished the sight of that asphalt stretching before him with a yellow dotted line down the middle. It was his own personal wide-open road that would take him as close to heaven as a man could get while still alive and alone.

"Maverick 1-3-7 Hotel Kilo departing, runway three. Downwind departure to the southeast."

"Cessna 45 Echo turning left base for runway three."

Hunter pushed the handle forward, blowin' up the gear.

The plane shot forward, faster, faster...

He would be out of the Cessna's way before he could turn "final for three." In one minute, he could be 8,000 feet above the earth. He could climb out at 250 kts if he wanted. And shoot all the way up to 41,000 feet. He'd tried her out, a couple times, taking her all the way up to 30,001 feet, going the full climb 250 kts.

But this quick return trip to Lexington didn't require all that. As he accelerated along the runway, those dotted yellow lines disappeared faster and faster under his plane, and the runway in front of him narrowed. The lines blurred into one.

Whoosh! In one floaty moment... 96 knots... lift off!

Hunter savored the pressure against his chest, the entire length of his six-feet, two-inches of sculpted muscle, as the force of his single engine thrust his 5600 pounds of airplane up toward the sky.

"Woo-hoo!" he exclaimed. "Do your thing, Baby Doll!"

The sultry, computerized female voice answered, "You are now flying at 3,556 feet and climbing. Your speed is 215 knots. All systems are 'in the green.' Bearing is 45 degrees."

Yes... this was the feeling that he had anticipated back on the tarmac. That familiar rush of excitement jolted through him as the plane sliced through the sky. The humming vibration of the single jet engine beneath him, and the visual of magenta, lime and orange graphics on the high-tech panels before him, left no doubt that he had achieved aviation Nirvana.

Hunter had just one word for the thrill of piloting his Maverick SoloJet between the snow-covered earth and the bright blue sky: *fly-gasm*.

5. Miami, Florida

In an orange Corvette, John-John cruised past a yellow dump truck that had been pulling out of a beachside construction site. But the truck wasn't moving. Because crunched up under its giant black wheels was the anniversary boy's Mercedes.

"Da's wha's up," he said, nodding as the deep bass beat of a rap song vibrated through his 28-year-old body.

John-John would have to tell Freddie, that special clear coating on the inside of a dude's windshield was the shit! Rub a little a' that on while these rich m'uh fuckas be inside all they fancy clubs—*didn't they know, leavin' they ride in valet parking was the easiest way for a thug like me to mess wit' they shit?*—and *bam!* First sign of oncoming traffic, them headlights hit that coating, and that dude be blinder than a mug.

And John-John was five K richer. Add that to the slip-and-fall he'd engineered earlier today on an old bitch's twentieth floor balcony... and the food poisoning he'd served up at a restaurant, and John-John was bankin' a sweet 15-grand. Not bad for a Monday in February. Especially for a ninth grade dropout who was the only dude in his family who had a job in this fucked up economy.

"Business be boomin'!"

He imitated the voices he'd heard through the gumdrop-sized microphone that his boy had planted in the Benz at the valet. John-John imitated the wife's voice:

"Sorry, Lois, no party tonight for Lukas. There's been a little ax-c-dent."

6. Lexington, Kentucky

As Hunter Knightly completed push-up number 200, a strong-from-the-inside-out-sensation burned away his bad feelings. He dreaded the moment that Meredith would come home from work tonight. He wanted to watch the Vice President in peace, without being nagged. Plus, his father's scolding kept replaying in his head. And he was just plain bored.

Need to do 200 more push-ups to clear my mind... Inhaling as his face lowered to the hardwood floor, exhaling as he pushed up, all that oxygen in his brain launched his thoughts into super-sonic speed. The rush was as close to flyin' as he could get here on the floor of his family room. And he'd already had his fix today with that trip to Indiana.

"Two-oh-five," he said raspily, his accent making the "five" sound like "faaahhhve." So what if he was in his suburban hometown in the middle of horse country. He was still a stallion, as fit in brain and body as he'd been as a SEAL.

Right now the only threat he faced was his bride, coming home with a mouthful of attitude, yakkin' at him about always working, always working out, always flyin' off someplace, not spending enough time with her or caring about "society." Meredith's latest campaign was to use her Southern Bell charms to coerce him into taking her to the Lexington Ball out at Donamire Farm. But being around all those rich muckitty-mucks was about the last thing Hunter wanted to do. Raised up in that, didn't want anything to do with it now. Had to find a reason to be out of town, way out of town, when that event rolled around. But since the cause was admirable, he'd send a check.

"Two-oh-eight," Hunter groaned, not with pain but with pleasure. Pushing himself like this was the opposite of that rich boy life of leisure. He could have it easy if he wanted. But he craved adventure. Stimulation. Freedom.

Nobody can do your push-ups for you. Commander Buck's hard voice rang in his brain, flashing him back to sleepless Hell Week, the culmination of the 24-week Basic Underwater Demolition/SEAL (BUD/S) selection at the Naval Special Warfare Center at the Naval Amphibious Base on Coronado near San Diego.

There, he and the other BUD recruits did more push-ups with 100-pound backpacks than anybody could count. That, plus four weeks of Cold Weather Survival Training at Kodiak, Alaska, had sure given Hunter the adventure he'd sought by signing up to be a bad-ass on Sea, Air and Land, straight out of high school in 1983. And the thrill of rescuing the *Achille Lauro* passenger liner from Palestinian terrorists near Egypt in October 1985, had been the icing on the cake for Hunter's nearly five years of service as a SEAL.

But it was during his grueling, year-long training that Hunter had realized, a guy could buy all the gym equipment in the world, but all he really needed was his own body weight and the ground to sculpt the strongest muscles. *Every man has to carry his own body weight,* Commander Buck always said.

And it was during those horrific hours of sloshing through icy, black water at 3 a.m. in full fatigues, weighted down with gear, then cramming his whole face into cold mud until the Commander said he could get up, that Hunter discovered whom he was. A real man. A survivor. A winner.

"Two-10," Hunter grunted, sounding like "two-tin."

I'm on turbo! On the polished pine floor before him sat his laptop computer, logged onto *TheInsuranceGazette.com*. The reporter was interviewing an insurance broker about increasingly popular arrangements called viaticals or life settlements.

Beside his computer was his BlackBerry Storm, which could buzz with a new assignment anytime, so he could fly off across the southeast quadrant of the United States to solve a mystery. His phone also had special security features bestowed on former Navy SEALS. And for every company that contracted him to investigate claims, he set a different ring tone, each recorded right off 137 Hotel Kilo.

Man, ah cain't wait to get to flyin' again.

His trip next week would take him to North Carolina to investigate a small plane crash on a notoriously dangerous landing strip, a mile up in the mountains. Hunter had to pinpoint the cause, so the life insurance company could decide whether to pay or subrogate the claims on the insured. His role was routine, to determine whether any of the claim could be "laid off" on another party, such as an aircraft manufacturer, etc. When the crash happened, he'd seen the report on his flat-screen TV, beside the fireplace, which was now on low volume and showing a documentary on *History TV*. Hunter had also read about that crash in *The NTSB Investigator*; he routinely scoured every edition for details about crashes and how to avoid them. Safety was priority one in his pretty little Maverick SoloJet. Sounded like this one landed too "hot."

But even that trip would not quench this hankering for adventure. Hating that Dad was right, he scrolled through his phone contacts to his SEAL mentor, Commander Joseph Buck.

"Hunter Knightly, you keepin' outta trouble?" Commander Buck boomed jovially through the phone.

"Yes, sir. Callin' to see if you might need my services down there in Florida."

"Spoken like a true Frogman," said the Commander of the 4th Fleet of the U.S. Naval Forces Southern Command (NAVSO), which patrolled the Caribbean, and the waters surrounding Central and South America with Navy ships, aircraft and submarines. "Ready to lead, ready to follow—"

"Never quit," Hunter said the motto in unison with the older man.

"I can hear it in your voice," Commander Buck said, "Civilian life and all that insurance work is borin' you to tears. Even that little airplane isn't excitement enough for you?"

Hunter chuckled. "I think I could enhance your operations on a special mission here or there."

"I'll tell you what, Stallion Six. The world's fiercest terrorist of all time has us jumpin'. You'll see it on the news today—new video from Sheik Sunami il Tabbul. After I implement these new mandates in response to his threat, I'll see what I can do. Can't promise anything, though."

"I appreciate it, Sir," Hunter said. He hated the sound of another terrorist threat. But it presented an adventurous opportunity to serve his country.

Man, I wish I could go now.

7. The Sea Palace Yacht Club, South Beach, Florida

Juan Pantera Diablo was living like a king, surrounded by beautiful women in bikinis, here on his 200-foot yacht, *The Black Panther*. He expected nothing less as he lounged with the women on huge red velvet chairs arranged theatre-style facing the giant flatscreen. All the while, he repeated his mantra in his mind:

I deserve to live like a king and will do anything to maintain my empire.

Those words had gotten him through Hell, and come to fruition once again, during this second chance at the glamorous life that he desired and deserved. Stolen from him once, returned like magic, never to be taken from him again. Ever.

"Turn to channel six," Felecia exclaimed, jumping up in her white crocheted thong. Her tits bounced as she dove over the chair to snatch the silver remote from Blanche.

"Stop your mischief!" Blanche squealed with her sexy British accent. She slapped Felecia on the ass. In response, Felecia climbed on the back of the chair and wrapped her long, tanned legs around Blanche's neck. Her ass cheeks spread; Juan's gaze traced up the white crocheted strip in her crack, then over the two arches around her supple hips. Her long, dark hair danced down her back, with fat curls swishing at her tiny waist.

Juan's dick responded accordingly, as he laid low on the chair, arms outstretched on the plush velvet. With Gigi holding his drink as she balanced her bare ass on his right knee, and Cheyenne in the chair to his left, holding his cigar, Juan only wanted one thing. To see his secret queen live on his enormous TV screen.

"No, Blanche," Felecia teased, running her fingers through Blanche's platinum spiked hair. "Miss America is on channel six. Hurry up! We don't want to miss Tiffany."

"She'll kill us," Gigi snapped, "if she comes back here and we say we missed it, because of you, Blanche!"

"Yeah, Blanche," chimed the six other girls, lounging in varying degrees of nudity. They all turned to Blanche and shouted, "Turn it!"

"Get her, girls," Cheyenne ordered.

Like a litter of playful kittens, they all climbed over the chairs toward the remote in Blanche's hands. The recessed lights spotlighted a stomach here, a titty there, flailing legs as one girl fell over a chair. They became one writhing mass of T & A.

Juan chuckled. This was his life. And he loved every second of it.

He never thought too long or too hard about the work he had to do in return for this privilege. The few times he had, anger had singed his senses in a way, he was sure, that could jeopardize the deal altogether. Power and control were always a prerequisite for The Panther. But in this enterprise, he lacked both.

The pile of women on his yacht—and the Hell he'd escaped just one year ago—inspired him to focus on his work via laptop, cell phone and airplane. He was a virtual CEO, hired to handle this top-secret project called Eldorado. They'd arranged for his hands to stay relatively clean, except when he loaded all those crates of cash onto his plane. Those splinters were so bothersome.

And once he did the work, he had all this time to take these *mamacitas* to the clubs, gourmet restaurants and celebrity parties here on the playground of the world's rich and famous.

Yet another perk was the good fortune of jetting over to his private island. Repossessing his *paradiso* after a 15-year absence was as simple as a single phone call, thanks to his many generous "investments" with Bahamian officials. Today, he was reaping the huge dividends. Knowing what a bad ass The Panther was, they'd preserved the island's pristine privacy of Casuarina Cay for his inevitable return.

Now, Juan's deep, guttural voice cast an immediate silence and stillness over his personal pile of the primest pussy in Miami as he ordered, "Turn to Global News Network. I need to watch the news. Now."

"I love your voice," Gigi leaned back and whispered.

Cheyenne leaned in, too. "I hear Colombian," she said seductively to Gigi, "a hint of French. But such proper English."

Gigi kissed his right cheek; Cheyenne kissed his left cheek. Their hot, full lips on his face, and their perfumy deliciousness made his manliness even harder. They were his top girls, and brought new meaning to the term ménage à trios. The three of them all twisted together had taken Juan to erotic heights higher than he'd ever dreamed.

I deserve to live like a king and will do anything to maintain my empire.

And right now, he needed to watch Her, the girl he'd wanted since his first day in ninth grade at Episcopal High School back near Washington, D.C. With his line of work, he couldn't get anywhere near her squeaky clean image as a national leader. Lucky for him, though, she was coming to him... tonight, live on TV.

"I said turn to GNN," Juan said, reaching back to pull the black satin ribbon from his ponytail. He raked his long fingers through his raven-black, thick, shoulder-length hair. Gigi and Cheyenne played with it as it fell around his shoulders. The other girls retreated from their attack on Blanche, who pointed the remote.

The screen flashed. The blue GNN logo appeared at the bottom of the screen. And Carrie's beautiful face appeared, larger than life, more beautiful than she was even 30 years ago. She had all these bitches beat hands down in the beauty department. These were girls; she was 100 percent hot-blooded woman. And knew what to do with it to get what she wanted. How else would a woman become Vice President of the bastion of white male dominance known as the United States government?

"The speech isn't even on yet," Gigi said. "This is like the preview show or whatever. Do we have to—"

"Quiet," Juan ordered.

"Juan, baby, since when do you give a hoot about the news?" Cheyenne nestled against his shoulder.

Her face mesmerized him as she spoke to a reporter, saying, "Tonight I'm going to announce a way for America to preserve the system that will take care of all of us into our golden years."

I would spend my golden years with you...

Carrie's sultry voice made Juan's six-feet-one-inch of thin brawn sink deeper into the chair. Watching her washed away the sights and sounds of the day's work— flying to Vegas and Palm Springs to orchestrate the K.C. Teams to do what needed to be done. And yesterday, during his meeting in that elegant restaurant in the French Quarter, Juan took his orders and asked no questions to identify the Emperor who controlled the power for his life in Eldorado.

His fingertips traced the soft curves of Gigi's ass on his lap as he thought how grateful he was to this mysterious Emperor who gifted him with this dream life of cash, chicks and flying. That's all he cared about, and this gig had infinity of all three. He didn't know why he was anointed to do this work, or who was calling the shots and footing the huge bill, but he didn't care.

With more international clearance than James Bond and the new Secretary of State, and all the state-of-the-art toys he needed to make it happen, his every cell radiated omnipotence and invincibility. That was what he was born to feel—and when this knowing was all he had in the dark, lonely cell for so many years—it had kept his heart beating. Because even then, Juan had known he would reign again. Bigger, better, bolder than ever.

And here I am.

8. Lexington, Kentucky

Hunter felt a chill as the reporter on *TheInsuranceGazette.com* referred to groups of life settlement policies as "death bonds." He felt cold, despite the sweat soaking his white shorts and tank top emblazoned with the UK Wildcats.

"Quite a controversy is brewing over these increasingly popular arrangements called viaticals or life settlements," the reporter said. "Cynics and critics are referring to a grouping of these policies by using the term 'death bonds.'"

"That's rather morbid," the broker said, "but if you think about it in terms of the AIDS patient, I can see why someone might coin that term. As you know, life settlements became popular back when people started dying of AIDS. Here's how they worked. About half of a patient's life insurance policy would be given to him in cash, to spend on his health care and improve the quality of the last few months of his life."

The reporter asked, "And the insured would sign away all rights of the policy?"

"Yes," the broker said. "In today's world, life settlements are a perfectly legitimate investment for people who no longer need their life insurance policies or can no longer afford the premium."

"Sounds like an invitation for fraud," Hunter grunted as sweat dripped from the tip of his nose onto the floor. Seemed like those greedy insurance guys were always thinking of new ways to sack big bags of cash from the rich folks, coming and going.

The report reminded Hunter of that death claim he denied to Chrisma Corporation back in December for Stony Wilkerson of Connecticut. The 15-million dollar policy had only been in force for 23 months before he died. No policy could be paid before the two-year incontestability period expired. Those probationary 24 months lowered the chance of a person who was suicidal or secretly terminally ill, for example, from signing up for life insurance, then dying soon thereafter, so his family could get the money.

Besides the timing, the Wilkerson case involved clear-cut fraud as well. Someone had forged his signature six times on the application. The blood type on his labs didn't even match his Red Cross donor card blood type. Denying that claim was a no-brainer. No carrier would have paid it.

"Brazen acts of fraud, and the potential for it," the reporter said, "have prompted 12 states to outlaw STOLIs, or Stranger Originated Life Insurance. Take a listen to the Ohio lawmaker driving Ohio House Bill HB404 to limit STOLI use. He's leading a national crusade against life settlements."

The screen showed a lawmaker, in a navy blue suit and green tie, saying, "Viaticals, life settlements, STOLI, IOLI and death bonds, same difference. They invite unscrupulous people to essentially bet on someone's life, and collect a huge jackpot when the person dies. Life insurance is intended to aid families and businesses in the event of the loss of a loved one or key employee."

Hunter never trusted a politician. That guy was probably being paid by somebody to speak out on this. Viaticals had been around for a long time. So had schemes to kill somebody to get their life insurance money. As for the fear factor here, *I don't think so.* It sounded more like paranoid fiction.

Hunter glanced from the computer to the television, where *History TV* showed a smoke-filled room full of British men in white wigs and powdered faces, debating something. The narrator was describing Parliament enacting laws in 1774. Hunter would have to catch that show in its entirety another time.

Because the lawmaker's voice drew Hunter's attention back to the computer. "Abuse of STOLIs does occur," the lawmaker said, "and they invite a rather macabre 'Guido factor' that should send a chill down the spine of every wealthy retiree in America."

The report showed the journalist for *TheInsuranceGazette.com*, who said, "Is that lawmaker making a mountain out of a molehill by calling for a ban on STOLI-type policies?"

The insurance broker shook his head. "Nonsense. I'd bet that poor man is one of those conspiracy theorists who think Apollo 13 was staged, that our own government planned 9-11, and that Washington allows drugs to flow into our country to keep the masses of poor people in a perpetual underclass. Oh, and don't forget that all of Africa was deliberately infected with AIDS." The broker let out a hearty laugh. "The reality is that the insurance industry is so tightly regulated, so meticulously investigated on multiple levels, there's no way such mass corruption could occur. Nonsense! Our industry does an excellent job of policing ourselves."

But it did make sense. Hunter had seen enough schemers try to sucker Dad into shady deals, especially with insurance and other investments, that he knew there was plenty of room for abuse. Heck, that was what Hunter did for a living. He'd unraveled some pretty cockamamie schemes by folks tryin' to connive their way into some dollars.

The reporter let out a cynical laugh. "Come on, Jake. We both know the industry is rife with abuse—"

"Not on the scale that the gentleman in Ohio is describing. I think he should switch careers and become a science fiction filmmaker—"

The more push-ups Hunter did, the more he wanted to do. All this energy roused his libido; if by some miracle, Meredith came home in a good mood, he'd have a real treat for her. Like when they were first married. When was the last time they'd really made a night of passionate lovemaking? Oh yeah, back in October, when the Keeneland Races opened and he took her to that fancy-schmancy dinner with the Who's Who of Lexington. He was only going because Dad wanted him there. Couldn't wait to leave, but that scene was the ultimate aphrodisiac for his bride; she was a 25-year-old pistol all over again that night, all night. But ice-cold, except for short interludes a couple times a week, ever since.

But Hunter was hot right now. Beads of perspiration rolled over the contours of his biceps, zig-zagging between the sandy-blond hairs on his forearms, pooling between the bones on the back of his hand. His fingers fanned the floor, flashing him back to endless hours of treading water, and seeing his SEAL classmates' hands glowing white and waterlogged in the salt-stinging ocean.

Now, he did 10 clapping push-ups, just for the fun of it.

"Hunter Knightly—still a bad-ass at 44!" Unlike all the fat, balding, slouchy guys at his 25-year high school reunion last spring. Those guys were smoking, drinking and eating their way into the grave. Lorraine Lee, the diving champ, had blown up like a hippo. Ron Jones, the master debater, had had so much plastic surgery, his face had taken on a clownish puffiness. Juan Pantera Diablo, their senior class President, had looked half-starved and pale as if he'd been in a cave for 20 years.

Carolyn Snedegar Taylor, however, who had joined Hunter for an early morning run during reunion weekend, was as fit and youthful as ever. Man, did she look good. The daughter of former U.S. President Thomas Taylor, the brunette beauty had stolen Hunter's heart with her first "Hi" back in ninth grade at Episcopal in Virginia. At the reunion, hiding his crush and playing it cool under Meredith's watchful eyes had been torture.

Man, what if I'd married Carrie instead? Bad deal. He'd hate the high profile lifestyle. She'd used the reunion to campaign for Vice President, even having her running mate stop by to rouse the crowd. She probably loved living in a fishbowl as America's first female Vice President. Carrie lived for the spotlight; if Hunter wanted that, he'd be running Knightly Farms and showboating with his winners at horse races across America. Carrie had given him her cell phone number; he'd flirted with the idea of calling her, but never had. Maybe someday.

"This is a pretty serious charge," the reporter said. "How can you laugh when a respectable lawmaker is crusading to ban—"

The insurance broker's laughter mocked the reporter in a way that rubbed Hunter wrong. That slickster wouldn't admit there was room for abuse because he was whistlin' Dixie all the way to the bank, probably making millions off these life settlement transactions himself.

The hum of the garage door opening made Hunter glance past the plump brown leather couches, toward the kitchen door. Dread seeped through him, darkening his euphoric endorphin rush.

Meredith.

9. Palm Springs, California

Barbara Lawrence always loved to take a sauna before hosting one of her famously decadent dinner parties. Nothing was more relaxing for her to cleanse her pores and sweat out the anxiety of having the A-list social group at their French Provincial mansion at the edge of the golf course. Her husband thought she was crazy, wanting a sauna in a house in the middle of a desert.

"It's a sauna outside," he'd grumbled, "why do you need one inside, too?"

"Steam heat," she had said. It was far better than the dry heat of this sun-baked valley. Plus it kept her 71-year-old complexion looking dewy, with her plastic surgeon's help, of course.

Now, Barbara peeled off her sweaty tennis outfit and slipped into the sauna. The kitchen staff was getting everything ready for tonight; the maids were making sure everything was spotless. She would be in and out, ready to supervise the valet team's arrival and welcome the caterers into her gourmet kitchen.

"Mrs. Lawrence," called the young maid, who was as pretty as a Barbie doll with her classic California beach girl looks. She was working her way through college. Now, in her white uniform, she handed over a chilled bottle of water. "Remember the last time you got dehydrated from exercising, then sweating in there." The girl smiled, fingering the crucifix on a silver chain at her neck. "Scared me to death."

"Alison," the older woman said, "you're so sweet. I was going to get water after—"

The girl playfully waved her index finger.

Barbara squeezed the bottle cap and turned it to break the safety seal. She gulped the cool water. "See, Mrs. Lawrence, you were thirsty already."

"Thank you, Alison." As the girl walked away, Barbara felt grateful for such a dedicated staff. Especially since her friends were always singing the blues about how hard it was to get good help.

The redwood door of the sauna, with its glass oval, enabled her to peek in at the heavenly delights of steamy heat that awaited her. Wrapped in a white towel, she stepped inside, water bottle in hand.

"Aahhh," she exhaled, sitting on the hot wood plank. She loved how the sweat literally bubbled from her pores in little mounds of liquid. She admired them all down her arms, on her legs, on the backs of her hands.

The timer on the wall said she'd only been in two minutes, and already she was drenched. Divine! She'd sweat off at least two pounds in here, to feel extra slim in her little black dress tonight. Boy, was she exhausted, after that brisk tennis match with Sharon at the Club.

Barbara laid her head back. The timer would ring, after 10 minutes, letting her know it was time to get up and out of this wonderful heat. It was so relaxing. So sedating...

10. Lexington, Kentucky

Dread quickened Hunter's push-ups as the door leading to the garage burst open. A big bouquet of lilies wrapped in clear, crinkly plastic appeared, framed by Meredith's ironed-straight blond hair and white sheared-mink coat. It extended just above her knees, where her loose black trousers extended down to sharp-pointed black boots that angled toward him in a way that was far more ominous than his commander's combat boots had ever been.

His thoughts scrambled to remember what he had undoubtedly forgotten to do or get ready for. Something that would surely get him bitched out—

"Honey, you reek! Bless your heart," she said with her sing-song voice. "Don't tell me you forgot the Rogers are coming over for wine and appetizers tonight."

Breathing hard, Hunter sucked in a mouthful of her expensive perfume and the scent of tiger lilies. The sweetness tasted sour on his tongue. He coughed.

"Shit the bed, honey, you're so lost in your multimedia He-Man routine," she said, her big blue eyes lobbing icicles down at him. Bitter undertones soured the sweetness in her voice as she said, "You forgot all about poor little Meredith again."

Damn, how could such an ugly attitude come out of such a beautiful face? Even at 39, Meredith reminded him of his sister's porcelain dolls — pouty red mouth, skin smooth as china, cheeks rouged, big blue eyes sucking him in under those long, dark lashes.

She dropped the flowers on the square leather ottoman. Snatched up the remote. Switched off *History TV*. Touched the top of his laptop to close it.

"Now honey, we have exactly 30 minutes," she said, her pointed boots just inches from his left fingertips, "to get you cleaned up and presentable. Hit the shower, soldier."

An acidy sensation burned in Hunter's gut, even though his abs were feeling tight and tingly, thanks to the countless crunches he'd done before the push-ups. As for all that arousal, Meredith's arrival had just splashed a huge bucket of ice on it.

"Up, Mister. Don't you humiliate me by giving southern hospitality a bad name."

Hunter did a one-handed push-up as he used his right hand to flip his laptop back open. He held down the volume key, turning it up, as the insurance broker explained the finer points of life settlements.

Hunter's life, it seemed, had settled in a bad spot in the marriage department. But he was going to hold his ground. He focused on the screen, heaving his body up and down, up and down, heart hammering, lungs pumping. He imagined Commander Buck calling with a mission. Then Hunter could fly away as quickly as his bride was now stomping out of the room, mumbling about his lack of love and social graces.

Man, I can't wait to get back on my airplane and fly the hell outta here.

11. Lexington, Kentucky

Meredith Knightly wanted to burst into tears as she dashed into the kitchen. She seethed as she laid the stems of the flowers on the wooden cutting board, then took a butcher knife to the bottoms. Nothing in her life was turning out the way she wanted. She'd married one of the richest boys in the county, but here she was, living in this little house, going to work every day, staring down the big 4-0.

The knife pressed through the stems. She set a vase in the sink to fill it with water. Her wedding ring glimmered; that should've been her first clue to run. A measly one-carat diamond from a multi-millionaire? Little did she know at the time that this symbol of their eternal bond was setting the standard for his stingy, let's-live-the-simple-life-honey attitude.

The hissing sound of water drowned out the sob that escaped her mouth. Darn, now she'd have to go freshen up her make-up before company. And she damn well didn't want Hunter to see her crying over him.

I couldn't even have babies. If she and Hunter had been able to conceive, she'd be a stay-at-home mother, like so many of her friends, carpooling to soccer games, swim meets and football matches. She'd be fussing over their clothes, their meals, their social activities. Maybe their daughter would even be a cheerleader like she was.

"Hunter!" she shouted over the small kitchen island into the family room, where he was still goin' at it on the floor.

The way he used to go at me. His buff body going up and down, up and down, facing the floor, sent a shiver through her. Boy, what she wouldn't do to revive the spark. Maybe her 39-year-old ovaries still had a chance to bless them with a baby or three.

But no, Superman over there refused to let her try fertility drugs. Even though Sue Ann next door used them and now she and Andy had those adorable twins. Every time Meredith saw her friend pushing that stroller around their cul-de-sac, she wanted to spit bullets. At her own body. At her husband. And at God for depriving her of the chance to do what a woman was supposed to do: birth babies.

She shoved the flowers into the vase. It was Waterford crystal, etched with a frosted maiden and a hunter, received as a wedding gift, almost 16 years ago. Meredith's insides felt like a candle, melting under the hot sadness of her fate. She wished her mother were still alive to console her and say, "Put on a happy face, girl. Nobody wants to be bothered with a Sad Sally."

But her sadness turned to rage. Rage that had been festering for nearly 16 years. Rage that a southern lady was never supposed to show. Rage that shot out of her mouth anyway, with vicious velocity.

"Hunter Allen Knightly, I am warning you!" What did she have to do to get that man's attention? Her skinny heels tapped the floor as she stormed toward him. She crossed her arms, glaring down at his tousled, sandy brown waves. His smooth, suntanned skin on his shoulders— thanks to all those trips to warm climates he took without her in the middle of winter — glistened with sweat as his muscles rippled. His T-shirt clung to his back, outlining the vee-shaped taper down to his slim waist and hips and his shapely behind. Such pretty legs, with just enough soft, light-colored hair to look manly over those long, lean muscles. But his sweat on the floor, and his sneakers that he'd been running all over kingdom come in, made their family room look, feel and smell like a gym.

She put just as much effort into staying slim and keeping those wrinkles from creeping any deeper around her eyes and mouth. But what was the use?

He doesn't even look at me!

"Honey," she drawled with sing-song sweetness to mask the certified nagging bitch voice that she wanted to use. "Do I have to turn into an airplane for you to look at me? Maybe a sleek little V—" she cooed, "L... J?"

He turned his head just enough to train those gorgeous brown eyes up at her. His nose was long and sharp, his cheekbones glistening and super-chiseled, his clean-shaven jaw framing those full, rosy-red lips. The side of his mouth rose in a slight smile. His eyes twinkled up.

"Oh, I said the magic three little letters," she cooed, bending down to kneel beside him. She pressed her palm to his rock-hard triceps, wrapped her fingers around them in admiration. "My, my," she cooed as her body reacted to his brawn. But that geeky stuff he was watching on the computer... it just didn't fit. It was so not macho.

Meredith's gaze trailed the length of his body. She raked her fingers through his hair, from the back, pressing her fingertips into his damp scalp, lifting her fingers to watch the waves part between them and fall in sexy clumps around his head.

Boy, was he a beautiful specimen of manhood. None of the men who came into the agency, any day of the year, could come close to being as handsome and athletic as Hunter. And his confidence made him all the more irresistible.

But he doesn't want me. Her melting sadness hardened back into searing rage. The rage that she felt every time he left town on his little airplane that cost way more than this house. The name SoloJet said it all. It was his escape hatch away from her, that let him jet away into the wild blue yonder to probably tryst with a different bimbo in every port of call, from Louisiana to Florida and up to D.C. Yeah, he probably had 20-something ditz-brains hidden away in apartments. He could afford that, easy, with his family's money. Meredith hated that her brain was flashing into a fear fantasy of some tramp opening her apartment door, wearing a see-through negligée, yanking Hunter inside...

Stop it. Hunter wouldn't do that.

His friend, Robert, at the club, had gotten busted doing just that. Always flying off to see his mistress in Naples. But he got caught, and paid dearly for it in divorce court. No "Poor Janice" for his wife. She was riding high in that little red two-seater Benz with her boy-toy *du jour*.

"Hunter," Meredith cooed, training an acrylic fingernail down the valley of muscles on his back. They were shiny red, done fresh during her lunchtime manicure. Why couldn't she be like Lee-Anna? Her college sorority sister had married into a whiskey dynasty. Lived in a mansion over in Bourbon County. Drove a Porsche. Said she and her husband hadn't had sex for months, but she had all the credit cards and spa trips and society events a girl could ever dream of. "Forget about all that messy sex," Lee-Anna had said from the next manicure chair today. "I'm happy as a clam full of pearls."

He was facing the floor again, probably imagining that he was on top of one of those bimbos, humpin' away like there was no tomorrow. Yeah, all that energy and manpower had to be going someplace, because it sure wasn't getting spent in their bed.

"Hunter! Stop ignoring me!"

"ShShShShShShSh"! His BlackBerry rang with the sound of his jet engine starting up. That meant a job. A trip.

And another chance to leave me here all alone.

12. Lexington, Kentucky

Hunter didn't answer until Meredith had stomped away, sobbing. He wished it were Commander Buck, but Caller I.D. flashed EMERSON INSURANCE COMPANY.

"ShShShShShShSh"! He loved to hear that kitten purr. It would ring seven times before going to voicemail. After one final push-up, he pressed the tiny button for speakerphone, laid on his back on the floor and clicked on the TV. He muted *History TV.*

"Randy, Man!" Despite his enthusiasm, Hunter kept his voice low and his pace slow, so folks really had to pay attention to hear him. "Tell me you're callin' with the job of a lifetime so I can crank up my Baby Doll and fly—"

"Up, up and away, my friend." Randy's laugh reminded Hunter of their adolescent prankster days back in middle school. Like sneaking into empty lockers in the girls' locker room and watching, through the tiny holes in the gray metal, as the girls toweled off and pranced around nude. Randy's voice still had that same mischief as he did at age 12. Even though he was pushin' 45. "You're gonna love me for this one, Fly Boy. Best place you can go to escape from February. South Florida."

Hunter grinned. "What 'cha got for me?"

"A biggie," Randy said. "This one come across my desk, I say, there's only one man for this job. Hunter Knightly. All my 15 years of workin' with you, you get it right every—"

"The suspense is killin' me, man." As was the dread of Meredith coming back to nag him about company. Why couldn't she remember that he wanted to watch Carrie's first national address about Social Security? His friend, for Christ sakes, was second in command of the country. "Randal, what's the story?"

"A retired dentist is workin' on the pool behind his 10-million dollar winter home. Gets electrocuted. Wife sees him, drops dead. Heart attack. Both in their seventies. Both in perfect health three years ago when they got their new insurance policies."

"What kinda red flag am I lookin' for?"

"That's for your sneaky-smart ass to find out," Randy said playfully. "If it's legit, you'll know. They can't get nothin' past you."

"You know I live for the thrill of the chase," Hunter said, as he set the story to ticking inside his head. He loved the challenge of piecing together clues, making them fit like a perfect puzzle, to solve a mystery if there was one to solve, a theft, a crime—and now, an insurance claim. Yeah, maybe it was less glamorous, less macho than his SEAL days. Back then, he wore fatigues and an ammo belt; now he wore khakis and carried business cards. But then and now, he was always armed with his best weapon: his brain.

The triumph of figuring it out was as exhilarating as flying. Just like, after a series of clandestine meetings and cryptic communications, he bagged bad guys in South America, Asia and Africa. Nothing beat basking in the glory of his good defeating somebody else's evil.

"So Fly Boy, you think you can take them Colombo instincts you got, and go check out this life insurance claim for the poor old dentist and his wife?"

"Where at, exactly? You want me to iron out the facts, I gotta know where I'm goin'." He said *iron* like *arn*.

"West Palm. A community called Diamond Lagoon."

"Randal, you *are* the man."

"I know," he said playfully.

"Ah cain't b'lieve the number a' life insurance cases I'm gettin'. Used to be one a month. Now, one or two a week."

"Blame the economy," Randy said. "Stress is killin' 'em. With 50-percent portfolio losses, folks are desperate. Maybe they see an insurance claim as their big payday. Even if they gotta kill somebody—"

Hunter had a hunch that it was more complicated. "I'm gonna do my darnedest to find out. While I'm down there, I'll check out one of those life settlement seminars that have been comin' under scrutiny."

"I've actually been lookin' into a serious case of fraud," Randy said, "where a guy attended one a' them fancy lunches, signed in, but decided it wasn't for him. Next thing we find out, the company had gotten a big, fat, 20-million dollar policy on him—forging his signature. Bought a policy that he didn't even know about. And to top that, a loan in his name to pay the premium on it. They call it premium financing!"

"How'd he find out?" Hunter asked. "Seems like that policy could've just sat out there in the system until he died. Then somebody would get paid."

"Divorce. The wife hired a private investigator. Found this 20-million dollar life insurance policy. And get this. The guy is 70. Supported four mistresses, each with a condo. So the wife wants to know *who* he wrote the policies for."

Hunter said, "Makes me tired just thinkin' about keeping up with all that mess."

"Well, he couldn't. His lawyer called me, claiming the guy never signed up. I subpoena the files; turns out, somebody had forged his signature and took out a policy he never even knew about."

"That's so brazen."

"Now the guy is suin' for fraud," Randy said. "The broker, the life settlement company and the insurance company. He says they stole his identity when he attended one of those wealth-planning seminars down in Florida. While he was visitin' his girl in Naples, of course."

"I'll check out one of those life settlement seminars while I'm down there," Hunter said. "The whole thing just sounds way too aggressive."

"I wouldn't put anything past these insurance agents," Randal said. "They'll strong-arm anybody who gets in their way. Remember the last guy who tried to cramp their style. They set him up with a prostitute and brought him *down* with a capital D."

Hunter wasn't sure if he believed that. But the rumor just proved the industry's bullyish reputation. "Don't know if that's fact or fiction, Randal."

"That's what a whole lotta folks are sayin' about that terrorist video on the news tonight," Randy said. "Sheik Sunami il Tabbul claims he's to blame for sendin' our economy on this kamikaze flight. Go over to GNN."

Hunter logged onto Global News Network's website. He clicked the triangle in the center of Sheik Sunami il Tabbul's face. White text at the corner of the video said: February 6, 2005. Sheik Sunami il Tabbul spoke Arabic; a translator with an English accent said, "Four years from today, the American economy will become a pile of rubble. Just a short distance from the graveyard of the World Trade Center, Wall Street will become a smoking pile of financial catastrophe. The American people will suffer—"

"Oh, mah gosh," Hunter said softly as President Anderson came on the screen, saying the government was working aggressively to protect the country from another terrorist attack, financial or otherwise.

"The pilot community's known for awhile," Hunter said, "that the threat level has been escalated to red, and some more crazy shit is gonna hit the fan from those terrorists. Just don't know when."

"That is some scary shit," Randy said.

"Who you tellin'?"

13. Miami, Florida

Rosalee's stiletto sandals tapped the marble floor as she carried a tray of cocktails into the chandeliered ballroom. Wispy white sheers billowed in the ocean breeze in the two-story arched doors open to the beachside terrace. Classical music, a waltz, actually, played as hundreds of old men danced with their nipped, tucked, Botoxed and surgically enhanced wives. It was some kind of charity ball, and the ladies all wore diamonds and sequins and designer dresses that cost more than Rosalee's whole family would make in a lifetime.

But finally, she was gettin' paid. And several of the people down on that dance floor were making it happen. Not all at once. Patience would pay great dividends. Anything else would be too obvious. No, right now, she'd handle the Order for a Mr. Nathaniel McLane. 74. Retired banker from New Jersey. He and his wife, the one in the red gown and rubies, had just ordered a fresh round of drinks. And Rosalee was there to deliver.

She stood at the top of the marble stairs that led down into the ballroom, which literally sparkled with gowns and jewels.

"Bring more champagne to table 34," an old witch ordered with that look like she was the queen and Rosalee was a piece of trash on the floor. Most of them looked at her that way. But it wasn't so much about class. It was a woman thing. Rosalee was a hot 24-year-old with perky tits, a tight ass and a smooth face. Oh, and her whole life ahead of her. A life that looked better than ever, thanks to Freddie Buford.

"Did you hear me?" the woman snapped with a glare. "And make sure it's chilled. We had to return that last bottle because it was luke-warm."

"Yes, ma'am," Rosalee said with fake cheerfulness in her smoky deep voice. She hoped that bitch would be an

Order someday. Rosalee didn't know how or why any of these people made the K.C. Team's list. The only thing they had in common was that they were old and filthy rich.

And this old woman, who couldn't have weighed more than 90 pounds, looked like a clothes hanger in her blue dress. As she stepped down the marble steps toward the party, Rosalee smiled and thought, whoops, don't slip and fall. There had been a few of those lately. Like the one she'd arranged in the museum lobby. Why the museum's janitors hadn't cleaned up the oil that had mysteriously slicked the top of a stone staircase, was the question everyone wanted answered. Especially the family of dead-ass Emanuel Jenkins, a 75-year-old retired doctor from Wisconsin. Hell, he was old.

Old people trip and fall. Cha-ching!

The happy expression on Rosalee's face—as she caught her reflection in a huge mirror to her right—was so foreign that it took a second to realize, *That's me!* She loved how her peroxide blonde hair was pulled up in a tight, high bun. Her eyeliner was black and thick, Audrey Hepburn style, going up in the corners. And she wore a slim-fitting black dress like all the other waitresses here. She was making her own money, finally feeling in charge of her own life. And lovin' it.

"Your hairdo is lovely," a man's voice said behind her. "It shows off your long neck."

She turned. A man who was as old as salt ogled her exposed cleavage. The creases in his forehead were so deep, she wanted to fill them in with some of that spackling that they used when her kids' father punched holes in the drywall of that dingy little rat hole where he loved to smack her around. She was a new person, free from terror and trauma.

"Can I help you, sir?" she asked.

"Well that depends on how much you're gonna charge me," he said, his gaze never leaving her chest. "And whether you can keep a secret from my wife."

Rosalee smiled. Thank God she didn't have to turn tricks anymore to pay the rent. She had the best hook-up she could imagine. And it was time to get to work.

"Excuse me, sir," she said, stepping down the stairs.

Hell yeah, she was gettin' paid, thanks to hookin' up with Freddie Buford. Nobody could believe little ol' Rosalee had moved her kids and her momma outta the trailer park and into a spacious ranch house with a pool. Thanks to the messed-up housing market, even in Florida, she'd bought way more house than she could ever have dreamed for the price.

Everybody thought she'd sucked up on a rich boyfriend at that law firm where she'd been working as a receptionist. No, the only thing she got outta that place was very proper speaking skills that she was putting to excellent use with every Order. The K.C. meeting was coming up; she couldn't wait to tell Freddie how easy it was to stir that new drug—the untraceable one that shut down the lungs—into a drink at a big party.

Right now, she strode past the fancy tables, to the one in the far corner where the McLanes were sitting.

The wife smiled. "There you are, dear."

Rosalee handed her a crystal flute. "Your champagne, ma'am." She lifted a scotch on the rocks and handed it to Mr. McLane, who took it and sipped eagerly.

"Thank you, sweetheart," he said. Rosalee looked into his suntanned face. His eyes, nose, mouth and other features blurred. Like those streaming words on the TV screen during the news, Rosalee imagined big green dollar signs dancing all over his face, along with the number 5,000. Because to this hard-ass chick from way across the wrong side of the tracks, that's all that old bastard meant.

Another big, juicy payday.

14. Lexington, Kentucky

In the kitchen, Meredith Knightly turned on the tiny countertop TV to block Hunter's happy talk with Randy. And all that chatter about insurance from his computer was so irritating. The national news wasn't much better; it showed that Middle Eastern terrorist in a cave, talking about destroying America's economy.

Terrorism seemed a million miles away. Just like her husband, flying all over kingdom come. Could he have picked a more boring or less glamorous line of work? Where was the glory for Mr. Navy SEAL in all that paperwork? Why in the world he hadn't partaken of his daddy's wealth—

We could be livin' in our mansion on that beautiful horse farm, right now... Hunter's father had built them a dream home on the 600 acres of Knightly Farms, where his sister and brother-in-law were enjoying the life—

That's supposed to be ours! The elder Mr. and Mrs. Knightly had given Meredith and Hunter a grand tour after the wedding, and handed over the keys. But then Hunter dropped the bomb on everybody, announcing that no, they had a house of their own. And no, he would not be part of Kentucky's horse farming aristocracy; he was becoming an insurance investigator!

Well shit the bed. That was how everyone, especially Meredith, had reacted. That man loved to take everyone's expectations and smash them to bits.

And this kitchen, this house, were constant reminders of that. As she pulled a container of pimento cheese from the fridge, she remembered their argument last week, because Hunter refused to upgrade to stainless steel appliances like all her friends had in their renovated kitchens. What was he trying to prove? He was wasting his brains on the work that he did. And she was wasting away in this little house that Hunter had described as "brand new, with columns and stone work." Well that described his parents' mansion. Even the barns, with their stonework exteriors and beautiful stained wood interiors, were more opulent than this.

So when he'd said they weren't living at Knightly Farms, Meredith was expecting *at least* one of those mini mansions over on the golf course in Andover Farms. But no, Mr. Millionaire drove her up to this 1800 square foot ranch on a little cul-de-sac. Three bedrooms, one and a half baths, an unfinished basement. One measly column stood by the front door—not free-standing, but halved and attached to faux stonework around the window.

That morning, in the passenger seat of his Jeep, Meredith had felt like life had played a cruel trick on her. She was the homecoming queen, the campus sorority princess, voted prettiest and peppiest girl in school. Her beauty and charm were supposed to be rewarded with a life of luxury after she earned her simultaneous B.A. in General Studies and her M.R.S. degree as the number one draft pick of the Richest Boy in the County. Especially after the heartbreaking disappointment when her first college beau broke his leg, lost his NFL deal, and broke off their engagement, all in a matter of days. The miscarriage, the embarrassment of it all.

But Hunter was supposed to be her knight in shining armor to rescue the princess from such grim tragedy. The first time she slid down into his blue two-door XKR Jaguar, and took a ride in his airplane, she had been sure that he would whisk her away to his castle and they would live happily ever after. Oh, how wrong she had been!

That day after their honeymoon–at least *that* was at the Four Seasons in Tahiti—when he'd driven her up to this house and jingled the keys, she'd burst into tears and sobbed harder with every room that they entered.

She always thought he'd change his mind and they'd move to Knightly Farms. But here they were, 16 years later.

And he acts like I'm invisible.

15. Lexington, Kentucky

With Meredith clangin' around all mad in the kitchen, Hunter couldn't wait to hear more about this trip down to Florida.

"Listen, Fly Boy," Randy said, "I'll send the particulars about this case in an email. The who, what, when, where and why."

"Let's start with the 'when.'"

"Tomorrow, if you can," Randy said. "This couple's daughter is on a rampage. Thinks there's foul play. Says her parents were in perfect health, that her father was meticulous about safety around the pool. That he'd never do anything so stupid—"

"The daughter, is she the beneficiary?"

"No," Randy said. "And even if she were, this family was so loaded, she doesn't need their piddly 10-million dollar policies. She's got her own mansions in New York and Florida. Don't think she's got a motive—"

"Any greedy siblings or spouses? Some black sheep of the family who wants what Mom and Dad had?"

"That's for your nosey ass to find out, Fly Boy."

"Randal, log onto the Very Light Jets website."

"Oh man, don't tease me! I'll stick with my twin-engine Bonanza," Randy said. "I'll leave the fancy high tech stuff to you, Fly Boy."

"She's a beauty, ain't she?"

"I can only dream. Unless we find all that cash they brought back from Saddam Hussein's palace. Then I can buy my own little jet."

Hunter laughed, remembering how, over beers, his Navy buddy, nicknamed A-K, had shared allegedly classified information that cargo airbuses full of United States currency had been flown back to the U.S. after American troops raided Saddam's palace. And about nine billion dollars were missing from the 12-billion dollars that President Bush had authorized to disperse in Iraq to stimulate their economy.

"Where the hell is all that money?" Hunter asked.

"That *Vanity Fair* article I read said a house near San Diego and a P.O. Box in the Bahamas was as far as they traced the missing billions," Randy said. "Did that nine billion end up in Saddam's house, then on American airplanes, back to the U.S.?"

"America giveth, and America taketh away," Hunter said.

"And if it's a secret, they can't just pull up to the U.S. Treasury and make a deposit." Randal made a play voice: "'Uh, hi. I just flew in from Baghdad. Got a couple planes out back full 'a cash. I'll need a couple forklifts—'"

Hunter laughed. "You're right. Even with Electronic Funds Transfers, it has to start with cash somewhere. Can you imagine bein' the pilot of *that* plane?"

Meredith huffed. "Airplanes. It figures. Forget all about the agency's banquet Friday night. Maybe I can find a date—"

Hunter closed his eyes. The last place he wanted to be on the planet was that fundraising banquet for the non-profit where Meredith worked. Those people were constantly trying to squeeze another big check out of him and his father to support their literacy foundation. Hunter loved to help, but suspected they hired Meredith to do their marketing just to use the Knightly name and generosity.

Hunter couldn't wait to drive his SUV exactly 17 minutes to the Air 51 FBO, beside the commercial Blue Grass Airport, and fly away to Florida.

"Sure thing, Randy. I'm outta here tomorrow morning. Anytime I can escape the cold Kentucky snow and streak through some cloudless Florida sunshine, it's a great day for Hunter Knightly."

"You owe me a ride," Randal said.

"You're on! Maybe we can fly over to Louisville, grab a hot brown for lunch."

"…assurance," the narrator said on TV. Then the bewigged, powdered lawmaker said: "Hail ye fellow lords. I pray thee shalt declarest into law mine desire to protecteth each man, woman and child from those wretched souls who would gambleth on their lives—"

Meredith blocked the screen. She snatched the remote from his hand, turned off the TV. He pushed the mute button on his phone as she snapped, "You nitwit! All you care about is work and that gosh-darn airplane a' yours. Company's comin' in 15 minutes and you're a sweaty wreck. I'll tell them you're sick. Pukin' your guts up or somethin'."

What a relief. He couldn't stand that pretentious Darlene and her stiff-assed husband. Besides, he wanted to pack.

"Fly Boy, you there?"

"Meredith," Hunter said, "I'm on with a client."

"God forbid," she snapped, "you waste a minute to talk to your wife." The anger in her eyes, burning down on him, made him question why they even stayed married. But they both knew the answer.

"Hey," Randy said, "don't forget to watch Pretty Lips at eight. That big talk on Social Security—"

"Wouldn't miss it," Hunter said. "That girl was always comin' up with the wildest ideas back in high school. We voted her 'Most Out of the Box Thinker' our senior year. The crazier her ideas were, the more successful she was. Had balls as big as a bull, and a knack for doing the impossible."

"She might be the VP," Randy said, "but I just like to watch that pretty mouth wrap around all them big words she uses."

"I'll tell you what," Hunter said. "If she gets up there and says she's gonna save Social Security, but falls flat on that pretty face, them boys in Washington'll chew her up and spit her out. Don't care who her daddy is."

Randy laughed. "Unless she's growin' money trees back at the Taylor estate in Virginia Sound, or she's Robin Hood, takin' from the Treasury and givin' it to the elderly, then she's lyin' through her teeth. Guess she's gotta say something so we don't think America is goin' to hell in a hand basket."

Like my marriage. Hunter plunked down into his big leather chair. Above the fireplace, his face stared back from a huge gilt frame. In their wedding picture, Meredith was beautiful beyond words in her white dress and veil. Her eyes glowed with sweetness and confidence that a blissful eternity awaited.

"Wonder why the V.P. never married," Randy said. "Probably doesn't want to play second fiddle to a husband."

"She's not the marryin' type," Hunter said. "My Dad always says, two race horses don't belong together. Too competitive. A race horse belongs with a show pony that just wants to sit and look pretty while he wins the blue ribbons—and the money."

Randy laughed. "Sign me up! I'll be her house-husband any day. Would sure beat workin' for a living."

Meredith appeared, staring down with questioning eyes. Her beauty — a perfect "10" — made him feel a sudden need to put a happy sparkle into those big blue eyes. He stood, took her delicate jaw into his palms… planted his mouth on her pink-glossed lips… and kept them there until he felt her melting. He pulled away. Her eyes sparkled up at him. Her lips trembled.

"Oh my," she cooed.

"Let me pack in peace, darlin'," Hunter said with a sexy rasp as his gaze smoldered down on hers. "I'll show 'ya, there's plenty more where that came from." He winked, then dashed down the hallway.

16. Washington, D.C.

She stared straight into the camera, right into the eyes of the American people who would, in four years, elect her as the first female President of the United States. Because right now, as second in command, she was about to unveil a miracle plan that would establish her as a hero and a history-maker, beloved by men and women for generations to come.

"Ladies and gentlemen," said Carolyn Snedegar Taylor with slow, practiced enunciation that virtually erased her Virginia accent. Her speech coaches had warned to always read the words on the teleprompter before saying them, just in case a saboteur or authentic typo got in there. She had memorized the speech backward and forward, but for such a momentous occasion, she needed the guidance of technology. "You know that Social Security has been on a collision course with disaster for many years. Now with the economic downturn and more people choosing retirement, along with the baby boomer bubble beginning to draw from it, action must be taken immediately."

This is divine. She was the most important person speaking in the United States right now. People around the world were watching her on live TV. After tonight's flawless delivery of her perfect speech, she would only move onward and upward. Like no other woman in world history.

Carolyn trembled with excitement as she glanced at her image on the monitor just beyond the teleprompter. The thrill of this moment made goosebumps dance across her skin under her tailored navy blue suit, pantyhose and silk blouse. She just looked so downright Presidential with her long, dark hair twisted up and her eyes trained on millions of people with such sincerity and concern. And she was just getting started. She focused on the rows of capital letters streaming across the teleprompter—a black and white screen that was about a foot wide and high, shielded by black awnings to prevent glare from these bright studio lights.

Those sentences were her magic formula for success. She had obsessed over every word with her speechwriter. And thanks to the brilliant technology of a teleprompter right above the camera, it looked like she was speaking naturally and looking straight into the eyes of her viewers, even though she was reading every sentence.

"As your Vice President," she said with a smooth, deep voice that she had practiced with her coaches to radiate authority and warmth, "I am coming to your rescue. I am implementing a bold new initiative that will preserve and build the Social Security Trust Fund, and insure your financial security during your golden years. This mission is my passion and my purpose for the next four years. And I'm doing it for you, the American people."

She paused to smile slightly, letting her eyes gleam with the confidence that her secret plan would work magic for America. Nobody had to know the details. They just needed to see the results. And they would. Soon.

"I have a rescue plan that will redistribute, in a sense, the resources required to rebuild the Social Security Trust Fund so that it can be self-sustaining to take care of your grandparents, your parents, your children, and their children." Standing behind the podium, she shifted on her high-heeled pumps. Couldn't wait to take them off and put her running shoes back on. She hoped that all of her rivals were watching this triumphant moment in the global spotlight. From that prissy little bitch who pushed her in the mud in third grade... to her ex-boyfriend at the University of Virginia who dumped her the night of the homecoming dance so he could take a stripper instead... to all the Republicans who said she would never get elected, much less do anything important as a politician.

Now they could all kiss her 43-year-old, extremely firm and fit behind. Among those cheering her on tonight, besides her family, would be her classmates from Episcopal High, where she was the youngest member of her class. Also watching were the key players in her plan. They were a team and together they would triumph.

"My rescue plan will require the nonpartisan support of Congress. And since our victorious election in November, the President and I have been working behind the scenes to invite every lawmaker from across America to join us in this mission. Ladies and gentlemen, I am thrilled to announce tonight that we have succeeded. This is an awesome accomplishment on its own." Carolyn allowed her eyes to project into the camera in a way that would earn the love and adoration of 300 million Americans and countless more around the globe.

"Any nonpartisan venture for the good of our country is impressive," she said, "but this one is even more so. Because it will require the assistance of the most wealthy among you, the ultra wealthy, to make a personal sacrifice for the sake of the less fortunate."

Oh, wait 'til they hear this! Her heart hammered with excitement; her mouth wanted to fast-forward to the good stuff.

And her success was so palpable, Carolyn literally had the sensation of champagne bubbles on her tongue.

Sure, she would celebrate tonight with her benefactor and lover. He was already waiting for her in the Presidential Suite in the East Wing of the Washington, D.C. Four Seasons. Tonight's pinnacle moment would spark the momentum for her to ultimately catapult into the Oval Office—and the history books as America's first female President.

"I am calling this rescue plan SOS," she said with a tone that was both somber and celebratory. "It stands for 'Save Our Social Security.' And I pledge to you tonight, America, that I am going to do that for you. I will be successful."

Carolyn gloated. She'd named her plan SOS on purpose, as an affront to the new Secretary of State. Why the hell the President had insulted Carolyn by appointing a woman—*that* woman—to such a prominent position, she would never know. Especially Sue Bookman, who had seduced Carolyn's former fiancé out from under Carolyn's influence, causing an important business deal to collapse. It was a blessing in disguise, it turned out, because the guy was later indicted. Not to mention, Sue made no secret of her ambition to become America's first female President.

Dream on, bitch. Someday, Carolyn's vengeance would make Sue Bookman wish she'd never even come to town. Someday.

For now, though, Carolyn loved that the media's inevitable obsession with her SOS Plan would constantly remind Sue Bookman, and every other ambitious woman in Washington, just who was the HBIC—Head Bitch In Charge—in American government.

Me. Not her. Ever.

17. Lexington, Kentucky

That delicious dinner, and the sight of his clothes laid out neatly on the bed for his trip, left no doubt why Hunter stayed married. They were in their bedroom, with the Vice President on television, talking about Social Security. After company had cancelled, Meredith cooled off and served up some of her best cooking as a kiss-and-make-up meal that had ended here on the bed.

"I love you, darlin'," he whispered, kissing her forehead as she approached with his leather toiletry kit.

"I filled up your shampoo," she said, wrapped in a baby blue satin robe that made her eyes even brighter.

"Hey, Meredith," he said softly. "You know I love you 'til death do us part."

"Unless we kill each other first," she said, squeezing her arms around his bare waist. Showered, wearing boxers, he pressed his nose into her hair and inhaled the floral scent.

"Why am I afraid that I'd be the one goin' down first?" Hunter teased. "The way you were comin' at me with those pointed boots tonight—"

She pressed her cheek to his chest. "I'm sorry, honey. Sometimes I just want everything to be perfect. But when it's not, I just lose it. And when I drove up tonight and saw Sue Ann playing with her twins all bundled up in the yard, that really set me off."

Hunter cast a sympathetic gaze down at her. But kids, with her, just were not on his wish list. If they'd had 'em, great. All his friends with kids, though, were always griping about the downside of parenthood: the worries, the disappointments, the terror that something could happen, then all the other wildcards like allergies and autism and 22-year-olds moving back home after college. Not to mention, softball, tennis, football practice and games—all that took a lot of time. And then there were the soccer moms. *Save me.*

But deeper than these feelings, Hunter had something bigger on his mind: guilt. It twinged beneath his lovey-dovey façade. Guilt that the only reason he kept Meredith around was to serve as his glorified housekeeper. That sounded so harsh. But that was the truth. Crazy thing was, he could afford to live alone and hire three maids if he wanted. But he didn't want employees in his house. He wanted a wife who was there for him, no matter what.

He stroked the back of her head with both hands. His chest felt damp; she was crying.

"Ssshhh," he said, his gut aching with guilt. "It's okay, Meredith. It's okay."

He did love her. But based on true confessions from friends and colleagues, the reality of marriage was nothing like the fantasy they'd grown up to believe in.

Whoever had coined that phrase "wedded bliss" had to be smoking crack or strictly referring to the honeymoon or describing someone like that Saudi Arabian prince who was buying up horse farms here in Kentucky. Every time he came to town, he brought his four wives and a huge entourage that catered to his every whim. *That* would be bliss. Four women to choose from, and all eager to please, would leave no time for anybody to have an attitude. But that was too complicated. Too much work. Too many people to keep organized.

"I think we're gonna be just fine," Hunter whispered, holding her close. He was luckier than most of his friends, though. His work was his excuse to fly away for days, and on rare occasions, weeks at a time. He couldn't wait to do just that come 0800 hours tomorrow, also known as 1300 Zulu, in pilot lingo.

"Sounds like it's comin' to an end," Meredith said.

Hunter froze for a moment. But Meredith pointed to the TV that they'd been watching while packing; she was talking about the Vice President's speech, not their marriage. Or was she?

"So tonight I'm asking you to join me in making history with this bold new initiative," Carrie said. "Join me to revive our dying Social Security system. Help me pump new financial life into the trust fund. And together we will make certain that all Americans live comfortably and securely throughout their golden years."

Would he and Meredith still be together during their golden years?

"I think she has a good plan," Meredith said. "People like your dad don't need that itty bitty little check from Washington every month. That wouldn't buy feed for a single horse in a month."

Hunter shook his head. "That's for Dad to decide, not the Vice President."

"Maybe they'll make it voluntary," Meredith said, pulling away to place his clothes in his leather travel bag. Compact and light, it was perfect for his plane.

"You were out of the room when Carrie said they're proposing legislation, by some senator from Louisiana, to make it a law across the board. It's wrong. Government messed up the Social Security funds. You break it, you fix it."

But who had broken their marital bonds? Him? Meredith? The modesty of her ring and this house were his way of testing her, to see if she'd married him for money. Her frequent bitch fits, even during the engagement and now about the Lexington Ball, seemed to indicate a resounding "Yes." Plus, when they married, he'd been entertaining Dad's offer to live in the new mansion and ultimately take over as CEO of Knightly Farms. But the secret that she'd kept from him had cost her all that.

Yet it was no secret, based on a comment here, or a demand there, that being the First Lady of Knightly Farms was Meredith's goal. Being his loving wife was secondary, it seemed, to her striking gold at the altar.

His plan had been to discover that she loved him for him, then reward her with the mansion, the cars, the luxurious trips that she craved. But she had flunked his test. And kept flunking. She didn't love Hunter Knightly for Hunter Knightly. She loved him for his name, his family, his wealth. Wealth that he was too smart to squander on the gold-digger that he had married.

"She's so smart," Meredith said, casting a proud smile at the television. "The girls and I were talking after yoga the other night. She makes us proud to be women. Finally, beauty and brains that show women can be great leaders, too."

Meredith looked gorgeous, standing there in her silky robe, smiling. Hunter grabbed her, swung her up into his arms. She shrieked gleefully, until he kissed her pretty, pouty mouth. Out of the corner of his eye, he glimpsed the clock on the nightstand. The red digital letters said 7:35. In less than 12 hours, and he'd be outta here, flyin' to his heart's content, all the way down to the warmth of the Sunshine State.

For now, he'd share some heat between their own Southern parts. With her shaved and him manicured in their private erotic zones, they were about to soar up, up and away...

And in the morning, so would he, to Palm Beach International Airport.

PBI, here I come...

18. Washington, D.C.

Flawless. That's how I have to be...
And this speech epitomized Carolyn Snedegar Taylor's flawless execution of her plan to revolutionize America.

"I have a bold new initiative," Carolyn said, loving that she would soon have the power to obliterate some of those financially slick Republicans whose backstabbing had robbed Daddy of a second term as President. Those rich bastards didn't deserve to live so long, while sucking the Social Security system dry, year after year, when they didn't even need the money. They were among a growing and useless class of elderly who were living forever and a day, contributing nothing, just drawing down the government dole. Now was the time to put America's resources to better use.

"And I need the assistance and support of our nation's wealthiest people who are above the age of 65," she said with her most confident and convincing tone. She read the next sentence as it streamed across the screen of the teleprompter: "If you can find it in your home—"

No! It was supposed to say *heart.* Not *home!*

Somebody's ass is gonna fry tonight. Anger jolted through her, making her nerves feel like sparking electrical wires. Carolyn bit down hard, keeping her face and eyes perfectly diplomatic and poised. But her mouth was twitching to shoot out the kind of language she would hear from those fishermen on the docks of Chesapeake Bay as a little girl, when her parents let her go down with the cook (and bodyguards) to fetch lobsters. Oh, if America could hear those down-home expletives fire like buckshot from her perfectly lipsticked mouth.

No, I'll save it for the idiot who fucked up my speech!

Carolyn remembered a golden nugget of wisdom that her father often shared with her: *"I do not know the secret to success, but I know the secret of sure failure: trying to please everyone, all the time. Someone has to pay."* And they would. Later.

For now, she corrected the line in her head and said: "If you can find it in your heart to put the good of less fortunate Americans ahead of all else, then together we will rebuild the Social Security system. It will become robust and rich and self-sustaining to provide the security that every senior deserves. Together we can make history by helping our fellow Americans."

She inhaled deeply. "To do this, I am asking that people over the age of 65, who are fortunate enough to rank in the top one percent of our country's wealthiest people, our ultra wealthy—to donate your monthly payments back into the system."

She stared into the camera. "That is truly the American spirit of giving and helping and caring. Because we are all our brother's keepers. And our sister's keepers. Countless Americans have given their lives in war to protect the United States. Many people have already expressed that they would be glad to give up their Social Security for the greater good."

Her heart raced with the thrill of making this happen, her way. "And what a tremendous example we can show to the rest of the world, that we can come together to share resources and provide financial security for our seniors in need. That is the kind of America that we need to rebuild and celebrate."

Carolyn beamed into the camera.

Screw that one percent. Because that leaves 99 percent to vote for me! The Oval Office is mine.

19. Diamond Lagoon, Florida

Ernest Bloomfield watched in disbelief as the Vice President spoke live from the 65-inch flat screen TV in his media room.

"Did this girl just escape the mental ward?" he asked, turning to his best buddy and their wives. Each sat in a plush taupe recliner in the two-story room overlooking the ninth hole of the Diamond Lagoon Golf Course. "I work my whole life and pay into Social Security, now she wants to keep my money?!"

"Oh Ernest, it's not like you need it," exclaimed his wife, Stella. The gold charm bracelet on her right wrist, jingled with starfish, dolphins, mermaids and other ocean creatures as she tapped his arm. "You use it for golf. Some people live off that puny little check."

"Be a little philanthropic, will 'ya, buddy!" said Herschel Goodman, wearing a green polo shirt embroidered on the left breast with Diamond Lagoon Golf Club. Bald with full cheeks that shook when he talked, he shifted his long, slim body and said, "You give millions to The Children's Charity Classic back in New York, but you don't want to help out your fellow elderly? Whaaaat, Ernie?"

"I'm not elderly," Ernie said. "I'm 75. Elderly, that's 95. And it's different. I give money to the inner city kids out of the goodness of my heart."

"And your tax return," Stella teased. "The write-off."

Ernest turned to his wife as she stared right back at him with her cheerful eyes. Framed by a jazzy fringe of blond hair, her face looked 40, thanks to the Botox and other treatments, but her neck, he didn't look so much at her neck, a victim of gravity. She smoothed down her short, sea green cotton dress, running her hand over her slim, petite shape. With her ankles crossed, her matching sandals with the gold sand dollars rested on the beige carpet just past her adorable pedicured feet. Ernest's gaze lingered on the shiny pink squares at the tip of each toe. He just wanted bite them like little pieces of candy. He would, later. But right now, he was too mad about this young girl's insane idea to keep his money.

Ernest grumbled, "When I give money to Uncle Sam, I want it back."

"Her plan gets my vote," declared Herschel's wife, Margie. Always looked puffy, like she'd had too much salt. Could stand to lose 20 pounds from the midsection, but she kept it neatly concealed under loose shorts and flowy shirts that, if she wasn't in her early seventies, would look like maternity tops. "I like what her father did to help Israel when he was President. Bent over backwards to make good things happen and protect innocent people. Sounds like she's cut from the same cloth."

"Pretty girl," Stella said. "When I first saw her, I would have guessed Native American, with the dark hair and olive skin."

"Earth tones," Margie said. "Her make-up is there, but you don't notice it. Such clear skin—"

"They had a profile in *Retirement Magazine* about her, how she looks so young to be 43," Stella said.

"That is young!" Margie exclaimed, fluffing her auburn coif. Her hazel eyes became little slits as she smiled.

"I hear she runs every day," Stella said. "Never touches sweets. Never got married."

Margie snickered playfully. "That's why she looks so great."

They laughed.

"Ladies," Ernest said. "Let's talk about the substance, not the style. That's the problem with America these days. It's all about the—what's that word the grandkids say, Stella?"

"Bling, Ernie," she said. "Things that sparkle, and razzle dazzle, they call it bling. Diamond watches, big earrings, fancy cars. Bling, bling!"

Margie laughed.

"I watch my share of those music videos with the girls," Stella said. "Rachel, she's 14. Eats it up. Gets straight As, but loves the videos."

The Vice President's voice drew their attention back to the screen. "Now, in order to enact a law that will make this plan possible," Carolyn Snedegar Taylor said, "I am partnering with my dear friend, Representative John Donaldson of Florida, who will introduce the bill, and Senator Gerald Boxley of Louisiana, who is Chairman of the Finance Committee."

Ernest snickered. "Ugh, that Donaldson. Slippery as they come. My son saw him in a club, doing cocaine in South Beach. Out in the open!"

The Vice President continued, "Together as a historic bipartisan team, we are crafting legislation that will enable the United States government to begin to transfer this vast wealth into a fund. Your investments into that secure fund will make it grow. Your small commitment will secure the financial futures of our elders for generations to come."

Herschel shook his head. "Funny she didn't say a word about this when she was campaigning with the President. Then she comes out, a month after inauguration, and drops this bomb on us hardworking Americans. It's outright thievery."

"Shush!" Stella said. "Listen."

"As we know, our advances in medicine and healthier lifestyles," the Vice President said, "are enabling Americans to live longer. While this is a blessing to us and our families, it's a curse to the Social Security system. It was not designed to support so many people for so long."

Margie shook her head. "Remember that movie, *Logan's Run*? Where they killed everybody after age, what was it? Thirty-five?"

Stella corrected, "Twenty-one!"

"I'm thinking more socialism," Herschel said. "Take from the rich, give to the poor, even everything out. That's not the American way."

"Robin Hood is a story that I read to my grandkids," Ernest said. "I don't want him wearing a dress in the White House, comin' after what I earned to subsidize those who failed! I'd call this redistribution of wealth. That's what it is."

"Oh Ernest, just listen," Stella said. "She has a smart idea. Maybe it's better to do a good deed. You never know when your time is up."

"Who are you tellin'?" Herschel said. "This is a banner year. How many, Ernie, we counted—"

"Seventeen," Ernie said. "From our club alone, 17 didn't make it back down for the season this year."

"Oi," Stella said somberly. Ernie squeezed his wife's hand as an eerie silence fell over the group. Because at their age, death would come calling sooner, rather than later.

20. The Sea Palace Yacht Club, South Beach, Florida

Juan barely heard his women's chatter as he watched Her on television. She was his mirror image, the female version. Her eyes flashed *Power*. *Cunning*. *Cojones*. *Win at all costs*. And that made him want to step through the screen and take her...

"I will do everything in my power to achieve this mission," Carrie said. "If saving Social Security means that we must—"

"Juan, baby," Felecia whined, still sitting on the chair in front of them and tilting her head to make her long dark hair tickle his arm. "News is so boring."

Marla, who was kneeling on the floor in a red, white and blue bikini, giggled. "I have no clue what the hell Social Security is."

Carrie said, "My rescue plan will implement this revolutionary solution over a five-year transitional period. For example, someone who is entitled to full Social Security today will notice a 20% reduction per year over the next five years."

Blanche snickered, "I don't understand a bloody bit of anything she's saying."

"However, for the ultra wealthy," the Vice President said, "we are looking to implement a system that will enable you to exercise your patriotic generosity by contributing those funds back into the system, to help your fellow Americans. Just as our 18- to 25-year-old soldiers risk their lives and fight for our country, I ask that you make a significantly smaller investment in the financial future of our country. "

"Okay," Blanche said, "I like the sound of 'ultra wealthy.' But she lost me after that."

Josette, topless in a pink g-string, added, "You know it, girlfriend. That confusing-ass shit is for old people to worry about."

"Bo-ring!" Cheyenne added. "Baby, we want to watch Miss America—"

"She *is* Miss America," Gigi said with a tone like the other girls were all idiots. "She's the freakin' Vice President!"

Juan almost smiled. "Go watch in my room," he ordered with a deep rasp that belied his long, lean build and reminded him, with every word, of the horrors he endured at the hands of—

No! He never allowed himself to think about that. But it manifested in an angry tone as he told the girls: "All of you. I'll be down later." He smiled. These women were under his complete control, thanks to that magic white powder that made his every wish, their command. He'd learned long, long ago that his Panther power could attract and keep a whole litter of sexy little female cubs—as long as he kept them purring on the high of cocaine. Allowing them to live on a yacht in one of the world's sexiest cities made it even easier to control them.

"We'll have our own Miss America pageant," he said with sexy gruffness. "The winner and the first runner-up get me all to herself for the night."

Gigi and Cheyenne planted symmetrical kisses on his cheeks. They handed him his cigar and his drink, then hopped up with the other women—cheering now—as they filed down the circular staircase to the master suite. Moments like this made him feel certain that he was the next Hugh Hefner—undercover, of course—but surrounded by his own sexy little Panther cubs all the same.

But as their prime T&A paraded past him, Juan's focus did not leave Seniorita V.P. These chicks were half her age. They were all about tits, ass and partying. Carrie had that, too, beneath her professional front, but it was her brains that turned him on.

"My plan is unlike anything America has experienced," Carrie said, "but given our dire economic times—"

Juan paused, applying her words to his enterprise.

What if Eldorado fails? Then what happens to me? He had no name or face for the mysterious, god-like person who was calling the shots for his fantasy life. *What if it suddenly shuts down? I'd be out on my ass...*

"—a bold new creative solution is our only hope," Carrie said, "And I will do everything in my power to achieve its success."

"A bold new creative solution," Juan repeated, loving the sound of that. He held up his drink to toast the way her great mind thought just like his.

I deserve to live like a king and will do anything to maintain my empire.

21. Diamond Lagoon, Florida

Ernie wanted to change the subject from death to something more cheerful, but everywhere they went, someone was constantly talking about another dead friend, acquaintance or stranger. So of course he couldn't get his friends—or himself—to shut up about it here at home.

"And that's just Diamond Lagoon," Herschel said. "We were talkin' with the golf pro, with the Swedish name—"

"Lars," Ernie said. "Works at golf clubs and resorts all over America. Arizona, Las Vegas, Palm Springs, the Carolinas—"

"Big retirement spots," Margie said, nodding. "People with money."

"Lars was telling us over burgers at the club," Ernie said, feeling a chill as he spoke, "it's become a common story everywhere. This year, it just seems like a lot of people are dying. A lot of accidental deaths. Car accidents and weird stuff, like the dead lady in the airplane bathroom—"

"Awful," Stella said. "Nobody helped her?"

"Didn't know she was in there until they landed," Ernie said. "Lars said he's heard all kinds of stories. Passing away in their sleep. Trip and falls with a killer concussion. One poor fellow choked on a steak."

"It's some kinda natural cycle," Margie said. "Mother Nature is hard to control. We know that from the ocean."

"Oh don't start with your astrology bullshit," Herschel said. "Or biorhythms or that psychic mumbo-jumbo." He turned to his friends. "I hear this constantly at home. Drives me nuts! We are getting old-E-R. The older we get, the more friends we lose. It just seems like more because we know them."

Margie's huge diamond ring and shiny coral fingernails sparkled as she waved him off. "The universe goes in cycles. You see some years, the trees or certain bushes are strong and thick. Other years, they're thin or don't grow at all. It has nothing to do with socioeconomic boundaries; the California fires proved that. So just like the moon affects the ocean tide, the universe affects human life, too."

"These are people, not shrubs or tides on the beach, Margie," Herschel said dismissively.

"People," Ernest said sadly. "Mark and Suzie."

"Oi, right next door," Stella said. "The poor daughter—" her bracelet jingled as she raised her hand to her chest, "—a complete mess."

Hershel's cheeks jiggled as he shook his head. "Freddie was anal about safety around the pool. Electrocuted, I don't buy it. Unless he was drinking—"

"Never," Ernie said. "He did oral surgery. How precise of a guy is that? He just didn't make mistakes."

"The hot tub was malfunctioning," Stella said. "One night we were with Suzie after bridge. It just wouldn't heat up."

"So you call a professional, don't try to fix it yourself," Herschel said with a puzzled expression. Then, playfully, he said, "The schmuck."

The foursome laughed, Ernie was sure, to keep from crying.

Margie chimed in: "Suzie, my God, I'd drop dead of a heart attack, too, if I found my Herschel like that."

"Freddie, fit as a fiddle," Stella says. "And Suzie, yoga every day. Perfect health when they got their exams—"

"Death happens," Herschel says with a *just shrug it off* tone. "So we enjoy while we're here. The auction for that house, everybody at the Club is talking about it. Hottest property around. Monday, they'll be like piranhas, bidding."

"Life is a gamble, too," Stella said. "You never know."

Ernie glanced back at the Vice President on TV. "So maybe she has a good idea. Maybe we help the system, we can buy some more time."

"I don't know if the Grim Reaper is keeping track like that," Herschel said. "Think of Barry, the most miserable, malicious guy—"

"Ugh, everybody hated him," Stella said. "Why he came to the banquets, I don't know."

"And the guy lives to be 102," Herschel said. "And active! Played golf 'til he was 100 years old!"

"He gave," Stella shrugged. "Carnegie Hall, Rockefeller Center, his temple, the Wharton School—"

"He put that good karma out there," Margie said. "He started that program for kids with cancer to go to Disney World and get all the latest video games in their hospital rooms. A good guy."

The Vice President said: "Our nation's economy is undergoing a tremendous shift. When children in the future read our history books, they can learn how *you* helped save our Social Security system—"

"Can you imagine depending on that for your income?" Margie asked.

"I built the business," Ernest said, holding up his palms, "with these calloused hands, so my family would not have that nightmare."

Stella laughed, play-slapping his arm. "Oh Ernie, those calluses are from playing golf and tennis every day!"

For Ernie, his wife's smile inspired a silent prayer of thanks for the bounty in his life. His grandparents had died in Auschwitz. His emaciated parents had come to the United States for a better life. Exactly the life that he had created for his family and future generations. And he wasn't going to let the democratic government that he loved, enact some law that was a throwback to Nazi takeovers of Jewish businesses and bank accounts.

"I don't like her plan," Ernie said. "Not one bit."

"Oh come on, Ernie," Stella said, "not everybody has your Midas touch."

Herschel laughed. "Yeah, not everybody can lay on their living room floor for an EKG, then a couple months later collect a 50-thousand-dollar check for it!"

"And a TV," Margie chimed.

They all looked at the flat screen TV. Its sleek silver frame said in scroll engraving across the top: "We're here for YOU, because we appreciate your business! The Genuine Insurance Group."

"Easiest money I ever made," Herschel said. "The flat screen? Everybody who comes over says it's the nicest they've seen."

"Not everyone has such good fortune," Stella said. "My cousin's husband worked for that company where the CEO stole the pension fund. He's working the popcorn stand at the local movie house to make ends meet."

"Nightmare with a capital N," Margie said.

"Meanwhile," Stella said, "the four of us get 50-grand apiece for some life insurance policy that we don't even need."

"Those viaticals are becoming really popular," Herschel said. "Those companies, they have huge advertising budgets, with the full page ads in all the papers, just about every day."

"Free money," Ernie said, "no strings attached. Sounded too fantastic to be real. But here we are, three years later, with the money in the bank and the TV right there in front of us. And never paid a premium."

Margie smiled. "That seminar at Luxury Suites, with the stuffed lobster tails, and that dessert buffet in the suite where we met with the broker after. A dream. Too bad we can't buy more!"

Herschel added, "Imagine, life insurance, all sold out!"

"Stranger things have happened. I remember sitting in that seminar, thinking, 'This sounds too good to be true,'" Ernie said, nodding at the Vice President on TV, "but so does Miss Lady's plan."

22. The Sea Palace Yacht Club, South Beach, Florida

Juan's body burned with lust; his mind sparked with intrigue. He barely blinked as he watched her larger-than-life face on his huge TV.

I have to have her. The feelings were as intense as they'd been the first time he saw her in ninth grade science class.

"This divine mission is bigger than any of us can imagine," Carrie said. "My immense need to serve the American people was instilled in me at my father's knee, literally, when he was President and I played under his desk in the Oval Office. I feel that his record of helping people ordained me to do the same."

Juan chuckled.

Yeah, I feel the same way about my father. But I never met him. Nope, the senior Juan Pantera Diablo, according to his mother, was killed by guerillas while hunting in Colombia when their son was only three. As a child, Juan had created his own fantastic story that his father had been a heroic heavyweight in the Medellin drug cartel. That his dad had made all that money to help the poor people in the villages of Colombia, by feeding hungry children and building safe houses and even founding a school for the peasants to learn to read and write.

Meanwhile, his mother had brought him to the United States, where she worked as a secretary in the *Embajada de Colombia,* the Colombian Embassy, in Washington, D.C. They provided a nice apartment and financed Juan's private schooling at Sidwell Friends School, then Episcopal High. Juan always imagined that his dad had been such a powerful motherfucker that he had somehow arranged for the government to take care of his family, far away in the safety of America.

He dreamed of someday meeting his father. But over the years, anecdotal evidence and even some newspaper articles had filled in the sinister yet fascinating blanks in Juan's vision of his father as a powerful drug kingpin. He was no hero. Just a money-hungry hustler whose tactics to seize power and accumulate wealth knew no moral bounds.

"It's in my genes," Carrie said, "to serve the American people. And to follow in my father's footsteps to execute his vision so that each of you can seize the American Dream and celebrate it every day. I am giving you the power to live your best and most meaningful lives, so that your golden years are golden in every way."

Juan groaned, "Well said, Carrie." Because it was in his genes, too, to rise to power and wealth—and to help the spoiled rich kids, the egotistical professionals, and the straight-up fiends who craved cocaine—the same way his father had.

Even though his mother had done everything possible to protect him from reliving his father's fate. An American educated in France, she instilled in him a passion for opulence. Gourmet food, exotic trips, expensive linens on his bed. And, with his excellent math and science skills, and a natural knack for navigation and aviation, his mother had bought him is own twin-engine Baron at age 15. Right after he'd earned his pilot's license. Little did she know she was preparing him for the very life of crime she was trying to protect him from.

Because Juan Pantera Diablo had found his life calling during his freshman year at Episcopal, during a school ecological summer program in the Bahamas. The program should have been called, *Cocaine 101: How to Become a Drug Lord Before High School Graduation.* Because Juan's encounter with some Colombian dealers there, who perhaps saw his father's features on his face, or simply sensed one of their own, taught him the ropes and indoctrinated him into the intoxicating power and profit of the booming 1980s cocaine trade between South America, the Bahamas, Florida and the rest of the United States. Perhaps this had even been Juan's way of connecting with his absentee father, or reliving the legacy of the senior Juan Pantera Diablo.

For Juan, his new business had felt as natural as breathing. And boy did he have a built-in market back at school. All the rich American kids were already addicted to blow. So it had been wickedly easy for Juan to become the supply for their huge demand. Of course, Juan was too smart and calculating to use the stuff or get addicted, until much later in his grand career. And it did lead to his downfall and ultimate incarceration.

Before that, selling and rising up the ranks of the hierarchy, had come so easily to him as he breezed through the academic demands of high school, then excelled at the University of Miami, that Juan was sure he had inherited some kind of drug dealer gene from his dad. After one semester of college, he was already credited as a second semester sophomore. But aside from all the chicks, college was boring. He was ready for a more exciting and rewarding life in the Caribbean.

Now, Juan inhaled the length of a Cohiba. Yeah, it was time to take a little trip down to his old turf to reflect further on where he'd been, where he was now, and where he was going.

"She's so fuckin' sexy," Juan said aloud, staring at Carrie. He loved her confidence. And the way she wore her hair twisted up. Looked like she could become one wild seductress with the snatch of a hairpin.

"Thank you, ladies and gentlemen for—" she paused, looking perplexed. But only for a split-second.

"The teleprompter jammed," he groaned. He'd hop in his jet and fly to Washington himself—right now—to pop the punk who messed it up. Anything to wipe that stress out of the Vice President's eyes.

He chuckled. He'd spent most of his life nursing this crush on her, and she never even knew it. Didn't know it back in high school. Didn't know it at the 25-year-reunion last May, even when he'd given the keynote as the former class President, congratulating her on her bid for the Vice Presidency. Of course, he had looked like shit back then. No sun, too skinny. Now, though, he was tanned by the Miami sun, and filled out to his ideal look of long, lean and muscular. Irresistible to her, he was sure.

"It's our little secret," Juan said playfully, holding a silver lighter so that a tiny flame danced around the tip of his Cohiba.

Most of the suckers watching her probably didn't notice the glitch. Because she was so smooth with her excellent segueway: "I pause to allow you, the American people, to remain confident that I am coming to your rescue, to take care of you more gloriously and more generously than you ever imagined, to establish the security of Social Security Trust Fund forever."

The tip of his cigar glowed red as Juan inhaled. He blew a Knightly stream of smoke toward the screen. It billowed under the spotlights of the recessed lighting.

Everything she was saying was bullshit. There was no such thing as security from someone else, especially the government. In America, you had to get your own. Like all the rich motherfuckers in yachts all around him at this marina, and the folks he knew down in the Bahamas and in Colombia. Getting a mind-blowing fortune—by any means necessary—was the only insurance anybody had for real lifelong security. Perhaps a quick trip down to his beloved Bahamian retreat would help him brainstorm a brilliant solution to secure his retirement.

"You talk good game, Carrie," Juan said, squinting through the smoke.

"With me as your Vice President, I want you to sleep peacefully at night, knowing that Social Security is your insurance for a good life. Mark my words."

Juan sucked on the cigar. The sizzle of tobacco and the glowing red of its tip underscored her words. Words. And Eldorado. They could go up in smoke in an instant.

That's why he had to get his, and get out, because nothing lasted forever. Especially something this good. And the bigger and better it was, the easier it was to crash and burn. Or get burned.

"I don't get burned," he said. Never again.

23. Washington, D.C.

Now that the camera was off, the Vice President kicked off her shoes as she stepped down from the platform. The media was waiting for her in the next room, for a press conference. And dozens of her staff and supporters were applauding her here in the studio. But Carolyn had only one thing on her mind.

"Brittany!" she shouted. "Brittany, where the fuck are you?" Words blasted out of her mouth 10 times faster than the slow, rhythmic pattern she had just used during her speech. "Somebody find me my speechwriter!"

She did not give a shit about how this would feed the rumor mill about her bitchy attitude. It was time to crack down on the 25-year-old who had come from one of the best families in the Tidewater Region and highly recommended by Carolyn's advisors.

"Yes, ma'am," Brittany said, scampering out of the crowd of men and women in conservative suits. Her dark ponytail hung down the back of her slim brown skirt suit. Pale as the stack of paper that was shaking in her hand — *my perfect speech* — she looked up with guilt roiling in her eyes.

Carolyn towered over the girl, who couldn't have been more than five-four. Glaring down, holding back the urge to smack this stupid little shit in front of all these people, Carolyn shouted, "Tell me how the hell you changed 'heart' to 'home'?"

"First, Madame Vice President," the girl squeaked, "I'm sorry. Ah apolo-gah-ze from the bottom of ma heaaa-art."

"An apology does not erase mistakes on live television around the world!" Carolyn's Virginia accent, which had been barely detectable during her speech, sounded thick and twangy. Her "does not" came out "d'unt" and her "world," a drawn out, two syllable "WER-rald."

Brittany spoke fast: "I think when I went into the computer to make the last minute changes, I was so excited for you that I typed the wrong—"

"Didn't they teach you to proof-read up there at Harvard?"

"In all honesty, Ma'am, nobody would ever guess they were there," Brittany said. "Your delivery was smooth as silk."

"*Snagged* silk! Exquisite, rare silk with two ugly snags that made it worthless. And I have to be perfect! Right now every critic in America is on TV or on a blog, ripping me to shreds."

A six-foot-five tower of navy blue wool stepped between Carolyn and the girl.

"Carrie," said Russell, her chief of staff. He was an Episcopal classmate and former point guard for the Charlotte Hornets; his father had worked in Carolyn's father's administration. He was now her right-hand man who always had her back. In his mid-forties, he had a boyish, freckled face and side-parted, auburn hair. "Carrie, give her a break. No harm done. Two little typos—"

"One miniscule typo is unacceptable," Carolyn shouted up at him. "And you'd be having a fit right now if I had actually said 'home' instead of 'heart.' What if the mistakes had been even worse, and I said them on live TV?"

"No harm done," Russell said. "Ask any viewer, I bet they'd have no idea. Besides, you need to appear human, not a perfect robot."

"I am nothing less than perfect, Russell!"

He shook his head. "Come on. The press is waiting—"

"They can wait." Carolyn turned to her speechwriter and spat: "You are finished."

Russell cast a sympathetic glance down at Brittany. "Give her a break, Carrie. She's only 25."

Carolyn glared up at him. "If you weren't always flirting with her and every other woman within a five mile radius, maybe you could think straight and understand the severity of her offense!"

Tears streamed down Brittany's cheeks.

"Dry it up!" Carolyn ordered. "You'll have plenty of time to cry on your next job. And plenty of time to think about how a successful woman must be perfect. Flawless! If she wants to make it all the way to the top."

The girl grimaced as if she'd been punched in the gut.

"And do *not* call the White House for a reference. Because I will tell your prospective employer how you fucked up the most important speech that any woman has made in modern American history!"

Carolyn spun on a bare heel, pursed her lips and walked with hard steps toward the door behind the set. The cold cement studio floor felt good under her burning hot feet, and that blister she'd gotten while running a sixth mile this morning.

"Carrie," Russell demanded, "the media is waiting. Your press conference goes live in three minutes."

"I'll be back with bells on," she said, her voice slowing again. She dashed behind the curtains, into the green room, where she sat in the make-up chair facing the mirror.

"A little powder," the make-up artist said as she dusted Carolyn's nose with a big brush. "Don't want to be shiny."

"I have to shine with brilliance," Carolyn said, staring at her reflection. Her mind was like a run-away radio dial... zipping past blaring stations: *"...meeting with Boxley... prepare speech for Middle East trip... go to the gym tomorrow morning at five... forgot to take my vitamin... speech tonight will make Daddy proud... gotta call him after the press conference... need a bottle of cold water (or a shot of bourbon)... golf Saturday with the President."* Then, for a moment, she was calm. Because she knew she'd go down in history for saving Social

Security, because she and she alone had brilliantly conceived the perfect solution.

The stylist's TV was on mute.

"Turn it up," Carolyn said, watching the conservative Republican white male commentator—the one who hated her most—on Global News Network.

"—problem is that what person in their right mind would actually forfeit money that they've given to the government throughout their working lives. Taylor's plan is ludicrous, at best."

She snatched up the remote, clicked it to the next network, where that bitch from that economy website was ranting: "—I don't know what economics class Ms. Taylor took in college, but she's sadly delusional about the generosity of our nation's upper class—"

"Bitch," Carolyn snapped as the stylist moistened her lips and spritzed her hair. She clicked to the next channel:

That bull-dyke-in-the-closet Republican senator from Texas whined, "This is a bold-faced tax increase. She promised, Ms. Taylor promised the American people during the election campaign, that she would support only minimal tax increases. Well this is major! Her deceitful trickery will backfire—"

Click!

"—Americans are desperate for a solution to so many failing systems. I think the Vice President is absolutely brilliant to propose a new way of solving our government's problems." It was the super liberal Gen-X blogger who'd never written a negative word about her. "She is protecting citizens' estates from deflation, which printing money does to all of us," the blogger said. "I've gotten emails from a lot of folks, in the last few minutes, who say they'll sign over their Social Security checks in a heartbeat, if it helps put this nation back onto firm economic ground."

Click!

Carolyn's picture was on a big screen on the set behind three 20-something chicks on the entertainment channel. "Her make-up," one girl said, "those muted earth tones, were just so hot. I wish I could look that gorgeous and sound so smart at the same time!"

"Rah, rah!" Carolyn said sarcastically as the stylist adjusted her collar. "You gotta use it, baby, 'cause we will lose it!" Carolyn had to take her vitamin and eat a big green salad tonight. All the pressure of today, she could almost feel it etching deeper lines around her eyes. Where the hell was Russell with her vitamins?

One of the chicks said, "What a great role model for the younger generation. Our Vice President shows a woman can do and be anything. I wonder why she never got married, though. Bizarre!"

"I don't like to share!" Carolyn snapped. She twisted her face with disgust. "Or compromise."

"Tell me about it," the makeup artist said. "My guy was just reamin' me a new one today about how I don't know the meaning of compromise. I told him to pack up and GTFO."

"What's that?" Carolyn asked.

"Get the fuck out," the makeup artist said.

Carolyn laughed. "Love that."

Click!

On TV, that Wall Street bastard who was always sounding the death knell for America's financial future was sitting in some money-green studio with Carolyn's face on freeze-frame, with her mouth open, on his monitor.

"Could he make me look any less dignified?" she snapped. "I oughta go up to New York and slap the shit outta his ass!"

The stylish laughed.

"Shh," Carolyn said as the commentator spoke.

"At first glance, I admit, it sounded radical. But now that I think about it, Ms. Taylor's proposal could redistribute resources in a way that grows significant security for our seniors' futures. By soliciting the support of the 'ultra rich' and implementing changes over five years, I think Americans will be open to doing this. We truly are in unprecedented economic times. The stock market is at a 15-year low. If I were a Congressman, she'd have my vote."

"Well halelluja!" Carolyn declared, throwing her hands up as Russell came through the parted curtains.

"You okay?"

"That tight-ass who does his commentary in front of the Stock Exchange, he just gave me a thumbs up."

Russell high-fived her. "Let's go," Russell said as another commentator talked about how, as a woman and as a former President's daughter, she was under immense pressure and scrutiny to succeed.

"Russell, soon as we're done, get me links to all the network analysis, so I can study what they're saying tonight. Tell Shari to buy me a new pair of running shoes for the Middle East trip. I think I've already broken down another pair. I felt those calf cramps again on the end of today's run."

"Geez," he whistled.

"Give me my talking points for tomorrow's press conference. Where are my vitamins? I forgot to take my vitamins yesterday. I'm way off schedule. Supposed to take it with breakfast. It's damn near eight o'clock at night! My cells need to repair—"

He pulled the bottle from his suit jacket pocket. "This was all they had at the corner drugstore. We'll get your usual kind when—"

She stopped at the curtain and grabbed the bottle. "This isn't my brand." The label said 1-A-Day. She turned it over, scanning for directions and the dosage. "Why the hell doesn't it say how many I should take? They think I have a whole damn hour to stand here reading this label!"

"Carrie," he said calmly, taking the bottle. "You take one a day. As the title suggests." He opened it, handed her a tablet and a bottle of water. As she tilted her head back, and chugged the water, he said, "Now, your cells can repair while you talk to the press."

She swallowed, then playfully cut her eyes at him. "If that reporter from *The Times* rips into me, I'm gonna rip right back at his ass. I'm not in the mood—"

"Carrie," Russell said as she reached to part the curtain and step through. He offered her shoes. "You'll need these."

"Not if I need to kick that reporter's ass, I won't. I'm still spittin' bullets over that article he wrote last week about the comments I made about Russia. I'd like to see that nit-wit do my job for an hour and see how brilliant he can be."

Russell gently squeezed her upper arms, looking down with a soothing expression. "Deep breath."

She inhaled, then exhaled. That was nice, but she knew what would mellow her out, all the way. A couple hours in the arms of man who was helping her make all of this happen, in a way that was far more spectacular than anybody would ever know. Especially these reporters.

As she stepped before the cameras and dozens of journalists from around the world, she envisioned herself bedazzling them with brilliant answers, then wooing the pundits into endorsing her proposal. Because she was about to make a miracle happen for America.

24. The Sky Over Kentucky

Hunter soared over horse country—an endless quilt of brown and dark green squares of earth and grass boxed in by miles and miles of white and black horse fencing. Enormous mansions reigned over vast rolling plains of horse pastures, the land dotted with barns and ponds and clusters of trees.

"Knightly Farms," Hunter said proudly, "even prettier from the sky." The 600-acre parcel of America where Hunter had grown up looked pretty as a postcard from up here. The main house had a regal French provincial design of gray brick with a stone slate roof and massive chimneys for its multiple fireplaces. The same house, though slightly smaller, also graced the rolling property.

Guilt panged in Hunter's gut. His father had built that house just for him, his gold-digging wife and the children they didn't have. His sister's family was doing just fine there; her husband loved horses more than air, so why couldn't Dad just be happy with that?

Hunter gripped the yoke, hand-flying his Maverick for the first few minutes. It felt good to control his airplane, as opposed to sitting back and letting autopilot do the work, as he often did.

Wrapping his palms around the yoke made him focus harder on flying, and forget the angst that was trying to kill his joy right now. No, he would not allow guilt to sour the sweetness of doing what he loved most—flying. He looked down at the house where he grew up. It sure did look like a chateau, with all those manicured hedges in the garden out back, and the patterned-brick patio where his mother loved to host receptions.

The life of a horse breeder and aristocrat in that mansion was just not the life Hunter wanted. No matter how hard his father had worked to build it. Hunter wanted things simpler. Or more exciting; like flying over the ocean, if Commander Buck called with a mission with the 4th Fleet, to patrol the Caribbean or South America. Or climbing into a cave to capture a terrorist, as he'd done in Afghanistan. Or bagging that drug lord in Nicaragua.

Now, the world stretched before him like an enormous mosaic of square fields bounded by roads, rows of trees and ponds. The huge Toyota plant was a cluster of white buildings to his left. Groupings of white boxy buildings held whiskey and bourbon that would age for years to perfection.

Flying a million metaphoric miles from the gloomy conflicts at home with Meredith, even though the night had ended on a mutual high note, he was literally sailing into sunnier skies. He'd checked the weather between here and West Palm Beach; it was clear as crystal all the way.

"Severe clear," he said aloud.

His route—a straight magenta line between the center of Kentucky and the edge of Southeast Florida—stretched across the colorful map on the Garmin G1000. Just like a GPS system in a car, that amazing piece of technology used satellites to pinpoint his location and his destination to Palm Beach International. He knew that straight line as he had "flight planned" his trip would be amended, as they would vector him in South Florida. They always did.

Between him and his empty co-pilot's seat was a black box with a keypad; he could enter all trip data to essentially program the plane to fly to his destination. Hunter scanned the other screens and various knobs. He pushed the audio button, one of the state-of-the-art bells and whistles he'd had loaded as a special treat. "Tell me somethin' good, darlin'."

A sultry, computerized female voice answered, "You are now flying at 13,500 feet and climbing. Your speed is 250 knots. All systems green. Estimated fuel remaining at your destination, 525 pounds."

"Ready to rock!" he said, ogling the control panel with the same awe as when he was a boy, staring at the huge candy display at the dime store in town with his sister. Always knew what he wanted—a Snickers bar and some plain old Hershey's chocolate—but he sure loved to look at all the choices. Colorful wrappers, suckers in every size, shape and flavor, bubble gum with exotic flavors like watermelon paradise. All that candy was just like women; he'd stick to the flavor he knew—his wife—but it sure was fun to look.

"Baby Doll," Hunter said, smiling at the control panel, "drive me wild!" Just like a woman, a plane could have some unpredictable behavior. "Kinks are still bein' ironed out," the guy had said when he'd delivered the new plane to Hunter's hangar in Lexington. Handing over the pilot operating handbook, the guy had said, "Keep that P.O.H. nearby at all times. Never know when she might decide to throw a little tantrum."

Hunter's P.O.H.—which according to the F.A.A., must remain in the airplane at all times—rested on the floor between the pilot seats. He had a programmer loading the P.O.H. data into his aviation note pad as an electronic version. Space was limited and precious here in the cockpit; the less paper, the better. But he had nothing to worry about in this flawless machine. So far, he'd logged 165 hours on this beauty. Not a single whisper of a problem.

One glance at the state-of-the-art avionics suite here in the cockpit, and he had a split-second reading on all the important variables for a safe flight. It was nothing like the "steam gauges" on Dad's twin-engine King Air 200, or the Twin Bonanza that had served as Hunter's training plane for flying. Only 14, he wasn't legal to drive a car, but he sure could zip across the sky like a pro. Thanks to the landing strip Dad had on the farm, they'd take her up two, sometimes three, times a week. Hunter couldn't get enough. Mom hated the idea, so he and Dad always took off when she was in town, out of town, or busy in the house. The noise always gave them away, but at least they were up and out before she could stop them.

Hunter laughed. Women were always trying to stop him from doing something he loved. Meredith's bitchin' this morning, about how long he was going to be gone, and what he'd be doing all by himself down in Florida, and when would he take her there with him for a vacation—

Hunter tightened his grip on the black yoke. Yep, just as he'd told Mr. Williams, this plane had been the Mother of Marital Discord in the Knightly home. Meredith had had a fit when she found out he was buying himself a two million dollar airplane. She didn't know anything about the couple hundred grand avionic suite that Hunter had added as custom-adds. But she had a fit all the same. Her mouth was like a demonic calculator, spewing numbers about her puny little salary and how she could be using all that airplane money to try one last-ditch effort with *in vitro*, and quitting her job, having babies and taking care of the family, never working again.

She seemed to have forgotten that the doctor had said she had zero chance of conceiving, thanks to scarring from that abortion during college. The abortion that she'd conveniently forgotten to tell him about until she was his wife, sobbing in the doctor's office, hearing the bad news about how her greed had damaged her womb. The father, she confessed, had been her one and only sexual partner, her college sweetheart that she'd just broken up with when she met Hunter. The guy's parents had a hardscrabble life, working on a tobacco farm, but his future was lined with millions because he was, thanks to an athletic scholarship, the star of the UK football team. He was all set to sign a seven-figure deal with the NFL—and Meredith had insured her part of the deal with the baby growing inside her, and the engagement ring sparkling on her finger—when he smashed up his leg in a car crash on Paris Pike. Having no professional athlete's insurance, he was financially ruined.

Meredith miscarried, she told him, and returned the ring around the same time as his NFL dream crashed and burned.

Those memories were stealing Hunter's joy up here in the sky. But his gut still cramped with the devastating realization, years ago in that doctor's office, that he'd married a lying, conniving, manipulating schemer whose singular goal was to bag the rich guy and live the glamorous life.

"You got me," Hunter said, "but I'm gone, baby." Air Traffic Control cleared him of all speed restrictions. He accelerated the plane, closing his eyes as the delicious pressure pressed him back into the plush leather folds of his pilot's chair. Autopilot was now engaged to level him off at flight level 370.

He focused on the dazzling colors and textures of the horizon. Dark green earth, blending with a band of silver-gray haze between land and sky, then shades of blue that started pale and intensified into the clearest, deepest blue. The same shade as his plane.

I'm one with the sky.

He scanned the avionics. All readings were right where they should be. He could already make out the edge of the Atlantic Ocean, after only 45 minutes at 37,000 feet.

Now, on to the dead dentist and his wife, down in Diamond Lagoon. Had to figure out whether it was accidental or foul play. Then he'd decide whether the insurance company should pay the claim, and if so, to whom it would be paid, and whether another party could be brought in to share in the financial claim.

Then he'd fly over to the Gulf of Mexico side of Florida to check out the type of "wealth planning" luncheon where Randy's client had fallen prey to big-money fraud.

Hunter couldn't shake thoughts about that report on *TheInsuranceGazette.com*. Were these life settlement arrangements good or bad? Were they helping people, or being used to take advantage of people? The insurance companies had heavy-duty advertising in all the retirement hotspots. In particular, Hunter had handled a case of fraud that originated when an insurance salesman met new clients at Luxury Suites in Naples, right on the Gulf of Mexico.

The case, flagged for fraud in the system, involved the client committing a common sin in the insurance business—lying about one's health on the formal application. Just last week, Hunter had denied a claim for an Arkansas man who claimed he never smoked, but the autopsy showed classic smoker's lungs—gray/black, full of soot instead of pink and healthy. And the ultimate "kiss of death" was his doctor's records that showed, just three weeks before his death, that he should quit smoking and take a prescription for Chantix. How stupid.

Hunter agreed with Randal that this trip would be an ideal time to get a feel for these ostentatious productions by insurance agents who were possibly preying on super-wealthy snowbirds. He'd seen their splashy ads in the Florida papers, promising free lunch seminars. But nothing in life was free. Especially if it involved life insurance.

As he scanned the vast terrain below, Hunter's thoughts spun a million miles a minute. Those wealthy snowbirds were the ones that Carrie would be asking to forfeit their Social Security payments. Hunter couldn't wait to casually bring that up in a conversation. How in the world did she think she was going to pull off something so radical? She would either be hailed as a hero, or stopped dead in her tracks.

Hunter checked his altitude, his speed, his fuel. He could hear his father warning over and over, "Always stay ahead of the airplane." Hunter loaded the correct approach plate for landing, still 15 minutes out. He confirmed that all systems were good.

"What the—" Gray static, like "snow" on a TV screen, filled the avionics panels. It wiped out the maps, the brightly colored numbers and diagrams and maps on the flat screens before him.

Short circuit? Electrical failure?

"Hell no!"

"Warning," said the computerized female voice. "Warning. Electronic malfunction. Total system failure. Warning."

25. Washington, D.C.

Her whole body hummed with frustration and hunger. The little blue digits said 8:45 a.m. on the screen of her BlackBerry. Here in her luxurious hotel suite, Carolyn Snedegar Taylor hated this familiar feeling that things were moving too slowly. That nobody would take her seriously as a leader. That she would never satisfy this immense hunger for power, for money, and for erotic fulfillment.

During her entire five-mile run starting at five o'clock this morning, she'd stewed over every detail of her SOS Rescue plan. Potential pitfalls. Her overall strategy. And the intoxicating fantasy of actually pulling it off.

"You will succeed," Neal had said at six a.m. when she romped back into bed with her benefactor for another pathetic round of Minute Man sex. Last night, amidst the champagne and praise for her speech, he'd gotten her all wet and wild, did his business lickity split, then dozed off like a baby. Just like a man, it was all about him.

Didn't give a rat's ass about her needs. Sexually, anyway.

Carolyn didn't much care; this physical transaction was as much a part of their business deal as handling paperwork and talking during strategy sessions. Because she wasn't with this 55-year-old billionaire for mind-blowing sex. No, her motive was much bigger. And as such, her sex power was better spent by channeling it up to her brain. She'd handle the hot mess between her legs at a later time. When she was really ready to celebrate. And that wouldn't come a day sooner than when the world would celebrate her as the savior of Social Security—and the first female President of the United States.

"I've got the deal of the century for you," Neal had said last year when he first proposed this idea. With his all-American good looks, and super-intelligent but calculating eyes, he had laid out how Magna Corporation could offer a sale of this valuable company to just the right political suitor.

Batting her best doe eyes, sprinkling the conversation with her sing-song confessions about how economics had always been her most baffling subject in college, she took him up on his offer. And was in the process of taking that manipulative motherfucker to the cleaners.

"President Taylor," she said aloud.

A short while ago, as she'd eaten her usual oatmeal, fruit and egg whites, she was sure that every bite would taste even more delicious if a waiter said, "Your Breakfast, Madame President," before her meal.

Just minutes ago, the briefing with Russell about her day's meetings had filled her head with 50 more things to think about. He had given her talking points for two meetings today. And he knew about her next meeting, but would sit that one out. Because Russell knew nothing about the content of the next item on her agenda: a top secret meeting with the beautiful window dressing around the shiny package of hope and help that she was offering to the America people.

"Where the hell is he?"

Sitting at the long, shiny table in the five star hotel suite's dining room, she flipped open a laptop and scanned the websites for *The Washington News, The New York Journal*, the major TV networks, and every other place that would have something to say about her, her speech and her SOS Plan to rescue Social Security. She devoured every word of praise and criticism, vowing to use it all to hone both the content and delivery of her next speech.

"Madame Vice President," said one of her Secret Service guys said from the doorway. "He's here." The tiny numbers at the top of her laptop screen said 9:00.

"Gerry, darlin'! You're late!" she accused, standing up to greet Senator Boxley, impeccably dressed in his usual blue pinstriped suit. His adorable dog strutted in alongside him.

"I am exactly on time," he said, bending to kiss her hand. His full, pink lips were warm and soft against her skin. As were his fingertips under hers. He looked up and said, "Nine o'clock on the dot."

"My daddy always said, 'On time is late. Early is on time.' But your people have a different schedule. You're better than that! We don't operate on CP time here in our nation's capitol."

Boxley let out a bellow of a laugh. He stood a good six inches taller than her, even in these gosh-darn heels that were already hurting. Why couldn't she just wear her running shoes all day? Why did he get to sport the comfortable flat loafers while her feet were scrunched in these pointed, three-inch monstrosities? Especially since she was doing all the major thinking here. Come to think of it, why did he get to wear slacks and she was confined to these damn pantyhose and a skirt so narrow she couldn't take a big stride?

Stop it! Thinking about the vast unfairness between men and women on every level made her feel like steam would blow out of her ears. That's why she would get even, by beating them at their own greedy, lying, cheating game.

Boxley's dark orange silk tie and starched white shirt complimented his exotic complexion. Its color always reminded Carolyn of the luscious golden-brown tops of those buttered buttermilk biscuits that she grew up on. The kind their cook, NormaJane, used to knead with her plump brown fingers and bake to flaky perfection. Then she'd set them out in a basket on the big kitchen table. Carolyn loved to spread them with butter, drizzle them with honey as Daddy read the papers and talked about international crises and the bills he would sign into law that day.

Hell, if she ate like that today, her ass would be as wide as this table. Better to indulge the flavor and texture with the adult pleasure of—

Mmmm. The sight of this man, with her body hungry for a real hammering... No! She could not get distracted by lust. That's what ordinary people did, and ended up stuck in the hellish mediocrity of their lives as a result.

Carolyn's mind still felt razor-sharp as she stared at his delicious color. Boxley had the look of a fancy African American man, perfectly groomed, not a hair astray from those pretty black and silver waves shining against his head and ending in a neat row of tiny curls at the top of his always-shaved neck.

"Madame Vice President," he said with the utmost formality that he'd no doubt practiced as an international business student at Oxford University in England. "I did not become a U.S. Senator by following Colored People's Time." He held up his left wrist; a band of gold and the sparkle of 12 diamonds around the face shimmered from beneath his white, monogrammed shirt cuffs clasped by gold cufflinks. "I'm on Rolex time today. Other days, Cartier does the job quite well."

"I'm just teasin'," she said. "I can do that; I was raised by three different black women, my nannies. Damn, my heart hurts every time I think about Miss Mable. Died 'a cancer over Christmas. The sweetest lady—"

Carolyn stared into the sympathetic expression in Boxley's hazel eyes. They were almost the same color as his skin, but less yellow, more topaz.

"Your Creole people down there in Louisiana are the most fascinating blend of genetics," she said. "I swear."

"You're looking at French, Indian, Black—"

"That last one is all that counts," she said, waving a hand toward the silver coffee service on the table. "Need a jolt before we get started?"

"Seeing you is all the jolt I need, Carolyn," he said, flashing straight white teeth.

She guided him to two chintz armchairs by a large, paned window overlooking a courtyard. The dog nestled at his feet.

"Katrina, you're so cute," Carolyn said, reaching to pat the short, gray-brown fur on the Catahoula Leopard Dog. She growled slightly, pressing her head against Boxley's leg and looking up with gray-blue eyes. "Well excuse me, little missy. You just love your daddy. Nobody else."

"Loyalty," Boxley said. "Ever since I pulled her from the floodwaters—"

Carolyn waved her hand. "I know, I know, darlin'. I saw the story on GNN with the rest of the world. That one picture was worth a million votes for you."

And he was worth many million votes for her. He was the politically correct, financially beneficial face on her SOS Plan that would launch her into the history books, and into the Oval Office. She leaned close, using her most seductive voice: "Gerry, darlin', your life depends on this goin' off without a hitch. Ya hear?"

"I assure you, Carrie, the word *hitch* has no place in our plan."

Yes, this was the perfect man for her plan.

26. The Sky Over Georgia

Hunter watched in shock as all three avionics screens flashed intermittent red, then snow, and back to red, like a TV channel with no programming.

His body switched into the most serene state of calm that men who were born to fly seemed to have hardwired into their systems. It was as if the sights and sounds of danger flipped him into super-calm autopilot, so that he could concentrate on a solution without the distraction of panic.

He could almost hear the calm drone of Charles Yeager, who was famous for saying, while flying commercial: "Aw, folks, we seem to have, aw, a little red light flashing up here."

Hunter's calm was bolstered by memories of a flight with his dad when the engine died. Only 10 years old on that blustery September day over Kentucky... *Hunter was amazed at his own calm as his father had assumed an almost zombie-like trance. Dad steered and coasted as Hunter watched the altitude drop from 3,350 to 3,001 to 2,900...*

They were still moving at 87 knots. With the prop slowly windmilling on the nose of the aircraft, they had to coast and figure out the problem before they hit 57 knots; that's when the plane would stop flying. The ideal would be for that to occur just above the ground at the runway.

Dad quickly opened his Pilot Operating Handbook. He pulled some knobs and flipped some switches. Vvvrrrrroooom! That baby came back to life at full speed.

"*Yessiree!*" Dad had boomed as they ascended back up toward the deep blue sky.

"*Woo-hoo!*" Hunter cheered.

"*Son, that's what you call being a real man and a real pilot,*" Dad had said. "*When crisis is at hand, you find out if flyin' is in your blood. Or not.*"

"*How do you know?*" Hunter had asked.

"*A man who's born to fly,*" Dad said, "*like myself, I shift to a mode where I think about every move, before I make it. You don't just touch something, just to be doing something.*"

"*What if you get scared?*" Hunter asked.

"*Just like them fuel lines are feedin' gasoline into the engine,*" Dad said, "*You let that fear fuel your brain to think, calculate, anticipate the outcome of your every move. You gotta think what is right and what is wrong with each and every action, because it's all happenin' so fast.*"

"*A pilot doesn't freak out. 'Less he wants to make the newspaper the next day, and his funeral a few days after that.*"

"*You're a real pilot, Dad,*" Hunter had declared. "*And I'm a real pilot, too.*"

Then why the hell was Baby Doll trying to short circuit on him right now? Though the three blood-red screens on the avionics panel across the entire front of the cockpit were quite ominous, the plane was not losing altitude. In fact, the turbine was still spinning. And the engine was still generating proper thrust. So all systems were not failing. So why were his avionics screens filling with that electronic snow, as if he'd suddenly turned to the wrong channel on television?

Every cell in Hunter's body became focused on the landing. His body and brain were one with the flying machine around him; the razor-sharp focus on every detail exhilarated him because it left no room for thinking about the mundane problems of life. Heck, most times, he didn't even want to eat when he was flying.

"All systems 100 percent," the computerized voice said as the three panels repopulated with all of the information. The map with his flight route reappeared; the magenta line stretched across the chart for his final 10 minutes into Palm Beach International.

"Estimated fuel remaining at destination: 545 pounds. Altitude: 15,000 feet."

Hunter's quick mental calculation on burning less fuel was that he must have had a tail wind as a result of this most recent cold front moving through. And since he'd never experienced such interference right over NASA and Merritt Island, his gut told him it was something more.

"What the hell was that?"

27. Washington, D.C.

The Vice President needed to lay it out for Boxley so he understood exactly what was expected of him. Or else.

"The bill is written," she said. "On Monday, Donaldson will officially introduce it to the House. I expect the Republicans in the Senate to get behind you like they did on the Education Initiative. This is a slam dunk."

"I agree wholeheartedly," he said, nodding. "Pardon my rather crass reference, Carolyn. But this situation reminds me of what my fraternity brothers used to say about a man's prowess: 'It doesn't matter what kind of nail you have, if you don't have a hammer.'"

Carolyn laughed. "With the Republicans, we've got a jackhammer nailin' support for us."

Gerald smiled that she got his joke. "Republican support is paramount, since their constituents more often than not include the ultra rich, who'll have to make the sacrifice. Although it's laughable to call $1600 per month a sacrifice for a multi-millionaire."

His words punched Carolyn's mad button, which released an array of images... all those wealthy CEOs who lived like Louis XIV while downsizing hardworking men and women into foreclosures and bankruptcies... or raiding the retirement funds so grandparents had to spend their golden years serving up burgers and fries at the local fast food joint... or asking the government to bail them out after years of financial recklessness. She hated those stingy conservative capitalists who had made life hell for her father's administration. Now was her time to shove all that grief back up their asses.

"Nobody gets that rich," Carolyn said, "without screwin' somebody over. You know that, Gerry. So, think of this as us helping the universe and its little law on karma: 'What goes around, comes around.'"

Boxley's eyes glimmered. He understood exactly what she was thinking.

"We're two of a kind, darlin'," she said. "The alliance of a lifetime. Not to mention, your work on the Senate Finance Committee showed me you've got the financial savvy to comprehend the enormity of what we're doin' here."

"That I do," he said. "I have an overwhelming respect for the billions at stake, and the sophistication of our arrangement."

"You couldn't be more invested in this, Gerry," she said, staring hard at him. If he fucked this up, he wouldn't live to enjoy the huge fortune that was his for the taking. He crossed his legs, letting his shiny black shoed foot dangle from over his long leg, with the perfectly creased cuff swaying above it. He laced his fingers together, his gold wedding band shining, as he rested his praying hands mid-thigh and cast a cool, concentrated gaze right back at her.

Protective body language. Fake confidence in his eyes. Good. He's scared shitless. Knows if he fucks up, I got his fancy ass on a silver platter.

She leaned forward slightly. "Here's another word for you today, Gerry: Trillions. I want you to remember, every hour on the hour, every day of the week, that we're talkin' about more than 14 trillion dollars! How many zeroes is that, Gerry?"

"Twelve zeroes."

"Doesn't that just blow your mind? Fourteen, followed by 12 zeroes, with a dollar sign in front. All that money, just waiting for us to put it to good use. And we only need a fraction of it—"

He grinned. "Sing my tune, sweetheart."

Carolyn smiled. His sexy tone and the sparkle in his eye reminded her of some of the steamier moments that had helped her convince him that this was the secret alliance of a lifetime, and that he'd best say yes and do everything she needed him to do.

"I am going to do everything in my power," he said with a sensuous rasp, "to show you perfection at every turn. In fact, we've identified an added bonus: estate taxes. This is an added windfall to the tax base. That's a benefit even we failed to realize as a bi-product to our plan."

He paused, staring with a calculating glint. "Of course, the only two things that are certain for anyone are life, death and taxes. So thinking about this: 45 cents for every dollar transfer in an estate over three million dollars. There's a few more zeroes for you, Ms. V.P."

Carolyn squealed. "Now that's music to my ears." She leaned forward, letting her blouse part slightly to reveal creamy mounds of cleavage. "You know, Gerry," she said softly, "when all this goes down, you'll be livin' like a king. Set for life in some Caribbean villa."

"The French Riviera," he corrected playfully. "Already picked out my chateau."

"I love a man with vision," Carolyn said. "Now apply that to getting our stamp of approval." Her tone hardened: "That's the big picture. The little picture is the day-by-day tasks to make this happen. One by one, two by two. Smooth as glass."

"Understood. With perfect clarity."

"You get your people to do this right. No questions. No glitches. No problems. Ya hear?"

He nodded. "I have to relay, however, we did have one small problem. But it's since been resolved. And will never happen again."

She pursed her lips. "What problem? That word is not anywhere on the vocabulary list for this alliance, Gerry, darlin'. And while we're on the subject, I hear you had a cozy little dinner with Sue Bookman over at Le Bon Dîner. The chef himself served up your meal."

He looked bewildered.

"I know everything," Carolyn said.

Boxley nodded meekly. "The Secretary of State invited me—"

"Stay away from her," Carolyn said. "Or you can kiss your chateau on the French Riviera, your cute little dog, and everything else, goodbye."

28. The Sea Palace Yacht Club, South Beach, Florida

With his yacht docked at this high-security boutique marina, Juan stretched out on a huge white mattress on the top deck. Pillows propped up his back; before him stretched the glistening blue Biscayne Bay and the Miami skyline of sleek hotels and million-dollar condo towers. But Juan was not taking in the scenery that made Miami a playground for the world's rich and famous.

Instead, he focused on the task that enabled him to live this glamorous life: the portal where lists of names and pictures of faces provided him with his daily work. With his laptop on his thighs, he navigated to the web page that looked like the face of a black Panther. Its smoky green-brown eye provided the spaces for him to type his user name and password.

A panther's roar indicated that access was granted. There, on endless spreadsheets for each city and region of America, he input information for each Order that was complete. Boxley's company had set up invoices, Order forms and online databases for each K.C. Team Leader to log on as a vendor, place an Order, submit an invoice and retrieve other pertinent information, such as a personal profile for each Order.

Payment was always in person; Juan's jet enabled him to deliver compensation quickly and discreetly across America.

Subcontracting with the electronic surveillance company helped, too, by providing all the vendors with the materials required to do their quickest, cleanest and most efficient work. The logs and information could not be printed. The "print screen" did not ever work and once a contract was complete, no cyber record existed. The name and picture simply disappeared.

They were all the same: rich old people. At first, he'd thought about his grandmother down in Bogotá. She was a sweet old woman who deserved to enjoy as many days as she had left. What if someone wanted her dead? They didn't. And all these Orders were strangers. Juan had no idea why they were the targets. He simply had a job to do, and the rewards cleared his conscience—

"Juan Baby, come on the jet skis with us," Gigi—wearing a tiny red bikini, appeared at the foot of the mattress. "Can Juan come out and play? Why are you still working?"

"My work lets you play," Juan said, "so go, have fun. I'll have plenty of time to join you later." As she strutted away, her ass looked juicy enough to bite.

"Adios, mamacita," he groaned, as lust burned through his body. She turned back and smiled. Maybe he could take a break and—

The computer beeped. Across the screen, green letters flashed URGENT MESSAGE. Juan typed in his user name and password yet again to access the message. The black space where the sender's name should have appeared was always black. Blank. Juan assumed the directives in these periodic emails came from his Angel. The message popped up:

"URGENT: Due to a sudden change in circumstances, you must immediately double K.C. Leadership nationwide. Portal will deliver twice the number of current Orders for each state through December 2009. Immediate expedition of Orders required."

Juan read it again. He was already working his ass off. In a short while, he'd jet off to deliver payments up the coast of Florida. Now he'd have to double this? It meant twice the money, but—

They want to work me to death...

Juan read it one more time.

He whispered *Go to Hell* in Spanish. "And I'll go to heaven. Casuarina Cay."

Doubling the Orders could mean two things. First, that Eldorado was in trouble. Were the feds threatening to expose it and shut it down? Second, an accelerated pace could simply indicate greed. By the Angel. By Boxley. By whoever the hell was behind it all. And Juan had seen far too many times, greed led to disaster.

I gotta get out. After I plunder Eldorado... But how?

Juan clicked the X in the corner of the email. A pouf sound accompanied a small, animated dust cloud that sparkled as the email disappeared. Gone forever. Untraceable. They simply evaporated in cyberspace. The same thing happened with every Order after he read it and sent the information via benign-looking invoices.

And he had so many today...

Red-hot rage pulsed through his veins as he stared out at the turquoise bay. It led to the Bahamas, and his island paradise. They just upped the ante on him. Yeah, he'd double his workload. And double his efforts to find the Emperor of Eldorado, conquer that *conchetumare*, that motherfucker, and fly away forever.

Juan almost smiled. Because he had already interviewed a second tier of K.C. Leaders across the country. Always needed a back-up crew if the first one got caught, killed or otherwise disqualified.

Yeah, he'd win, but the sooner he got down to his island to figure out how, the better. One quick phone call, and he'd take the helicopter to the airport.

Juan pulled his BlackBerry from his belt and called his personal intelligence assistant, known only as K. They'd never met in person. Didn't need to. But Juan could call him at 3 a.m. for a background check on somebody... or take a peek through the government's satellite surveillance on a particular house... or check on the cash pick-ups... and K would have the information within minutes. Always.

"You got the background check on Ricky Perkins in Phoenix?" Juan had interviewed the mid-level drug dealer to become a K.C. Leader, but something about the guy didn't add up.

K always answered before it rang even once. His deep voice reminded Juan of metal grating against metal.

"Since he worked for you the first time around, he's copped a real renegade reputation," K said. "Bad news."

"Next," Juan said. "Malinda Reeves, Chicago."

"A-plus material for you. Former high-end call girl. Has some kids. Looking for easier work, less risk."

Juan chuckled. "Everything's relative."

"As for the sailor you told me about," K said. Juan had called K to find out about a pest who'd shown up on the port side of a 45-foot Sea Ray, staring at Juan through binoculars. Some of the girls were sunbathing on the mattresses when the guy yelled, "Josette! I'm comin' to get your slutty ass!"

Topless, she had sobbed that the guy was her obsessed ex-boyfriend. Juan didn't need K's report anymore, but let him talk anyway. As K described the guy as an unemployed mechanic from Minneapolis, Juan sent an email through the secret portal for K to check out all the bitches on this boat. He couldn't be too careful about who they were, what they wanted, or why that asshole from Minneapolis might be looking for them.

"Right away, Mr. Panther," K said. "I'll have what you need on all eight, back in a flash."

The deep chop noise above let Juan know that the helicopter was landing on top of the yacht. Both the yacht and the chopper were driven by some of the trusted crew that once guarded his turf during his previous reign in quite a different business. He could trust these guys with his life. And to service the yacht, captain it, serve the food and take care of unexpected tasks. During Juan's 15-some years in the pen, they had remained loyal.

"I guess they didn't see all the Coast Guard warnings about the coral reef a short way out," said Juan's top crewman, who had driven the mechanic's boat out, smashed it up, and climbed up onto the helicopter piloted by another of Juan's crew. "That shit can tear up a hull and sink a boat in a couple minutes flat. Them sharks are havin' a good lunch today."

Juan nodded. *Fresh cut mechanic, flown in from Minneapolis.*

29. Washington, D.C.

Carolyn's tone turned downright bitchy as she ordered: "Now tell me *exactly* what kinda problem you're talkin' about, Gerry, darlin'."

"A miniscule kink in the system," he said too confidently. "Call it a growing pain that's since been massaged away."

"Well if any more kinks come along, you use the FBI, the CIA and whatever else you need to smooth that baby out, ya hear? Whatever you have to do."

"Understood," Boxley said. "Carolyn, our state motto down in Louisiana is 'Union, Justice and Confidence.' I live by that. Especially in our shared endeavor."

"Of course you do," she said.

"To further assure you," Boxley continued, "I've called a meeting with my team to reinforce the absolutely imperative need for flawlessness in every assignment."

"Now you're talkin'," she said. "The future of America depends on our perfect execution of this. Not a single failure."

"Absolutely, Carolyn. Absolutely."

Carolyn stared hard into his eyes. This operation was mammoth. They had to maintain strict control, lest it become unwieldy. What with so many people handling the nitty-gritty details.

"Gerry, darlin', don't you let me hear about one single monkey wrench gettin' tossed into our perfect machine, ya hear?'

"Loud and clear," he said with a grave stare.

"Now you know," Carolyn said, "I am one heartbeat away from bein' the Commander in Chief. The President is so stressed out about this newest terrorism drama, you know it's takin' a toll on his ticker. Shoot, after 72 years, that sucker could give out any minute."

Gerry shook his head, but his eyes glowed with the thrill of that very realistic fantasy. "He looked quite pallid when I saw him last week at the Tribute to Literacy."

"Pallid," she snickered. "Downright corpse-like. The old man could fall over dead right now. And if he does, I've got it."

"Madame President," Gerry said, bowing dramatically.

"Either that way, or our way, when my SOS Plan makes history. I rise; you rise with me, as a reward for your loyalty and dedication in handling such delicate and—" she let her eyes smolder at him, "—clandestine orchestrations."

He held her stare, smoldering right back in a way that made a hot, sexy bolt of lust zigzag through her middle, exploding in a tingle between her legs. She hated that her body was still aroused—and excruciatingly unsatisfied— after that blink-in-time interlude with her benefactor this morning.

She thought about Boxley's hammer-and-nail comment. Neal had both, in a metaphoric sense, with power and money. But in the bedroom, he had more like a staple, with a jammed stapler that failed to penetrate and hold down the sheets.

Instead, Neal's stamina was concentrated in his brainpower and in the boardroom. Fucking him was little more than an exercise in getting aroused, faking it for a few minutes, then after his Minute Man performance, pretending she loved it. If some women got mad over being all dressed up with nowhere to go, Carolyn got furious when she was all wet and throbbing—with no way to come. A woman of her beauty and charm and intelligence shouldn't have to do it herself. But this hunger for satisfaction, on days like today, would be better utilized when redirected into getting rewards that were far bigger and better than the fleeting thrill of the moment.

Because sleeping with Neal wasn't about the Big O. It was about the Big D—as in Dollar. And the Big P. Power. And Presidency.

With Boxley though, she knew from past experience, she could get the deal and the great cock, all in one discreet package that never failed to satisfy. In the bedroom, Boxley had the jackhammer and the super-strong nail, all in one...

"You are baaaaad, Senator Boxley," she whispered.

"Only a very select few have the privilege of knowing that," he said, tilting his chin up to a cocky angle. "The rest of the world can continue to appreciate my squeaky clean reputation as a family man, a reformer, an advocate for the people—"

"Image is everything," she said. "And when you introduce this bill, the media's gonna be buzzin' around you like bees at a Sunday picnic. So I'm gonna have you meet with the consultants, to coach you on exactly what to say."

"Appreciated." He unlaced his fingers, uncrossed his legs. She took that to mean he was totally open to her ideas. Her orders.

"Meanwhile," she said, "all those greedy, rich bastards who don't need their Social Security checks anyway, might need a little persuasion. The genteel Southern kind that you're so good at giving. Couldn't believe when you sweet-talked Donaldson, that conservative prick, into siding with you on the schooling issue. We sure got him by the short curly ones now."

She smiled, loving that this conservative Republican who once rallied against her father, and who led an aggressive campaign against her and the President in Florida, had a sudden change of heart about her and her ideas. America would chalk that up to her nonpartisan appeal; she would forever credit those text messages that she retrieved from the cell phone company. That married "family values" guy definitely didn't want America to read the virtual romance novel he'd composed with his multitude of gay lovers across the country. Seemed like the closer they got to South Beach, the nastier they got. It helped, Carolyn smiled, to have the photographs to back her up—literally—the thousands of text messages that both scheduled and described at least one tryst per day.

"Having the support of the most conservative man in the House," Carolyn said with a sneaky smile, "makes us look like heroes."

"It's all about finding common ground," Boxley said with a knowing smile. "And money is the most common denominator we know."

She said, "Some key words for you to sprinkle any- and everywhere: 'ultra rich' and 'patriotic.' The masses of 'have-nots' are gonna love thinkin' they're getting somethin' for free from the 'haves.' So we've got 99 percent of America in need, and one percent of America livin' the good life. Let's use guilt, peer pressure, fear, love for our fellow man, and anything else you can think of, to make America buy into this SOS Plan. By any means necessary. Ya hear?"

"Understood," he said.

"Now, Donaldson owes me a jumbo, juicy favor that's been a long time comin'. I'm gonna work on him, while you pretty up to the media, and all your Democratic friends."

"Indeed," he said. "Remember at baseball games, when everyone did the wave? A whole section would stand and raise their hands, and it would go all around the stadium? That's how I envision the groundswell of support for Vice President Taylor's SOS Rescue Plan."

"I love it!" she exclaimed, smiling for the first time this morning. Because it was only a matter of time before everyone would be calling her "President Taylor." Whether it would be four years or four weeks, it didn't really matter to her; she would enjoy the ride, regardless of the price.   "Success is a journey, not a destination," her Daddy always said.

30. SURFN Intersection in the Sky Over Southeast Florida

Hunter Knightly marveled at the breathtaking majesty of flying over the green land that extended up to the vast blue Atlantic sparkling to his left. The sky was bluer than blue as the sun beamed its high noon brightest. The airways were abuzz with small aircraft: private jets for both training and sightseeing, with many whisking men and women to business meetings, or families on vacations, or pilots just out for a joy ride.

"Awesome!" he exclaimed, loving every second of the parade of planes in this bedazzling sky show. A beige King Air 350 zoomed in the distance to the right. A Delta 747 cruised like a silver bird above. A twin-engine Cessna 421 zipped along to the left. And—

"What the hell is that?" Hunter gawked at the sexiest little piece of composite aircraft he'd ever seen. Fire engine red, sleek. Definitely a VLJ. But not a design that Hunter recognized from his favorite magazines and websites. That hot momma even gave his pimped out Baby Doll a run for her money. And fast! Here and gone in a heartbeat. A red streak in the sky.

"Oh no, you don't!" Hunter said playfully. He pushed a button, canceling his I.F.R. flight plan, so he could change directions.

Whoosh! The power of acceleration pressed him back into the warm embrace of his leather seat. The blue numbers became blurs, then registered 275 knots. And that guy was still going faster. Hunter accelerated to 385 knots. In a flash, he caught up behind the red beauty. He needed to go a little faster, and get beside the plane, so he could see the tail number. He'd type it into flightaware.com and find out what she was, and who was in the pilot's seat.

But just as he approached from the rear left quadrant of the little red plane–almost formation flying less than 1,000 feet away from it–the plane shot away.

Like a shooting star.

A red one, firing toward the ocean.

In less than a minute, the aircraft was a silver dot that disappeared against the infinite blue of sea and sky.

"What the hell?" Hunter had seen plenty of shooting stars over the farm as a kid. They moved so fast, and seemed so far out and mysterious, that they always left him wondering if he'd really seen them. That sexy red bullet in the sky had the same effect. It reminded him of a military Stealth, definitely faster than the speed of sound. So fast that Hunter had not gotten the tail number. Had to be military. But military planes were gray, or camouflage or black. Red was about the flashiest color in the spectrum. And the military was not flashy.

Hunter slowed back down to 250 knots. He corrected, back on course. But that plane stayed on his mind. Now, he shared the sky with a G-5 painted in airbrushed reds, browns and greens—with a rapper's face and the name Big G—along with a pink, twin engine Seneca with a breast cancer awareness ribbon painted on its tail.

Down here in Florida he was liable to see anything—even in the sky. But that red hot rod, that left him downright baffled.

Though he'd been flying most of his life, it still struck him, at times, that up here in the sky, nothing was underneath him. Nothing holding him up. The engine power, of course. But unlike a car's tires on the road, or a boat's hull in the water, the only thing beneath an airplane was, well, air. The mechanics of his engine, the wings, flaps and trim tabs, plus plenty of Jet A fuel, kept him flying like a bird.

But the true magic of flying was faith. Faith that this airplane would carry him safely through the sky and back down to Earth. Hunter passed over velvety green golf courses... rugged swampland... small towns and mansions. Winding inlets, ponds and lakes.

"Wow," he said, looking down at a golf course community whose greens looked bright enough to glow in the dark. Surrounding them were palatial homes on large lots with swimming pools. That was probably a gated community because it looked so perfectly contained by a ring of trees. And compared to the surrounding developments, it really stood out.

"You are now seven-point-two miles from your destination," the airplane voice told him. "Glide slope engaged." He glanced at the monitor. The nose of the airplane on top of the magenta line from Lexington to West Palm was almost to the tip of the ocean. Baby Doll said, "Deploy landing gear."

Hunter marveled at how little he had to think up here, thanks to modern technology. He was sure the day would come when he could program the plane to automatically deploy the landing gear when the GPS system detected its proximity to the destination airport.

"Not yet," Hunter said. Besides, this plane already did so much for him, he'd be sitting up here with nothing to do.

The control tower operator said, "Maverick 137 Hotel Kilo, contact tower now 119.7. Goo' day."

"Maverick 137 Hotel Kilo," Hunter responded. "Airport in sight. Request side step to 27 left."

"Maverick 137 Hotel Kilo. PBI Tower clear to land, number two, 27 left. Caution, wake turbulence. Boeing 747 short final. Nice ride."

Hunter responded, "Clear to land, 27 left. Thanks." That runway put him closer to his regular parking spot.

Looking down at the landing strip, Hunter exclaimed, "There she is." It resembled a giant black asphalt road with white dotted lines down the center. He envisioned the smoothest landing for this spectacular flight. He had to slow the plane down to 80 knots, or 88 miles per hour, for her to stop flying and touch down. He deployed the landing gear, which hummed beneath him as it descended.

"Maverick 137 Hotel Kilo," Hunter told the control tower. "Ready to land."

"Cleared to land. Now number one for 27 left," the control tower operator responded.

Thank goodness for his excellent vision; anybody with a depth perception problem could not land an airplane. The ground came up so fast, a guy could crash in a split second if he wasn't paying attention.

The wheels touched the ground. The plane slowed.

And Hunter smiled. One of his smoothest landings ever. But who the hell was flying that red hot rod in the sky?

31. BOSAR Intersection at the North End of the Exumas, The Bahamas

Juan Pantera Diablo was so furious, it felt like a thousand matchsticks were igniting under his skin. As his airplane soared over the Caribbean, his high-tech cockpit, with its colorful flat screens and simulated terrain, made him feel like he was playing a virtual reality video game. The objective? The evil Emperor tried to work The Panther to death, then toss his carcass to the sharks below. But The Panther always won by creeping up on the Emperor to plunder the fortune of Eldorado.

"I always win," Juan groaned.

He would never relinquish this intoxicating feeling of control and power here in the single pilot cockpit, with the avionics suite that rivaled NASA's best rockets. The bubble of glass around his head and shoulders provided unobstructed views from his periphery and on up to heaven.

Where I will stay.

From the sky, the 700-plus islands of the Bahamas looked like a submerged black and blue mountain ridge whose peaks had surged up through the sea's surface as violently as Juan's thoughts now ricocheted through his mind. Ringed by every imaginable shade of turquoise, the cool colors failed to temper his red-hot rage.

But like the lush explosions of green foliage and white sand atop each island, the depths of his mind would, during this short get-away, erupt with ideas for Operation Vanish. All the while, that email had burned into his brain and now streamed like a stock ticker across his thoughts:

"...Due to a sudden change in circumstances... immediately double K.C. Leadership nationwide.... twice the number of current Orders... through December, 2009. Immediate expedition... required."

Juan couldn't wait to for his disappearance to serve as an urgent newsflash for the Emperor. No more Eldorado to do the dirty work. The motherfucker could take *that* for "a sudden change of circumstances..."

Below, a row of tiny islands dotting the water in a claw shape indicated he was nearing his three-mile long, one-mile wide tropical sanctuary. That phrase, *No man is an island,* popped into his thoughts. That phrase was correct. That's why, back in the day, Juan's small army of gun-strapped guards had patrolled every inch of Casuarina Cay by foot and by boat. They'd taken care of the island ever since, even now.

Laying claim to this island years ago was one of his best decisions ever. When he bought it, the Bahamas

Investment Board had said that his conveyance was to the shoreline at high tide. That way the beaches remained public property and any Bahamian could use the beaches on any island. Even the nearby ones that were owned by famous singers and actors. But no locals would visit Juan's beaches.

Because The Panther's soldiers never let anyone—even innocuous-looking vacationers in luxury sailboats—come within half a nautical mile of this place.

Just like he hadn't let that little blue and white jet fly up on him north of West Palm. It had probably been a harmless gawker; Juan's one-of-its-kind red jet was always making other pilots stare with envy or admiration. Still, nobody got close to The Panther in the sky. Especially a guy who might fantasize that his plane could compete with the best aviation technology the United States military had to offer.

Dream on, bastardo.

But was Juan's plane one-of-its-kind? Another blast of anger singed his senses.

Am I the only Eldorado? Or had his Angel and her Emperor pulled a whole battalion of brilliant criminals from their prison pissholes—to oversee the extermination of filthy rich retirees?

"Bastardo!" Juan's deep voice shot through the cockpit, muffled by his headset. Didn't they know he had the balls and the brains to outsmart them? They had set Juan up with everything he needed to simply vanish. Starting with this plane—and his special Black U.S. Visa. The only other people on Planet Earth who shared that privilege were the President, the Vice President, the U.S. Ambassador to Great Britain, and the heads of the FBI and CIA.

That little booklet let him, along with his passengers and his cargo, fly direct from the Bahamas and completely bypass the mandatory departure from an Airport Of Entry, such as Nassau or Freeport. That A.O.E. stop was mandatory for regular people arriving in the U.S. from the out islands. Because any regular American needed to show a passport to get back into the United States. With no exceptions, since 9-11.

Except for The Panther, of course. In true king-of-the-jungle style, he loved to make a game of it when flying back into the States. First, he'd drop below radar coverage and turn his transponder off, giving the airport officials no clue that he was coming in. Then after landing, he'd walk straight past customs and immigration officers. A machine scanned his Black Passport, and he was in.

He needed no clearance to land. And he needed no clearance in the air. Because the military-issued Green Box on his plane enabled him to literally disappear from the U.S. government's radar. The government tracked *everything*, every boat and every plane that crossed the American Defense Identification Zone to enter the U.S.

But The Panther's comings and goings never made a single footprint on the ADIZ radar screens. That had made it so easy to take several trips down to Bogotá to visit his grandmother, the only living relative that he knew of.

"You're invisible," his Angel had said. "You don't exist."

That would soon be even more true than she and her bossman would ever know.

He would slip right past them. But nothing ever got past him. Because his private jet had synthetic vision, just in case. Amazed by the technological advances in aviation technology while he was locked up, Juan couldn't get enough of the latest gadgets and features that the airplane designers and tech geeks invented. His new favorite was the Garmin-based "Perspective" avionics system. Juan was always impressed with the products that L-3 put on the market.

Yeah, he had Panther eyes. Saw everything. Now synthetic vision took him to a superhuman level. Thanks to the infrared "enhanced vision" feature, Juan really could see in the dark.

"Aye, mamacita!" he exclaimed at the sight of his island. Long ago, he'd named it Casuarina Cay, after the Casuarina she-oaks, whose needles dropped to the soil and made the surrounding ground so toxic that no plants could grow in their shadow. Except the razor edged "Love Vines," which could thrive. Somehow the symbolism of that, with Juan's line of work back then, had made the name irresistible. As was Panther's Peak, the house that he'd built at the highest point of Casuarina Cay, giving him 360-degree views of the island and the ocean.

Only a cement slab of the original house remained; beside it, Juan's new luxury digs were nearly complete. Through the palm trees and thick vegetation, a beige stone staircase sliced through the green to the white powder beach. And nearby—

"Paradiso." His personal landing strip, a 5,000-foot white strand that he'd built for his cocaine empire, beckoned from the thick green foliage.

Very soon, he'd make it an impenetrable—and invisible—fortress, once again. Because right now, American government satellites could see his hide-away. He'd have K do something about that.

I need this place to disappear into thin air. So I can.

32. Singer Island, Florida

This was an easy one, behind this mansion at 401 Bamboo Road. As Elijah Hanna stood in the garden beside the tiny old lady, he secretly gloated that he was making so much money by using his creativity and strategic planning skills. He was as smart as his cousin who'd gone to college and was always using those career terms, like *strategy* and *long-term goals.* Well Elijah had all that, and was making 10 times more money than his suit-wearing, arrogant cousin.

No office for me. Looks like I'm standing in the Garden of Eden. The roses, the green grass, the white trellis nearby dripping with vines and flowers, the mansion just past the swimming pool. Very appropriately, Elijah's official task right now was to stand on snake watch, to spare the matron of this garden the evil trouble of encountering a snake.

"This is relaxing for me," the woman told him as he stood beside her in his red landscaper's jumpsuit. With his right hand, he held a net, a pole with a pincher on the end, as well as a bag that hung—with amazing stillness—beside his leg.

As she knelt on her little gardening pad, and snipped leaves from her flowering plants, Elijah asked, "Why do you do this yourself when you have a landscaping crew?"

"I love to get down here in the dirt and nurture these plants and enjoy the satisfaction of a job well done," she told Elijah, as he eyed the exposed stretch of flesh between her slim green pantlegs and her white ankle socks. Hunched over in her long sleeved white blouse and floppy flowered hat, she turned and cast a hard look at him. Her eyes were like two blue marbles set in crinkled tissue paper.

She was 76, according to the Order, and looked 86. Had all this money, but let herself go in the looks department. Wouldn't matter much after today, anyway. "Keep your eyes on the ground," she snapped. "Some of the snakes, they're so camouflaged against the dirt, you don't see 'em 'til they've got their fangs in your flesh. Like my brother, God rest his soul."

"I'm watching," Elijah said as his bag jiggled. "Soon as Raoul gets back from lunch, he'll be back on the job."

"Good, you look like you're daydreaming. Raoul is sharp. The other day he caught a big orange snake. It was coming at me fast as lightening. But Raoul was faster. We buried it right over there." She pointed her gloved hand toward the edge of the garden. Then she looked back up at him. "Now that rascal is bougainvillea fertilizer."

The old woman half-smiled. "Such a cute little boy. It's so hard to tell what you folks are these days. Let me guess, Cuban?"

Elijah smiled. He felt no fear that he'd be recognized. With his caramel skin and straight black hair, he blended in with the legions of Hispanic yard workers who groomed the grounds of mansions, golf clubs and hotels. Anywhere that flowers and grass grew, a small army of Latino men would be scattering like ants with lawnmowers and clippers, from dawn until dusk. Guaranteed. That made it easy to blend in.

"My dad was a trailer trash jailbird," Elijah said, amused that she'd called him a "little boy" even though he was 28. But his boyish looks and his shortness for his age worked to his advantage in this line of work. "My mom, she come from a good family. Her dad was the first black accountant in his town in Mississippi. But Mom, she made some bad choices."

"Bad choices," the old lady said, yanking a drooping flower. "Pay attention to the ground! I told you, my brother died from a rattlesnake bite, out west. When he retired, he wanted to live out this cowboy fantasy from when he was a boy. Bought a ranch, rode around on a horse all day long."

"Sounds fun," Elijah said. "My Pops, I mean the dude who kind of adopted me, we ride around on motorcycles all day."

"Dangerous," the woman hissed. Deep down, Elijah hated women like her. They had treated his mother like dirt when she cleaned their houses to support him as a kid. Most times, Elijah could justify his Orders with some bad experience or feeling they brought to mind. The old white guys, they reminded him of his dad or his grandfather or his great grandfather. Never met any of those losers. Elijah had more vital stats and bios on his Orders than he had about his own bloodline.

As for the women, all he had to do was remember how the rich people would look down on him and his mom. Especially the day she got fired for going to her doctor's appointment. She returned with four-year-old Elijah, pleading for her job back so she could feed her child. But the lady called the cops, who treated his mother with even more disrespect during the arrest and questioning at the police station.

If these people wanted to treat his mother like a common criminal when she was only trying to take care of her baby, then her baby was back, a quite uncommon criminal, getting some sweet revenge. She now had the prettiest marble headstone at the cemetery; it was the Madonna holding a baby and it was engraved, *I love you, Mom. Your son, Elijah.*

Now, he glared down at this old bitch doing her gardening.

"Motorcycles," she spat. "You be careful, young man. You got your whole life ahead of you. So you're black?"

"Half, anyway," Elijah shrugged. "Doesn't much matter to me. People are people. Bad comes in every color."

"You can say that again. My husband was lily white and evil as all get-up. But what goes around, comes around. That's why he suffered until his dying day. That cancer put him through hell for three years. Ate him from the inside out."

Elijah glanced toward the enormous house, then down at his silver Breitling watch. The scar that stretched from the palm of his left hand to the top of his knuckles made him say a prayer of thanks for finding a line of work that was easier, less dangerous, and paid a helluva lot more loot. It was 12:29 p.m. Raoul would arrive any minute.

Once he scored on this job, Elijah would do the usual and pick up some lunch for himself and Freddie. Then he'd go take care of another Order. Man, this life sure beat the hell outta the crazy he was doin' when Freddie first snuck up on him at the burger joint on Marathon Key.

He loved that place. Paradise Burger. Best burgers around. No cops. And not many people, considering there were only two outside tables. Elijah flashed back....

One of his favorite things was to sit there and think about how much money he'd made on his B&Es that day down at Big Pine Key. And that was sure less risky than that copper shit he was doin' awhile back when he fried his left hand when some jerk at Florida Power & Electric turned on the juice before Elijah was finished strippin' the wires out of that new house.

No risk here, though, as he savored his burger and looked out at the Straits of Florida between the Keys and the southern tip of Florida. Since he was on the north side of the island, he could almost see the shoreline of Homestead.

So he didn't like it too much when this skinny dude in sunglasses with pockmarked skin and a brown buzz cut sat down and interrupted his pleasant late afternoon meal.

"Hey buddy," the guy said as if he were a long lost friend. "My name's Freddie. How's that burger? I try to get down here every few weeks to enjoy one myself."

Elijah shrugged, in no mood for a conversation as the adrenaline rush from the recent theft had long diminished. Though he looked and sounded vaguely familiar, Elijah ignored the guy, finished his burger, and stabbed his fork into a piece of apple pie. He wanted to get the hell outta there. This guy, staring like he knew him, was giving him the creeps. He had something in his pocket for him, if a problem were to arise.

After the waitress brought the guy a burger, he took a bite, then paused. "You know, Mr. Hanna, the day will come when you're gonna get hurt stealing other people's flat screens." Then he slowly bit into his Paradise Burger.

"What the Fuck are you talking about, pal?" A piece of piecrust flew out of Elijah's mouth as he spoke. Yeah, he somehow knew this guy, but until he could place whether that was good or bad, he wasn't about to bust on himself. "I don't know you and you certainly don't know me."

He wiped his mouth and stood. That motherfucker could cover the $8 tab for interrupting his meal.

He stepped away, then froze in his tracks. That dude was his old boss, his old partner in crime, who had the copper hook-up with the insurance money. He looked different now with hair and no beard.

"So what's the price of copper these days, now Mr. Hanna? Or perhaps you don't keep...." the guy's voice trailed off to a whisper. "How's the hand?"

33. Washington, D.C.

Senator Gerald Boxley was playing a dangerous game. He was spinning the proverbial roulette wheel, where losing would cost him everything. His entire political career, his family's financial security, his future, his life.

So he was playing to win, at any cost. And whatever little monkey was trying to be that wrench in the system, it was time to silence it, stop it, squash it. No matter who it was.

And that was exactly why he was meeting his favorite FBI fix-it man here at a restaurant in Union Station. This man's father, back when they were young Marines in that hell of leech-infested, bullet-riddled jungle known as Vietnam, had saved Boxley's life. And Boxley had returned the favor just a week later, by saving that soldier's life. Now, their bond was thicker than blood or money. They credited each other with every beat of their hearts. So the son was always happy to help his dad's savior.

"I need you to find out the proverbial who, what, when, where, how and why," Boxley told him over cobb salads. "I need a name, a motivation, the whole deal." Boxley handed the seasoned agent a document detailing the names, dates and other pertinent information.

"I need to know what went wrong here, so it never happens again."

"Senator, consider it done."

34. Singer Island, Florida

Now, Elijah said a quick prayer of gratitude for the day he met Freddie Buford. Because that dude changed his life. Became more of a dad figure than he'd ever known. And elevated him to a spot where he was making easy money. More money than he'd ever imagined. Especially today, with several jobs lined up.

So he needed to make this deadly snake bite happen fast. He loved tailoring each job to the specific person. Like a few weeks ago in Miami, after planting the listening devices in that old dude's Porsche while it sat in the valet parking lot at his yacht club marina, Elijah had listened to his conversations and picked up the best way to proceed. Turned out, even though the dude was old as fuck, he had a mistress in that waterfront condo tower just over the bridge. So every time he went to see her, on Tuesdays, Thursdays and Saturdays, he'd pop some Viagra. He got the pills one by one from his doc—arranged over his cell phone from his car, so Elijah heard it all. And of course, the dude was operating on the down low; never wanted to get busted by his younger wife, who was always nagging him about flirting with other women.

"You're 75 already," she'd bitched one night, "you're probably trying to squeeze in all the extra tits and ass that's humanly possible."

"I do you everyday, baby," he'd said. "You think I have any energy leftover? It'd kill me if I tried to bang every skirt in South Florida."

"Oh, so you've thought about it!" the wife accused. "Great, have a heart attack in some slut's bed!"

Elijah heard it all as they drove back and forth to the Club. He and the rest of the K.C. Team were well-trained in home security, electrical stuff, landscaping and any other job that enabled them access into people's homes. This lady's house, for example, had security cameras everywhere. Except way out here—a football field away—from the mansion. They were surrounded by trees that bounded the enormous lot and would provide cover for Elijah to slip away.

He loved feeling like a chameleon. Like he could slip into one scene, then out just as quickly. Doing what he needed to do, and making ridiculous money at it. That's how he got all the high-tech hook-ups that made him even more efficient and sly at what he did as an entramanure... extraplanner... or whatever it was called. A business man! He had a whole room full of gadgets and monitors back at his little house. It was actually the guesthouse behind

Freddie Buford's sweet-ass place. Elijah had decorated his little house as cool as anything he'd seen on *MTV Cribs*. All the latest video games, a huge flatscreen with surround sound, a bar. And of course, the tools of his trade. That's how he'd been able to listen to the retired moviemaker's conversations with his wife, and his mistress.

The electronics made Elijah's work so easy. For that job, all he'd had to do was sneak into the parking lot of the yacht club, find the one little blue pill hidden in the secret compartment in the Porsche, and replace it with a blue pill. A blue pill that Elijah had "doctored up" with that wicked lung-paralyzing shit that Freddie was about to officially introduce to the K.C. Team. Elijah had the privilege of testing it out. And sure enough, that Saturday evening on the news, they announced that retired movie producer Albert Nichols was found dead of a heart attack in the high-rise condo of an unidentified woman.

Some bad news was about to strike this little old lady, too. Because that black beetle scurrying across the dirt, right toward her knee, was his cue to make this happen. Now.

"Watch out!" he said, loud enough for her—but no one else—to hear. He dove for the bug. At the same time, he dropped the bag next to his leg, allowing the top to fall open. As he grabbed the beetle, he dropped scented snake food that the guy at the pet shop said was guaranteed to attract any snake in the area. Especially the two hungry, venomous ones that slithered out of Elijah's handy gardening bag.

"I got it," he assured the woman. "These bugs are so big. Like they eat radioactive waste for dinner."

"Beetles!" she snapped. "They're next on my list after snakes. Then come these tiny little biting flies," she said, waving her hand in front of her eye. "We call 'em 'no-see-ums.' They sting like nobody's business. And you can't see them."

"I can go get a swatter," Elijah lied.

"No thank you, young man. I need you here."

"Just here to do my job," Elijah said, watching one snake under a big green leaf. It was still, staring straight at that juicy chunk of ancient leg.

The guy at the exotic pet shop said this type of snake was so venomous, death would occur within seconds. The victim would have no time to scream, or even know what happened.

He was right. In a split second, both snakes dove at her. Widened their mouths around her leg. Sunk those fangs into her flesh.

And she keeled over. Right on top of her pretty flowers.

Elijah felt nothing. Except excitement that he'd just earned another fat wad of cash for a job well done.

Cha-ching!

35. The Sky Over Casuarina Cay, The Bahamas

Descending toward his landing strip, Juan was sure he had one of the best pieces of real estate on the planet. Similarly, his yacht was docked in the exclusive marina in the heart of the international playground for the rich and famous—South Beach.

"Location, location, location," the yacht club manager had said when he'd inquired about dock space and security.

He repeated those words as he looked down at his future sanctuary from the wicked world. Owning real estate, especially a tropical island, was the most empowering ego trip a man could have. All through history, land ownership had been key to building wealth and empires.

"Real estate," he said aloud. "That's it."

Was America's economy so desperate that the government was having him kill rich old people—to get their real estate? With the government and its housing crisis, Juan hadn't paid much attention to that confusing barrage of bad news about Freddie Mac and Fannie Mae. It didn't concern him; he was living the high life and that was all he needed to focus on. But now, what could Boxley and his higher-up partners in crime be getting from these hits?

The government is taking back its real estate. Sort of a new manifest destiny, that term he'd learned in history class about how the U.S. government had expanded ever westward during the pioneer days, calling its plan Manifest Destiny, to possess the land all the way to the Pacific Ocean.

Repossessing property was what the whole foreclosure ordeal was about. Juan had ignored the endless media drumbeat about that, too. But from what he did know, those repossessed houses weren't necessarily owned by elderly or wealthy people. That was hitting everybody hard. So what was Uncle Sam up to this time?

Whatever was going on, Juan was going to find out, and take a big slice. Because the lush tropical paradise below him was where he belonged until his last breath. Not to mention, this airspace was free and clear of the FAA. The sky over Casuarina Cay had Class G airspace classification, which required no communication whatsoever with the FAA.

This was all far easier than running up and down the coast for the Cartel. No more sneaking. Now it was wide open and wild.

The powers that be trusted him. However misplaced that trust was, he would use it to his advantage. And get paid. This payday would make his Cartel days and the cases of cash piled head-high, look like chump change. Once cash was king, but now tax-free electronic funds ruled the world.

36. Miami, Florida

In a split-second glance, Freddie Buford knew Elijah had scored. Something about the glint in the little dude's eyes as he walked—no, Elijah sort of bounced when he walked, like he'd gotten laid—into the game room carrying burritos from the place up the street, told him it was time to celebrate.

Freddie, who was on the phone with The Panther and playing a game of pool by himself, nodded toward Elijah.

"I got it, Boss," Freddie said. Leaning over the red velvet pool table, he drew back the cue, then rammed it into the white ball, which smashed into a cluster of striped and solid balls. The crack and clatter underscored his ominous tone of voice. "No more fuck-ups. That shit'll be handled tonight."

"We're expanding," the Panther said. "Double the K.C. Team. Orders are coming in fast and furious. Get more supply to handle the demand."

Freddie let out a sinister chuckle, glancing at his Number One Recruit as Elijah opened his burrito at the mirrored bar. The delicious scent of cheese and beef and Mexican spices made Freddie's mouth water. "In this economy, Bossman, I can get you an army in a day."

"You never disappoint," the Panther said. His deep, gravelly voice came through the phone as if each word were a rock, blasting into the side of Freddie's head: "You'll keep it that way."

Click.

Freddie threw down the pool cue. It bounced off the table, onto the floor. "Fuckin' A!"

"Freddie, dude!" Elijah exclaimed, shooting off his bar stool. Sour cream and guacamole dotted his upper lip. "Bad news?"

"Naw, just disrespect." Freddie hated when the Boss hung up like that. Plus, The Panther he never said goodbye, and always ended the conversation with a semi-threat. Now, Freddie's whole body stung inferiority. After all, Freddie suspected he was just one of dozens of other K.C. Leaders across the country. As much as he dreamed about being the Boss himself, Freddie knew deep down that he just didn't have it in him. The brains, the balls, the brilliance.

As Freddie pulled a joint from his pocket and lit up, he realized he'd had the same feelings of inferiority back in the day, when he worked for The Panther's private and international pharmaceutical enterprise. *I was just a street level drug dealer then.* And in-between, while The Panther was down, life had been rough. Two-bit cash here and there, but nobody wanted to hire The Panther's people. They knew he'd be back someday. And they knew he'd be mighty pissed off at anyone who'd taken his crews.

Then Freddie had risen, on his own enterprising skills, in the late 90s, thanks to Florida's home building boom. When that crashed and burned in 2008, The Panther came along, just in time, to save Freddie from a second bout with ruin.

And ever since the call last year, life had been good. This house, the electronic toys, the motorcycles, the chicks—and the power trip. Yeah, so what if this was about as high as Freddie Buford could climb, and he had to constantly remind himself to be glad about that. He sucked down more sweet smoke. His words rode a plume out of his mouth as he said: "We're kickin' ass down here. Ain't we?"

"Project Snake Bite," Elijah said, his face glowing like Christmas, "pulled it off like a dream."

"Little Dude!" Freddie high-fived him. He offered the joint, but Elijah shook his head. "I'm proud of you, my man."

"Hey, Freddie, brought you a burrito to celebrate," Elijah said, stepping back to the bar to retrieve Freddie's treat wrapped foil.

Freddie's emotions did a 180 as he gazed at his Little Dude. Rescued that thug from a life of crime and put him on his way to makin' real money.

"Not to sound like a sissy or nothin'," Freddie said, putting his hand on Elijah's shoulder, "but you know you're like a son to me, Little Dude."

"True dat," Elijah said with a play thug voice. He set down his burrito and banged his right hand over his heart. "To da grave, m'uh fucka." Elijah bust out laughing in his boyish way that had first endeared Freddie to him. The kid had been through hell as far as fights, changing schools, stealing food to eat when his mom was in jail. Fending off that abusive aunt and uncle who kept him.

"That old bitch today, she asked if I was Cuban," Elijah said, taking another bite. "Love bein' a chameleon, man. Hated it as a kid. Now it helps me bank fat loot."

"It's there," Freddie said, pointing at a white canvas bag on the bar. He wrapped his fingers around the tortilla and took a huge bite. "Little Dude, I remember when I first met you at that burger joint last year. You had this look in your eye like you'd much rather figure out how to steal a dollar than spend half the time earning two dollars."

Elijah shrugged. "I'm a survivor. Love the challenge. My white-collar cousin with his bank job was always tellin' me I would be shit. But look who's livin' large now. He's always cryin' the blues about cut-backs and mergers. Might lose his job."

"Tell him to come work for us," Freddie said through a mouthful of spicy beef and melted cheese. The weed, as it soothed his senses and boosted his confidence, transporting him into a thought pattern of being the biggest, baddest motherfucker in South Florida, "tell him to talk to the king maker, Freddie Cash."

"I sure don't miss the copper business, though," Elijah said. "I thought I was the shit, sellin' that stuff for $3.95 a pound. Couldn't believe how easy it was to strip it outta those unfinished houses—"

"Always helps when it's an inside job," Freddie said. Despite his inferiority complex in comparison to The Panther, Freddie knew deep down he was a bad motherfucker. That's why folks called him Freddie Cash. Yeah, that hook-up during the housing boom was the shit. Freddie loved the air of mystery he kept around himself. It was rumored that he was in the home building business, but nobody really knew. He also loved that he had so many connections—from politicians to business owners to guys who worked in gas stations—who were always happy to help him out in exchange for a Benjamin or two.

Come to think of it, some of those state politicians still owed him some favors. Even they had come to Freddie Cash for loans and schemes to cover up their extramarital affairs or business bribes. Turns out that wad of cash in his pocket had impressed street guys and lawmakers alike. Because everybody had a price.

"Little Dude," Freddie laughed as Elijah chugged a beer, "I remember how big your eyes got when I pulled that rubber band bank outta my pocket."

"Hell yeah," Elijah laughed. "Man, you had the best hook-up in town."

Back then, Freddie would put up new construction, and the boys would come along and generate a little pocket money unwiring each house, sometimes as many two or three times during the building process. Freddie would file a claim and rewire the house. Nobody got hurt, other than a little hit to the deep pockets of the insurance industry. Who the fuck cared? Everyone knew the insurance companies and banks had all the money anyway. Hell, even the copper market was depressed now. $1.25 a pound. An economic downturn, for real!

Freddie said, "On to bigger and better shit now that the housing industry's in the fuckin' toilet."

Elijah took the last bite of his lunch. "What I do now, it sure beats the hell outta carjacking, B&E and robbin' the snowbirds. That was too much work."

"Dangerous, too," Freddie said. "Your hand was fucked up when I met you."

Elijah rubbed the scar on his left hand. "Dude, that shit coulda killed me!"

Freddie laughed and spasmed. "ZZZzztttt!"

"Third degree burn," Elijah said, "Good thing I'm right handed."

"Lucky you survived, and I came along to save your little ass."

"Oh yeah," Elijah said. "Back then, I was all about booze and blunts. Now it's the big boy toys. Got my eye on this bike, dude, you gotta see it. A Yamaha. Neon green with chrome, makes the crotch rocket I got right now look like a tricycle."

"You da man, Little Dude." Freddie smiled, then sucked on his joint. "We're 'bout to take it to the next level. You and me."

37. Washington, D.C.

Carolyn Taylor had no time for Russell's cautionary approach. She hated how he was always holding her back from making a decision.

"We have to weigh every aspect of the potential outcomes," he said, sitting at the conference table in her office. "The media is watching your every move, waiting for the chance to rip you to shreds. So please, Carrie, heed my caution on this one."

She shot to her feet and paced. "The court of public opinion needs to have a unanimous ruling in support of my

Rescue Plan before Donaldson introduces the legislation. We need every citizen in America calling, writing, faxing, texting their Congressmen and Congresswomen—to tell them to vote for my plan."

Russell nodded. "You're right. And we can only do that by showing Mary the hairdresser and Jim the bus driver that this plan is in their best interest."

Carolyn stared down at him, her whole body humming with frustration. She was a racehorse, ready to bolt out of the gate and win the race, so fast that if folks weren't paying close attention, they'd miss it. She'd leave all the other horses, owners, trainers and handlers in the dust. Perhaps too fast, she thought for the first time.

Russell was a trainer, a handler. Not an owner. No one owned her. That's why she would never marry. She was like Queen Elizabeth. Certainly no virgin, but enjoying solitary reign all the same. Refusing to succumb to suitors' promises of wealth or power or privilege. Men were all liars. Once they "got" a woman as their own—as girlfriend, mistress, or wife—it was only a matter of time before they were tramping off with a bevy of courtesans, concubines and downright whores. Even married women.

Carrie would never forget her roommate, Tess, at boarding school. They were best friends; Carrie was her maid of honor and would frequently visit Tess' beautiful house in Biloxi. Every year on their anniversary, Tess and her well-to-do husband would host the entire bridal party of 12 for a weekend of fun, food and friendship. Well one night, when all the women gathered in the kitchen, sipping wine, Tess said, "Let's all go shoppin' tomorrow. My personal money is burnin' a hole in my purse! Time for a new dress."

"What's personal money?" asked a bridesmaid, who, with her Southern accent, said personal like *PUH-sonal*.

"Why," Tess said, looking surprised, "you don't get PUH-sonal money from your husband? I'm so sorry to hear that."

"What is it?" the bridesmaid demanded.

"Well," Tess explained with a flustered smile, "that's the money mah husband puts under mah pillow for favors, in the bedroom."

"Like a prostitute?" Carrie blurted. Needless to say, Carrie had, at Tess's very sugar-coated request, packed up her bag and made an early departure from her last bridal party weekend at Tess's house.

I'll never be like her—or Mother. Carolyn adored everything about her father except the way he had abandoned Mother in the White House while he tended to the Presidential duties of bedding a mistress at every port. All across America, her dashing daddy was rumored to have women at his beck and call, in every city, in every state. Do the math on that one, and her father's collection of women could rival the harem of any Arabian sheik.

All the everyday men she knew—like the ones she had seen at her high school reunion, or the pages and assistants of lawmakers here in Washington, and the guys at other tables in restaurants—they were all the same. Rich or poor. Insatiable fiends for pussy.

And she had no use for any of them. Unless they were the chairman of America's largest bank. Or a lawmaker who could serve as the perfect pawn in her game. Or a young stud bad boy who knew how to make her body quiver all night long.

Even Russell here, poor thing didn't know it, but if things didn't work out her way, it would all be his fault. It was always good to have extra layers of insulation. Yeah, a whole row of fall guys would always stand between her and a problem, however small.

"You won over the working class and middle class with your speech," Russell said, "for the everyday Americans. Now we have to convince ultra wealthy—"

"Estate taxes!" she claimed as if it were the answer. "This huge tax break for the rich expires in 2010. Any wealthy person who dies in 2010 will not have to pay any estate taxes. So rich people will be happy about that. Let's twist it around so it feels like the government is helping them out."

Carolyn was done with Russell. She needed another secret meeting with Boxley. This realization just jolted her with a new sense of urgency.

"What are you thinking, Carrie?" Russell asked, furling his brow. "You look like the cat who just swallowed the canary."

"I'm just ready to move full speed ahead," she said. "You can go meet with the team about our PR strategy with the ultra rich."

As soon as Russell left her office, Carolyn phoned Boxley.

"Step it up," she ordered. "I know you said estate taxes are an added benefit. But not in 2010. Any rich bastard who croaks in 2010, the family is free and clear of estate taxes."

Boxley said, "I have already doubled productivity."

"Always one step ahead," Carolyn said. At least she'd allow him to think that. "You're the best man for the job. By the way, I neglected to ask you this morning, is everything finalized for Chrisma Corporation?"

"As I expected, even with our high level clearance," Boxley said, "the red tape involved when the nation's largest financial institution sells an entity like LivesVest, it's more than a notion."

"Gerry, darlin', are you sayin' there's a problem?"

"None whatsoever," he said. "I'm saying that we've successfully sailed over that hurdle."

"Smooth sailin' is all I want to hear about," she said. "The benefits we get with you as a minority business owner is the icing on the cake. Secret icing, of course. With the holding company, not even the dirt-hungriest reporter can sniff up on the real deal here."

"I love the sound of that," Boxley said. "Now, back to estate taxes. "Would you consider a sabbatical on our plan for those 12 months in 2010 when we receive no estate tax revenues?"

"Hell-double-no!" she exclaimed. "I haven't done the math, but I need us to keep movin' along at a steady clip. Delay is a four letter word in my book."

Boxley let out a sexy chuckle. "You always have a way with words, Madame Vice President. Of course, in 2011, estate tax revenue should get a great boost, blessing our dear Uncle Sam with 55 percent for every estate over a million dollars."

"I love the sound of that," Carolyn said. "Hey, Gerry, let's toss in a little white lie. Something like, my SOS Plan includes a full repeal of estate taxes in 2011. That should inspire them to give up the Social Security money!"

"HMmmmm," Boxley said. "Your creativity is magnificent. Let's do it. Although, we're making out quite well right now, with the death tax raking in 42 percent of any estate over three million dollars."

"I need to do some convincing in the Oval Office," she said. "The President promised the American people that he'd let this tax break for the rich expire. I'm about to tell him that's just a plain old bad idea."

Carolyn hurried behind her desk. At her computer, she called up the article about how 2010 was a great year for rich people to die because their families would be taxed zero percent on their estates, compared to 45% in 2009 and 55% in 2011. She read the article verbatim to Boxley.

"Sick bastards," she snickered. "They're calling 2010 'Throw Grandma Off the Train Year.' Just let the old bag die so they don't have to pay taxes on her money. The things people do."

Only then did she realize Russell was standing beside her.

Covering the receiver with her hand, she glared up at him. "Darlin', didn't your momma teach you it's downright rude to eavesdrop?" Her sing-song tone barely masked the bitchy undercurrent in her voice. "Especially when a lady is on the phone with the President of the United States!"

She was sure that Russell's stunned expression was just an act to cover up his nosiness. Maybe he was sleeping with that bitch speechwriter and was now out to get revenge for firing the little typo-plagued tramp.

"Carrie, calm down," Russell said in a patronizing tone. "I just walked in." He held up the phone in his hand. "I was on the phone, didn't hear a word you said."

"I've interviewed three speechwriters," he said, "I need you to meet them and pick a new one."

She covered the receiver and whispered angrily, "Don't you ever sneak up on me again!" She turned away from him, then spoke into the phone. "I apologize, Mr. President—"

38. Casuarina Cay, The Bahamas

The cave looked exactly as Juan had left it two decades ago: A five-foot arch of gray volcanic rock, covered with a tangle of vines, lush green leaves and pink flowers. All leading into darkness here on the windward side of his island.

But were the cash and cocaine still hidden inside? He'd just taken a walk across the island, under the hot afternoon sun, to clear his mind after making phone calls to some K.C. Leaders back in the States.

I need to beat the Emperor at his own game. Seize my fortune. Disappear without a trace. And come back here forever.

But how? Tiny bits of craggy rock scraped his fingertips as he ran his hand over the chest-level edge of the cave. The salty breeze made a few thick leaves dance over his knuckles as he peered into the ominous blackness.

The cave reminded him of his life. On the outside, it looked so beautiful and exotic: the women, the jet, the yacht; the personal FBI hack getting him any information at any hour; and the teams of obedient servants nationwide, executing his Orders every day, or else.

The sun blazed on Juan's bare shoulders; it heated the gold crucifix that his mother had given him, burning a hot spot where it hung on a chain on his lean, muscular chest. If he stood here too long, he'd get burned. Just like his "assignment." Despite its glamorous appearance, the grim reality of his existence singed his soul. Like tiny flames in his gut, anxiety charred his peace of mind. Because this dream life could be snatched away as quickly as it was given. As for the nasty and evil nature of his work, well, if that was what it took to enjoy this lifestyle—and please the Emperor to keep his freedom—then so be it. But Juan hated the uncertainty, the mystery, the vulnerability.

Courage and creativity, those would serve as the engine to drive him from this phase of his life into the next one. And, just as he'd had the creativity to hide cash and coke in caves all over this island, to preserve his stash for future use, he would do the same with his immense resources now.

Juan stepped into the cave. It was cool and smelled musty. A flying insect buzzed past his face. He pulled the flashlight from the right pocket of his black cotton cargo pants, which also held bottled water, a pocket knife, keys to his plane and house, his phone and his gun.

If the loot was still here, he'd take it as a good omen that he'd hatch an immaculate plan here on the island. Today.

Juan turned around, shining the flashlight. Over the mouth of the cave was a sort of shelf, formed of a great volcanic bubble of lava, that created a round cove. The tree branches, now dried and covered with spider webs, still covered it, along with small boulders that he'd placed there.

Juan positioned the flashlight to illuminate the space while he cleared the brush and rocks. Two little lizards scampered out. And there, glistening in the yellow flashlight beam—bricks of cash and cocaine wrapped in plastic.

"Aye, mamacita!"

Twenty bundles of cash and cocaine. Still intact, untouched by humans, animals or hurricanes. For 15 years. The coke was no good. But the cash sure was. With his knife, he sliced through the plastic. Benjamin Franklin stared up from the crisp $100 bill on top.

"Senor Franklin," Juan groaned. "Mi amigo íntimo. My trusted friend."

The corners of Juan's mouth rose up, just like Benjamin Franklin's. The former President wasn't really smiling, but his expression always made Juan think old Ben had a juicy secret, with a somber warning at the same time.

I deserve to live like a king and will do anything to maintain my empire. Now.

39. Diamond Lagoon, Florida

Hunter Knightly couldn't pinpoint what was wrong as he stood behind the dead couple's lavish, super-contemporary mansion on the ninth hole of the Diamond Lagoon Golf Course.

"It happened right there," said their daughter, Lauren Price Miller. She pointed to the spot by the blue-tiled swimming pool where her father had been electrocuted and her mother had dropped dead.

"Daddy was a drill sergeant about safety," she said, her red-rimmed eyes trained on the tangle of wires protruding from the electrical utility box beside the cabana. She watched the electrician that Hunter had hired as he examined the wires. "Even when we were kids, he'd get hysterical if we even carried the scissors wrong."

This 35-year-old mother of three was nothing like a woman who had been convicted of fraud a couple years ago, after his investigation proved she had arranged her parents' deaths to collect their hefty life insurance policy. That family's wealth was a mere fraction of this. The winter home here in Florida was worth 10-million dollars; the Price's townhouse mansion on New York's Upper East Side was 25-million dollars. Plus they had properties in Aspen and the Hamptons. When Hunter figured in the value of their investment portfolio, plus their art collection, this family's wealth ranked them among America's most privileged.

"You said kids," Hunter said as the electrician knelt and shined a flashlight into the wires. "How many brothers and sisters do you have?"

"Three girls," said Lauren, a slender brunette with a round, pleasant face that might have been pretty if it weren't so pale from crying. "All married with kids. Lisa is a trader on Wall Street. Has her own firm. Lillie, she's an interior designer. Ask anyone on the Upper East Side what designer to call, you'll hear her name first. Me, I own a baby boutique on Fifth Avenue. Maybe you saw the feature in *Vogue*?"

"My wife probably saw it," Hunter said, noting that she looked almost airbrushed. Perfect haircut. Diamonds sparkling in each ear. Manicure and pedicure. Subtle but flawless make-up. Black leather belt cinching her waist just so. Every word enunciated just right, despite the slight New York accent. She reminded him of something—

"My husband had the article framed for me," she said. "Mom and Dad were so proud."

"Your husband? What does he do?"

She shook her head. "There's no motive for money here, Mr. Knightly. Zero. My sisters and I, we're set for life. Ten lives, if we could live that long. Our husbands are honest."

"Sometimes greed is a wolf in sheep's clothing," Hunter said. "I've seen it. Had a case. Looked like the culprit was set for life on her own. But she wanted more. Now she's got all the time in the world to think about it. In prison."

"Look," Lauren said, crossing her bare arms over the black tank top she wore with Capri pants and sandals, "I need you to figure out what happened here. My parents were as healthy as you and me. No enemies. My mother wouldn't just drop dead."

Hunter stared down at the wires covered in red, yellow and green plastic. Now the electrician he'd hired was unscrewing the back of the utility box, to examine it from another angle.

"Don't see nothin' outta the ordinary, buddy," the electrician said. The nametag on his gray jumpsuit said John. "Only thing I can think of, is the man had wet fingers when he went to reachin' around in here, and zzzzt!"

Lauren winced.

"I can see here," the electrician said, "where it sparked at the edge of the box."

Lauren shook her head. "No, Daddy was the type who called a professional to fix things. Once when I was little, the light bulb in the refrigerator burned out. My father told the housekeeper to call the repairman. She was like, 'Dr. Price, I get a bulb from the drawer. Do it myself.' He was clueless about how to fix anything. Except teeth, of course."

"Just gotta take a few more pictures," the electrician said, aiming his digital camera at the wires. Then he shoved everything back in the box and screwed the panel on. "That utility box is in mint condition. Not a wire out of place."

"Tell me this, John," Hunter said as the electrician knelt to return his screwdriver to his toolbox. The guy kept futzing with his tools. "John!"

The electrician looked up with a puzzled expression.

"Whose uniform did you borrow today?" Hunter asked.

"Sorry, buddy." He tapped the nametag. "I'm makin' a name for myself in country music, so most folks call me by my stage name so much, I stopped answerin' to the name my momma gave me."

Hunter scanned the guy's thick fingers for signs of burns or cuts that might indicate a third line of work. B&E. Stealing cars or copper wire off newly constructed homes. All thanks to casing houses during his day job as an electrician. Besides a little dirt under his nails, the guy's hands looked clean.

"Oh yeah?" Hunter asked, not believing a word this guy was saying. "What's your stage name?"

"Lonnie Cool," the guy said. "My first CD's 'bout to drop. It's called Cool."

"I'll check out your MySpace page." Hunter feigned a congratulatory tone. Any 20-something musician would be crazy not to have a MySpace page to promote his work.

"'Course." The guy looked down, then over to the pool. "My girl's hookin' me up with all that."

Liar. Hunter said, "Show me your electrician's license. I told the company I only work with licensed contractors."

The guy pulled out an I.D. for Beachside Electrical Services. It showed his picture and his name: John McDaniel.

Lauren huffed. "Listen, Mr. Knightly, I asked you to come down here because I heard you're the best. Now I need you to find some answers. Whatever you have to do—"

"Lauren!" an older woman's voice called. Through the lush landscaping around the pool came a woman in a short pink cotton dress. She had spiky blond hair and a jangling gold bracelet.

"Hello Mrs. Bloomfield," Lauren said as the woman embraced her. Another woman, rounder, with auburn hair, and two men in their seventies, followed. Each hugged her and whispered words like "shocked" and "so sorry."

"Mr. Knightly, these are my parents' best friends," Lauren said. "Stella and Ernest Bloomfield. Margie and Herschel Goodman." Hunter shook their hands.

More perfect-looking people walked into this backyard that looked camera-ready for a luxury homes magazine spread.

Hunter felt like he'd driven his rental car onto the lot of a fake town on a Hollywood studio lot. He'd been to Universal Studios out in California as kid. And he'd grown up on a horse farm where one stud fee could get half a million dollars for his daddy. So Hunter was no stranger to big money. But back in the Bluegrass State, the rich people felt real.

Here, something felt plastic.

"We did everything together," Mrs. Bloomfield said as Hunter marveled at their modern cosmetic procedures.

This woman had to be pushing 75; the speckled white, beige and brown skin on her thin arms and legs left no doubt. But her face, thanks to Botox, plastic surgery and who knew what other procedures—she looked as young as Meredith. Dozens of half-carat diamonds sparkled from side-by-side gold circles that formed her necklace.

And there was no way a woman this old could have a rack of tits that sat up so firm and full.

Margie grabbed Hunter's hand and squeezed. "Herschel, I'm gonna trade you in for the newer, younger model." She smiled up at Hunter. "Such a hunk!"

"Thank you," he said playfully. "My wife will appreciate your praise. Mrs. Bloomfield, let's talk about Dr. and Mrs. Price."

"I'm not buyin' this freak accident explanation," said Mr. Goodman. "Freddie was anal about safety. Seventy-eight years old, and the man refused to replace a water filter in his fridge! He said water and electricity don't mix."

"And Suzie," the auburn haired lady said. "We used to tease, her slogan was '76 is the new 36.' Yoga, wheat grass, so much energy, her personal trainer quit on her. I kid you not."

"Let's go inside," Lauren said. She led them through doors that were white frames around glass planes. Three more sets of these doors stretched across the back of the house, opening onto the pool deck. Huge paned windows stretched above them to the peaked roof. The all-white interior had marble floors, a two-story atrium lit by skylights, and a curving staircase to a balcony overlooking the pool and golf course.

"Let's go in the kitchen," Lauren said, leading them to leather and silver stools at the center island. The kitchen faced an open, sunken family room with a marble fireplace stretching up to the ceiling.

A fireplace for those cold South Florida nights. What a waste...

Beside it sat a huge flat screen television. Its sleek silver frame said in scroll engraving across the top: "We're here for YOU, because we appreciate your business! The Genuine Insurance Group."

Hunter said, "I've never seen such blatant or upscale advertising. Most companies I come across, they give out baseball caps. Or coffee mugs. Pens. The Genuine Insurance Group gives out top-of-the-line flatscreens?"

"Oh, that damn viatical settlement," Lauren said as she poured ice and lemonade into jumbo tumblers, and set out a tray of fresh fruit, gourmet cheeses and fancy crackers. "Everybody got them."

"All of us," Ernest said. "The TVs, the money." His tone became mocking as he said, "The young agent, he told us we had, quote-unquote, *unused capacity* for life insurance."

Stella's bracelet jangled as she touched Hunter's arm. "Because we're healthy and above a certain net worth."

Margie smiled. "We go to these beautiful luncheons, they tell you all about it. Quite a production. Turns out, you get money, basically, for taking an exam to prove your healthy, and signing up.

"Signing and signing," Ernest laughed. "How many trees did they kill? So much paperwork!"

"I was extremely skeptical," Lauren said, "when Mom and Dad wanted to sign up, what, this is February, it was two years ago, last month. In January. They got down here for the season, in November, and all their friends were talking about this great deal."

"That would be us," Herschel said. "All four of us."

"Then, after two years, this investment fund takes over, and you get your TV."

Hunter wondered if these couples spoke in such synchronicity with each other because they'd been friends forever, or because they had rehearsed a sympathy show for Lauren and the insurance investigator.

"Marilyn got a car," Mrs. Goodman said. "And the Thomases got a cruise to Bermuda."

"Tell me more about this Serenity Insurance Group," Hunter said, wondering if any of them had any stake in the company.

Ernest drew his brows together and spoke in a scolding tone: "Mr. Knightly, you're an insurance investigator and you've never heard of this?"

Hunter slipped into his best *aw-shucks, I'm just a simple Southern boy* act. He chuckled and said, "I have, sir. But I leave the complicated stuff to the big boys. When it comes to the life insurance cases that I investigate, like this one here, my specialty is fraud."

Lauren cast a worried look his way. "If you're in the dark about these viaticals, why'd they send you—"

"Fraud is fraud," Hunter said. "No matter what fancy name a company is puttin' on the policy."

"Viatical," Lauren said. "Sounds so creepy and vague."

The confusion and fear in her eyes inspired Hunter to say with a soothing tone, "Viatical is just a fancy word for an *arrangement* where a third party buys a life insurance policy in exchange for part of the death benefits on the insured. In this case, your parents."

Anger flashed in Lauren's eyes. "Who is this third party? Why would my parents do that?"

"Your parents, the insured, got an 'advance' on death benefits," Hunter said, "in cash—"

"The check," Stella said. "We all did."

Hunter added, "And the investor gets the balance of

the death benefit, upon the insured's death."

Lauren shook her head. "Who thought of this? It just sounds wrong!"

"Viaticals started back in the eighties when AIDS first showed up," Hunter said. "The idea was for the terminally ill person to get the money in his hand, to pay medical bills and improve his quality of life. Viaticals added dignity and financial security for folks who were going through Hell, dying from AIDS. It was a legitimate arrangement."

Ernest asked, "So how'd it get from that to us?"

"The insurance agents realized this was a good deal and decided to expand their market," Hunter said. "They softened the name to Life Settlements or Senior Settlements, and deals evolved into what your mother and father purchased, a STOLI or IOLI, Stranger Owned or Investor Owned Life Insurance arrangement."

Lauren sighed. "That sounds even worse than viatical!"

"It comes from the Latin word *viaticum*," Hunter said. "That's the Eucharist, or Last Communion, to bless and protect a dying person on their journey—"

"Not if you're Jewish!" Lauren shouted. Her tear-glazed eyes hardened on Hunter. "There's something bad going on here. Now tell me what happened to my parents. And who did it!"

40. Washington, D.C.

This surprise summons to the Oval Office sent Carolyn's imagination spinning a thousand directions. Would President Anderson reveal that he was terminally ill, and in a few months, she'd assume his position? Or would he say he'd just discovered some god-awful glitch with her SOS Plan?

"This way, Madame Vice President," an aide said, guiding her toward the couch where the President sat. Russell stood behind her. A handful of his top aides, including the heads of the FBI, the CIA and the Secret Service, remained standing as she sat down. In the two armchairs facing them were the Secretary of Defense and that conniving seductress Sue Bookman, the Secretary of State.

"Goodday, Carolyn," the President said. His cheerful tone belied his somber eyes. "Excellent work on the SOS Plan. I'm hearing more praise than criticism."

"Why thank you, President Anderson. I'm working hard to make your administration shine. Now and in the history books." Though she felt everyone staring at her, she focused only on him.

A sudden ashen pallor spread across his face as he said, "Carolyn, I'm afraid there's more to the Sheik Sunami il Tabbul video about the economy." He focused hard on her. "He said a high-ranking American government leader will be abducted."
The words hung in the tense silence.

"He's a crackpot," Carolyn said confidently. "Sitting in a cave, spewing psychotic ramblings into a camera. Doesn't scare me one bit." Carolyn glanced up at the intelligence leaders. "Any idea who this high ranking official might be?"

The President said, "We're afraid it might be you. The translation is fuzzy, but he makes reference to a President's daughter. I have three sons. And as you know, your father's relations in the Middle East—except for Israel—were quite strained."

The Secretary of State practically gloated as she said, "And that's a generous euphemism." That conniver was probably scheming to convince the President to make Carolyn step down—citing safety concerns—so *she* could become the interim Vice President.

Never! Carolyn had enough security, with Secret Service agents watching her every move. She didn't need even more people scrutinizing her every blink and breath; she had too much work to do to secure her SOS Plan.

"Well I sure appreciate this advisory, gentlemen," she said in a way to wrap up the conversation and leave. "But I don't run and hide. I don't get spooked by some terrorist on a grainy videotape that's four years old and appeared out of nowhere."

The Secretary of State corrected, "Oh no, it did *not* come out of nowhere. This videotape was in a safety deposit box at Magna Corp. Sheik Sunami il Tabbul has people here, operating right under our noses."

Carolyn maintained her perfectly diplomatic visage as her eyes shot daggers of hate at that snobby bitch. "Then find them and send them back to the caves where they belong."

The President cleared his throat. "Carolyn, you need to see the tape for yourself." He nodded at a Secret Service agent, who pushed a button on a hand-held video screen; the Middle Eastern terrorist appeared, speaking Arabic.

"America will pay for many sins of her fathers with a beautiful sacrificial lamb," the translator said in English. Static crackled as he spoke, making the next line inaudible. The static ended as the interpreter said either "she" or "he," then, "...will be abducted and never seen again on this Earth."

Carolyn shook her head. "That doesn't mean me," she insisted as goosebumps of fear prickled across her skin. "He doesn't say my name or anything about me. You can't even tell if he said 'he' or 'she.' Not everything he says comes true."

The Secretary of State, with her pompous deep voice, said, "In this case, he was right about the economy. And we can't take any chances."

The President nodded. "We're going to ensure your safety with extra surveillance and security measures, at least for a time. Until our intelligence officers can verify whether this is a direct threat to you."

Carolyn shook her head ever-so-slightly. This was a direct threat to the flawless execution of her plan to elevate herself right back here, as the boss, in the Oval Office. Surveillance would mean people snooping on her every phone call and meeting.

Not to mention, it could increase the chance of someone discovering her relationships with Neal and Boxley. Carolyn wouldn't put it past Sue to unleash her temptress wiles on Boxley, who in the heat of the moment, could whisper a sweet nothing about their dealings—

Hell double no!

Or did the President already know something, somehow—

Stop it. It would be impossible for anyone to know anything about what she was doing behind closed doors. Russell didn't even have a clue, and he was with her 98 percent of the time.

The silver-haired Secretary of Defense added, "We all know what horrific things happen to those abducted by the Islamic terrorists. The beheadings, the torture, we can't risk that. With you, or anyone."

The Secretary of State added, "It's imperative that we double your security."

"I'm afraid I agree," the President said.

Carolyn nodded at the Secretary of Defense. "I appreciate your concern for my well-being, sir." Then she focused on the President. "Sir, I'm confident that my Secret Service protection is sufficient. If not, my Daddy didn't nickname me 'Annie Oakley' for nothin'."

41. Casuarina Cay, The Bahamas

The sound of Boxley's arrogant commands through the phone made Juan's blood boil here on the beach. He'd been striding across the talcum-soft sand, toward his hammock strung between two palm trees near the water's edge, when Boxley called.

"You need to appreciate the sense of urgency here," Boxley repeated. "We cannot afford to waste a single minute. I need you working at maximum capacity."

"Trust me," Juan said over the squawks of two free-soaring tropicbirds, whose long white tails resembled feathered swords protruding from their backsides as they streaked across the blue sky. "I've kept a reserve of K.C. Leaders in every state, just in case. Already called them up for duty."

"Let's remember not to sacrifice quality for quantity," Boxley said. "We've had one slip-up. None will be tolerated."

"My work has been impeccable," Juan said confidently. "Clarify what you mean. Slip-up."

"Nothing that concerns you. Just maintain the same quality recruitment efforts."

Bastardo!

"If there's a problem, I need to know about it," Juan said as the hot sand burned his bare feet. "To take care of it."

Boxley mumbled affectionately to his dog, then said, "Juan, the cause of the problem cannot be blamed on you, the K.C. Leaders or their members. But perhaps we can use this to send a strong message that we do not tolerate errors."

"Now you're talkin'," Juan said. "Fear has a way of motivating excellent work."

Boxley laughed too loud, for too long. Juan had heard such nervous laughter many times. That uncharacteristically shrill sound shot up from deep inside a man, shattering his most sophisticated and confident exterior. It revealed a man's fear and opened him up for manipulation for stronger men such as The Panther.

Boxley was scared. And unaware that he'd just signed up to become Juan's answer man to get to the Emperor.

42. Diamond Lagoon, Florida

Hunter projected his best poker face to the grieving daughter. The urgent need to find answers for her—to confirm the suspicion roiling in her eyes and in his thoughts—that foul play had, in fact, caused her parents' deaths.

Mrs. Bloomfield grasped Lauren's hand and said, "Honey I know you're upset, but I think it just happened. A freak accident, call it what you want. But I don't think Mr. Knightly here is going to find any smoking gun."

"Nobody had a motive," Ernest said. "Mr. Knightly. Tell us what kind of motive you usually find."

"Money, of course," added Hunter, who would neither confirm nor deny foul play until he had hard facts in hand. "The most common type of life insurance fraud I see goes like this. A man lies on his application, saying he's never smoked a day in his life. Then he dies of lung cancer, and the autopsy shows his lungs look like dirty sponges. Or the wife who puts arsenic in her husband's coffee every morning. He dies, she tries to collect on the policy. I come along, examine the facts, and say, no deal. Claim denied. Wife goes to jail. I must say, most death claims do not come with foul play. This investigation is routine."

Lauren asked, "So what do you think about my parents?"

"So far, no proof of foul play," Hunter said.

"My intuition is never wrong," she said. "I'm also extremely suspicious about the life insurance deal they did. Just a few months after they sell it back to some company that I can't even find the name of, they're dead. Does that mean some mysterious company gets to collect on their 10-million dollar policies? Each!"

Fear and suspicion filled her bloodshot eyes.

"It might sound strange," Hunter said, "but these life settlement companies operate like the blind investment funds that high ranking politicians use. Their investments are actually shielded from them, so no impropriety can be called."

"Just because politicians do it, doesn't make it right," Lauren said. "I want to know who has my parents' policies. But when I called the life settlement agent that Mom and Dad worked with down here, he kept telling me they had willingly signed their contracts over, and since it's a 'blind' fund, it couldn't be identified or traced. How can that be?"

"Didn't your sister, the stockbroker, explain—"

"A million times," Lauren said. "It still doesn't make sense. Seems like there was a 20-million dollar price on my parents' head. They die in a suspicious way. Now nobody can tell me who gets the money."

"Oh Lauren, stop it!" Margie scolded.

"So paranoid!" Herschel snapped. "Do you really think all four of us—and your parents—didn't think about every aspect of these policies before we signed up? Give us some credit here!"

"Two seasoned businessmen," Stella said, "experience in finance all their lives. Your father, he was an investor—"

"Honey," Margie said, putting an arm around Lauren. "Put that worry out of your head. It's outrageous."

"Half the people we know at the Club did this deal," Ernest said. "All got their money and all are still walkin' around today."

Hunter remembered the Ohio lawmaker speaking about the sinister nature of life settlements. Now, it was making sense—for someone who believed in far-fetched conspiracy theories. It just sounded too sci-fi—too wicked—to endorse as a theory for the Price's deaths. This community was definitely where he should focus his search for fraud.

"Mrs. Miller," Hunter said, "the insurance industry is regulated like you wouldn't believe. It is very unlikely that any connection links your parents' deaths directly to their insurance policy."

"This morning I reviewed the autopsy reports for both your parents," Hunter said. "Everything was consistent with your father being electrocuted, and your mother having sudden cardiac arrest."

"That can happen," Margie said. "Harry, last summer, out on his boat around Manhattan—"

"And couples," Stella said, "I know two, when one dies, the other goes right away. My cousin, Adelle in Newark; when her Bernie caught pneumonia and died, she literally curled up, went to sleep, and never woke up. She was in fine health, too."

Hunter still couldn't pinpoint what this place reminded him of. The plastic perfection in the conversation, the houses, the polished and sparkling people.

That's it! The Stepford Wives. Hunter remembered watching both the 1970s version and the modern remake of the movie about a small town where rich men transformed their wives into beautiful, subservient robots. Here, though, these women definitely let their opinions be heard. But moreso Hunter got a sense that their lives revolved around a money-makes-everything-perfect theme. And the more money, the better. Even if your neighbors had to die.

Yeah, something strange, perhaps even sinister, was going on in this surreal enclave of wealth and privilege called Diamond Lagoon.

That word, lagoon, kept conjuring up images of *Creature from the Black Lagoon*. As a kid, Hunter had watched the movie over and over, fascinated by the dangers lurking in the murky darkness. Now, it felt as if danger were hiding here, behind the sparkle of diamonds and within the gated walls of prime real estate.

"My parents grew up together," Lauren said.

"Next door neighbors," Stella said, "their mothers would take them to Central Park in the baby carriages together. What a story."

"It's possible," Ernest said, "that your mother just died of a broken heart. The sight of losing Mark was just too much for her heart—

The doorbell chimed. Lauren sighed, "Ugh, who is that?" She turned toward an archway leading to a two-story foyer, then leaned back enough to see through glass panels on each side of the double doors. "The realtor. She's early."

"Let her in," Margie said. "The sooner you settle the estate, the better."

"This morning she said they got five unsolicited bids on the house already," Stella said. "No housing crisis here."

"Five bids?" Hunter asked.

"You betta believe it," Ernest said. "This is Florida's answer to Silicon Valley in terms of real estate. Hot! People would kill to get these properties. Oh, I didn't really mean to say that."

Hunter showed no reaction as he looked into the elder man's eyes. Would this man want his own friend dead—so he could somehow get his hands on this house and sell it? Hunter didn't quite get it, but that vague sense of wrong in his gut was no longer vague. Something here was just plain wrong.

43. Casuarina Cay, The Bahamas

Annoyed that Boxley's call had interrupted this rare get-away, Juan sprinted up the stone steps. He needed to get his laptop from the plane to see if the portal was, indeed, bursting with twice the orders as usual. If so, he'd disperse them immediately. Only then would he hit the hammock to brainstorm Operation Vanish.

He'd be like the little crabs on the steps, scurrying under lush green leaves of vegetation surrounding the staircase. Everything about this island was sexy. Like the plants that could be combined—according to Juan's Bahamian bodyguards years ago—to make "hard dick" tea. And the Dildo Cactus that could grow 20 feet high. Not to mention, seductive tropical fruits and vegetables that were his for the taking, by pulling pineapples, bananas, tomatoes and cucumbers from trees and plants.

And he'd made sure that a vine called Queen of the Night was growing around his house. In just a few months, in the Spring—

I'll be a permanent resident of Casuarina Cay by then...

—the vines would blossom with huge white flowers that made the air smell like vanilla cake. Juan would never forget that night during his high school trip to the Bahamas, when Carrie and his other female classmates were all excited about the flowers on the hotel terrace.

"Look how the Sphinx moths are fluttering from flower to flower to pollinate them," Carrie had said, looking up with those smoky brown eyes that made Juan's 17-year-old body melt. She was a year younger than their classmates, due to her smartness; he was a year older,

thanks to emigrating from Bogotá as a small child and getting held back a grade while he mastered English. But that Kentucky country boy had a crush on her, too. And he'd cock-blocked by inviting everybody back inside to watch his father's horse race on television. That milk-toast motherfucker was always talking about horses like they were real people.

Bastardo. Still had that same wholesome American rich boy look at the high school reunion back in May. He looked just as boring as he had in high school, in his khaki pants and clean-cut yuppie style. Didn't say what he did for a living back in Kentucky, but was probably running his father's horse farm so he could keep talking about those stallions like they were people.

"Who would she pick today?" Juan wondered aloud as a foot-long lizard stared at him from an eye-level step. "Me or him? The good guy or the bad guy?"

Me. He and Carrie were two of a kind and belonged together. But she was the Vice President. And he was a high level hit man. The mis-match of the millennium. But the fire in her eyes revealed that she was more like him than anyone would ever believe. Maybe she would indulge a secret affair with him here.

Juan had to hatch a plan. Now. Halfway up the stairs, he turned around. The computer could wait.

Minutes later, Juan laid in the shaded hammock, rocking with thoughts of another woman—the beautiful Angel who'd lifted him from Hell. He closed his eyes, drifting back...

"Today's your lucky day, Big Guy," said one of four official looking guys—clean cut, in dark suits—who escorted him out of his Hell hole and into a limousine.

"Somebody decided you'd serve your country better on a secret mission, than in a prison cell," one guy said, not looking up from a palm-sized, black and silver square that had buttons with numbers and letters, and a tiny TV screen. It vibrated, and he answered it like a phone! Juan—feeling like he'd just stepped into the prop room on a James Bond movie set—wanted to see what the hell it was, but he waited. If this hook-up were as good as it sounded so far, he'd get his own little vibrating typewriter TV screen that fit in his palm and worked like a telephone, too. A better one. He restrained himself even more when another guy pulled from a leather attaché a silver rectangle that was no thicker than those substandard bologna sandwiches in prison. The guy opened it—a computer! The keyboard was flat and metallic. His picture flashed on the color screen with his name and information about him.

All the while, Juan copped a "speak when spoken to" stance. He'd find out soon enough, and it'd be better than he could have ever dreamed. Surely this was not a dream. As they drove, he repeated his mantra: I deserve to live like a king and will do anything to maintain my empire.

But there had to be a catch. The federal judge who'd sentenced him to life in prison had called him "the face of depravity" and "the epitome of money-hungry evil." So what work had they lined up for such a character? Was there some trial where they wanted him to snitch? Do spy work? Take an undercover DEA job?

Juan was sure that all those government pay-offs he'd made 15, 20, 25 years ago had somehow influenced this miraculous release. Did those crooked politicians—state and federal—think he had a stash of millions that they could now raid? Investing in lawmakers always paid dividends, sooner or later. And all that money he'd paid to the Bahamian officials to protect his private island... had they honored the agreement after all these years?

Juan's heart raced with excitement when the limo stopped on a dark, rainy tarmac and they boarded a government-issue Gulfstream 550, the finest private business jet produced at a price tag of roughly $40 million.

He hadn't flown since the feds had shot down his plane over Florida, just coming back from a mission with a shitload of cash and cocaine. His downfall happened shortly after that ex-Narc from Kentucky had parachuted to his death in Knoxville, Tennessee with 60 pounds of cocaine strapped to his body. After that, the U.S. and DEA cracked down hard, making an example out of The Panther.

As a result, Juan went from flying the Florida skies, to rotting in solitary darkness for 23 hours a day. One hour in the outdoor dog-run kept him in shape. And sane. All he'd had was his mind. And he relived every minute of his life that he could remember, over and over, forcing himself to recollect even more details each time.

For example, he'd think about his mother, who died of pneumonia two weeks after he went to prison. There, he thought about not just her presence, but the scent of gardenia perfume that she wore when he was a boy. He remembered the tickle of her long black braid on his arm when she served his meals. The strand of pearls that his father had given her, that she never took off, the way they hugged the base of her long, caramel-hued neck, snugly just above those two points of her collarbones, and the single pearl that dangled in the hollow of her neck.

Soon, Juan was reviewing his life, like a Dolby surround sound movie in the clearest Technicolor, over and over in his mind. He relived his reign in the cartel. Every deal. Every word. Every nuance that spoke volumes between partners, between enemies. He relived every tryst with countless whores, every freckle and hair. His mind's eye recollected their perfume, their lips, their nipples.

Now, in this airplane with four mystery men, Juan silently mused, I could write a book called "How to Stay Sane in Solitary." *Because his mental exercises had made him smarter than ever. With every deal or betrayal or seduction that he relived, he learned. With every flight he* revisited, he thought of new ways to perfect his flying. Always knowing he would be free again.

And here he was, on this luxury, private jet with plush leather passenger seats and a shiny teak door in the back that probably—according to Juan's experience as an international titan of commerce—led to a bedroom suite.

"Come with me," the escort said, leading Juan through that back door. To the left, a bathroom. Straight ahead—a plush bed.

"You stink," the guy said. "She wants you to clean up."

"Who is she?" Juan asked.

The guy pointed toward a silver tray with shaving supplies. On another tray were expensive colognes, deodorant, lotion, mouthwash, toothpaste and a toothbrush, and nail clippers.

"She wants you to leave your hair long," the guy said, leaving. "Your clothes are in the bedroom."

For the first time in 15 years, Juan looked in the mirror.

"Aye mierdo," he whispered "Oh shit," in Spanish.

His sunken eyes shimmered with shocking power above the sharp peaks of his cheekbones and pale skin. It was clear but thin-looking, like beige tissue paper stretched over a skull. His shoulders, despite daily push-ups in his cell, appeared thin under his beige wool sweater. His superior genes had kept his skin clear, his hair thick and jet black, despite his 45 years. It hung in a matted mess down his back.

"You have the eyes of a black panther," that drug lord had said during Juan's beachside encounter during a high school field trip for an ecology project in the Bahamas. "Work for me, and I'll make you the most feared and respected king of the jungle."

That power still glowed in Juan's hazel eyes that looked like they'd been peppered with gold and copper and jade. Sometimes darkening, sometimes lightening, always intensifying the fear of a foe or the warmth of a woman. Framed by thick black lashes and naturally arched brows, the unusually large irises had the power to stun—even their owner, as they were doing now. Deathly still, with focused intelligence, his eyes emanated the arrogant dominance of a predator.

And his next prey would be whoever "She" was. If this were a business meeting, why would she care if he were shaved or not? A miracle was happening, and Juan expected nothing but the best. But what price would he have to pay?

44. Washington, D.C.

Carolyn hated the extra Secret Service guys watching her every move here in her office. But President Anderson had refused to let her leave the meeting in the Oval Office without them. With Sue Bookman in the mix, Carolyn distrusted everything about it. She wouldn't put it past the Secretary of State to pay or seduce one of these guards to "find" incriminating information about the Vice President.

I need to stop her before she tries to stop me.

While Carolyn refused to indulge a paranoid fantasy about failure, this whole new development with the abduction threat had gotten her thinking about a Plan B. Carolyn's usual *Modus Operandi* was to hatch a Plan A and believe so faithfully in its fruition and success, that she never needed a Plan B. In fact, as she had climbed the career ladder, she never considered failure as she rose from one position to the next. She always got what she wanted.

And in this case, her SOS Plan would succeed. She would become President. Period.

But it sure wouldn't hurt to have a back-up strategy. Her mother's weak voice, sharing words of wisdom on her deathbed a decade ago, whispered through Carolyn's mind: *"Honey, remember. You always win. Even if it looks like they're chasing you, you turn it around and chase them."* Carolyn had gripped her mother's hand, hating the cancer that had rotted her from the inside out. *"In other words, steal their guns and blast back at 'em."*

So how, if necessary, could Carolyn use this high security mandate, and this threat of abduction, in her favor? If the President hadn't stamped the matter with "classified" before her guarded dismissal, then she could use the threat—which would be all over the media in a split second—to garner sympathy from the American public. And of course she would translate that sympathy into support for her SOS Plan.

I got it! If the abduction threat "leaked" to the media—and it somehow looked like the leak was Sue Bookman, the Secretary of State—Carolyn could kill two birds with one stone.

45. Diamond Lagoon, Florida

The real estate agent fluttered into the Price's kitchen like a hummingbird fiending for nectar, the sweet, green kind that came in the form of money for mansions. Hunter maintained his friendly expression as he watched her with complete awe. She was small and pretty and fast-moving like a hummingbird, but her vibe screamed vulture.

"Ciao, my friends," gushed the gold-haired maven with bright pink lipstick. She woke a slim, pink linen suit with matching patent leather pumps and carried a white leather briefcase. Her hair–teased on top and swooping up at ear-level—was shellacked in place like a helmet.

Her fake eyelashes reminded Hunter of awnings over her brown eyes that flitted from person to person far too quickly for his comfort. Her nose literally looked chiseled in a taut face that contrasted dramatically with her tanned turkey neck. The skin over her chest was crinkled, like paper that had been balled up, then flattened—except for the exposed mounds of her breasts. That skin was stretched to the max over silicon torpedoes that made her look top-heavy.

A gold chain around her neck held a gold charm in the shape of a house that glimmered over her cleavage. A heart-shaped ruby sparkled in the center of the golden house.

"Polly Chesterfield," Lauren said, "this is Hunter Knightly. He's trying to find answers about how my parents died."

The real estate agent's hand felt tiny in Hunter's grip, but she squeezed and shook hard.

"It was an accident!" Polly said. "Everybody I know is being so careful around anything electric. My last client, she won't even screw in a light bulb by herself."

"Pleasure meeting you," Hunter said.

Polly talked fast as she set her briefcase on the kitchen island. "Mr. Knightly, are you looking for real estate in South Florida?"

"Polly," Lauren said with an annoyed glance at the briefcase as it bumped the fruit platter, which screeched across the white marble countertop. "I need to finish up with Mr. Knightly before we talk about the house."

"No, I need you to sign these papers for the auction on Monday," the real estate agent said, pulling documents from her briefcase. "My phone is blowing up for this property. Everyone wants to bid on this house. You'll make a mint!"

Where's the grief? Hunter couldn't believe how all this talk about money and real estate had made everyone forget about the deceased. Except Lauren, who moved the fruit platter away from the briefcase.

"The house, money, I could care less about that right now," Lauren said, turning her back and walking to the sleek stainless steel refrigerator. She grasped the handle, bowed her head, and sobbed.

"Aw, honey," Stella said, dashing over with a jangle of gold to comfort her. Margie followed.

Polly held up some documents and glared over at Lauren. "Ugh," she exclaimed. "There's a time to grieve. And a time to take care of business. The two don't mix."

Ernest said, "Her husband, he's finishing a deal in New York. He'll be down tomorrow. Maybe handle that with him." Ernie leaned toward Polly and said in a low voice, "Her husband's just as pushy as that insurance agent was, truth be known."

Polly quipped, "Today's Friday. We have the weekend to finalize this paperwork. Somebody help her compose herself in time for the auction. Every auction is exciting, but now we have so many."

"Next Wednesday," Herschel said, "the Philips place, on the 18th hole. That auction is gonna be vicious."

He turned to Hunter and said, "He was an amateur pilot. Crashed in—"

"North Carolina," Ernest said. "Killed them and their best friends."

Hunter was going to North Carolina to investigate those deaths next week. With home bases in Hampton, New York, they had several other properties, including a winter home in Florida. Hunter didn't remember what town, though. He had planned to review that file as soon as he returned home. Could those cases involve the same dead homeowners that these folks were talking about?

"The Berkleys," Polly said, "the auction for their house is next week, too. They're all hot properties, but this one, this one is an absolute masterpiece."

She focused on Hunter. "You look confused, my friend." She handed him a business card; it was thick and glossy with her name and that gold house with the red heart in the center.

"Why do the houses go to auction?" Hunter asked.

Ernest shrugged. "That's just how we do things around here. It's a special place." He nudged his friend. "Herschel, don't forget, we got a tee time at one."

The other man looked at him like he had turned orange. "You're telling me, 'Don't forget golf'?" He turned to Hunter and said playfully, "Next he'll tell me, 'Don't forget to breathe.'"

"Actually the truth about our auctions is somewhat," Polly said, lowering her voice, "incestuous." She stepped closer to Hunter, bringing with her a choking cloud of too-sweet perfume. "It kind of violates one of the 10 commandments. Though shalt not covet thy neighbor's—"

"House!" Ernest laughed. Herschel joined in, then popped a cracker and a lump of gorgonzola into his mouth.

"Years ago," Polly said, "the residents decided two things. One, they wanted to maintain the elite atmosphere of residents and homes. And two, they liked to 'move up' to a nicer home when one became available."

"Actually, Polly," Herschel corrected, "they buy the house, tear it down, and build a bigger, better one. Rarely does anybody 'renovate' here. Why renovate when you can rebuild? Nobody wants to look out-dated in The Diamond Lagoon Club."

Hunter was sure this was the community he had noticed during his descent into Palm Beach. He still couldn't believe how bright green the golf course appeared from 3,000 feet; even up there, the houses looked enormous.

"The homeowners association prohibits renovating," Ernest added. "New properties keep everyone on their toes. Someone builds Versailles. The next guy builds the Taj Mahal. Pre-terrorist attack, of course."

"I should hire the both of you," Polly said. "Make my job so easy—"

"We closed off Diamond Lagoon real estate to the general public," Ernest said. "Nobody knows about our auctions, except us insiders, so we keep this little slice of heaven all to ourselves."

This place was getting more intriguing by the minute. Could there have been any connection between the Bloomfields' deaths and their covetous neighbors' greed for this house? Were these people so property-hungry that they'd kill for it?

And what about the other two couples—and their houses? He'd call Randy to get the details about those cases as soon as he left here. That would be far beyond coincidence if he were investigating three dead couples—all in their 70s, all who had houses in this picture perfect retirement community.

"Lauren," the real estate agent called as the daughter sobbed into Margie's shoulder. "Your parents enjoyed a wonderfully loving and long life." Her tone hardened: "I'll leave these papers on the counter. When you get yourself together, sign them. Fax them to my office ASAP."

Hunter wished his mother could see this lady in action. Polly Chesterfield was the opposite of everything he'd learned about good manners, both personally or professionally.

"Polly," Hunter said, "how 'bout we take a spin around the neighborhood and I talk with you about the hot properties in the area?"

"Oh, I'm afraid you may not qualify," Polly said. "These homes are only available to families and close friends of current residents. Once in a blue moon, a frequent visitor *might* win approval by a residential vote.

But the odds are against you. Five hundred voters versus one little outsider. Sort of like the old black ball initiation into a country club. One 'no' vote from a resident means total disqualification to live here."

This exclusivity didn't feel desirable; it felt sinister.

"Are you buying, Mr. Knightly?" she asked. "Where are you from?" She scanned him from his brown leather loafers, up the creased legs of his khaki pants, over the brown belt around his slim waist, and up his crisp white dress shirt. She checked out his clean-shaven face, and his neatly tousled tumbles of wavy hair. She closed the briefcase. "I have nothing less than five million. All the way up to 25-million. That's for the property before tear-down and rebuild. Can you afford—"

"Actually my parents are looking for a retirement place," Hunter said. "They always say, 'Location, location, location.' And this little utopia you got here is just what they're looking for. But if it's closed to outsiders—"

Delight danced in her eyes. "Lauren, I'm coming back tomorrow to talk to your husband."

"Thank you, Gentlemen," Hunter said, shaking hands with Ernest and Herschel. "I'll see you tomorrow. If you think of anything, here's my card. That's the cell. Call anytime, day or night."

Hunter gently squeezed Lauren's arm. "I'm sorry. I'll come back at a better time."

Tears spilled from her bloodshot eyes as she whispered, "Thank you."

Minutes later, after Hunter followed the hummingbird through the huge white marble foyer with the curving staircase, onto the lushly landscaped lawn and into her enormous black Mercedes, he got the feeling she was out to suck the nectar out of every possible person and deal that came around.

"Your parents," she said, squeezing the steering wheel at two and 10 o'clock. "What do they do?"

"My dad," Hunter fudged, "he owns an aeronautics company. Designed the P-450 airplane engine back in the '60s. That sparked an avalanche of government contracts. He swore it was like gettin' his own key to Fort Knox."

Polly getting an eight percent commission on all real estate deals down here, now that would be like owning Fort Knox!

Her voice was seductive: "Your dad, I love this man already." She drove past mansions, two men in a golf cart and well-coiffed couples walking expensive dogs.

"So does my mom," Hunter said, fudging more and having fun with it. This had nothing to do with his official investigation, and everything to do with getting this lady to tell him everything he wanted to know about real estate in this eerily perfect community called Diamond Lagoon.

A pang of guilt registered in his gut. He could hear his father lecturing him as a 10-year-old: *A winner never lies, Son, because the lie always catches up with him and brings him down.* It happened the one time Hunter had ever fibbed to his dad. He'd told him no, he hadn't been the one who'd let the stallion Best Bet out and run wild, risking injury before the Derby. But the security cameras had shown that yes, Hunter had been the culprit. *Don't ever lie,* Dad had said, *because somebody or somethin' is always watchin'. Might be God who's watchin'. Might be a camera. Or someday, your wife. Never lie, Son.*

But, here with this real estate agent, this fib was as harmless as the fake identities he'd used as a SEAL to sneak wherever he needed. "Yeah, my mom, the quintessential Southern Belle, she hails from an oil family down in Louisiana. Silver spoons, that's how we live."

Polly smiled. "Well, then, I don't have to speak the unspoken about whether your parents would be welcome here. They say money talks. I say money sings!"

As they passed yet another manicured lawn, Hunter said, "No FOR SALE signs. Why is that?"

"Discretion," Polly said. "On the surface, anyway. Diamond Lagoon residents can smell an available home a mile away."

Sort of like sharks smell blood.

46. Casuarina Cay, The Bahamas

As the salty breeze rocked the hammock, Juan reviewed his recent past in order to plan his future. The night of his liberation, he'd known it would carry an enormous price.

No such thing as a free lunch...

Or for him, a gourmet meal on a private jet...

A huge Porterhouse steak, two enormous lobster tails, pasta, a loaf of sourdough bread, buttered asparagus, and New York style cheesecake with strawberries on top.

"All your favorites," the escort said. "You better believe, we did our homework on you."

Juan repeated his mantra as he savored every bite.

Thunder crashed as the plane landed hours later. Blue lightening crackled across the black sky as a limo took them up to the Medieval-looking fortress that was the luxury hotel, The Chateau Frontenac, overlooking Quebec City in northeastern Canada.

"You'll be briefed on everything you need to know," the man said as they led Juan into a suite where he sat on a couch for the first time in 15 years. It faced a fireplace in which flames danced over white-hot logs and red embers. He inhaled the scent of burning wood. He would never go back to that cold, damp cell. Ever.

"Good luck," the men said, leaving. Almost immediately, a woman walked in from another room.

"The Panther lives," she said, stepping toward him in a black business suit that opened just enough to hint at full breasts. "Mr. Diablo, welcome back. Call me your

Angel, because I'll be watching over your new life. You're about to serve your country by putting that brilliant brain of yours to work."

She looked like a Playboy Playmate of the Year who was about to undress her corporate costume for a provocative photo shoot. Platinum hair tumbled down her back and chest in waist-length locks whose curled ends boinged up and down as she walked. Her black pumps were pointed at the toe and sky-high on pencil-thin heels. Her body was curvaceous yet athletic. Cleopatra-style black liner ringed her big blue eyes that glowed even brighter against her deeply suntanned skin. And she spoke with a slow, smooth voice unlike any he'd heard. This was a world-class seductress. But far too intelligent to be an ordinary whore.

That alone made Juan's dick hard. As she stepped closer, he inhaled her until his lungs ached. His tongue twitched with the need to taste her.

"Angel," he said in a way that made it sound like the law. "Tell me your real name. Your parents did not name you Angel."

"For you, they did," she snapped, leading him to a table displaying papers and gadgets. "In two months, you'll go to your high school reunion to get re-acclimated to the world. Other than that, you are now Eduardo Rodriguez." She handed him a spiral-bound report. "Here is your life. Memorize every detail. Date of birth, parents, siblings, where you grew up, the bike accident that broke your arm when you were six, etcetera. Then burn it."

He took the document.

"You're in charge of a special project called Eldorado," she said. "I don't have to tell you what that means."

"The Golden One," Juan said, remembering how his grandmother would tell him the legend that originated *in the Andes Mountains near Bogotá. His beloved* Abuelita, *Spanish for "little grandma," loved to weave fantastic tales while she cooked; each food inspired a different story. And when she made churros, Juan got a double treat: the sweet pastry* and *the legend of Eldorado. She always reached the part about the Muisca tribal chief dusting his body with powdered gold, as she lifted long strips of pastry from the fry pan, then rolled them in sugar and cinnamon. As Juan ate the delicious churros, she'd explain how the chief spent a long period alone in a cave, then in all his gilded glory, dove into Lake Guatavita. He'd also throw golden objects into the huge lagoon—all offerings to the tribe's demonic god.*

"So I'm your gilded man," Juan said. "Does that make you a Conquistador? They plundered the Muiscas, you know. Or am I your golden offering to some demonic god."

She smiled. "I knew we could put all that brainpower of yours to good use!"

"We?" Juan was sure she was the sexy assistant to some mysterious Emperor on a secret throne, issuing orders to usher Juan into the Land of Eldorado.

"Tell me what type of use," he said. "Eldorado implies a great fortune."

"Your passport," she said, handing it to him. "Notice it's the same as an ordinary citizen's passport. Except it's black and contains multiple miniature electronic clearance properties. That will grant you access to the highest echelons of intelligence and power in the world."

No, she was no whore. The whores he knew didn't use words like "echelon." Or so skillfully evade his demands for information.

"Only the President of the United States and a handful of the top government officials have the privilege of a Black Passport," she said. "Let no one see it. It goes without saying, everything you do is not only classified, it's nonexistent, ya hear? It does not exist. This is not happening."

Yes, yes, it was. And whatever "it" was, he was going to milk it for all it was worth. And win.

"Now, while you were away, a fascinating new world of technology developed. This is your laptop computer." She opened it on the table; it was the same style as the one in the limo, except this one was shiny black. "You can do anything but cook dinner on this machine. Here, electronic mail—it's called email—will send your notes anywhere in the world in the blink of an eye. Completely wireless. No trail whatsoever."

Juan couldn't wait to play with that baby and explore all her features.

"Click here," she said, glancing up at him, "I mean you touch the pad here with your thumb—" she pressed his thumb to the pad "—and you make the cursor, that little arrow, you make it move."

The heat of her body, her intelligent yet sultry energy, the touch of her hand to his... made flames of lust shoot up and down his body.

"Double click—that means, press your thumb down twice—with the cursor on this Internet Explorer icon," she said, "and you can hop onto this global computer system called the Internet. It's also called the world wide web or the information superhighway. You can visit the Louvre, take a safari in Africa and chat live with your friends around the globe, all in an instant."

She logged onto a site that showed his hometown in Colombia. "Google Earth—it works by satellites and these ground pictures they take—will show you any- and everywhere you can imagine. We have access to a system that's far more powerful; you'll need it in your work. Here's the front of your grandmother's house," she said, turning to him as if she expected to hear a gasp, or see disapproval in his eyes.

Anger flamed within him, but his expression was cool. Juan didn't like for anyone to know anything about the innocent people in his family. Especially his Abuelita. He would go visit her as soon as possible, and make sure she was safe. Juan would maintain his policy that anyone who harmed his family would pay with blood.

"Just as they said," she marveled, as her blue eyes—an almost artificially dark blue—reminded him of the deep part of the ocean. "No reaction, whatsoever."

"Who are you." His words hit the air like hooks that usually had the power to extract whatever facts he desired from anybody. He never asked a question; he demanded information with his tone of voice and inflection.

"Your Angel," she said softly as she turned and typed. A blue screen flashed. A computerized voice said, "Please provide your User Name and Password."

Juan steeled his face, his eyes. He would show no surprise, no delight, no intrigue.

Bending over the computer, she tossed her hair over her shoulder as she looked back at him. The tiny slit at the back of her skirt revealed two stockinged sets of sculpted hamstrings; this woman definitely did her time in the gym. Juan imagined lifting her skirt over the perfect mounds of her ass, and—

"This is the portal where you'll operate," she said, shifting slightly. A band of white lace flashed in the slit of her skirt; she was wearing garters.

Juan's insides melted as all of his blood rushed to the hot, throbbing rod in his pants. He bent slightly, staring at the computer. Every heartbeat blasted more fire through his veins.

"You'll retrieve assignments here," she said. "You'll input data regarding every mission. They will all be successful." The look in her eyes hardened as if she were a seasoned drug lord, issuing a wordless warning about the deal. Juan had seen that too many times, and though he always triumphed, no matter what, that expression was a warning that he was doing business with one ruthless motherfucker. Even if she called herself an angel, looked like a Playmate, and was resurrecting The Panther.

"Here are your User Name and Password," she said, typing. Each letter showed up on screen as a black dot.

User Name: ElDorado.
Password: Conquistadores.

"You'll have a top intelligence agent at your service, 'round the clock," she said. "You'll master these electronics within 48 hours."

"Tell me what I'll be doing," he said. "Tell me the nature of these assignments and missions."

She leaned past him to wrap her hand around that small electronic phone device that he'd seen in the limo. "This is your phone, a mainstream BlackBerry, enhanced with impenetrable military-grade technology. Agent K will contact you for a tutorial."

She handed him a glossy picture of a small red airplane. "Tomorrow you'll get your plane."

"My plane?" The words rode a surge of excitement that shot through Juan's lips before he could stop them.

"I hear you're quite the Top Gun," she said. "Your experience with small aircraft over a vast array of terrains in every season will help you in your work."

Juan had never seen a plane so sleek and small. ""What type of plane is this?"

"It started off as a Maverick Military, Very Light Jet. That's a relatively new class of personal jets that anybody can buy for a couple million bucks. Yours, however, has technological and power plant enhancements that make it fly faster and longer than any plane out there."

Questions jammed Juan's brain.

She looked into his eyes and said, "Don't worry—"

"I don't worry," he said with a tone that was so cold, the words seemed to freeze mid-air. She read my mind. She saw the emotion behind my thoughts. No one is supposed to do that. *He squinted down at her.* "Who are you!"

Her eyes twinkled up at him. "Your airplane has the latest technology in your avionics suite. Flat screens with every kind of map and monitor, different colors, it's amazing. Makes me want to get my own damn airplane."

Juan smiled. *To hear her talk about flying ignited yet another burst of lust within him.*

"We equipped your plane with a hidden military Green Box," she said. "It's nothing like the Black Box that records flight data. The Green Box makes your plane invisible to radar, so you can cross international borders without detection or advance clearance. And it emits a military-friendly beacon code."

"Describe 'we'."

"We," she whispered, casting a smoldering look up at him, "is you—" she leaned closer "—plus me."

He wanted to taste her lips, to press his hungry mouth to hers and suck like there was no tomorrow.

"Here," she whispered, closer, leaning up. "Tonight." She tilted her mouth toward his. "Alone—"

Juan's parted lips pressed into hers. Lust burned through his body. He was about to make a devil of this Angel.

47. Diamond Lagoon, Florida

For Hunter, the surreal feeling of this community intensified as the real estate agent pulled up to an ornate black gate leading to a pale orange Mediterranean villa. Humid heat gusted into the icy air conditioning as she rolled down the window, pushed a button and said, "Polly Chesterfield. Heart Real Estate."

The gate opened. She drove onto a cobbled courtyard centered by a fountain. She parked behind two trucks—one from a carpet company, one from an "interior reconstruction" business.

As she and Hunter walked toward the enormous double doors of carved wood, she whispered, "Not to jinx the deal, but the previous owner died. Burglary. They stole mostly electronics and some cash. Then killed him. Horrible. He was 69. Houses in the Hamptons, Aspen, Connecticut. Down here, he was always playing tennis or, crazy—" she laughed "—once I saw him rollerblading with these hot young babes on South Beach. Young at heart, gotta love 'im."

"How long's the place been on the market?" Hunter asked.

"Longer than any other house, ever," she said. "It's not the 25-million dollar price tag. It's the tragedy. And the delay of his nephew coming long distance to clean up the mess. Come to the auction. Bring your parents." She flitted through the huge door as a butler opened it. "I've gotten 15 phone calls since the day this house went on the market."

"Thank you," Hunter said to the butler.

Polly barked, "Mr. Mathers is expecting me."

"Polly!" exclaimed a flamboyant brunette in a velvet smoking jacket. Tall and thin, he floated toward her across a brown marble floor that stretched like a tarmac between walls of intricately carved dark wood that arched two stories above them. Heck, Hunter could probably fly his plane through this place, it was so big and vaulted. Another man, shorter and bald but wearing a similar jacket, dashed out of a side hall and hugged her.

"This is Mr. Knightly," Polly said. "I'm showing him the house."

"Hi, I'm Seth Mathers. This is Zack. You're so wholesome!" the tall man said with a sweeping gaze from Hunter's head to his feet. "You must be from the Midwest."

"You're close," Hunter said playfully. "Why 'yawl movin'?"

"Vegas calls," said the shorter man. "I design costumes. Got the gig of the century with a fabulous show."

"Polly's helping us find something that's more low maintenance," Seth said. "Paying 750-thousand dollars to join the golf club, just to eat dinner there a few times a month, is just so excessive."

"That's the membership fee," Polly said to Hunter. "You have to join to live in the neighborhood. We have to maintain a certain exclusivity."

"No," Seth said, "this is another planet altogether. Foreclosure crisis? The people here say, 'What foreclosure crisis?'"

"All my friends back in Seattle," Zack said, "they're always griping about gas prices and the cost of a gallon of orange juice. Here, we're insulated. In a bubble made of money."

"A seven million dollar median," Polly said, "for houses here. It's so competitive. Sometimes residents bid double the market value, just so they can get a specific location—"

Hunter remembered how his parents would harp about "Location, location, location." The only time he'd considered location for his own home-buying needs had been the house for Meredith. Her greed had landed her in the wanna-be version of Lexington's best neighborhoods.

"It's like sport," Seth added. "Almost barbaric, the competition. It's so amusing to watch these high-class society ladies get rabid over a house. That auction last month—" he turned to Hunter "—it was better than watching that movie Gladiator. All these oxygenarians, we call them—"

"You know," Zack laughed "old enough to need oxygen!"

"Why do you guys live here, then?" Hunter asked.

"Oh, since my uncle died last Fall," Seth said as men trampled past with a huge roll of carpet, "we've had to fix the place up before putting it on the market. This house is not a tear-down/rebuild." He cast a questioning look at Polly.

"It's okay, I told him," she said.

"Hope that doesn't creep you out," Seth said, "that someone died here."

"We've totally redone the master bedroom," Zack said. "You'd never know—"

Seth glared at him. "We're also going through his 10 centuries' worth of stuff. The man collected junk from all around the world."

"You're lucky," Zack said. "Usually an outsider can't bid on these properties."

"Come again?" Hunter said.

"When the surviving spouse dies," Polly said, "an outsider can bid on the property. But Mr. Mathers never married."

"Complicated, isn't it?" Zack said. "But it preserves the elite-ness. Elitist-ness? What's the word?"

"Elitism," Hunter said. That's how his buddies jokingly referred to Hunter because he grew up on one of the biggest horse farms in Kentucky.

Polly glanced around. "We usually don't allow a property to sit unsold this long after a death. But since Seth and Zack had so much clearing out to do—and that god-awful clean-up—we made an exception."

Seth nodded at Hunter. "Could be your lucky day."

Hunter's mind whirled a million miles a minute with all the names, faces and details of the past few hours. Why did that name, Mathers, sound so familiar?

48. Diamond Lagoon, Florida

On the green at the ninth hole, Herschel Goodman maneuvered into his best stance. He loved this hole because it faced the picturesque clubhouse, with its pond and fountain, its deck bustling with people talking, eating, and chatting on cell phones. Rippling in the breeze above them: flags for the United States, the state of Florida, and Diamond Lagoon Golf Club, forming a perfect trinity.

A plume of barbecue smoke rose from the huge outdoor kitchen where the chef was sizzling up juicy steaks that Herschel, Ernest and their two partners would enjoy after 18 holes. So what if they had to pop an extra Lipitor and keep their beefy indulgence a secret from the wives. A man had to live, and enjoy life!

And he was doing just that, lacing his fingers over his custom-made club, and gripping his number four hybrid just right. He straddled the ball with his new white saddle oxford loafer-style golf shoes. Bent his knees. Envisioned a hole-in-one. He and his buddies always joked that only Superman could hit the ball hard enough to make it land on the deck of the Club. Besides, the hole was just east of the Club, so balls were never really flying toward it, for safety reasons.

That was a good thing, because Herschel felt like Superman today. Like he could hit that ball from here to eternity.

"Get ready to lose all your money, fellas," Herschel declared. "It's been a long time since I had a hole-in-one." He said it with the confidence that he was due another one today.

"Twenty years and counting," Ernie said.

"Gotta say it once during every round," Herschel said. "Just in case." He drew the club back, swung with all his might, and...

Whack!

The tiny white ball whizzed toward the hole near the Club. An explosion of red sprayed at the center of the upper deck.

Screams. Shrieks. People scurried like insects.

"Oh my God!" Ernest groaned. "Oh my God!"

Herschel tried to focus. He went numb. His ball had gone so far left... into a group of people... it hit somebody in the head. Busted open their skull. That was blood, flying everywhere.

"No!" Herschel shouted. "No, no!" He could never live with the guilt of killing someone. Especially with a golf ball. He was moving and thinking in slow motion as the three men around him talked and turned on their own cell phones, which were normally banned from use on the course. But this was an emergency.

Ernest shook his head as he pressed his phone to his ear. Then he nodded and said, "Okay, okay." Eyes wide with shock and relief, he turned to Herschel and said, "It wasn't you. Something blew up. Killed the guy."

49. Miami, Florida

Freddie Buford had a point to prove. And his name was Chico, that tattooed piece of shit who was swaggerin' up the beach right now like he had balls as big as Texas. Had to, in this business. But that arrogant M.F. in his saggin' jeans and wife beater tank top needed to come down a notch or 10.

"Chico, my man!" Freddie exclaimed, rising from a bench to dude-hug this bitch. Chests barely touching, reaching around to double thump each other on the back. Then quick separation. "You been workin' hard."

"Workin' my ass off," Chico said, pulling off his turquoise Miami Dolphins cap to rake his dark hair into the messy ponytail down his back. His brown eyes were bloodshot; his breath smelled of beer. "I was hittin' it with this hot momma named Nina when you called. Said, 'Gotta go, Baby.' Take my work serious."

Freddie stared hard into Chico's long, thin face. He had a baby-soft goatee that made him look 15 instead of 25. But the silvery scar across his neck, where a rival gang had tried to slit the life out of him, made it clear that he was no innocent boy. Chico stared back, his thumb hooked in his silver belt buckle—a marijuana leaf spreading up over the white cotton hugging his skinny groin.

"Sit down," Freddie said, motioning toward the brown paper bag on the bench. "Grab a 40."

Chico removed the gold cap and chugged the malt liquor. With his head tilted back, his Adam's apple moved up and down behind the scar with every gulp.

"Ah," Chico sighed. "That's some good shit. Boss, why'd you want to see me before the meeting? Thought you were gonna pay me there. I got my talk all ready for the new recruits about my techniques."

"Got a new system," Freddie said. "Checkin' in with everybody one-on-one. Quality control, you know?" He probed Chico's eyes for any sign of suspicion. Or early reaction. He needed to drink all the beer, just to make sure.

Freddie sucked down some brew, then tilted his bottle for a toast with Chico's bottle. "Just wanna recognize hard work where it's deserved," Freddie said. "'Preciate you, dude."

Chico grinned, but stared at Freddie like he'd lost his mind. "What's with the warm and fuzzy thing, my man? You ain't gay, is you?"

Freddie doubled over with laughter. "You stupid fuck. Can't you take a compliment?"

Chico chugged more beer. And chugged, until the last little bubbles slid down the inside of the thick glass into his mouth. "Stop laughin' at me, my man."

Freddie sat up, catching his breath. "You got a bonus comin' tonight. Just caught me in a generous mood."

"Hell yeah!" Chico pumped his arm. "Yesssss."

"From here on out," Freddie said, patting Chico on the shoulder, "we're only gettin' bigger and better, stronger. Thanks to you."

Chico's grin withered as Freddie projected his best *you're-in-deep-shit* glare down at him.

50. Washington, D.C.

Carolyn ordered the Secret Service guys to wait outside her office while she met with Senator Boxley to discuss the SOS Plan. He was sponsoring the legislation in the Senate, after all, so by all appearances, their meeting was perfectly legitimate.

Her stereo played Mozart just loud enough to block their voices for anyone who might try to listen, physically or electronically. One could never be too careful.

"You're about to hear somethin' on the news about me," said Carolyn, who earlier today had sent off a note to GNN—on the Secretary of State's stationery—about the abduction threat. "Turns out, the President has informed me, there was more to the Sheik Sunami il Tabbul video. About me."

"What, pray tell?" Boxley asked as that adorable little dog of his, Katrina, curled at his feet.

"Gerry, this is beyond classified."

Mischief glinted in his eyes. "We're used to that."

She explained the videotaped threat and the President's reaction. "Sounds bad, but I don't believe the hype. If that crackpot wanted to inflict some more collateral damage, he would've done it by now."

"If the tape is correct, he has, on the economy," Boxley said.

"Oh," Carolyn said dismissively, "Anybody who was payin' attention coulda seen this recession comin' a mile away. Nobody wanted to look. And that works to our advantage."

The dog whimpered; Boxley pulled a packaged treat from his pocket and gave it to her without losing eye contact with Carolyn.

"That little beauty never leaves your side, does she?" Carolyn reached down to pet her, but Kat nuzzled Boxley's leg.

"Well that's an improvement from growling," Carolyn said sweetly. "Okay, okay, you love your daddy. Nobody else. She knows the meaning of loyalty," Carolyn said, staring hard at Boxley. He'd have to be crazy to defy her or jeopardize their plan, should he fall under the influence of schemer like Sue Bookman or anyone else. That letter to GNN, right about now, should take care of that.

"If the abduction stuff leaks to the media, we find every angle to milk America for sympathy, and we turn that into support for SOS. Ya hear?"

"Loud and clear."

"Good. Now how's the workload?"

"Smooth as silk," Boxley said. "We're right on target to meet the revised goals for 2009."

"Security?"

Boxley said, "Our updated server has the very latest Secure Socket Layer. The new SSL is the absolute safest way to protect Internet transactions."

Carolyn smiled. Everything was going so smoothly, she would let nothing and no one stop her now. "And the financing?"

"Withdrawals and deposits are increasing in frequency, in relation the workload."

"Sing to me, Gerry! This is music to my ears."

51. Diamond Lagoon, Florida

Ernest couldn't believe his eyes as the paramedics rolled a gurney through the front door of the Clubhouse.

"But how in the world can your cell phone just blow up?" he demanded as he and the fellas chugged their third round of drinks. "Makes no sense."

"Sure it does," said Stanley Goldstein, who was in from Naples for a few days. "My brother was in the military. It's easy to make a bomb from a lithium battery, if you know what you're doing. Newer, longer-lasting lithium batteries are unstable. Saw it in an article the other day."

"What," Ernest asked, "does it overheat? And spark—"

"You know they say you shouldn't use your cell phone while you're pumping gas," said another man at the bar. "Something about static electricity can spark the gasoline fumes—"

"Herschel," Stanley asked, "you okay?"

"If I can offer some comic relief," Ernest said, "your expression when it happened—" he grasped his gut, laughing "—you actually thought you hit the ball that far!"

"You'd be upset too," Herschel said, "if you saw blood spray—"

"I'm sorry, guys," Ernest said, "I think I'm laughing so I don't cry. After Mark and Suzie, this is just too much."

Another man, standing in the semi-circle of shocked golfers around them, added, "I hear it was the uncle of those gay guys. They're just here until the auction, and the uncle, I think he was from Nebraska, he was just down for the week."

Stanley pulled his phone from his belt. "I wanna know what kind of phone he had. The manufacturer, the carrier, the make, the model. Everything. I guarantee, all of us will get rid of ours if it's the same."

Ernest waved him off. "It's just a fluke! I remember growing up in Pittsburgh. My neighbor's house blew up in the middle of the night. Looked like match sticks all over the street the next morning. Faulty furnace. In a split second, a whole family blown to bits."

The ice cubes chilled Herschel's lips as he drank the last drops of vodka. "Hate to say it, fellas, but I agree. A fluke. When it's your time to go, it's your time."

Herschel shrugged. And shivered. Not enough for his friends to notice. But enough for the hairs on the back of his neck to stand.

52. Miami, Florida

Freddie Buford felt like the dean of Killer College, and tonight's secret meeting with his six new recruits and veterans was called Killing Without a Trace. They were about to get a lesson they would never forget. And that dumb motherfucker Chico in the front row had no idea that he was the living, breathing—at least for now—example.

"You boys ready to get paid?" Freddie called out like a sports coach would pep up his team before a game. But in the front row, that chick's breasts, all squeezed up in that tube top and tattooed QUEEN BITCH in black scroll ink over the tops, reminded him that he was an equal opportunity employer. Yep, he was taking applications from hot Hispanic mamacitas, black thugstresses from the 'hood, and the best trashy white chicks the trailer park had to offer. All of these hard-ass females wanted to rock. They were coming in handy for special jobs that needed a lady's touch. Besides, who would ever suspect a girl of being a hit man?

He chuckled: "You boys and girls ready to get paid?"

All of them exploded "Hell yeah!" and "Fuck yeah!" Some rose from their chairs along the long, gray tables in this conference room. A blue cloud of cigarette and marijuana smoke shrouded them under a single strip of fluorescent lights. The haze thickened as plumes rose from three students puffing cigarettes and joints.

"You!" Freddie ordered, ogling the front row girl's breast-top tattoos instead of her eyes, "help Elijah pass out the Training Cards. They don't leave this room," he said, looking each person in the eye. "Five cards, all numbered, come right back to me before you leave."

His lusty gaze returned to the girl. She was Cuban or Puerto Rican or some damn place where her people spoke Spanish. With her long dark hair in a high ponytail and big silver hoops swaying in her ears, she rose. Her tight ass popped in her skin-tight jeans that she had peeled off for him just an hour earlier. Freddie lit a cigarette, watching her walk through the aisles between tables. Elijah, in his usual New York Yankees cap, jersey and baggy jeans, handed her the three-by-five cards labeled Death by Natural Cause.

This crazy-ass cast of characters, and the reason they were here, made Freddie bust out laughing. "Hey, class, can you imagine if this was a reality TV show?" He deepened his voice to sound like an announcer: "Stay tuned for the next episode of Killer College! What creative deathtraps will Suzie set for rich old men this week? And how will Johnny plan the accidental death of the retired tennis pro?'"

"We makin' sick bank!" a black dude said from his seat in the middle of the room. He was slouched down low, like the hood rats cruising in their pimped-out cars, almost as low as the damn Hobbits. The handle of his black nine millimeter protruded from the waistband of his jeans; a sequined dollar sign sparkled on his black baseball cap. It cast a shadow over his eyes that shined against his ebony-black babyface.

"Keep kickin' ass like you are, my number one dude," Freddie said, "and you'll keep the cash flowin'." Freddie reached inside his pocket and tossed a leather bag to the black dude, who caught it. "My man here did the most Orders this week. Tell me your most creative job next week, and you'll be the one catchin' a surprise five-K."

"Tha's what's up," the guy said, nodding as he peered into the bag of Benjamins.

"I'll take the money, my man—" Chico coughed, "—but fuck a reality show. I don't want no video cameras nowhere near my wild-wild-west ass." He coughed, sounding like a cat with hair caught in its throat.

"You okay, dude?" Freddie asked.

"Throat just feels scratchy," Chico said, rubbing his scar.

"Smokin' too much weed," another guy whispered beside him in the smoky room.

"No wonder this place is shut down for renovations," Freddie said. "The ventilation ain't worth shit. Somebody might choke to death tonight."

He turned and glared at Chico.

53. Casuarina Cay, The Bahamas

Sitting in the only overstuffed lounge chair on the whole island, Juan dialed his newspaper buddy at *USA News*. It helped to have friends from his previous life who still owed him big favors.

"Is the article ready?" Juan stared out at 100 shades of turquoise water.

"Set to run tomorrow," his buddy said, "from sea to shining sea."

"Cool," Juan said. "That report helped?"

"Always makes a story more believable when you have a government report warning of the dangers. Causes a nice little panic. Just like the Sheik Sunami il Tabbul video."

Juan nodded. K's powers knew no bounds; that would help him execute make Operation Vanish. Meanwhile, Juan didn't care if anybody figured out that he was the mastermind behind this cell phone hysteria. It would take all those idiot investigators forever to trace any of this back to him, if they ever did. Juan gently raked his fingers through the warm sand. He'd be right back here, with a fortune and a new identity, by the time anybody discovered anything about what he was doing.

He relished his sense of invincibility and fierce pursuit of the life of luxury that he deserved.

"Listen," his buddy said, "let me call up the story on my computer. Here, I'll read it: 'A national government inspection of lithium cell phone batteries says they can become unstable and dangerous. All consumers are being warned to take extra caution with overusing and thus overheating cell phones that use the new, longer-lasting lithium batteries. Scientists say the batteries can become dangerously hot and melt some components in your cell phone. The slightest bit of moisture in the wrong spot can cause tragedy.'"

He continued: "That's what happened in Diamond Lagoon, Florida, where a 77-year-old Nebraska man died after his cell phone exploded while he was holding it to his ear. Now government inspectors are urging consumers to take their phones into the nearest cellular services outlet to have them inspected immediately. And they urge, always use a Bluetooth headset as an extra safety precaution."

"News you can use," Juan said, loving that America's obsession with cell phones made his work that much easier. Every cell phone company had countless subscribers, that undoubtedly included his Orders. It would be simple to match the hit list to the phone owners who were Orders.

To facilitate that, the K.C. Leaders were working with dudes in cell phone stores across America, to wire certain phones to ring with a special ring tone that would warn consumers that their batteries were overheating. That ring tone, the consumers would think, would mean they had to head back to the repair shop and get a new battery, compliments of Juan's special-order government Consumer Product Safety Commission.

Little did they know, the ring tone would play *Taps*. And the caller would be The Grim Reaper. *Bammo!*
Nothing like providing state-of-the-art tools for your staff to make their jobs easier.

54. Miami, Florida

Freddie was such a smart businessman. That was some smart shit he pulled, having this secret meeting in the conference room of the yacht club that was closed this season for renovations. Those fancy motherfuckers would be mad as hell if they saw all these killer thugs in here smoking. But one of Freddie's hoes was a receptionist there; she gave him the keys and *presto!* A free meeting room for his Killing Clan.

"Listen up!" Freddie shouted, standing in the center of his five students. "Memorize these top secret tricks of our trade. Everything's in code. You gotta speak that way, so nobody has any fuckin' idea what you're talkin' about."

Freddie said, "Somebody tell me what I'm saying if I tell you, 'My Order was an E2 with a faulty generator, during a black out, after a storm one night.'"

"The shit blew up in their face," a guy said. He pulled the toothpick from between his thin lips. "Put too much gas, make it spark, shazamm, muh-fucka!" His chocolate-brown face beamed as brightly as his bald head. Rhinestones sparkled in his ears. Scarface appeared larger than life on the T-shirt draping his huge Fat Albert ass.

"You got it!" Freddie high-fived him as Chico coughed. Right on time. "Now, if you know anything about South Florida in the winter, and the majority of our targets, you can see that our work is pretty easy. The hobbits—"

Freddie had his back to most of the students when he heard a deep voice: "What the fuck is a hobbit?"

"Don't interrupt me, shitface," Freddie shouted as he turned around. "Raise your hand. This is a serious class. Who said that?"

A white chick raised her hand; smoke plumed from the cigarette between her fingers. When Freddie hired her, he had bought her a hamburger. Poor thing looked like she hadn't eaten. But, she said with her redneck twang as her stringy peroxide-blond hair blew in the breeze, she'd always been the "runt" of the family. And cigarettes made her lose her appetite.

"I'm sorry, Mr. Freddie. That was me." All that smoking had fried her vocal cords; she had a whiskey-hard voice like a man. Suddenly she sounded like a lily-white receptionist, speaking The Queen's English: "Sir, if you could please be so kind to explain, what is a hobbit? Please."

The class laughed.

Another guy, in his head-to-toe silky white jogging suit and spotless Air Force Ones, ran his fingertips over his chin like he was thinking hard. "Ain't that some kinda character in a book? Seem like I heard about it befo' I said, 'Fuck school.'"

"You'd sure make your teachers proud if they saw you now." Freddie glared down on him. "Stupid wise-ass. Shut the fuck up and listen." Freddie paced, savoring every second of being in control and the center of attention. The authority figure. Sure beat all those days of gettin' the crap beat out of him by his mom, or teachers telling him he wouldn't amount to shit in life because he was too dumb.

"A hobbit," Freddie said, "is one of those old fucks who sit so low in the car you can barely see their head over the dash board. Old as dirt, shouldn't be drivin' anyway, and rich as all get-up. Our typical Order. They're already killing themselves. Trying to drive in South Florida traffic."

"Eat or be eaten," Elijah exclaimed.

Freddie smiled at Elijah, then said, "Somebody tell me some smart ways to knock out a hobbit."

"Sic a gator on 'em!" Chico shouted as the students eagerly offered a barrage of violent ideas. He laughed, then coughed.

Freddie shouted: "Everybody repeat after me: ACCIDENTAL!"

"ACCIDENTAL!" they roared. "NATURAL CAUSES!"

"You don't get paid for two reasons. One, it looks like murder. Two, they don't find a body. Got it? We need the bodies!"

"Got it!" they answered.

"So, no missing bodies," Freddie said, "or bodies that can't be identified. That means you don't get paid.

Now those old fucks already get in car accidents every day. That's an easy one. Let's get creative."

"Freddie," the Hispanic chick said, "What about the money?"

"You get paid half when you complete the assignment," Freddie says, "the other half, if you do it right, three months later. Gotta make sure nobody investigates or comes up with a way to say it was murder. Nothing suspicious. That's why we're giving you the tools for success. You can bank more loot with a two-for-one deal or even a three-for-one deal."

Elijah smiled. "Joey got paid that sweet-ass, four-for-one deal, for sinkin' that sailboat in the Greek Isles."

"I thought all our work was right around here," Rosalee said. "I got two babies to feed. I can't be goin' to no damn Greece—"

"That was a special situation," Freddie said. "You can make more dough if you wipe out a couple at a time. But they both have to be an Order. Say a dude is home alone, eating dinner. He chokes on a chunk of meat. Wife comes home, sees the dead motherfucker, and she keels over, too. From shock or rich bitch drama or whatever. But there has to be an Order for her, too."

"How you gonna make somebody drop dead?" a guy asked.

Coughing drew everyone's attention to the front of the room. Freddie took long strides toward Chico. Couldn't stand that punk anymore. Too cocky. Too messy. Fucked up an Order, now everybody would learn from it. He was the perfect candidate for the sacrificial lamb. Tonight's lesson on doing good work. Kill three birds with one stone. Eliminate, dominate and intimidate.

"Class, I got a special lesson tonight," Freddie said, standing beside Chico, whose eyes were huge with fear. He had turned in his chair so he was leaning on the table behind him, facing Bianca, who leaned back as if she thought he was going to puke on her.

"A live demonstration," Freddie said. "An example of what happens if you're—" he looked around at the students, then shouted, "—fuckin' sloppy!"

He slammed a hand on the table. "Or somebody comes sniffin' around to investigate because it didn't look accidental! Let this also be a real-life example of some killer drugs that leave no trace."

Chico's eyes grew huge. His chest was still.

"Everybody look at Chico. He fucked up a job. So he's our demonstration for tonight. Just a little peek at what happens to motherfuckers and bitches who fuck up."

The class was still and silent. All eyes focused on Chico, whose face was screaming agony and anger and mercy. But his body was motionless as he sat there, weakly holding himself up with his arms stretched over the table. They had all joined a fraternity with only one way out.

Freddie felt nothing as he stared down at that lowlife punk and said, "As you know, especially in this economy, you're all a dime a dozen. I can replace Chico 10 times over by tomorrow. You can't make this kinda money any other way unless you're robbin' banks or slingin' dope."

Chico's eyes moved back and forth, as if he were screaming for help. But these punks were just as scared as Chico. And they wanted to live.

"What the hell is wrong with him?" asked the guy in the dollar sign cap.

"What's wrong with Chico is that he messed up his last mission. Nobody got paid. You hear that? Nobody's gettin' paid for that wasted assignment. Why are we here?"

"To get paid!" they chanted in unison.

"Damn right," Freddie said. "Now this is the price that Chico's gotta pay. You're seein' it right now."

"Daaaaaaaang," another guy sighed in disbelief.

Freddie pointed to Chico's face. "Notice how his eyes are moving. He can hear us. But he can't talk. Can't breathe, either. This is a great way to demonstration a new drug I'm introducing to The K.C. Team tonight."

All six of them stared without speaking a word. Didn't try to help. Didn't question what was going down. They just watched and learned, exactly like Freddie wanted.

Welcome to the new fraternity! There's only one way out...

55. Washington, D.C.

Carolyn knew the news had hit the airwaves because her phone started ringing nonstop. The news would spread like wildfire around the world, and everyone would rally behind United States Vice President Carolyn Snedegar Taylor in every way possible.

Curled up in her plush bed in her luxurious penthouse—with round-the-clock security in her living room, in the hallway and in the downstairs lobby—Carolyn clicked on GNN and took the calls.

Russell was angry: "This has Sue Bookman written all over it. To defy the President! She's playing with fire."

But President Anderson was downright furious: "Whoever is responsible will regret this day! Carolyn, I apologize that our own government servants, even at the highest levels, lack the loyalty to respect and protect classified information."

After that, her father called: "Carrie, you protect yourself at all costs, understand? Go to the gun range, do your target practice. Even though there's no way anybody can get to you with the best security in the world. You know how to do it yourself—"

Next, Neal phoned: "Carrie, sweetie. I can come over—"

Best of all, GNN started playing clips of her SOS speech, along with video of her at the Inauguration, during the campaign, and even playing as a little girl under her father's desk in the Oval Office. Boy did she love that picture of herself in a dress, making her frilly doll drive a toy dump truck.

Pretty as a girl. Tough as a boy.

56. Washington, D.C.

A glittery green and gold Mardi Gras mask sat on Senator Gerald Boxley's desk as a reminder of the huge celebration in his hometown later this month. How symbolic that the documents he was reading were masking his business endeavors as well. Specifically, he reviewed paperwork for the holding company that cast a bureaucratic veil over his name on all documents involving ownership of Chrisma Corporation. Carolyn left nothing to chance.

But that was a double-edged sword. Their alliance of a lifetime, as she had called it, was so brilliantly crafted and orchestrated that it would succeed in complete secrecy. The staggering wealth that Boxley would receive—and was already receiving in increments via secure EFTs—made his whole body tingle with confident anticipation. The downside, however, meant that should anything go wrong, Carolyn would have already designated a scapegoat, a fall guy. Someone to blame.

That would be me. She could easily manipulate the paperwork to show that he was using a holding company to hide his illicit activities that were taking advantage of the system and America's senior citizens. She would play up resentments that festered in the mainstream against the perceived perks that minority businesses received from the public and private sector. Everyone seemed to forget that those so-called perks were to help even the playing field on which black businesses couldn't even step foot on for centuries. Maybe that's why she picked him in the first place, because it would be so easy, in the end, to dispose of him.

Yes, just as Carolyn was using the abduction threat as a PR perk—she was all over the media—she would find a way to twist that around in her favor. And survive. She'd use her charming Virginia accent, her lilting female voice, her endearing way of speaking, to convince the world that he was the culprit, and that she was squeaky clean.

"Here you go, Katrina." Boxley tossed a biscuit; the dog stared up with glassy eyes that pleaded for more treats. Boxley never wanted to appear that way to the Vice President. Even though, of all the money that Carolyn's plan was raking in, she was tossing him a mere biscuit. But that was a golden biscuit compared to his senatorial salary, subsequent pension and money from the Boxley family farm back home in Louisiana. She would probably also find a way to incriminate him for the huge vault of cash that she had charged him with protecting. Despite this risk, he felt satisfied with his take on the deal.

Pigs get fat and hogs get slaughtered. My position in this organization is just fine.

That's why Boxley was determined to work his ass off and execute his duties in the "alliance of a lifetime" to the absolute best of his ability. It would be flawless. Everyone would win, and he'd sit back—someday very soon—and live the fine life in his French chateau.

The phone buzzed; his secretary said, "Senator Boxley, I have Agent A here to see you."

Boxley smiled. "Bring him in, please." His most trusted FBI agent stepped into the office, wearing a dark suit and holding a folder. After the secretary left, he sat down at Boxley's table and opened the folder.

"Quite an interesting fellow, this Hunter Knightly," the agent said. What a fitting name. The guy had a pasty oval face that reminded Boxley of his grandchildrens' Mr. Potato Head. How many times had he watched them switch noses, eyes, mustaches and glasses to give Mr. Potato Head a whole new identity? Even Agent A's hair—a neat Beatles-style mushroom of straight black hair—looked interchangeable. Was his British accent even real? Didn't matter. Agent A always delivered the goods, quickly and accurately. In fact it was his work that had helped to convince Donaldson to sponsor the legislation for the SOS Rescue Plan.

"Hunter Knightly?" Boxley mocked. "Sounds like a TV character."

The agent pulled out an 8x10 headshot, then full body shots, of Hunter down in Florida. There he was with his plane on the tarmac, and entering a Mediterranean style mansion on a golf course in Diamond Lagoon.

"He's got the movie star good looks to match the name," Boxley said. "But he's picked the wrong drama to star in."

"Well that is, indeed, the name of this chap who investigates insurance claims for a number of companies. And just so happened to be the one who denied the claim here."

"I need to know, was this a fluke?" Boxley asked. "Was he just doing his job or is there more to it?"

"My first hunch," Agent A said, "would be affirmative on that. According to his employment record for the past 15 or so years of insurance investigations, he's not had many of these types of claims. It appears as though he was simply going by the book."

"What's his profile?" Boxley asked.

"At first, he looks like an ordinary chap from central Kentucky," Agent A said. "Lives like the proverbial ordinary Joe. Except he flies a two million dollar personal jet. Pity, plane crashes do happen every day."

Nodding, Boxley fed his dog another biscuit.

"And he's a former Navy SEAL."

"Oh Lord," Boxley exclaimed.

"Top of his class," Agent A said. "Perfect record. Stellar performances on every assignment around the world. Including the *Achille Lauro*. And with his family's financial background and political connections, he obviously became a Navy SEAL for a personal challenge."

"Find out everything about this guy. Was it a deliberate attempt to block us, or was he just naively doing his job? Tell me he has no clue!"

"I'd bank on the second one, but you never know," Agent A said. "If someone is two steps ahead of your plan, say for example if a phone line or office were bugged and they were motivated to sabotage—"

"No, we'll have none of that. Get me everything you can. His every move, phone call, text message, email. Everything for the next three days. That should give us a good look at what he's up to."

"If my work in the Cold War taught me anything," the agent said, "Truth is always stranger than fiction. That's why I like to come up with creative solutions that make Hollywood science fiction look ordinary and dull."

"I like the sound of that," Boxley said. "Let's take care of this right away."

"An easy stroll in the park," the agent said. "And such a helpful wife. When I called the house in Lexington, I told the little Mrs. I had some information for one of his insurance jobs. She gave me his cell number and said he'd be gone a couple days. Also gave me her work number in case I needed to reach her during the day."

"It's a beautiful thing when people make your work easy, isn't it?" Boxley smiled.

The agent nodded as he gathered up his papers and closed his folder.

Boxley crossed his arms. "You're going to find that this Hunter Knightly character is a one-time nuisance whose pilot program will be terminated, giving new meaning to 'airport terminal.' And if our detractors somehow have put him up to this—nobody could possibly know about the inner workings of Chrisma Corporation—then you will expedite his efficient removal from our radar."

57. Miami, Florida

Elijah's eyes glowed with sympathy and fear. But Freddie knew he'd never, ever have to consider this with Elijah. Too smart. Too good. Too loyal. Partners for life. And always followed directions.

"In a couple minutes, this low-life scumbag will be dead," Freddie said, looking at his diamond-faced gold Rolex. "You think anybody can trace the drug in his body?"

"Hell naw," a guy said. "I heard 'bout that shit on TV. It don't leave a trace of nothin'."

"That's right," Freddie said, staring down at Chico as he weakly reached up for his throat. "It's undetectable. It suffocates, paralyzes the breathing. Squeezes the life outta him. Can't trace it in an autopsy."

Chico turned, then slumped to the table, laying on his back. Bianca scooted away as Chico stared up at Freddie.

"This is a nasty drug," Freddie said with a matter-of-fact tone. "He knows he's about to die. Can't do a thing about it."

"His chest ain't even movin'," a dude said.

Chico's eyes closed. His body went limp and slipped to the floor with a thud.

"This drug is now available to you," Freddie said, feeling clever. He popped a DVD into the portable, battery-powered DVD player that Elijah just set up on a front table. "Everybody watch."

A reporter's voice on the DVD said, "This deadly drug is called Rocuronium. It's used in hospital procedures when doctors need to temporarily paralyze muscles. The patient is always put on a ventilator to help him breathe. Without a ventilator, an injection of Rocuronium causes slow suffocation as the lungs become paralyzed."

Freddie felt really smart that he found this technical information on the reports about spouses using drugs to kill their estranged partners and NOT get caught.

"Another drug that's commonly used in untraceable murders is succinylcholine chloride. While this drug is usually used during animal experiments and long surgical procedures that require extensive muscle relaxation, experts say it's undetectable in the human body."

Lastly, the report said that Nitrogen pumped into a room could kill within minutes, with no trace of cause of death.

"Snap out of it!" Freddie shouted. "You all look like somebody just died. Get used to it."

They sat up straight.

"Another bonus," Freddie said, "is more money if the mark is under age 70. There, I talk about some Benjamins and you perk the fuck up. If you're thinkin' about bailin' on this job, too late. You know too much. So unless you wanna end up like our buddy Chico—"

Freddie collected the cards from each person. "You're gonna be rakin' in a shitload of cash," he promised. "With every job, you'll get better, faster, smarter. Addicted is what you'll be. Hooked on the money, addicted to the thrill and the power. Now let's all get payyyyyy-ed!"

He counted the cards, then opened a duffel bag and pulled out three payments. Elijah already got his. The two new recruits hadn't earned it yet. But to the others, he handed five grand in cash, each, inside a large pink diaper bag, a backpack and gym bag.

Then he gave out the new Orders. "We're doubling up," Freddie said. "Got a big push to work faster. More jobs mean more cash for you. But don't rush or get sloppy." He turned toward Chico's dead ass, all crumpled up and still. "Or you see what'll happen."

Freddie loved feeling like a fuckin' CEO who was about to cash in on a huge bonus. Man, was he glad he got the call from The Panther last year that it was time to rock 'n roll once again.

Gotta love The Panther.

58. Diamond Lagoon, Florida

As Hunter entered his hotel room, a clog of questions sat in the middle of his thoughts; one by one, he tried to pry them apart and answer them. Was someone associated with that ritzy community called Diamond Lagoon really killing just to acquire real estate? And what was wrong in the double death of Dr. and Mrs. Price?

He remembered Dad's friend, Mr. Williams, who'd said during their chance meeting at Indi Metro that he specialized in high-end housing. Hunter called him, explained the situation down here in Florida, and asked, "Have you ever heard of folks killin' over real estate?"

Mr. Williams laughed. "Sounds like somethin' off my wife's soap operas. I think it could happen in one or two isolated cases, maybe. But a whole community in on it? That'd take some pretty evil planning. I'd get some hard facts in my hand before I started pointin' fingers."

Hunter nodded. "Mr. Williams, I appreciate your insight."

"Give me a ring back when you find out more," Mr. Williams said.

"Will do, sir." Next, Hunter called the mechanic at the hangar.

"Mr. Knightly," the guy said, "I've looked at your avionics inside out, backwards and forwards. From what you described, I gotta blame a gremlin on this one."

"Come again?"

The guy laughed. "Gremlin, that's what I call something that I can't explain. Like a ghost. Ain't nothin' there."

"Then," Hunter demanded, "tell me what the hell happened to me up in the sky."

"As for the white snow stuff," the mechanic said, "only time I hear tell 'a that is when you're passin' by Air Force One or flyin' over a high security military base. My brother over in Iraq, he says they use avionic scramblers against enemy aircraft during battle."

"None of the above," Hunter said. If anyone knew about military airplane technology, it was him. Didn't need to hear it from the mechanic. "There couldn't have been a scrambler within many miles of where I was." Boy was that a cool device, top level stuff. He'd used them back when he was a SEAL. That little piece of machinery on his plane would jack up any- and every avionics system within a five-mile radius. So he'd been untraceable. And sneaky as he wanted to be.

"Maybe the President—"

Hunter shook his head. "There were no TFRs," he said, referring to the Temporary Flight Restrictions that followed Air Force One. "Last night they said on the news he'd be stayin' in Washington to help with that Social Security rescue plan," Hunter said. He picked up the remote and switched on the TV. Had to get the latest on that, and the weather forecast. He didn't know when he'd be leaving, but if a storm were forecast, he'd wait it out.

"You can cook this up in a few minutes," a chef said on television. He clicked, in search of news.

Hunter would take his rental car to the airport tomorrow, and talk to management. He would insist upon having his plane checked by a mechanic with a more professional—

"Breaking news," a female anchor said on television. "Channel 3 just getting word of a freak accident at a local golf course." Video showed an aerial view of the community that Hunter had just left. "Chopper 3 now over the scene at the Diamond Lagoon Golf Club. Just a short while ago, authorities telling us, an elderly man died on the deck—" the camera zoomed into the outdoor restaurant where a white tablecloth lay across the floor. "You can see, investigators are working on the scene where they say, unbelievably, the man's cell phone exploded as he was using it. He died instantly. Counselors are on hand to help witnesses cope with the shock of this gruesome death at the exclusive Club."

Hunter watched in disbelief.

"Mr. Knightly?" the guy on the phone said. "You there?"

"Yes sir, I'm—"

"More breaking news for the Channel 3 viewing area," the anchor said. "Authorities are warning about deadly snakes that apparently killed a woman this afternoon in her garden. It happened on the upscale Singer Island near Miami. Police telling us that this type of snake was once common in this region. Families with small children are being warned to stay indoors until authorities can determine where this snake came from. Of course Channel 3 will be following these tragic stories—"

The dial tone buzzed in his ear. *At least the snakebite death didn't happen at Diamond Lagoon.*

"And now," the anchor said, "back to our report about Sheik Sunami il Tabbul's threat to abduct the Vice President."

Hunter froze. "Carrie?" As he watched the report, he felt an overwhelming need to protect her; perhaps this was a good excuse to finally call and see how she was doing.

59. Boca Raton, Florida

As Bianca supervised the maids in the gigantic master bathroom overlooking the ocean, she felt so lucky that her business was booming. With cleaning crews known for meticulous attention to every speck of dirt, she had contracts to clean mansions for the rich and retired within a 20-mile radius of her home. And that made it easy to check off two or three Orders a day, since many of her clients were showing up on Freddie Buford's list. And it was a piece of cake to get into the homes of other Orders with her company's free trial cleaning.

Now, as the maids scrubbed the Jacuzzi bathtub and its step-up marble platform, Bianca envisioned her plan. *I'll just spill some baby oil on the floor...* If the slip-and-fall didn't sufficiently smash Ms. Hill's skull on the rock-hard steps, Bianca could put a little elbow grease into the job. This would be one bathroom she wouldn't have to clean. Because she'd be too distraught over finding the 73-year-old body of poor Ms. Hill.

60. West Palm Beach, Florida

As Hunter watched yet another report about the Vice President, he scrolled through his address book on his phone. *Carrie 202-...* He pushed the dial button.

An annoying tone blasted in his ear. "We're sorry this number is no longer in service." Hunter was sure he could use his SEAL connections to track down a new number for her—

MEREDITH flashed across the phone; the ring tone chimed with their wedding song. "Hi Honey," Meredith said sweetly. "How's it goin' down there?"

"Meredith, darlin', you would have *died* if you spent three minutes with some of the characters I met today." He felt a sudden surge of excitement to describe the real estate agent, the gay couple, the weirdo airplane mechanic. "And this mornin' I saw the slickest private jet, zippin' through the sky—"

"I'm at the banquet by myself," she snapped. "Everybody's askin' where my husband is tonight."

"You tell 'em I flew off into *The Twilight Zone*." Hunter said playfully with a cutting undertone that was only half joking.

"Somethin' like that," Meredith said flatly. "Said you took your Baby Doll down to Florida for a little fun in the sun."

"I can send some pictures to your phone to prove it on the spot for all those inquiring minds who want to know," Hunter said, walking over to the table by the balcony door. He glanced down at the glossy magazines, the hotel's directory and three newspapers.

"Honey, did a Mr. Knowles call you? He called the house, I gave him your cell number. Said it was about one of your cases."

"No." Hunter activated speakerphone and set the phone on the table. He opened *The Palm Beach Gazette.* "Which case?"

"Didn't say. When you comin' home?"

Hunter studied a full-page ad for a seminar about life settlement insurance policies. He remembered that online report he'd watched yesterday, and all the questions it sparked. He turned a few pages, coming to another full-page ad by another company. He put the other papers on the bed, spread them open. Every one of them had at least one full page ad—by a different company.

"A full page ad in *The Palm Beach Gazette*," Hunter said. "Wonder what that cost."

The headlines said LEARN ABOUT GENERATING LARGE PROFITS WITH NO INVESTMENT! The ads also promised, "Up front cash now! Get a new car in two years!"

Hunter was bugged by the repeated promise that these deals were "Absolutely risk free." All of them offered free seminars over lunch at upscale hotels up and down the Florida coasts. Hunter shook his head, whispering, "My momma always told me, 'No such thing as a free lunch.'" This was the perfect opportunity to investigate if there really was potential for fraud at these events. Not to mention, he would get some "continuing education" in his industry, to bring him up to speed on these no cost life insurance and life settlements. All three couples—two alive, one dead—that he'd met with this afternoon were beneficiaries of these too-good-to-be-true-sounding deals.

What was the catch? And what was the connection to The Diamond Lagoon Club? Or that fluttery real estate agent Ms. Polly Chesterfield? Hunter turned a page in the statewide *Florida Times*. There, a full-page ad by The Genuine Insurance Group announced a seminar tomorrow, on the Gulf of Mexico side of the state in Naples. Free lunch at The Luxury Suites Resort & Spa. Limited seating. First come, first served.

"Honey?" Meredith snapped. He startled. "When you comin' home?"

"Probably have to stay the weekend," Hunter said vacantly, scanning the papers. "Things are more complicated down here than I would have ever suspected."

Click. The sound of her hanging up on him hardly registered. That just gave him more brainpower to focus on his work, now that their conversation was over.

"Enjoy your banquet, my bride," Hunter said sarcastically as the dial tone rang. The ad for the Serenity seminar said pre-registration was required. The small print said: "This seminar is closed to insurance agents and financial planners. You must be 65 or older with a net worth no less than $10 million to attend. Register by calling…"

Hunter dialed the number. "The Genuine Insurance Group, may I help you?"

"Yes, I'd like to attend your lunch seminar tomorrow in Naples, Florida."

"Excellent, Mr. Knightly."

"How'd you know my name?"

"Caller I.D.," she said with a smile in her voice. "Mr. Knightly, if you can kindly log onto our secure website and register this evening, that'll save you a significant amount of time tomorrow. It will also ensure that you meet all of the qualifying criteria to benefit from this tremendous opportunity."

She sounded robotic, reciting a programmed script that she was probably saying for the umpteenth time today. "Please log onto TheGenuineInsuranceGroup.com. Our advanced computer system will evaluate your application and respond within one hour whether you are qualified to—"

Hunter interrupted, "What sorts of qualifications are you looking for?"

She was quiet, as if she didn't know how to deviate from the script. "Mr. Knightly, your qualification will be determined by your net worth, which includes your investment portfolio, homes and vacation properties, art collections, jewelry, cars, boats, airplanes. In addition—"

Hunter pulled his laptop from his leather travel bag. He logged onto the website. Heck, the registration page was asking for everything about him except whether he preferred boxers or briefs. He glanced outside; it was dark, but he needed to take a jog and sort through the day's information. Running always provided him with solutions.

"Miss," he said. "I'm attending this on behalf of my elderly parents. I'll have to check with them and get back with you."

"Of course, Mr. Knightly. You're welcome to register onsite as well."

"I'll take you up on that. See you tomorrow."

Hunter called the hangar. The supervising mechanic promised his plane would be ready to fly first thing in the morning.

61. Lexington, Kentucky

For such a decorated SEAL, this Hunter Knightly fellow sure lived like a simpleton in the home security department. The modest ranch had an alarm, but it was not activated. From the back yard, the door into the garage was unlocked. As was the inner door between the garage and the kitchen! What kind of imbecile, in this day and age, even in the no-crime zone of this middle class neighborhood, left his doors unlocked?

At night! And being out of town, all the way down in Florida, leaving the Mrs. here alone, didn't he instruct his stunningly beautiful partner of 16 years to make sure she secured the house? After all, she'd be returning alone, probably well past midnight. It was a pity, at least on the issue of safety, that she lent credence to the dumb blonde stereotype.

Oh well, that simply made work faster and easier for a hardworking man in head-to-toe black to get in, find what he needed, and get out.

Mrs. Meredith Mae Brown Knightly, according to her less-than-romantic cell phone conversation with her husband a short while ago—and the blue dot on the surveillance screen that picked up a satellite signal from her phone—was inside a ballroom downtown at the Lexington Museum of Art.

That left plenty of time to collect video data here in Hunter Knightly's home office. The file cabinets and desk drawers were locked, but when one came equipped with devices for such an occurrence, the locks proved useless. The desk drawers contained files for insurance claims for a multitude of insurance companies. What a strange chap, choosing this work over his SEAL adventures or the excitement of horse racing.

This palm-sized video camera and its built-in spotlight meant a fellow didn't even need to turn on the light, which might draw the attention of neighbors. And should the Mrs. decide to return home early, all systems would indicate such with plenty of time for a clean departure.

This fellow must have been a laptop sort of worker who took it with him. No desktop computer. On his rather messy cherry desk and matching shelves were aviation magazines, a full-page newspaper ad about a seminar in Florida with a pink sticky note that said: "Check this out, Fly Boy." And it was signed, "Randy Man." An 8x10 picture of this Hollywood-esque hunk, beaming beside a small blue airplane, sat on his desk alongside another 8x10 of him in a tux, holding his smiling bride who wore a white gown in an old-fashioned carriage adorned with vines and flowers. Framing them were the rolling Bluegrass hills and white equestrian fences of Knightly Farms. Gold letters in the corner said 1993.

On the wall hung two diplomas. One from Episcopal High School in 1983. Another from the University of Kentucky in 1992. A multitude of plaques from the U.S. Navy were marked with the years between 1983 and 1988.

Now, to record all of these case files, one by one. Seeking a Republican connection. And any motive that might make him an enemy or saboteur of Boxley's endeavors. Any such evidence could and would be used against this Hunter Knightly fellow in a ruthless court that was entirely above the law.

62. Las Vegas, Nevada

As Juan strode past the sparkling pool at a world-famous resort and casino, all he could think about was jetting over to the Middle East to jack up Sheik Sunami il Tabbul. If the reports were true about the terrorist wanting to abduct Carrie, Juan would be first in line to rescue her and take her away to a secret hiding place.

For now, though, as he headed to his favorite poolside cabana, he had to handle business. While doubling his national staff to handle the accelerated pace for 2009, he was also scheming to pinpoint who held the strings to a giant purse that was getting even fatter, somehow, with all these Orders.

So here in Vegas—a mecca for Orders thanks to its wealthy retiree population—he especially needed productive and efficient K.C. Leaders.

Interviewing all these middlemen was time consuming, but that was the price of putting the best men in these crucial spots. And with the economy flat lining, it was easy to find eager workers. Juan's network of contacts from his previous life made this task as good as done. Still, the ax would fall on Juan if any of them fucked up. So he had to put each through his personal screening, which relied much more on the vibe a guy gave off than any words that were spoken. Either Juan trusted him. Or he didn't. His gut feeling was always right.

This guy, a clean-cut blond with a lean build and eyes that looked older and wiser than his dewy face, came from Boxley's endless list of people who owed him favors.

"You've come to my attention in a very confidential manner," Juan said, "from a very good friend. That's important, because the missions we're running are extremely clandestine. They're not high risk, even though the desired outcome is terminal."

Rick "Smitty" Smitherton nodded. His dark eyes never left Juan's; they reflected back eagerness and quick comprehension.

"My friend who recommended you said you have a team already assembled," Juan said. "A good two dozen."

"Right-oh," Smitty said. "I call it 'the empire.' We work outta my bike shop, so it's legit to have a bunch of guys runnin' in and out. Had a surf shop out in Venice, but needed to make a move inland."

Juan probed his face for signs that he was sweating heat of any sort. Local, state, federal, international.

Smitty laughed. "The cops didn't like my horticultural endeavors. Said I was growin' the wrong crop. I was lucky, though. My dad knew the right people. Got me off. Now my record is as clean as a white china plate. But I had to leave town. Miss the ocean, though. So I fly to Maui 'bout once a month to ride the waves like there's no tomorrow."

"The money you can make with me will make your 'horticulture' revenues look like chump change," Juan said. "You get 20-K per hit. Every K.C. Team Leader runs his business differently. Most give their crew members four or five grand per kill, then keep the rest. It's up to you."

Smitty asked, "How many orders are we talking about, in a month?"

"Between 15 and 50," Juan said.

"Rock that!" Smitty's eyes glowed. "I can get my own place on Maui with that kinda money comin' in."

"You'll find it's quite low risk for your boys," Juan said. "We're dealing with people who are 75, 80 and 85 years old."

Smitty looked perplexed. "Like, grandparents?"

"Think of it as a humanitarian mission," Juan said. "These people lived full lives, with wealth and privilege. You're sparing them the suffering of dementia and illness that inevitably strikes as they approach 90."

Juan's spoken words sparked a revelation about the King's motivation for murder.

Holy shit. Maybe Medicare... killing these people would save the government millions of dollars.

"Dig that," Smitty said.

"I'm only considering you for this position, and I have three more candidates to interview after you," Juan lied. He wasn't bout to spend all day doing this. He needed to jet off to San Francisco, hire another K.C. Team Leader there, and get back to Florida for his Sunday lunch meeting with Boxley at Sailfish Marina. "So if you have a soft spot for grandparents," Juan said, "then you won't be buying your Maui pad with my help."

"I'm cool," Smitty nodded. "Reminds me of that movie where they killed off the old people who were suckin' up precious resources. Hey, like that smokin' hot Vice President's plan for the government to take back your Social Security check if you're rich."

Smokin' hot. That's how this punk was referring to Her. As if he'd bang Her like a cheap piece of ass if he had the chance. Juan shot his Panther eyes at this dude. He didn't even need to say "Shut up." Because his eyes said that for him. In fact, Smitty sat up straighter. Turned a shade whiter, despite his tan. And looked like an attentive student, determined to earn an A-plus from a tough teacher.

"Now of course, Smitty, these are very secretive missions," Juan said. "You've heard that saying, 'If I tell you, I'll have to kill you.'"

Smitty turned white as that china plate he'd mentioned earlier. His voice sounded high-pitched as he said, "Yes, sir."

"Well that's a hint at how we operate. I've already told you what we do."

Smitty nodded. Looked like he had no trouble believing that was true.

"Now, all you and your boys need to do is simply help them have an accident, help them die," Juan said. "Besides the money, you'll get the thrill of the chase, the excitement of planning each hit for the specific person, being as creative as you want to be."

Juan glanced out at the pool, where hot women were splashing under a fountain. The water poured down on some D-cups in a tiny yellow bikini top. The girl shrieked and ran her tongue over her upper lip, casting a sultry stare at him.

Later.

"Now Smitty, you're an entrepreneur, so you'll understand this crucial rule that we operate by. Everything has to look like an accident. Or death by natural cause. If it looks like murder, you don't get paid. If it looks like murder, we have a big problem. A problem between you and me. And like I said, I've already told you how we operate."

The mix of fear and excitement roiling in Smitty's eyes let Juan know this guy was game for the long haul. "I can provide you with an endless supply of non-traceable drugs that result in deaths blamed on 'natural causes.'"

"Okay," Smitty said.

"You also have to make sure if your guys get caught, it never comes back to you or me. You're essentially insulating our operation with the dispensable street level guys."

The girl under the fountain got out of the pool. She was a perfect suntanned hourglass, with a diamond sparkling in her belly button. She smiled and waved for him to join them. Juan nodded just enough for her to know that he would, later. The Jacuzzi in his suite would provide all the splashing around they would need.

"Now Smitty, in order for us to ensure that each hit is executed with the utmost caution to look like an accident, I give you a significant amount of seed money to start the business. You pay your guys half as soon as they make the hit."

"And the other half later," Smitty dared to interject, "after there's no heat."

Juan cast approving eyes at this guy. "Three months is the usual elimination period."

"Sometimes I work with a partner," Smitty said. "Is that cool?"

"As long as the two of you separate the guys below you," Juan said. "Now Smitty, repeat back to me the three most important things about this work."

The guy nodded. "One, it has to look like an accident or natural causes. Two, if it looks like murder, we don't get paid. Three, if I fuck up, that's my ass. *Sayonara*, Smitty."

Juan allowed a smile to raise the corners of his mouth.

63. West Palm Beach, Florida

Hunter took a run, then returned to his room for push-ups and *History TV*, which was re-airing that documentary that Meredith had so rudely interrupted.

As he inhaled down, exhaled up, he scowled at the terrible health hazards those British lawmakers faced in the musty, dusty, smoke-filled chambers where their colleagues smoked pipes and cigars. How clueless they had been, back in the 1700s, of the carcinogens that they were both inhaling and inflicting upon their fellow lawmakers.

That guy in the wig, standing there debating, would have probably been doubled over coughing in the House of Commons and the House of Lords.

Hunter breathed deeply. If someone had orchestrated the deaths of Dr. Mark Price and his wife, Suzie, then it wasn't about their insurance at all. Even if they did have one of those mysteriously generous life settlement policies.

He would authorize payment on those tragic claims. But for the family, collecting on the combined 20-million dollars wasn't an option; the Prices had already released their policies back into one of those blind investment funds that Hunter had read were the "keepers" of these life settlements after the two year phase. Hunter would do some online research tonight, after his work-out, to further investigate what kinds of funds held these life settlement policies. From what he knew so far, they were enormous, holding billions, perhaps trillions, of dollars' worth of policies. Little did the average consumer know, that America's $14 trillion dollar life insurance industry would fail financially only second to the U.S. Treasury.

He thought about the real estate agent; she would make a huge commission on the sale of those luxury homes. Was she somehow linked with the insurance companies, so that she sold properties owned by people who had signed up for life settlements and divulged all of their real estate holdings? Did she somehow put a mark on their head, and a red dot on their property, like the red ruby in her necklace, marking the homes for sale as soon as they were knocked off? And why wouldn't she want to spur the housing market by any means necessary?

Here in surreal Diamond Lagoon, Hunter was sure that somehow, the Prices were victims of greed by someone who coveted their American Dream. Location, location, location.

"It's about that real estate," Hunter said, and the feeding frenzy it was apparently sparking amongst their neighbors. Instead of poker or slot machines, these multi-millionaire retirees were getting their kicks by gambling on houses. And getting rid of the owners, if necessary. The winner got the dead couple's architectural masterpiece.

The narrator on *History TV* echoed the theme of getting something from someone via unscrupulous methods, such as death: "… macabre nature of gambling in Great Britain prior to this law being passed. The Life Assurance Act of 1774 was one of the most important anti-gaming laws passed by the Parliament of Great Britain because it outlawed betting on human lives."

That brought to mind Lauren Price Miller saying: "… seems like there was a 20-million dollar price on my parents' heads. They die suspiciously. Now nobody can tell me who gets the money."

The documentary showed a bewigged lawmaker addressing 1774 Parliament: "Hail ye gentlemen. A most shocking and horrid occurrence hath scandalized the well-being of our citizens. At this fourth hour, I prayeth ye sympathetic gentlemen shall endevour to support the Life Assurance Act whereby arresting the grim occurrence of wagering on human beings. Sir Wilfred Barrington shall hereby read the proposed language of this most urgent matter of law."

Another man, whose curled wig was as white as the huge bow resting on the chest of his ornate blue jacket, held a scroll and read: "Whereas it hath been found by experience that the making of insurances on lives or other events wherein the assured shall have no interest hath introduced a mischievous kind of gaming—"

"Sounds barbaric," Hunter said, doing push-ups.

The narrator said the law was inspired by the frequent occurrence of people taking out perfectly legal life insurance policies on strangers, and putting in writing a date by which they expected the person to die, thus "gambling" on that person's death. "This invited the temptation to commit murder," the narrator added, "to cash in the life insurance policy."

"ShShShShShSh!"

With the phone near his hand on the floor, Hunter answered via speakerphone so he could continue his workout.

"Hey Fly Boy!" Randy exclaimed. "What's the 4-1-1?"

"Hell, where do I start?"

"That bad, huh?"

"Somethin' definitely doesn't smell right," Hunter said. "Dr. Price and his wife were too healthy and too smart to die the way they did. But as for who might have a motive, or what went wrong, I'm drawin' blanks."

"No clues from the daughter?"

"She's thinkin' the insurance company had something to do with it," Hunter said, "but I think that's pretty far-fetched. Hey, turn on *History TV*. Tell me what you think—"

"Already saw it, Fly Boy. Today in the United States? Hell no! I think that crazy shit might happen in one or two far-fetched cases, but it would take a conspiracy of mammoth proportions to pull that off on a big scale.

Even on four or five lives, and not in today's world, brother."

"You're right, Randal," Hunter said. But deep down, he wasn't sure. "I can release this claim to be paid. But find out who gets the money."

64. Washington, D.C.

It was déjà-vu as Carolyn stepped into the Oval Office. Same cast of characters. New anger on the President's ashen face.

"Someone in this room can't be trusted," he said, looking each person in the eye, stopping at the Secretary of State. "Madame Secretary, it appears that your office is responsible for betraying our trust."

Her cheeks were sunken. Dark circles ringed her eyes. Carolyn gloated secretly; that bitch hadn't eaten a bite or slept a wink since the news had splashed all over the media.

"We all know that sabotage is," the President said, studying each person, one by one, "always a possibility. That's why I'm casting a veil of suspicion over each of you, until we unmask Benedict Arnold and banish him or her from our team."

He looked so pale; Russell said he'd heard from a trusted White House source that a doctor had been called this morning to check on the President for chest discomfort. Maybe the stress of terrorism and the recession would clear him out of this office sooner than she thought.

The Secretary of State kept her shoulders square and her chin up. But her eyes left no doubt, Carolyn had scared that bitch into submission. For now.

65. Naples, Florida

All those question marks about the double death at the Diamond Lagoon Club still clogged Hunter's head Saturday morning as he flew across the state of Florida to Naples. Baby Doll behaved just fine, after the senior mechanic at the West Palm hangar assured him that "gremlins, indeed," were to blame for the bizarre occurrences the prior morning.

Now, after taking the courtesy car from Executive Flight, he entered the Luxury Suites Resort & Spa overlooking the Gulf of Mexico. Alongside him was a steady stream of seniors who drove up in expensive cars, wore country club attire, and glimmered with gold and diamonds. They strode through the plush lobby toward a registration area outside the ballroom.

"Good afternoon, Sir," said a 25-ish babe in a business suit and heels. She stood beside a reception table, where two women sat with laptop computers. "Your name?"

"Hunter Knightly." One of the women typed in his name.

"Mr. Knightly, I see that you spoke with our representative last night and that you visited our website for five minutes. It says that you prefer to register for yourself and your father here in person. Where is your father?"

"Oh, he's back in Kentucky, packin' up the horse farm," Hunter said with his best *Aw shucks, I'm rich as hell but humble as pie* demeanor. "He and mom are lookin' at properties in the Diamond Lagoon area, but they sent me down here to find out more about these insurance deals that all their friends are talkin' about."

The young woman at the table cast a questioning look at the hot one standing by Hunter.

The hot chick extended a pretty little hand. "Mr. Knightly, welcome. I'm Shelly Richards." He looked down into her honey-hued eyes and inhaled her spicy perfume. Her coral-colored business suit hugged her shape just right, and her blond hair was loose around her shoulders, but professional. He thought of how his buddies would make jokes about how they hoped she would "shell" it out.

"Pleased to meet you, Shelly."

She shook his hand like a man. Another woman, not nearly as hot, stepped close. "Mr. Knightly, you cannot attend this meeting if you're a financial advisor, an insurance agent or a banker. And you may not enter if your net worth is under 10-million dollars."

Shelly stood between him and the ballroom entrance. "And we ordinarily do not allow anyone to attend as a representative of the eligible parties. Mr. Knightly, may I ask you to wait a moment while I make a phone call." She said the question like an order, then pressed one button on her cell phone. She turned her back and spoke too low for him to hear.

Hunter exuded charm and confidence as his brain spun a plan of action. He had three goals here: to learn more about these life settlement insurance policies; to examine the legitimacy of the seminars and the seemingly wild claims the newspaper ads were making; and to see if somehow, the rabid hunger for Diamond Lagoon real estate could be connected to the human insurance industry.

The net worth Gestapo at the registration table was letting dozens of blue-haired ladies drenched in gold—and men in their 70s and 80s, just in from a morning round of golf or tennis—enter the ballroom. Hunter needed to get in there, no matter what.

"Alright, Mr. Knightly," Shelly said. "I have authority to allow you to attend. But we do need you to complete this personal financial statement." She handed him a metal square that had a computer touch screen in the center with a stylus attached on a wire. Her shiny pink fingernails tapped against the metal as she said, "Make sure you sign it to verify that the information is correct."

That slippery feeling crept over him again. They were really puttin' on a show here, and he was not about to leave without seeing the full production.

"Of course, Shelly," Hunter said, taking the electronic questionnaire. His personal information would not—even with his airplane figured in—qualify him to attend. And he didn't want anyone here to discover he was an insurance investigator, or he'd be banned from that ballroom. So he completed the form as if he were his Dad. That enabled him to qualify well above and beyond Miss Shelly's financial requirements. Dad, as private as he was, would be mad as hell if he knew Hunter was doing this. But he'd probably never know; Hunter entered his own phone numbers and email addresses. And if this company sent Dad any promotional materials, so what. No harm done. He could blame it on junk mail.

After Hunter completed the questionnaire and signed with the stylus, another pretty woman led him into the ballroom.

"Ladies and gentlemen," she said, to the nine people at the table. "This is Mr. Hunter Knightly. He owns an aviation business in Kentucky. He's here on behalf of his parents, who own a prize-winning horse racing farm."

"Oh, I love horses," exclaimed a woman with a jet black coif and ALICE in diamonds at her neck. Beside her sat a man in an all-white tennis outfit whose brown hair looked unnaturally detached from this forehead. Had to be a wig. "We're Alice and Stanley Goldstein. Stanley's an internist, retired. We're from Manhattan."

"Welcome," Stanley nodded.

"Such a handsome young man," Alice said. "What a treat!"

"It's a treat for me," Hunter said. "My parents sent me down here to check out the houses at the Diamond

Lagoon Club over near West Palm. They like the exclusivity of it."

"Good luck," said a woman with a blue-gray hairdo that swirled close to her head like a 1920s flapper. She wore a cameo choker and a jazzy red blouse. "If you can get in. Those people are like piranhas at those auctions. One house comes up for sale, they attack. Insane. I think they want to move more family and friends into the community, to increase property values at every sale."

Hunter listened, hoping to learn more.

"Be careful of exploding cell phones over there," joked a bald man across the table. Wearing gold half-glasses that barely concealed the I-know-everything glint in his eyes, he wiped the silver knife full of butter over his sourdough roll. "Propaganda! Those news reports that want us all to run in a panic to the cell phone store and get our batteries checked out? I won't do it. They're just trying to trick the consumer into going in there and buying a more expensive phone that's allegedly safer."

Hunter nodded in a way that showed he was listening but not necessarily agreeing. "And who, may I ask, do you mean by 'they'? I'm Hunter Knightly, by the way."

"Patty O'Shea. Yeah, I'm Irish. 'They'? The cell phone companies. I bet they paid somebody in the media to blow this one freak accident out of proportion. Then the network gets a kick-back when all the phone companies double their profits this year. Not to mention, the lithium battery companies."

Hunter chuckled. "Mr. O'Shea, if you think along those lines, then it seems you'd be pretty skeptical of the claims they're makin' in the ads for this life insurance planning and life settlement policy—"

"I was," he said, sipping black coffee. "Until all my friends did it and said there's no catch. They got the money. In, then out in two years. More cash or a gift—"

"A television," Alice said, smearing butter on her roll. "Flat screen or plasma. Your choice. There's no gimmick. Insurance companies got all the money. We all know that."

"That's my story, too," said a redheaded man with freckles and a thick gold chain glimmering in the vee of his green polo shirt. "Ralph Windstrom. Welcome. Didn't believe it, thought it was sure-fire false advertising. But I met too many people who proved me wrong. So I'm here. Healthy, 73-years-old. Nowadays, you have to be open minded to create extra income."

"Better do it now," said the lady with a shock of ice-white hair and dark eyebrows painted in dramatic arches over her sun-leathered face. She was one of the few who did not appear lifted, stretched, chemically peeled or plumped up with Botox. "Before Miss Missy the Vice President usurps your other money. Your Social Security check. Maybe this planning today can help me recoup the loss.'""

"That's the most absurd thing I've heard!" Pat said angrily. "My father came here with nothing but a dream for me. So I worked hard my whole life with my businesses. I earned my father's American Dream. I paid my Social Security taxes every quarter. Now the government wants to keep it!"

He made eye contact with everyone at the table. "All because they lack the kinds of money management skills that enabled us to build financial security for ourselves and our families!"

"Don't get him started," Alice warned. "Last night at the restaurant, he and his soapbox—"

"Stop it, Alice," Stanley snapped. "Let the man have his say."

She shook her head and speared a chunk of blue cheese from her salad. It reminded Hunter of those fancy salads served as a meal at Malone's in Lexington. But this was just the first course.

"I am one furious Irishman this afternoon," he said. "I won't do it. And I don't think it'll work."

Ralph held up his water glass to toast Pat's protest. "If there were a way to fix the system, they would have saved it already."

Alice glanced around the ballroom. "Nobody could save our friends from dropping like flies over the past year."

"Oh, Alice," Stanley groaned.

"I speak the truth," she said. "Haven't all of you noticed how many didn't return for the season this year? Seems like they're dying left and right—"

Stanley admitted, "Three of my friends. A car crash. A heart attack, and an electrocution from a blow drier in the bathtub, if you can believe that."

"I can't," Alice said. "It's eerie. Like a curse or something."

"No, it's just life," her husband said. "You've seen too many bad spy movies. Pass the salt."

"There's a couple more Social Security checks Miss Missy gets to keep," said the lady with ice-white hair. "The sooner we croak, the better for her greedy bean-counters."

Hunter wished he could talk to Carrie. Tough as she was, she had to be scared now that the whole world knew the most notorious terrorist in modern times wanted to kidnap her. Hunter would try to find a new number for her today.

"No coincidence that Sheik Sunami il Tabbul wants her," Ralph said over the clinking of silverware on china. "The timing of that report, it's rigged. To trick us into feeling patriotic and support her cockamamie idea. The girl is half our age, doesn't have a clue. I'm not givin' up *my* money. Already wrote a letter of protest to my Congressman."

How ironic that these ultra wealthy people were griping about checks that were maybe $1600 per month. They probably spent that on a set of golf clubs every year, or symphony tickets or new clothes.

Heck, it was $750,000 to join The Diamond Lagoon Golf Club. Now he was sitting in a room filled with dozens of tables, each seating 10 people just like this, each with net worths of 10-million dollars or more. And each owning properties here and elsewhere around America. A visual headcount tallied about 50 people. Fifty times 10-million, minimum, equaled half a billion. Then it would be safe to figure plenty of folks were probably worth far more than the 10-million minimum.

The people around him were easily worth a billion dollars! How astonishing that the wealth in this room alone, could have solved a multitude of America's financial problems. At the same time, they could represent a billion dollars' worth of life insurance. Carrie was right in thinking this money could be better used to help elderly men and women who had no savings and no income.

"It's just not Uncle Sam's decision," Pat said. "If I want to donate to a charity that helps old people who didn't work and save and plan, then so be it, but—"

"The Vice President says Social Security, it'll go broke by 2025 or sooner," the Flapper said as a black waitress refilled her water goblet. "By then, we'll all be dead anyway. Not that we need it, I'm just saying—"

A brown-skinned waitress served each of them plates of salmon stuffed with crab and dilled redskin potatoes.

"2025," Stanley said, watching to make sure the waitress had walked away, "I just read that's the year when we'll be the minority. The blacks, the Hispanics, the Asians, they'll be the majority."

"Didn't Nostradamus write about this?" asked the lady with ice-white hair. "Social Security goes broke, the Mexicans take over, and—"

"America goes to hell in a hand basket," Ralph said.

"Just a coincidence," Pat said.

"No coincidence," Ralph said, "that the Mexicans take over and Uncle Sam runs out of cash. I'm sure we'll be hearing about it from those civil rights clowns. Health insurance! They're all getting free health insurance at our expense."

"Ladies and gentlemen," said a man at the podium below a projection screen. "I'm Stephen Wuerthberg, and I want to thank you for joining us for this spectacular opportunity today."

Hunter flipped through the brochure that had covered his plate when he sat down. That guy's picture graced the front of the thick, glossy document that probably cost 40 dollars apiece, without the CD insert. One glance at the insurance broker, and Hunter's bullshit radar dinged at ear-piercing levels.

His auburn hair was slicked back. Gold glimmered at his wrists beneath monogrammed white shirt cuffs protruding from an expensive-looking, dark blue pinstriped suit. His Italian leather loafers had probably cost more than the suit. Manicured, polished fingernails.

Stephen Wuerthberg struck Hunter as the type of smooth-talking, Ivy League-looking, Northeast Wall Street type who talked fast with sentences so slippery, his prey never knew they were being tricked. The promises were bedazzling; Hunter was determined to sift the facts, if any, from what sounded like financial fantasy.

"Everyone here absolutely despises paying life insurance premiums," Wuerthberg declared. "Am I right?"

The audience clapped with agreement.

"Well how would you like it if we guarantee you 50-thousand dollars in cash if you sign up for a policy today?"

"What's the catch?" Pat demanded. "Sounds too good to be true."

"There is no catch," Wuerthberg said. "It's called a premium-financed life insurance policy. Each of you represents what we refer to as unused capacity for life insurance. Here's a way for you to make money, by simply signing up and agreeing to be insured on a policy—"

Alice leaned closer to Hunter. "Sounds like a STOLI. Stranger Originated Life Insurance. Buy a policy with someone else's money and sell that policy in two years as a life settlement. My brother-in-law told me. He's in insurance. This kind of scheme, seems to me, would really boost the Guido factor big-time, wouldn't you say?"

Hunter nodded. It sure as heck did.

66. Naples, Florida

The decadent spread of gourmet sweets on silver platters, plus the scent of fresh-brewed coffee, put some extra pep in Alice Goldstein's step.

"Please, help yourselves," Mr. Wuerthberg said, extending a hand toward the dessert buffet inside this waterfront suite at Luxury Suites. "Enjoy something sweet while I share an even sweeter opportunity."

The soft gurgle of liquid chocolate bubbling in the fondue fountain on the table nearly drowned out his voice. He was probably quite seductive with the ladies in romance—and persuasive with the men regarding money.

"Alice," Stanley barked, "you just had pecan pie."

To hell with both of them. Fifty grand, so what. It wouldn't make or break them. That was play money; if Stanley wanted to do this, fine. They and their kids, and grandkids, were set for life. Regardless of this. Regardless of the economy.

"Now, what would I like?" Giddiness tingled through her as she eyed the sweets on multi-tiered trays garnished with tropical blooms.

Just minutes ago, a dozen doubts had zinged through her head about this life insurance deal. But now those thoughts were melting and flowing away as smoothly as the chocolate bubbling in the silver fondue fountain. Cookies, strawberries and candies surrounded it, with a spread of tiny silver forks ready to spear and dunk.

"Look, Stanley, your favorite," she gushed. The longer Stanley focused on the deal, the less she'd have to hear his nagging about the stealth bomb of calories she was about to set off in her stomach—and get a to-go bag for a snack later. "Stanley, you love strawberries dipped in chocolate. Huge!"

"Ugh, so sweet." Stanley crossed his arms.

Mr. Wuerthberg stepped toward the table. "Dr. Goldstein, please indulge. At least a cup of coffee. So rich, it would make Juan Valdez proud."

"I don't drink Colombian," Stanley snapped. "Just Ethiopian. Grind it myself. One cup in the morning. Max."

"I admire a man with discipline and discriminating tastes," Wuerthberg said.

Alice half-smiled. Boy, did this Wuerthberg fellow probably earn A-pluses in salesman school. She picked up a silver fork; it clinked against her china plate.

"Oi, Alice, I don't want to hear you whine that you can't zip your dress."

"Hush." With her back to him, she smiled down at the luscious treats. Ever since his affair with that Barbie doll nurse at the hospital, Alice had been gaining weight, losing weight. A 30-pound yo-yo. While Stanley enjoyed his trysts with the tall, big-busted blonde, Alice had found just as much pleasure in both eating to her heart's content, and dieting as the numbers on the scale went down, down, down, and her clothes became baggy. Her closets boasted identical dresses, suits, pants, plus golf and tennis outfits—in size 4, 8 and 10. At five-foot-three, she felt best in a four. In a 10, she felt like a whale. But ah, the thrill of eating, then shrinking...

Stanley played women and the stock market. She played the diet game. One pound for every year, now, since his first affair that she knew of. Her attitude had been, *Fine. You're not attracted to me? Just look how fat and repulsive I can get!* Maybe this time she'd pack on even more pounds—during bathing suit season—just to get under his skin.

Not that he was interested in hers. After she had found the hotel room receipts and Barbie's hair on his clothes, their sex life died; food became her singular pleasure. Now, she literally experienced food-gasms when something tasted especially good. Everything on this table, she was sure, had the power to make her taste buds climax like never before.

"Alice, you'll go into sugar shock," Stanley said.

"Doctor says I'm healthy as a horse. Seventy-two glorious years young. Having my cake and eating it, too!"

Alice smiled at them.

"I love a lady who's not afraid to indulge," Mr. Wuerthberg chuckled. "I couldn't pay my wife to eat her own birthday cake."

"Oh, just you wait," Stanley said with a wiser- and older-than-thou tone. "Let's get down to business."

"Yes, sir." Mr. Wuerthberg stepped through the open French doors framing a picturesque view of the water. Sunshine, sailboats, sea gulls. Life didn't get much better than this.

"I'll be right out." Alice turned back to the buffet. She popped a chocolate truffle into her mouth. Closed her eyes.

"Mmmmmm." Her whole body tingled under her aqua blue sleeveless size 4 silk sheath dress.

"Delicious!" a young female voice startled her.

Alice turned. The woman standing beside her, staring down at her plateful of caloric abandon, was Barbie. The hussie who was Stanley's first affair. Alice shook her head slightly and focused on the girl's gold nametag: Shelley.

"Hello Mrs. Goldstein. I'm Shelley from the luncheon."

"So I'm not hallucinating," Alice said playfully.

"Pardon me?"

"Nothing, sweetheart. This chocolate's got my eyes playing tricks on me."

"I'm glad to know, our hospitality is appreciated."

Alice smiled, thrilled that she was no longer a 20-something with that Searching-for-Mr.-Right hunger in her eyes. "Sweetheart, my days of worrying about my waistline are over."

"Mrs. Goldstein, if you can eat like that and stay so small, you're lucky. You and your husband are extremely fortunate people."

Alice stiffened. "What do you mean?"

"Well, everyone who qualifies to attend our seminar is extremely fortunate. Financially, that is." She glanced at the terrace and the Gulf. "As is anyone who winters in South Florida, especially here."

Alice held a strawberry under the stream of chocolate. "Anyone who says 'winter' as a verb is pretty damn lucky, too."

The girl laughed. "Excuse me, Mrs. Goldstein. I have to chat with Mr. Wuerthberg. Enjoy!"

A bristling sense of annoyance dulled her euphoria. Why did these people seem to know so much about her and Stanley? Their I-know-all-about-you-but-you-don't-know-us rubbed Alice all wrong.

Stanley shook his head as Alice set her plate on the linen-covered table.

"So I'll take a swim at the club later," she said. "What's one cookie? And one piece of baklava—"

"Flown in from Greece today," Mr. Wuerthberg said.

"Diabetes on a plate," Stanley grumbled. "You're looking at a woman who'll order 'Death by Chocolate' for dessert."

The girl rushed back with a creamy cup of coffee. "Your coffee, Mrs. Goldstein."

"Thank you, Sweetheart."

As the girl left, Stanley said, "Now, convince me why we shouldn't do this."

Mr. Wuerthberg grinned. The sunlight on his bleached teeth made them look freakishly white, like a neat row of Chiclets gum squares. With practiced chumminess, he said, "This is a once in a lifetime opportunity to use your good health and your good fortune to make even more money."

Alice's chocolate chip cookie had split, oozing onto the baklava. Excitement sizzled through her, the same way she used to feel sexual electricity with Stanley. These days, the only things that got him excited were golf and money.

"First, Dr. and Mrs. Goldstein," Wuerthberg said, crossing his leg and looking Stanley in the eye. "I want to thank you for investing your time with me this afternoon. Clearly, you have a lot of choices on a beautiful day in South Florida. So I promise to make it more than worth your while."

Skepticism deepened the wrinkles on Stanley's sun-weathered face. Always so suspicious, that Stanley.

"Now, Dr. and Mrs. Goldstein, you're in a position to take an incredible opportunity. You're so uniquely qualified that very few people are in your position. You have what we like to call 'unused capacity' to purchase life insurance."

Stanley shrugged. "Don't need it. Don't want life insurance."

"Of course," Mr. Wuerthberg said. "Whether you want the life insurance is irrelevant. Because you're going to get a payoff. When the underwriting is complete, I'll write you a $50,000 check."

Stanley raised his brows, which after 45 years of marriage, Alice knew meant he was impressed. The desserts swirled on Alice's tongue in a symphony of sweetness. "Tell us something you didn't say down in the seminar," Alice ordered. "You told us this already."

Mr. Wuerthberg made an expression that looked like he'd just learned at an acting class for slickster salesmen. He was like a cross between a used car salesman and a wealthy Wall Street wizard. He squinted slightly, nodding. And he spoke with an overly familiar tone that reminded Alice of their sons, when they were little, trying to butter her up before asking to eat cookies before dinner.

"Mrs. Goldstein," he said, "you and your husband are entitled to $15 million dollar life insurance policies. Each. That is far above and beyond what many couples qualify for. As a result, I can write you a check for 50-thousand dollars."

Stanley raised a hand. "But what's this about two years—"

"Let me explain," Mr. Wuerthberg said. "At the end of two years, you decide, 'Do we want to keep the life insurance and pay back the loan at 14 percent interest?'"

"Not bad," Alice said, eyeing a white chocolate truffle.

"Absolutely!" Mr. Wuerthberg said. "In fact, that's a heck of a good deal. Because, should your health change, your family now has a $15 million dollar insurance policy, and you don't have to make a decision for two years."

Stanley asked, "What if I don't want the policy? Which I won't."

"Excellent point," Mr. Wuerthberg said. "That gets us to Part B. If you decide after two years that you no longer want the policy, you'll be entitled to even more money."

"How much?"

"We need to do some calculations," Wuerthberg said, "but I'd bet, at least your original signing bonus—"

Stanley raised his brows. "Another 50-grand?"

"Yes, sir," Wuerthberg grinned. "You like the sound of that!"

"Money for nothing," Alice said, "sounds as honest as saying these sweets have no calories. You better believe there's a downside—"

"She's right," Stanley said.

"This, Dr. and Mrs. Goldstein, I guarantee, is absolutely, 100 percent safe. We are even willing to make the loan on a non-recourse basis. That makes it virtually risk-free—"

"Lies." Stanley stood. "There's got to be a catch."

"Stanley," Alice said, not wanting to leave until she'd sampled everything on her plate. "Hear him out. You never know."

"That's the problem," Stanley said.

67. Naples, Florida

Something about that luncheon seminar made Hunter feel dirty. But he couldn't put his finger on exactly what. Was it the extravagance? Using the glossy brochures, the fancy talk, the pretty girls at the door, and the promise of cash... to bedazzle the seniors with bullshit? So that they'd be blind to the reality of this deal? But what *was* the reality?

All he'd heard so far, from the men and women in Diamond Lagoon who'd actually gotten the policies, was that they were a legitimate way to collect easy money. But what was the catch? What was the risk? Was it only, as it appeared, a way for creative insurance agents to generate huge commissions?

As he walked on the beach behind the hotel, Hunter's gut told him that beneath the impressive gilding festered a rotten core. Foremost in his thoughts, as he left Luxury Suites to return to the hangar, were Lauren Price Miller's questions about her parents' life settlement policies. She was furious that she had no way of knowing exactly who now owned the policies and would receive a $20 million payoff now that her parents were dead. After what he'd seen today, Hunter was starting to believe that it was above board.

But who did own those "blind" trusts that held the countless life settlement policies that were being purchased, churned and relinquished two years later? And if companies like The Genuine Insurance Group were doing high profile seminars in every senior citizen hotspot across America, then they were probably scoring hundreds of policies every week. It would be interesting to see who was holding them.

Facing the turquoise majesty of the Gulf of Mexico, Hunter pressed a single number on his phone. No tellin' where that cellular satellite signal would beam back down on Earth to find the man who was as close to a brother as Hunter had. The phone didn't even ring before a deep voice exclaimed, "Stallion Six!"

"A-K, my man," Hunter grinned, sitting on a polished bench in a cover of lush flowering bushes. "Ain't much better'n hearin' the voice that snatched me off death's doorstep."   Despite the 85-degree humidity, Hunter's face felt cold... *the assault of tiny hail pellets on his cheeks, the icy slap of waves against his ear, the sucking sensation that was pulling his body down into the black depths...* His heart pounded at the memory of that day, 20-some years ago.   "That's why we call you A-K. Strongest arms this side of the moon.   A human crane, that's what you are."

"Wasn't easy raising He-Man outta the Atlantic with my bare hands."   A-K's laughter shot through the phone like gunfire—deep, harsh, relentless—hence his nickname from day one on Coronado.   When he stopped laughing, the real sound of electronic gunfire shot through the phone.

"Sounds like you're on the set of *Star Wars* right now," Hunter said.

"Halo 3, man.   Fightin' aliens.   Coolest thing I've ever done.   If you don't count this chick named Shawna over the weekend.   Even a computer geek like me can get laid."

"What are you up to these days?" Hunter asked as he walked along the salty waves washing up, then fizzing on the sand.

That machine gun laughter shot through the phone. "Top Secret.   Classified.   The type of thing where I'd have to kill you if I told you."

Hunter laughed.   His buddy was probably doing Internet security for a big company.   "Well can you still find a couple minutes to help out your old buddy from Hell Week?"

"Not supposed to do any outside work right now," A-K said, "but if it's just a quick favor for a buddy, I don't see any harm in it."

"Cool," Hunter said, "I'm down in Florida tryin' to piece together a little insurance puzzle."

That laughter shot through the phone again. "Man, I love the way you talk. You need to call me more often. Read me the paper, I don't care. The way you emphasize the 'in' before the 'surance.' IN-surance."

"A Stallion can stomp an A-K any day, now." Hunter challenged playfully. "Don't make me have to fly up to your computer geek hide-away. My Baby Doll and I got the most sophisticated navigation system. We'll find you, swoop down, and kick your ass! For old time's sake."

The laughter shot through the phone so loud that Hunter held it away from his ear. "Seriously, Stallion, how can I help my buddy today?"

"Depends. You still gallivanting' the globe, masquerading as everybody and their brother?"

"Pretty stationary right now, but my portal takes me everywhere I need to go. Have Internet, will travel."

"I need to take a peek into what's probably classified like nobody's business."

"Just call me your humble servant. Whaddya need?" The electronic battle raged louder with gunfire and explosions. "Hold on. Let me turn this down."

It was quiet when Hunter said, "I came across a life insurance policy that's a little unique. There's a company that pays you to sign up and hold the policy for two years. After that, the policy goes into some blind institutional-size international investment fund. Need to put a name and a face on that fund."

"American?"

"Don't know. But I got a hunch it's huge. The insurance company is called The Genuine Insurance Group."

"One condition, Stallion Six."

Hunter chuckled. He hadn't heard that nickname in awhile. Got it for his six-pack abs, and being a stallion when it came to any challenge. Including orders to do dozens of "rocking chairs" during sleepless Hell Week.

That meant laying on your back at the edge of San Diego Bay, in the dark and in full fatigues. Knees raised, rolling back on the spine, dunking backwards into the water, then up, only to repeat the cold, wet exercise that left some guys pukin' up their guts and other guys deliriously dizzy.

"One condition?" Hunter teased. "What's that?"

"Take me flyin' next time I'm in your part of town. I'm comin' back to Chicago next month for my parents' fiftieth anniversary party. Next week, some TV show's doin' a special for Valentine's Day about couples who haven't killed each other—" machine gun laughter "—I meant to say, couples who've enjoyed a half century of wedded bliss."

"They're lyin'," Hunter said. Man, the water was so pretty today. He glanced up at the hotel, which was about a hundred yards away. Movement on a balcony caught his eye. It was Wuerthberg, sitting with a man, a woman with black hair and a sparkle at her neck. Alice and Stanley Goldstein, getting the private high-pressure sale, no doubt.

"My parents are happy," A-K said. "They've had their moments."

"Ditto for mine. There, that makes two happy couples that I know of."

"You'll see my left hand bears no symbol of matrichism." A-K laughed. "Get it? Matrimony plus masochism equals matrichism."

"I hear 'ya, buddy." Hunter thought of Meredith. She would just be more pissed off that he'd be staying for that housing auction on Monday in Diamond Lagoon. Annoyance cramped his gut for a split second, as he thought about calling her with an ETA. But why inflict that grief on himself? He wouldn't. She'd see him when she saw him.

"You got an airplane ride with your name on it," Hunter said. "It's a deal."

"But don't make me have to pluck you away from the Grim Reaper again." A-K laughed.

"Double deal."

68. Los Angeles, California

Juan looked into the terrified eyes of a stupid motherfucker.

"Your suicide will be celebrated by many," Juan said as two K.C. Leaders secured the rope around the Grecian column that rose in this three-story solarium over the indoor swimming pool. "Everyone will say your life of crime finally caught up with you." Juan lowered the noose around the guy's head. "'A taste of his own medicine,' they'll say."

"Please," the guy whimpered. "I'm sorry. I won't—"

Juan's fist thudded in his stomach. "A real man takes what's due to him. Strike out against The Panther, get too ambitious, you lose everything."

Turning to leave, Juan nodded to his helpers. They threw the guy over the balcony. His scream echoed off the glass ceiling. His body splashed in the water. And it was silent.

"Put the word out," Juan said. "The Panther says ambition is a bad word. Do the job, and live."

69. Naples, Florida

Stephen Wuerthberg would not let this couple walk away. He had to hook them on an appointment. Like the sweet temptations of this luxurious suite overlooking the ocean, he had to bedazzle them further—with confusing money talk.

"The non-recourse basis is a tremendous opportunity to avoid cost and risk," Wuerthberg said, "which theoretically make this far more competitive than any other investments."

"What?" Dr. Goldstein barked. "You say, 'Free money.' I say, 'Risk. Big risk.'"

"Ask your friends. Your referral slip mentions that your friends Herschel Goodman and Ernest Bloomfield both completed this process, got their money—"

"And flat screen TVs," Alice interjected.

"No catch," Wuerthberg said. "No risk. No problem."

"There's got to be more to it," Stanley said. "You want me to 'buy' free life insurance and give me money for buying?!"

"Think of it as a signing bonus," Wuerthberg said. "You get 50-thousand dollars for signing up for the policy. It requires no capital from you. My investors will—"

"What's in it for them?"

"What's in it for them, Mrs. Goldstein, is 14 percent interest. Either from you keeping the policy or from someone else who would be buying our policy. A lot of people like to get that 14 percent, especially in today's economic environment."

"What do we have to do?" she asked.

"We have to put you through an underwriting exam by a board certified physician. Not your physician."

"My doctor is fine," Alice said.

"Mrs. Goldstein, we have to use an insurance company's physician, to make sure we're doing this by the book. By using an independent third party, we make sure it's totally on the up and up."

Mr. Wuerthberg nodded. "All of your medical records will be released. Under the HIPAA rules, those records can only be used to underwrite your policy. A second company will be evaluating you for a possible sale of your policy down the road in two years."

"Still sounds too good to be true." Stanley pulled his cell phone from his jacket pocket. "If this is such a hot deal, why didn't my broker tell me—"

"Dr. Goldstein, this planning is so new and cutting edge, a brokerage firm wouldn't understand it. Please do call your broker. Invite him to meet with us." Wuerthberg bluffed, pulling a sheet from the glossy folder on the table. "As a matter of fact, here's a white paper. Share it with him."

"Will he fly down?" Alice asked.

"If I say, 'money,' he's on a plane," Stanley said.

Wuerthberg said, "I guarantee, he won't have a clue because this phenomenon is so new."

"You haven't met Jacob," Alice said. "Sharp as a razor. Always studying up on the latest—"

"Not this," Wuerthberg said. "It hasn't been introduced to the financial planning community. It's that new. And the few that are aware of it closed the door on it early, not understanding how it can help people like you."

Alice drew her brows together.

"You can be among the first to take advantage of this phenomenon that is sweeping the upper echelon of retirement communities across America."

Stanley nodded. "Ernest and Herschel said it's a no-brainer. Sign up, take an EKG, get a check, then a TV in two years. How can you sweeten the deal for us?"

"Excellent question, Dr. Goldstein. "They qualified for less coverage. You and your wife are so uniquely qualified that you may fare even better than your friends. Your significantly higher net worth—"

Stanley half-smiled at Alice.

"—in terms of your properties here in Florida and back home in New York."

"But the whole life insurance idea," Stanley said. "It bothers me."

"You have an astounding but unused capacity to capitalize on your qualifications for a tremendous policy. What I'm offering you today, Dr. and Mrs. Goldstein, is the chance to profit from that capacity, simply by signing up and agreeing to medical exams. That simple."

Stanley asked, "How often do people keep these policies?"

"Seldom! It's such a good investment. You're using an unused asset to generate additional retirement income. The life insurance policy is not that good of a deal for you," Wuerthberg lied. "This deal is as sweet as they come." He glanced at Alice, and grinned: "Without the calories. Without a cost."

"What about Uncle Sam's calorie count?" Alice asked. "Taxes."

"Excellent point, Mrs. Goldstein. This is ordinary income with full taxation. However, we may qualify you for a charitable deduction. We can talk about that later, because right now we don't even know what you qualify for."

"Later," Stanley said. "How long does all this take?"

"Because we are meticulous about handling every detail with excruciating accuracy and legitimacy," Wuerthberg said, "you should have your check in three months. During that time, we'll calculate how much you'll get in two years, when you sell the policy."

"Ballpark figure?" Stanley asked.

"The initial glimpse at your portfolio tells me, you'll probably get another check for 50-thousand. So all told, 100-thousand dollars for your signatures and a few doctor's exams. And we pay for everything. Including the gourmet dinner in three months when we finalize the paperwork and deliver your check. This is nothing short of superb."

Stanley stood. "I need to think about this."

Wuerthberg smiled. He was going to make money on this, with or without a deal. Not a bad way to make a living. It sure beat bagging and delivering groceries as a kid for the rich ladies back in New York. With Mom working three jobs to support three boys by herself, and their bum of a dad showing up when he needed a place to crash between poker games and drinking binges, Wuerthberg earned A's and became a millionaire living the glamorous life in South Florida.

All because a dude just like Dr. Goldstein took him aside one day, at the grocery story. "Stephen, you are the most industrious boy. Every day I come in here, you're earning extra money mopping the floor, straightening up the displays. Come to my office tomorrow."

Turned out, this old guy owned grocery stores across America. He made Wuerthberg his pet project. Taught him about the stock market. Paid for his college and MBA. And put him in charge of sales at this life insurance venture.

"Please, Dr. Goldstein, I have some more benefits to share with you. Sit, please."

Alice sunk her fork into a chocolate covered strawberry. Stanley sat down.

"Dr. Goldstein, I know exactly what you're thinking. 'Am I making a smart decision about my retirement?' Well, first the decision is three months from now. And the beauty is, it costs you nothing. We'll pay for everything. We paid for lunch. We'll pay for your medical exam, a nice dinner. Mrs. Goldstein, what's your favorite wine?"

Alice smiled. "Merlot."

"I promise, you'll enjoy the meal," Wuerthberg said. "With a sweet ending. Death by Chocolate, perhaps?"

Alice smiled. "It's a deal."

"Not so fast," Stanley said. "If Miss Piggy keeps eating like this, she'll flunk the medical exam." Stanley stayed focused on Wuerthberg. "What makes two years the magic number?"

"That's the length of time we're required to wait before we can sell a policy to an investment fund."

"Who's in this investment fund?" Stanley demanded. "I don't want some foreign group buying private information about me—"

Concern—the Academy Award-winning kind—washed over Wuerthberg's face. "Dr. Goldstein, I absolutely guarantee that these are blind investment funds. Your personal information will never, ever get into the hands of anyone but extremely confidential professionals. Confidentiality is our utmost priority."

Stanley argued, "I've read about some of these funds. They could be owned by Germans with Nazi connections, or some Middle Eastern sheik with ties to terrorism. Don't want any part of that!"

Wuerthberg shook his head. "I guarantee, the billion dollar investment fund that will hold your policy after two years is a blind institutional fund. Nobody knows who you are. It is confidential, completely anonymous. There are absolutely no shady characters hiding in the shadows. Florida laws are so strict, there is absolutely no room for abuse. I'll tell you who invested 400 million dollars in an international fund like this. The richest man in America, Andrew Pierce."

Dr. Goldstein said, "I did read about that. But that's not enough to convince me. Thank you for your time."

He walked out. Alice followed.

And Wuerthberg grinned. He could still make his 200-grand on them. Because Shelley had collected their electronic signatures at the luncheon.

I'm going to get paid whether Dr. Goldstein likes it or not.

70. Avoyelles Parish, Louisiana

Gerald Boxley opened the enormous metal doors on the beige farm building as Juan's jet streaked across the private runway here on the Boxley family farm. This building—which looked like a barn but was as big as a hangar and as secure as a bank vault—was newly constructed, along with the landing strip on these 10,000 acres of sugarcane, rice, wheat and soybeans.

"Welcome back to Creole Country," Boxley said, with Katrina at his side, as Juan used the tug to pull his plane inside the barn. This was their third trip here this week; Boxley arrived on his privately financed and piloted jet, which was outside on the tarmac.

Juan barely grunted a hello; his expression was grim.

"You may look overworked," Boxley chuckled, leaning against floor-to-ceiling pallets of shrink-wrapped cash. "But you certainly don't look underpaid."

Juan showed no expression as he opened the cargo doors on his plane.

"Palm Springs and L.A.," Juan said, stepping toward the wooden crates of cash that Boxley had prepared for these payouts to the K.C. Leaders.

"If it's any consolation," Boxley said, "you may get a reprieve in 2010."

Juan froze. His panther eyes always caught Boxley by surprise. The expression was so potent, it literally made the Senator hold his breath.

"Explain reprieve," Juan ordered as Katrina trotted over to him and rubbed her nose against his leg.

Good timing, Girl. Change the subject.

Juan pet her head.

"You're the only person Kat gives the time of day," Boxley said. "She even growls at beautiful women. But I saved her; I'll never forget that day, touring the flooded Ninth Ward, and this baby comes paddling along. Such sad eyes. I pulled her into the boat, and the rest is history."

Juan whispered to the dog in Spanish.

"She's a Catahoula Leopard Dog," Boxley said. "The official state dog of Louisiana. Breed the Indians's domestic dog with the Spaniards' war dog, and you get Katrina's relatives. Excellent family pets and guard dogs. Loyal to the owner. Aggressive to strangers."

Kat whimpered happily as she looked up at Juan.

"Strangers," Boxley said playfully, "not Panthers."

Juan shot his paralyzing gaze. "Explain reprieve."

"We've doubled up now," Boxley said, regretting that he'd mentioned it at all. His heartbeat quickened with worry that Carolyn would angrily disapprove that he'd divulged any more information than necessary. Then again, it wasn't like she was going to chat with this cold-blooded killer anytime soon. "But we anticipate a significant slow-down."

"Why?" Juan asked.

"That word appears nowhere in your job description," Boxley said.

"Then I'll ask *where* instead," Juan countered. "Where did this money come from, Senator?"

"If you're burned out or unhappy in your position, Senor Diablo, I'm quite certain that we can find an adequate replacement."

"Never," Juan said, lifting a crate onto the plane. "So tell me, where does one find a stack of cash that's three stories high and finds its way to the middle of Louisiana?"

Boxley crossed his arms and stared back with his cockiest air of defiance. But he wasn't looking at a silk-stockinged Republican in Congress during a contentious debate over legislation. He was looking into the eyes of a world-class drug lord turned high-class executioner.

"In three days, Chicago and Detroit will be due," Boxley said. "I'll text you an exact meeting time."

"Where'd the money come from?" Juan demanded, hauling another crate into the jet.

Nobody, especially Juan, would ever know that this cash was a sort of kick-back from Saddam Hussein. Here in this barn was part of the nine billion that disappeared after the U.S. Government dispersed 12-billion in Iraq to stimulate their economy between 2003 and 2004. While some of the cash may have helped, most of it was mismanaged, never tracked, and disappeared.

Investigators had linked some of the cash to a house in California, and a mailbox in the Caribbean. But that was as far as they would ever get. Because nobody would ever know some of that money was here, behind so many bales of hay on this wholesome farm that the Boxley family had operated for generations. The highly respected Boxley family tree was rooted in French-speaking blacks from Haiti and Napoleon's troops who settled here, thanks to a warm welcome from the Native Americans and Europeans. The resulting Creole culture—a unique ethnic blend of food, language and music—distinguished the Boxley family as aristocrats. No one would guess or believe that a conspiracy called Eldorado could possibly exist, especially here.

"You'd best eliminate the questions and focus on the task at hand." Boxley's deep voice echoed with confidence despite his pounding heart. Juan was capable of anything. Despite Carolyn's assurance that he would be so happy to have freedom and a life of luxury, Boxley worried that Juan could turn on them at any time. What if he had a crew of thugs who overwhelmed the intricate security here, and tried to abscond with this cash? Anything was possible. That's why technology was keeping a very close eye on Mr. Juan Pantera Diablo.

"If you recall what you were doing one year ago today," Boxley said, "you'll feel inspired by gratitude to forget the questions and simply enjoy your incredibly good fortune."

Juan stood still, staring with those cat eyes that glowed with things Boxley did not want to know.

71. The Sea Palace Yacht Club, South Beach, Florida

In the master suite of his yacht, a nightmare was sucking Juan back into the federal penitentiary, after his Angel confessed that his pardon and release were all a big mistake. In this dream, it felt like everything was going backward... to the hotel suite where his Angel confiscated the Black Passport. He was stripped of his phone, laptop, money, airplane, yacht and island.

"You've paid your debt to the United States," the beautiful blond told him. "You have accomplished our mission through high level activities of imminent importance to the White House. As I told you in the beginning, this never happened. Now, to ensure its secrecy, you will return to solitary confinement to serve out your life sentence—"

Suddenly, he was tossed into that concrete cell with double steel doors, no window and torturous solitude.

"No!" Juan screamed. "Never!" Fear burned through his veins. His ears rang with panic. "No!"

His father's deep voice boomed in his ears: "They're using you. They'll toss you back into the dungeon as quickly as they took you out. Do it, now."

Juan yelled, "Do it now!"

Thrashing, yelling, he woke up. Panting, he looked around the shadowy room. The lights of Miami sparkled beyond the circular wall of windows surrounding his huge bed. On the nightstand to his right sat his Black Passport and his silver Glock semi-automatic handgun. To his left, in the giant bed, Gigi and Cheyenne were sitting up, groggily staring at him in shock.

"Do it now," he whispered. "Get it and get out."

72. Sailfish Marina, Florida

Juan savored his grilled Mahi Mahi, the fresh catch of the day at Sailfish Marina on Singer Island. It was lunchtime, here with Boxley under one of several blue canvas umbrellas facing the marina lined with flawless white fishing boats that sprouted silver ladders, poles and antennas up toward the deep blue sky. And the boat names. What a classy yet egotistical exercise in vanity to describe one's life in three words or less. *Cash Flow. Lady Susan. Love The Action.*

"You were right," Juan said to Boxley over the chatter of people at the tables around them. Juan wore dark aviator sunglasses and a black baseball cap over his short ponytail. His direct questions at the hangar hadn't worked; Juan was going to extract information from Boxley in a more subtle way. For now. "This Cajun seasoning is superb."

"We know how to do things right in the Bayou State," said Boxley as he bent down to feed another piece of Black Angus Burger to Katrina, who sat with such canine cool on the cement between them. The black suitcase also rested on the ground between them, guarded by the dog and Juan's constant companions, Smith & Wesson. Smith was in the right front pocket, a .38

airweight; Wesson was in the top of Juan's left biker-style boot.

"Here you go, Kat." Boxley chuckled, glancing at the lunch plate that he had ordered just for the dog. "This girl loves her meat. Fish, too."

Juan studied his point man, who wore a Xavier University polo shirt and baseball cap with khaki pants and designer leather loafers. Boxley wasn't his boss. No, he was the middleman, if that. And the boss was insulated by many layers, protected from any wrongdoing up there in Eldorado. But Juan was about to figure out how to secure his own fortune.

Juan pulled a piece of fish from his plate and held it down for Kat. The dog licked it, then looked up with pleading eyes.

"She wants more," Juan said, lifting his glasses and casting his Panther eyes down at this animal that had found him irresistible since his first meeting with Boxley last April.

Juan fed Kat another piece of fish; she looked up at him the same way that Gigi and Cheyenne had this morning after the threesome's erotic romp on a sandbar during an early morning cruise.

"Bet she freaks out during storms," Juan said. "Reminds me of this big German Shepherd I had as a kid. His name was Duke, but he ran and hid under the bed during thunderstorms."

"Back in Colombia or when your mother worked at the Embassy in D.C.?" Boxley asked, sipping his milk. He held up the glass, "The official drink of Louisiana."

Juan reached for his bottled water. "Did her previous owners die in Katrina?"

Juan looked straight into Boxley's face as if he hadn't heard the question. He hated that Boxley seemed to know his whole story. The Emperor, or the next person down, had to have clued Boxley in to every detail. But

Juan sure as hell wasn't going to divulge anything beyond that. He was here for one reason: to get clues to figure out who was pulling Boxley's puppet strings. The bullshit conversation about the dog and the food, well, it was just that. And Boxley already knew that Juan was doubling the K.C. Leaders nationwide; this meeting was just a formality, probably, for the good senator to report back that he had a face-to-face with his Number One Hit Man.

"According to her tags," Boxley said, spearing the golden brown crab cakes on his plate with his fork. "Whimpers like a baby every night. Won't even sleep, my wife says, when I'm not in the house."

Juan glanced at today's *Washington News* and *New York Journal*, both of which laid on the table with front page stories about the nation's housing crisis. Boxley had been reading them when Juan walked up, always a few minutes after their meeting time.

"Rich get richer," Juan said coolly, "the poor get poorer. Doubling these Orders, though, we're certainly doing our duty for the economy by keeping otherwise useless people employed, and prosperous."

Boxley glanced around at the boats. "You know, Juan, you should invest some of your earnings in a minority company. The government's trying to right the sins of the fathers by giving all sorts of perks to folks like you and me. People of color. People who've been left out of the game."

Juan turned down the corners of his mouth. "All those applications, government regulations, audits, paper trails. Not my style."

"So you get a holding company," Boxley said. "It serves as a bureaucratic buffer between you and the business. Impossible for anyone to trace or connect you in any way. That's why it's a privately held minority company. I highly recommend it."

"I appreciate your advice," Juan said, "but I'm pretty content with serving my country exactly as I am."

Boxley laughed, holding a juicy bite of crab cake halfway between his plate and his face. "I love the way you make that sound so wholesome and patriotic. By the way, you know we had a claim denied." He put the morsel in his mouth.

"A what?"

"Oh, it's nothing that concerns you," Boxley said, chewing.

But the flash of oh-shit-I-shouldn't-have-said-that across Boxley's face let Juan know, it was something that concerned him. The word spun a thousand directions in Juan's brain. Claim. Real estate claim? Housing claim? Estate tax claim? Medical claim? Employment claim? Insurance claim? Social Security claim? It was time to get his FBI contact on the case.

"You are absolutely right, though," Boxley said, tapping the newspapers. "And the housing market is the most accurate barometer of the vast chasm between rich and poor. In the Florida paper I read earlier, they're starting 25-million-dollar homes in Naples, while the rest of Americans are getting foreclosures and evictions."

Juan dropped another chunk of fish to Kat. "If I were the Vice President, I'd be bailing out homeowners who have kids to raise," Juan said, "instead of senior citizens who've already had their chance." Juan took a bite of broccoli and summer squash. He'd rather be indulging in those pan-fried crab cakes on Boxley's plate, and the French fries. But a Panther needed superior quality fuel to prowl—and conquer—his jungle. He forked up some wild rice.

Meanwhile, Boxley's topaz eyes roiled; he pursed his mouth as if so many complex words were coming together in his brain, he needed to get his face to look official and grim about it. Juan wanted to tell him, It's okay, Senator, the TV news cameras aren't here. Don't have to spin a snappy sound byte like you did after Carrie's speech.

Juan also wanted to say, *and at the rate that we're killing these old people, they won't even need Social Security—*

"I'm working with several members of Congress," Boxley said, "on a bail-out package for homeowners. We plan to issue a federal moratorium on foreclosures. And provide funding to help people stay in their homes."

Juan nodded as if he thought that were a good idea. "Doesn't it stand to reason that the government could get a boatload of money by taking possession of all the foreclosed houses—and estates of the ultra rich when they die?"

There, Juan's question probed directly into what was happening to the property when the K.C. Teams knocked off all those rich men and women in their 70s and 80s. At first, Juan had wondered if the government wanted them dead because they were a drain on Medicare and Social Security. But no, the government would find a way, with some sneaky IRS rule or mega estate tax penalty, to seize the rich people's assets after Juan's K.C. Teams got through with them.

Juan wished he could pour a truth serum into Boxley's iced tea and get him to explain everything. Immediately and in detail. Then again, a Panther always loved the thrill of the chase. And he had much more intelligent means for mining diamonds of information from what seemed like impenetrable rock.

Boxley let out an important-sounding chuckle. "Oh no, the day the government seizes property is the day that we've lost all touch with democracy. Banks are private institutions—"

"But Uncle Sam just got custody of Fannie Mae and Freddie Mac," Juan said. "Seems like now he can raid their toy boxes all he wants."

Boxley laughed so suddenly that the dog startled.

"I've never heard it put quite that way," Boxley said. "We've been working feverishly on the Hill to find a quick, long-lasting solution to the credit crisis. I have constituents, young and old alike, who survived Katrina, but say their financial struggles are equally disastrous." Boxley sipped his tea. "But you do have a point."

"There, that takes care of the middle class," Juan said. "A couple IRS claims for estate taxes, say, on properties worth five million or more, and Uncle Sam is set for life." Juan wasn't exactly sure what he'd just said, but based on Boxley's expression, he'd struck gold.

Boxley cast a stone cold stare at Juan, whose Panther eyes reflected back confidence and knowing. Even though he was bluffing. Boxley pulled a pen from his pocket. On a napkin, he drew two side-by-side boxes. In one, he wrote his name. In the other, he wrote Juan.

"This is my job," Boxley said, sticking the tip of the pen in the center of his box. "This is your job," he said, poking the ink pen into the u in Juan. "Don't cross the line."

An ominous glint in Boxley's eyes let Juan know that the Senator would do anything to preserve the secrecy around his power.

He just didn't know how far The Panther would go to get what he wanted.

73. Sailfish Marina, Florida

The crowd waiting to eat lunch at world famous Sailfish Marina was bigger than Hunter expected, so he stepped into the gift shop to buy a pink T-shirt for his bride.

"Hey, didn't I meet you in up in the horse capital of the world?" a deep voice said behind Hunter. He turned around.

There stood the quintessential Scandinavian sportsman—tall, husky, blond, blue-eyed Lars Eriksson, golf pro and coach to the rich and leisurely.

"Didn't you promise a round of golf with a humble guy from Kentucky?" Hunter responded playfully as the cashier handed him his receipt and bag. "We could play a whole nine holes for the same time it takes to get through the wait list in the restaurant."

"I already got a table," Lars said, "come join me. They say a man should never eat alone."

"I'd be delighted," Hunter said. "Small world, i'n't it?"

As they left the store, stepping onto the boardwalk-style promenade where artists were sketching tourists' faces and families were enjoying ice cream cones, Hunter noticed a dog. Not a poodle or lab or bouvier, but a hunting-type dog, which looked strange in these ritzy surroundings. It walked alongside an African American man. He had a rich, caramel-hued complexion under a baseball cap that covered all but the curly bottoms of his silver-streaked black hair. He was tall, with regal posture and a gait that radiated authority. Didn't look like a tourist, but he was carrying a large black suitcase.

Beside him, a younger guy in all black, including the aviator glasses and baseball cap, was Latin, tall and slim. He walked with even more authority, exuding quiet confidence. A confidence that announced, he was such a cool dude, everyone knew it with one glance, but upon further visual inspection, no one could pinpoint exactly why or how. He gave off a vibe of privilege and wealth, with a gangster vibe. Like a former drug lord. Or one of those European playboys who were actually money launderers.

An air of wealth and power radiated around them. Even the dog had a cocky stride. And that suitcase. The black guy had a grip on it with his left hand; it hung next to the dog, which walked between the two men. Whatever was in that suitcase had two bodyguards and a guard dog. The scene looked like something straight off *Miami Vice*. Was that suitcase full of drugs? But if those two were up to something shady, would they do it in the bright Sunday afternoon sunshine in this crowd?

Hunter tried to watch those guys as tourists and restaurant patrons streamed past on the sunny boardwalk. The glare off the fishing boats and all their silver paraphernalia cast a blur over the two men.

Still, Hunter stared. They looked so familiar. That's who that was. Boxley. The African American was the Senior Senator from Louisiana who was helping Carrie with her new legislation to save Social Security. Hunter remembered the news reports, the night of her speech, that showed the key players in her bipartisan plan: Republican John Donaldson and Democrat Gerald Boxley. And the other guy, he looked like a guy Hunter had gone to school with. Juan Pantera Diablo, class President back at Episcopal High School. He'd see him at the reunion almost a year ago. No chance. The world wasn't that small. Besides, this guy was much more tanned and athletic looking.

Did he live down here? What were he and Boxley doing together? Hunter wanted to say hello. But Lars was two steps ahead of him, striding back toward the restaurant. Juan and Boxley were moving the opposite direction, even more quickly. And the crowd was so thick.

Something felt cold on Hunter's bare toes, in his brown leather sandals. He looked down.

"Mommy! I dropped it!" a little girl shrieked. Then she screamed at the sight of her blue ice cream scoop plopped onto Hunter's foot.

"Oh, Lindsey!" the mom fussed, "look what you've done to this poor man."

Juan and Boxley disappeared into the crowd. Lars turned around, scanning the crowd with a perplexed expression.

"Ah," he said, smiling, returning to Hunter as the mom bent down to mop the blue mess with tissues.

"It's okay, ma'am," Hunter said, smiling at the little girl. "Ill be fine." He handed a five-dollar bill to the lady. "Here, I think your little angel needs another scoop."

He bent down to the little girl. "Sorry a big clumsy guy like me wasn't lookin' where he was goin'. You get some more ice cream, okay?"

Lars laughed.

"Thank you, sir," the mom winked. "That's very kind."

A few minutes later, after Hunter had cleaned up in the men's room, he joined Lars at the table.

"Man," Lars said, "that Keeneland is the place to be. Hot chicks galore. Beautiful horses. Excitement."

"Come on back in the Spring," Hunter said. "The season flies by, gotta seize the moment while you can."

"Your friend Jake, the horse breeder—"

Hunter nodded. "Great guy."

"Well, tell Jake that his explanation of the difference between bourbon, whiskey and women—" Lars tilted his head back, flashed two perfect rows of exceptionally large teeth, and laughed for a good 20 seconds "—tell him I'm still laughing! Fast women and beautiful horses."

Hunter smiled. "Yeah, Jake's definitely got a unique outlook on things. You would, too, if you were the guy between the stallion and the mare come breedin' time."

Lars shook his head; a more serious expression took hold on his broad, clean-shaven, suntanned face.

"This might sound strange," Lars said, sipping a beer, "but after I left horse country, I paid closer attention to all the news reports about Eight Belles, right after the

Kentucky Derby Race. The way they have to put down a horse just because it has a broken leg."

"That's the reality of the horse business," Hunter said. "Even the best racehorse loses its value. Like Jake said, it's all about the insurance. Worth more dead than alive."

"I always think of that," Lars said, "when someone dies. And lately, a whole lotta people are passing away, in the places where I coach rich retirees. It's unbelievable."

The waitress handed Hunter a menu. "I'll have a beer, please," he said. As she walked away, he said, "You notice anything similar about these deaths?"

Lars shook his head in a way that made his slightly wavy, white-blond hair look unkempt.

"Some illness. One case of lung cancer for a long-term smoker. Another lady had a heart attack. Pneumonia from the flu. Most of the deaths," Lars said, glancing down at the cell phone on his belt, "are sudden, accidental or natural. Even more car accidents."

"I'm down here investigating some mysterious deaths myself," Hunter said. "Are there really more this year, or are you just more aware of it?"

"Oh, no!" Lars exclaimed. "I'm used to hearing about a couple deaths every year, in the retirement communities. Palm Springs, Phoenix, Vegas, the Carolinas, here in Florida. But this," he said, looking sad, "this sure seems above and beyond anything that's normal."

The waitress returned. Hunter ordered the grilled Mahi Mahi; Lars asked for a coconut shrimp appetizer and the grilled scallop salad.

Hunter, who set his phone in the table beside his right hand, set it to silent. If someone called, it would light up and he would decide whether to take the call.

"I'll give you some examples," Lars said. "First, everywhere I go, everybody's talking about it. At a golf club near Phoenix, as I was having dinner, you couldn't change the subject with a crowbar."

He looked down at his phone again. "Excuse me, Hunter. This person keeps calling." He answered: "Lars here." Listening, he turned chalk white, then shook his head and said, "Alright, I'll come by this afternoon." He hung up, then set the phone on the table. "That was another one. A client in Miami. Died in his sleep last night."

"Age?"

"Seventy-six but looked 56," Lars said. "A Jack LaLanne type. Had more energy than you and me together. Looks like sudden cardiac arrest."

Hunter leaned closer. "Lars, can you think of any strange angle between these wealthy folks dyin' and their real estate?"

Lars turned down the corners of his mouth. "Very wealthy people. A mansion for winter, a mansion for summer. More money than I could make in 10 lifetimes."

"Unless you marry one of their daughters," Hunter joked.

"Granddaughters," Lars corrected. "At The Golden Palm, the Maître De said 16 people came up missing this season. Gone. Dead. Now granted, The Golden Palm is a very large club. But he thinks people are so stressed about the stock market and the state of America, the stress is killing them in droves."

"You believe that?" Hunter asked skeptically.

Lars shook his head. "This Maître De, he gives new meaning to flamboyant. Tends to dramatize things. But all the ladies love how he fusses over the pretty details in the dining room. So he gets to know everybody's business—"

The waitress brought their plates.

"I think all these seniors dyin' could have a multitude of culprits," Hunter said. "Nice job on this fish. One thing is, with the baby boomers, we got more seniors than ever. So we hear about more deaths because there are just more people."

Lars stabbed his fork into a golden brown scallop. "No, my friend, I think there's much more to it."

An elderly couple in sailing clothes walked past.

"You want to know what I really think it is?" Lars said. "My girlfriend came up with this theory. And I believe it." He set down his fork and furled his brows. "Technology is to blame."

"Come again?"

"Technology," Lars said, as if it were obvious. "You and I, our bodies are used to all the radiation and crap that's being emitted from our cell phones, our TVs, the GPS navigators in our cars, our iPods, and everything else. Old people, their bodies can't handle it."

Hunter tilted his head as if that would help him grasp his friend's point.

Lars held up his hands and wiggled his fingers the way kids imitated falling rain. "Think about all the electrical currents in the air right now, connecting all of our cell phones to the satellites and the electrical towers. All those boats out there have radar and GPS and whatever else. You think all that energy is harmless? PFfffft! No way!"

Hunter was sure that all the electronics and energy charging the air couldn't possibly be a health booster, for anyone. But his friend's theory was a little out there. His avionics malfunction came to mind.

"We're all walking around in one giant microwave oven," Lars said. "Old people? Their bodies can't handle it. So they're dropping like flies."

74. Diamond Lagoon, Florida

This Hunter Knightly fellow really was getting around. Being privy to his seaside snooping was quite a treat for an old Brit who appreciated a nice winter get-away from time to time. Camera in hand, always, but not like all these tourists.

No, a fellow could sit at Sailfish Marina, eating lunch and watching the people—all while snapping dozens of candid shots of the handsome insurance investigator—and nobody would ever know it. Cameras came in all sorts of nifty disguises these days. The lens could hide in the brim of one's hat, or on a particularly funky pendant around one's neck, or even inside a lady's brooch. As a result, all sorts of husbands and wives truly regretted their naughty trysts with lovers, after such clandestine cameras captured their amorous wanderings.

But with this rugged chap, it was all business. The poor fellow didn't even know that—in addition to cameras—today's technology allowed the curious-minded to zoom in on a conversation, and record it from quite a distance, in complete secrecy. Not that he'd said anything especially interesting, but he sure was preoccupied with death and dying.

And unless he got wise and abandoned his snooping, it could be his own death and dying that would be preoccupying his conversations.

75. Diamond Lagoon, Florida

The auction for the Price's home was even more peculiar than Hunter had anticipated. The ringleader—real estate agent Polly Chesterfield—wore an eye-shocking orange suit with matching lipstick. Her voice seemed louder and her energy even bigger inside the packed ballroom at the Diamond Lagoon Golf Club. Hunter counted 20 tables of 10, so 200 people had shown up to bid on that house.

This shocked him in two ways. First, these folks were totally unaffected by the housing crisis that was kicking the country's rear end right now. And two, all of these ultra wealthy men and women already had a home here; now they wanted to acquire another one to upgrade in status and amenities.

Rather than the old-fashioned announcer calling out figures when bidders in the audience raised hands or cards, it was all electronic. Everyone held a palm-sized device that made Hunter wonder about Lars's theory. They entered their anonymous bids on the touch screen, which registered on the auctioneer's laptop computer up at the podium.

Behind him, a huge screen displayed the bids. It reminded Hunter of the tally board at The Crusade for Children Charity. Even though the room was silent as the numbers on the screen jumped from seven million to eight million and up, the room felt eerily electrified.

With each bid, Hunter could almost see a lavender web of electricity crackling over the rows of heads that were wispy silver, steel blue, shiny bald and unnaturally black. Stella's spiky blond hair stood out, as did her friend Margie's auburn pouf. Were they here to bid on their dead friends' home, or were they merely here as concerned spectators? Or were they simply watching to see who would become their next-door neighbors for six months out of the year?

As Hunter stood in the back, a hand squeezed his arm. He turned; it was Lauren Price Miller. Her eyes were even more bloodshot and her face was so puffy, it took a split second to recognize her. "Can I talk to you for a minute?"

Hunter followed her into a chandeliered hallway; she opened a door and entered an empty meeting room, then closed the door.

"I'm suing," she said, crossing her arms. "I talked with my lawyer and my family." She pressed a clump of pink tissues over each eye. Her voice was raspy and she spoke so fast, Hunter had to really focus. "First, we think our parents' death is suspicious. The police told us, they can't investigate anything because the night Mom and Dad died, their officer checked for clues. No struggle. No forced entry. No nothing."

"Do you think someone killed them?"

"They had no enemies," Lauren said. "But look out in that room. All those people want their house! And that bitch real estate agent—" Lauren sobbed into the tissues.

Hunter put his arms around her. She was trembling as violently as when he and his Bud unit spent too much time in the frigid water, and their lips would turn blue. On the verge of hypothermia, or past it.

"Mrs. Miller," Hunter said. "While it does look bizarre on the surface, even the autopsy reports showed no foul play. Sometimes unexplainable things do happen. I've even approved their life insurance claim."

She pulled away and glared up at him with glassy eyes. "We decided to sue the life settlement company that won't give us any answers."

"The life settlement company?" Hunter asked.

"Somebody is getting 20-million dollars now that my parents are dead," Lauren said. "I want to know who it is, and why we don't get it."

"You parents signed away their rights to that money," Hunter said, "after two years. They got paid to sign up, and paid to sign off. They even had an honest option to keep the policy. They were not forced to sell."

"Two hundred grand, compared to 20-million dollars?" She shook her head. "That's just one percent. It doesn't add up. But it will when I get through with this."

Hunter remembered the fraud case that Randy had told him about, when a broker forged the signatures of the womanizing soon-to-be-divorcé. But the Prices had willingly signed up. "I know these policies sound strange on the surface. But your parents' friends, obviously financially savvy people, couldn't say enough good things about them."

"My parents' friends? Their friends who are out there bidding on their dead neighbors' house?" Pain and suspicion and rage shot from her eyes so intensely, the hairs on the back of Hunter's neck stood up. *Somethin' ain't right at The Diamond Lagoon Club.*

76. Washington, D.C.

With a small army of security, Vice President Carolyn Snedegar Taylor stood at the podium in the White House Press Room, facing a sea of reporters from around the world. To her left stood Democratic Senator Gerald Boxley; to her right stood Republican Representative John Donaldson.

"First, I want to thank Representative Donaldson," she said, shaking his hand, "for your courage in introducing this bill that will change the fabric of America for the better."

"And Senator Boxley," she said, shaking his hand, "thank you for your tireless work to garner support for this endeavor all across Capitol Hill and the United States. I guarantee that the American people will reward you with an overwhelming outpouring of gratitude and generosity."

Carolyn turned back to face the podium that she would one day grasp as President. For now, this press conference would help to catapult her there. The Secretary of State had issued a formal apology for the information leak from her office. And the outpouring of cards, flowers and well-wishers from around the world—in the wake of Sheik Sunami il Tabbul's abduction threat—had accomplished exactly what she wanted. Publicity, sympathy, and a clear vision of Plan B.

"The President is so impressed with the nonpartisan support and cooperation of my SOS Rescue Plan," she said, "he signed it into law this afternoon." She didn't want to take questions or explain anything further. It was done. Period. The bill, the law, the press conference, this was all just a formality.

Russell, standing between her and the media corps, nodded and said, "Clarence."

The 30-something, clean cut *Washington News* reporter asked, "Madame Vice President, are you sticking with the five-year structure, that will gradually decrease Social Security checks rather than taking them away cold-turkey?"

"Of course," Carolyn said. "We need a smooth, fair and equitable transition that helps people adjust to the changes. We are doing what's best for America's future, and we appreciate the outpouring of support that we've received from seasoned—" she paused, shocked at her slip. "Excuse me, senior citizens in all 50 states."

Russell pointed to the x-ray thin, gray-haired woman wearing a black pantsuit in the front row. "Ethel?"

"Don't you think, Madame Vice President," asked the veteran reporter for GNN, "that it's rather greedy and cruel of the United States Government to expect hard-working, elderly Americans who earned their Social Security checks—to bail out a system that they didn't break?"

Carolyn radiated empathy. "No, absolutely not. I believe it's incredibly generous and kind-hearted of our ultra wealthy to assist their fellow Americans in meeting the financial demands of the golden years."

Russell nodded toward a young woman in a red suit and heels.

"Madame Vice President," asked the reporter for *NewsNow Magazine*, "Why would the government bail out wealthy financial companies, but ask elderly Americans to foot the bill for Social Security?"

Carolyn almost smiled. "Excellent question, Ramona. The huge difference here is—"

Russell looked up from his BlackBerry, stepped up on the stage, and whispered, "We've got an emergency."

"Ladies and gentlemen," Russell said into the microphone as Secret Service agents ushered Carolyn and the two lawmakers off the stage. "The President is going to speak momentarily about the latest development in the terrorist threats against the United States."

The press corps exploded with loud whispers. They pulled out cell phones, all chattering excitedly to editors and producers as Carolyn stepped behind the curtain.

"Perfect timing," she smiled up at Russell. "That little bitch thought she had me with her financial bail-out question." She turned to her two partners in changing America. "Two of my favorite men in the whole world," she said, slipping back into her accent. "Nice makin' history with you today, fellas."

"I am honored beyond words," Boxley said, beaming like it was his wedding day. Because they were wed in a way that was far more intimate than anyone would ever know. And if he stopped making her happy, she'd get the swiftest divorce that would banish him into silent oblivion.

As for Donaldson, he looked like he was about to heave. "You alright?" she asked sweetly. Oh, how she loved technology. Who ever would have guessed that some words pulled off a satellite—and some pictures taken by a camera the size of a shirt button of boys bein' boys together in the nude—could give a girl so much power.

Carolyn grasped Donaldson's arm as if she were concerned about him. "Sweetheart, you look white as milk." She glanced around. "Don't let anybody take your picture in this condition. We want to maintain the appropriate decorum of a family values Congressman that America loves."

She cast a triumphant stare down into his wide, fretful eyes. One wrong word from that little cocksucker, and he'd be downright disgraced off the Hill.

Carolyn's head swirled with the intoxicating rush of power and privilege and prosperity. Every bit of it whet her appetite for more.

77. Diamond Lagoon, Florida

Rosalee especially liked Orders that let her be creative. Like 78-year-old Edna Jacobs. Lethal allergy: nuts, nut oils, nut butters.

So, when Edna joined her girlfriends for their weekly Bridge game at their country club, she was always harassing the waitress about her food allergy. "Make sure my french fries are cooked in corn oil," Edna nagged to the same waitress, every Wednesday afternoon. The waitress, who was Rosalee's friend, would always recount hilarious stories about the spoiled seniors.

So it was easy, on her friend's day off, for Rosalee to pose as the new waitress and serve up a heaping pile of fries—fresh out of bubbling vat of peanut oil.

78. Washington, D.C.

As Boxley strode into his office suite, his top two aides followed, and briefed him on legislation that he'd need to review and vote on.

"Good afternoon, Senator Boxley," his secretary said from behind the large desk facing the entrance. To the left and to the right were hallways leading to office suites for himself and his staff. "Here are your messages, sir." She handed him pink slips as his dog came bounding down the hallway from his office.

"Hey Katrina," Boxley said, rubbing her soft head. "How's my girl?"

His aides spoke as he strode past dark bookcases and flags of Louisiana and the United States. They followed him into the huge, vaulted chamber of his office, where he hurried toward the large television facing his desk. All the while, he felt as though his oxblood wingtips never touched the floor as he floated with the euphoria of power and success created by his partnership of a lifetime with Madame V.P.

"I'm here to announce," the President said live from the podium where Boxley had just stood. "That we are intensifying security measures at all airports and waterways, starting now. You have all seen the videotape of Sheik Sunami il Tabbul that was recorded in 2003. That videotape was discovered recently in a safety deposit box at MagnaCorp's flagship bank in New York City. And on that tape, made two years after the September 11th disaster in 2001, Sheik Sunami il Tabbul promises to inflict economic ruin on the United States."

Boxley's staffers left the room; he sat at his desk with the dog at his feet. It was amazing how well orchestrated this day had become. From his press conference with Carolyn to the President's warning, this was the government's story and the government was sticking to it. The American people had no choice but to believe it all, whether it reflected reality and the truth, or not.

"Not," Boxley whispered jubilantly. After this press conference, he would log onto the website for his Swiss accounts and make sure his latest payment had cleared. Then he would make sure the other financial transactions were pumping into their appropriate places.

Agent K had installed the Secure Socket Layer to ensure the safest transfer of funds over the Internet. The key encryption on the Eldorado system was absolutely foolproof. It was secured by digital certificates—electronic files that served as a sort of online passport for entry. And only three people on Earth knew of the Eldorado SSL's existence—himself, the brains behind Eldorado and Agent A, who believed the transactions were routine government business. Juan certainly was doing the work to fill its coffers, but he would remain forever oblivious to anything beyond the portal and the crates of cash in his airplane. His inappropriate questions would go forever unanswered.

"...mastermind," the President said. Even the Commander In Chief was unaware of Eldorado. Boxley focused back on the television. The President, with his perfect silver coif and sickly-pale skin, stood behind the podium in a navy blue suit and red tie. "While we cannot directly pinpoint how he could have masterminded that financial crisis that is rocking the world of finance around the globe, we do know that he is a dangerous man who speaks dangerous words. And we are protecting America, and our Vice President, as the superpower that we will always be."

The furrows of age, worry and sun damage across his forehead deepened as he said, "Our war against terrorism continues in Iraq and the Middle East. We are continuing our efforts to find Sheik Sunami il Tabbul. But I am issuing a grave warning to you today. In this video," the President said, "Sheik Sunami il Tabbul vows to launch yet another attack on American soil. That is why, as you travel for business or pleasure in the coming weeks, you will experience increased security at airports, and international borders. This applies to both foot traffic, cars and buses, as well as boats and other water craft."

Boxley wished the previous President had been this vigilant about protecting his constituents from the promised wrath of Katrina. How many lives would that have saved?

"I am pleading with you now," the President said, "to please take your utmost patience and understanding with you when you travel in the coming weeks. The fine men and women who serve the TSA and NSA are only doing their jobs and following directions when they ask questions or search your belongings—"

"Only doing their jobs, poor chaps," a man said with a British accent. "A likely story."

"What'd you find?" Boxley asked without turning away from the Commander in Chief.

"This Hunter Knightly character, he's a real nosy nuisance," Agent A said.

"Who's behind him?"

"Independent contractor for a long list of insurance companies. Investigates all kinds of claims. Fire, theft, auto accidents, life insurance."

"Republican connection?"

"None. All the way back to grade school, the guy isn't the political type."

"Family?"

"Rich. Horse-breeders. Daddy's a registered Republican, but quiet about it."

"This Knightly fellow fancies himself as a real Sherlock Holmes. And he's getting a bit too close for comfort." Agent A handed over pictures of Hunter at Sailfish Marina, on Sunday—

Just 15 minutes after Juan and I were there.

"Why was he there?" Boxley asked as the agent gave him sheets of paper listing every phone number with which Hunter had sent or received phone calls and text messages.

"None of his calls raise a red flag for what you're looking for," Agent A said. "Except he did try to dial the Vice President. That number was disconnected on Inauguration Day."

"How'd he get Carolyn's old cell phone number?"

"They were classmates in high school. Attended a reunion together last April."

Boxley shook his head. "I don't like this at all. He's a SEAL. Could have an alias or some other device for communication. Find out." Boxley was sure that Hunter was sent by Republican agitators who hated the President, who wanted the White House in four years, and who wanted to crush any chance Carolyn had at success as a woman VP. This pretty boy investigator from Kentucky couldn't possibly be just that. "There's got to be somebody behind him. With a far deeper motive than his jive little insurance cases."

"We'll dig deeper," the agent said as Boxley scanned sheets detailing Hunter's Internet records. They showed his perusal of insurance sites, both for companies and for media reports about the industry, and a whole array of aviation sites. And a visit to The Genuine Insurance Group's registration page for a wealth planning luncheon in Florida.

"Way too close for comfort," Boxley said. "Find out what he knows and who he's shared it with. Hmmm. A pilot. Should be easy to bring him down when we're ready."

79. Diamond Lagoon, Florida

An unusual silence filled the black BMW sedan as Ernest drove and Herschel sat in the passenger seat. They had just enjoyed the "early bird senior special" buffet breakfast at Carmine's Café.

"That article," Ernest said, "It's got me thinking. I don't like the sound of these life settlements anymore."

"You got your money, so what?" Herschel said. "Don't jump on the paranoia bandwagon. Those lawmakers, that guy from Ohio, they gotta have something to crusade against."

"I did some checking last night," Ernest said, "online. Lawsuits are being filed. Twelve states have outlawed these things. Hedge funds are makin' out like bandits, so much money."

"Okay," Herschel said as they stopped at a red light on the Palm Beach Lakes Boulevard, lined with palm trees and colorful bougainvillea. A construction site at the bridge ahead had orange cones blocking one lane. Ernest and Herschel watched as crews wearing orange vests and hard hats used a jackhammer to break up huge chunks of cement on the bridge. Then a giant crane lifted each piece of cement and lowered it past the sloping banks, down to the edge of the canal.

With an impatient tone, Ernie said, "They're always working on the roads here."

"I know what's really bothering you," Herschel said. "The policies. Why worry about something that's over and done with?"

"Think about it, Herschel. Who gets the money on those policies when we die?" Ernest accelerated as traffic proceeded though the green light toward the bridge.

Herschel said, "I haven't thought—"

A huge yellow dump truck pulled out of nowhere. It blocked the road, just before the bridge.

Ernest's choices: smash into the truck. Or swerve off the road and risk bouncing down the ravine into the canal.

He swerved. The car went airborne, then careened down the slope.

Ernest and Herschel yelled. Their seatbelts held them upright. But they were heading straight down the ravine, toward the blue-gray water rushing through the canal.

The car stopped. It jerked, as if caught on something underneath, perhaps brush or a tree stump.

The car creaked, teetering just a few feet from the rushing water. Ernest and Herschel looked at each other.

"Are we dead?" Herschel panted.

"No, but I think somebody wants us to be."

80. I-95 and Palm Beach Lakes Boulevard, Florida

"Hell naw!" John-John shouted in his Corvette as he passed over the bridge. "Them m'uh fuckas ain't saved by a fuckin' tree branch!" As if the Grim Reaper had heard John-John speak, the crane lifted a giant chunk of concrete and—as it had been doing all afternoon—swung it down the ravine to drop it beside the water. This time, though, it was like a giant bowling ball—

Strike!

And the BMW goes down... upside down in the water... rushing down the canal... sucked under the surface.

"Double the money, baby!"

81. Kendall-Tamiami Executive Airport KTMB

Meredith's drama was about the last thing Hunter wanted to hear through the phone as he strode across the tarmac.

"I want a divorce," she cried. "I can't go on another minute feelin' like mah husband doesn't give a damn about me. I deserve better—"

He savored the hot sun on his face, the deep *whirr* of planes on the ground and in the sky around him, and the visual of so many outstretched wings, tails pointing up to the heavens, and perfectly curved bodies—all resting daintily on those little wheels, held in place by multi-colored triangular blocks. His every step crunched tiny pebbles on the asphalt. Hunter inhaled; the scent of jet fuel made him a little dizzy, as did Meredith's accusation:

"Admit it, Hunter, you got a girlfriend down there."

Hunter felt numb. Not with sadness or disappointment, but with complete indifference. Maybe it *was* time to free himself of this. If he weren't on the phone right now with Meredith, listening to her jealous rant that had absolutely no basis in reality, then he could be using his brain energy to answer all the questions in his head about the Price case.

And calling Commander Buck. Hunter had just watched the President's press conference about increasing security in the air, on land and in the water to protect against a terrorist attack. Just what a SEAL was trained to do.

They need me. Now.

Meredith's voice slapped his ear. "She's probably half my age. With hot poppin' ovaries that can't get enough of Hunter Knightly."

Hunter's plane glimmered in the sunshine about 100 yards away. It sat in a row of planes that included a banana yellow, twin-engine Cessna. It blocked the other aircraft so that they appeared as a mere line of noses and propellers. A red one, a black one—

"I bet she wears a tiny little bikini and has you chasin' her all over the beach," Meredith said. "You never want to go out with me 'cause you probably dance the night away with her."

Hunter strode past the yellow plane, holding the phone several inches from his ear. Why was he even still on the line with her? Why hadn't he just hung up?

"Let me know when my bride comes back," he said flatly. "'Cause I don't know this person who's on the line right now."

Click.

Hunter stopped and dialed Commander Buck. A Navy mission would take him far and away from the witch back home.

"Stallion Six," the Commander yelled over a siren. "I may have a job for you. Doin' a drill right now. I'll be in touch."

Hunter clipped his phone back onto his belt. But he froze mid-step. Because he was standing face-to-face with the most beautiful airplane—

The red hot-rod that left me in the dust a few days ago. And there, on the opposite side, below the plane, were two black boots extending from black denim pant legs.

Hunter had to see this guy. And this baby close up.

82. Las Vegas, Nevada

Smitty loved insects, snakes, rodents and anything else that qualified as a creepy crawly. As a kid, he was always dangling spiders in girls' faces. He had a pet snake until it died of old age.

So now, when his fact sheet for an Order said, "severe bee allergy," he knew exactly how he'd go after

69-year-old Robert Levy. The widower lived alone in a posh senior citizens complex. And he loved growing exotic flowers so much, he had a little greenhouse built onto the back of his condo. He tended his flowers every morning as he drank coffee and read the newspaper at that little café table amongst the plants. Of course he was adamant about keeping bees away from his flowers.

But that was like keeping dogs away from bones, cats away from mice, men away from women.

It just wasn't natural. So Smitty gave the bees their chance to pollinate all over those pretty flowers—by slipping a dozen of the buzzing little stingers through a ventilation slat on the greenhouse. He did it at night, after capturing the bees from that hive out behind the bike shop. All he'd had to do was shake them up, piss them off and turn them loose.

Then, he was pleased at the job well done when he heard on the news that day—his Order was found dead in his greenhouse after suffering an allergic reaction to multiple bee stings. A natural tragedy.

83. Kendall-Tamiami Executive Airport KTMB

In the bright Miami sunshine, Juan stood before the open cargo door on the right side of his plane. He was about to make a quick trip to handle some business that he'd been anticipating for a long time. His top-secret rendezvous would reward him for a job that, so far, was being executed with outstanding stealth and efficiency. And tonight it would give him another chance to pick the lock securing the secret of Eldorado's treasures.

An even stronger sense of urgency had sparked within him today, when the radio in the hangar announced the President's warning about terrorist threats. The Armageddon-type tone of that report had only intensified

Juan's impatience to get the hell out before war or some other disaster brought Eldorado to a screeching halt.

He never spoke to anyone at the airport, except for the one and only mechanic who was allowed to touch his plane. His Angel had made sure that this guy—a former military jet fighter—was the only person on the planet who could lay his hands on or inside Juan's flying machine.

Wearing his hair in a ponytail, Juan counted the wooden crates in the cargo hold. En route to his rendezvous, he was about to play Santa Claus and deliver these gifts for boys who'd been naughty enough to do a nice job as Santa's helpers. Juan had doubled his list, was checking it twice, and didn't need to be nice.

Not with crates of cash like this. Because for every Order, he got five times what the K.C. Team Leader took. Juan's cuts were coming fast and furious, all going directly into his secret and untouchable accounts in the Cayman Islands. But his take was nothing compared to the Emperor's fortune. It had to be huge.

Mine will be, too. Soon.

Juan counted the crates one more time. He inspected each one to make sure no greedy hands had reached in to grab a brick or two.

The sound of tiny pebbles grinding against the asphalt made him freeze. He listened—

Footsteps.

Juan's right hand went to his pocket. He could shoot right through it faster than anybody could blink. His Angel had made sure that practice on the range, with still and moving targets, had been a big part of his training.

A man in brown leather loafers and khaki pants walked around the front of the plane. He whistled, then said, "This has got to be the prettiest thing I've ever seen." He stepped around the wing and approached Juan.

The guy looked familiar. Wholesome, clean-cut, handsome. Cool if he wanted to be, but he didn't try.

Exuded confidence and intelligence. Fit. His round-neck, long-sleeved blue cotton shirt hugged his broad shoulders, cinched into the cut between his deltoids and his biceps, outlined his buff pecs and tapered down the vee from his chest to his small, flat waist.

His tousled, sandy-brown hair was just long enough to look rebellious, but just short enough to conform in the business world. Clean-shaven face, square jaw, chiseled features, big blue eyes.

And a sincere fascination with the airplane. Wearing gold aviator glasses—

It was Hunter Knightly, from Episcopal. That rich boy goody-two-shoes from Kentucky who was always cock-blocking Carrie. No wonder he'd registered a zero on Juan's threatometer.

Juan let his irritation at this interruption shoot from his eyes as he looked at Hunter and closed the cargo door.

"Just admirin' your plane," Hunter said. "That's my VLJ over there. The blue and white one."

"Nice," Juan nodded. So this was the motherfucker who'd tried to sneak up on him Friday morning.

Hunter removed his glasses. Recognition sparkled in his eyes. "Juan, man, you look different since the reunion. Put on some muscle, grew your hair, got some sun—"

"You don't miss a thing, do you, Hunter?" Juan let his former classmate give him a dude hug.

He flashed back to the reunion, last April, at the Four Seasons in Washington, D.C. Hunter and his wife, a hot blond named Meredith, had shared a banquet table with him, Carrie, and another guy from their class. He'd still looked pale and half-starved, two months after his pardon. And none of his classmates had known that, after college, he'd become a legendary drug lord who reigned up and down the coasts of North and South America, with his own Caribbean island in-between. None of them knew that he'd been in prison while they were climbing career ladders, marrying and having children.

And now, they certainly didn't know that he was sanctioned by the highest of the high powers as Eldorado, with a military-style airplane loaded with crates of cash that he was about to deliver to Killing Crews across America. And they would never know, in the very near future, how or when Juan Pantera Diablo disappeared from society— shockingly rich, immeasurably clever, and immensely pleased.

With all that on his mind, Juan couldn't stop the smile from lifting the corners of his mouth.

"What brings you down here, my friend?" Juan asked.

"Oh, I'm just investigatin' an insurance death claim," Hunter said, running his fingertips along the sleek red metal of the round jet cabin.

Those words wiped the smile off Juan's face. He could feel his Panther eyes sharpen and harden on this harmless creature that, suddenly, looked more like prey.

84. Kendall-Tamiami Executive Airport KTMB

Hunter became as still as those life-or-death moments when even the faint whistle of air up and down his windpipe could cost his life. In hiding, while stalking the enemy, Hunter had always had the ability to breathe with profound stillness and silence. Right now, in plain view, his instincts set his body on survival autopilot.

Because Juan's eyes could set fire to something. Or flash-freeze with a single glance.

"What's a death claim?"

Juan's tone was hard; every word felt like a nail piercing the air. He narrowed his eyes on Hunter in a way that the cats around the horse barns would look at a mouse before they pounced and clawed the little rodent to death.

85. Near Baltimore, Maryland

The private landing strip made it easy to get in and get out. But the icy wind coming off the Chesapeake as Juan stepped from his plane into the limo, made him wish they'd chosen a warmer climate for this rendezvous.

"I missed you," she said, her long blond hair forming a curtain around him as she straddled his lap as soon he got inside. Her dark blue eyes glowed with animal lust as she cupped his face and pulled his parted lips up to hers. The light was dim; her skin appeared darker than their previous meeting.

"This is your reward," she said, her lips close to his, "for serving your country."

Juan was loving every second of this erotic tryst. But he needed answers. Now. The first time, and the handful of sexy interludes since, he had been so thrilled to be free, and so bedazzled by his high-tech toys and mind-blowing privileges, that he'd been content to simply focus on the cash, the chicks, the airplane and the Orders. But things were different now.

"Who are you." Juan's voice was raspy as he spoke not a question but a demand. He grasped her stockinged legs and squeezed her hot thighs. Then he reached a hand under her hiked-up skirt. He ran his knuckles against the hot, damp expanse of silk between her legs.

"Ah," she cried, tossing back her head. She raked her right hand down his chest, his stomach. On the outside of his jeans, she grabbed the outline of his rock-hard rod. He pried her hand off.

"Who are you."

"Your Angel," she whispered. Her hot tongue trailed the edge of his ear; she sucked on the lobe. "That's all you need to know."

With a sudden jolt of machismo that was half angry, half lustful, Juan combed his fingers up into her hair, behind her ears. Tonight he would drill the answers out of her, giving her what she wanted, and getting what he needed: information that would help The Panther defeat the secret mastermind of Eldorado and execute Operation Vanish.

Tonight, he would get an explanation for what Boxley meant when he said, "You know we had a claim denied." Then, that rich boy classmate of his, on the tarmac today in Miami, saying, "insurance death claim." What the hell did that guy mean by "death claim." Who or what was he investigating? K was finding out just what that pretty boy from Kentucky was working on.

"Who do you work for?" he demanded as she did a slow grind on his lap.

"Who says a girl can't be an independent contractor?" she whispered with teasing eyes.

"Where does all the cash come from?"

"My friend. Mr. B.E.P. Look him up if you're so darn curious." Her fingers scratched at his belt buckle.

And her evasive sass set off a thousand explosions of rage inside him. He was going to make this *puta*, this whore, tell him everything.

She looked into his eyes, then tossed back her head, laughing. "Don't get mad, darlin'. I'm just teasin'. The Bureau of Engraving and Printing. That's where cash comes from."

He ripped open her blouse. Buried his face in her breasts. At the same time, he shoved his hands into her skirt and grabbed two handfuls of ass.

"Oh, yeah!" she moaned. "I *loooooove* that." Her fingernails raked through his hair.

"Tell me what I'm doing," Juan ordered, "having people killed."

She stiffened, then sharpened those dark blue eyes down at him.

"One more question out of you, Mr. Juan Pantera Diablo," she playfully touched her fingertip to his lips, "and I'll trade in your pretty little airplane, your yacht down in South Beach, your island in the Bahamas, and your freedom."

He glared up at her. How did she know about Casuarina Cay? That cloying paranoia, the kind he hadn't felt since his demise before prison when he was hooked on his own stuff, set off a barrage of fears.

She whispered, "And accidental deaths happen in Bogotá, too. I would hate for anything to happen to your sweet little *Abuelita*."

A red flare of anger exploded inside him. Nobody threatened The Panther or his family.

Was she tracking his every move? Was the Green Box on his plane also a device that enabled her—with K's help—to monitor him? All the electronic gadgets had the capacity to serve as spy tools for her to watch him. His phone, the laptop. After all, the Killing Crew Leaders had access to every kind of audio and video surveillance device one could imagine. And they all somehow came from the same source:

This horny bitch on my lap, who thinks she can threaten me and get away with it.

She kissed his forehead. "We've kept your old cell available, just in case things don't go right for you, out here in the lap of luxury." She touched her nose to his and looked into his eyes. "Now fuck me like you mean it, Mr. Juan Pantera Diablo, and I'll forget we ever had this little conversation, ya hear?"

86. Lexington, Kentucky

With one step into his home office, Hunter knew someone had been going through his things. And a single paperclip confirmed it. It was the small, standard silver kind, holding a copy of the insurance application that Dr. and Mrs. Price had filled out for their life settlement policies.

A paperclip always left a slight imprint on the top and bottom sheets of paper. That imprint was only visible if the paperclip moved. This one, it appeared, had both been moved and removed, because it was slightly bent. And once its looped structure was pried apart to hold a document, it could never be as flat as it had been coming out of the box.

But who the hell would have gone through his paperwork?

Meredith never gave half a damn about what he did in this office. In fact, he couldn't remember the last time she'd actually come in here, except at Christmas when she wanted more money to buy a dress for dinner at his parents' house.

Thank God she was staying with her mom on the other side of town. His "welcome home" last night had been a note on the kitchen counter saying she needed some time away. He would give the pink T-shirt from Sailfish Marina to his sister.

The Navy theme song played on his phone. That could only mean one person: Commander Buck.

"Yes!" Hunter exclaimed. Maybe he could turn around and leave home just as quickly as he'd arrived.

"Commander Buck," Hunter said.

"Stallion Six, we need you down here. I'm putting together a Special Forces unit for a clandestine mission that should be a piece of cake. Next week, expect to hear from

Rear Admiral Ellis. Be ready to come down here to Mayport for your assessment."

Hunter smiled. He would pass those evaluations for physical fitness and mental stress with flying colors. "Thank you, sir."

"We can use your brains and your brawn," Commander Buck said. "Let your wife know, you could be gone awhile."

Not a problem, if this silent house was any indication. After he hung up, Hunter felt a new urgency to resolve his open cases and figure out who the hell had been in his house. As he opened his laptop on his desk, he saw a hair. A black hair, about four inches long, across a white envelope.

Meredith would never have an affair. And if she were that crazy, she'd at least have the decency to go to a hotel.

He opened his laptop and logged onto flightaware.com, where he punched in the tail number for Juan Pantera Diablo's plane. That website enabled anyone to punch in a tail number and track the whereabouts and flight record of any plane in the air. The tail number could also reveal the airplane owner's name and address, and details about the aircraft, such as make, model and year it was built.

Hunter, of course, had made a mental note of Juan's tail number: PAN3R. He punched it in. Red letters popped up on the screen: "BLOCKED."

He punched into his favorite "people finder" websites that required special access codes that he had as a retired SEAL. But every time he typed in Juan Pantera Diablo, the response was "name not found" or "no matches found." He went to their mutual high school's website and clicked onto the REUNIONS page. Hunter knew a picture was posted there of himself with Meredith, Juan, Carrie and three other valedictorians. He had seen it. So had

Meredith. But now it was gone. The only hit he got was a 20-year-old article on a Juan Rodriguez, a Colombian drug lord. Wrong guy.

Hunter called A-K. "Hey, man, I need you to do a check on somebody."

"Anything for you, Stallion Six. I'm still earnin' that airplane ride."

"Name's Juan Pantera Diablo, D/O/B August 20, 1964, Bogotá, Colombia."

87. Las Vegas, Nevada

"Bingo!" Smitty's first list of Orders included an old couple that had just bought two top-of-the-line mountain bikes to ride around their huge property just outside of town.

Smitty just happened to know of a great trail for them to try. He even gave them a map, with helpful instructions to increase speed up the hilly little stretch that can be tricky for slow bikers. Oops, he forgot to tell them that just over the hill was a cliff…

"Double Bingo!"

88. Lexington, Kentucky

Hunter wasn't going to tell Randy or anyone else about his upcoming Navy mission. But his buddy sure could help sort through all the question marks clogging his mind. So he called Randal.

"How 'bout we fly over to Louisville for lunch? I got a hankerin' for a good ol' Kentucky Hot Brown?"

Randy whooped. "My lucky day. An airplane ride *and* a chance to blow to my diet to smithereens."

Hunter chuckled. "Meet 'cha at the airport faster than you can say, 'fattenin' as hell'!"

"Bye!"

Twenty minutes later, Hunter was sitting at the computer terminal at the airport, checking the weather between here and Louisville. The sky was broken, but calm. A short time after that, he and Randy were cruising at 4,000 feet, according to IFR altitude, over the snow-dusted horse farms of central Kentucky. Hunter looked down at the brown landscape dotted with mansions, frozen ponds, clusters of barren trees and endless wooden fences that separated one farm from the next.

"Man," Randy said, scanning the avionics suite. "This makes my plane look like something the Wright brothers flew."

Hunter chuckled. "Can you imagine if they were alive today and took a ride in one 'a these babies?"

"I guarantee they'd blow a wad at the first engine cycle."

"Don't let your momma hear you talkin' like that, Randal."

"You look stressed," Randy said into the little black microphone extending from his headset. "To the average observer, you look like your usual cool self. But to me? Somethin's jackin' you from the inside out. Spill it, Fly Boy."

Hunter gripped the black leather-covered yoke. He glanced at the GPS screen; a short magenta line extended from Lexington to Louisville over the lime green map. The gray airplane icon rested on the line just a millimeter outside of Lexington. "This is a 12-minute flight. We'd have to fly from here to Australia for me to tell you everything that's on my mind."

"Nope," Randy said, "got too much work waitin' for me back on my desk for a trip Down Under. How 'bout the abbreviated version of *The Life and Times of Hunter Knightly?*"

"I don't know, Randy. This is a big book. Pick a chapter: rocky marriage, suspicious life settlement seminar, mysterious death of wealthy couple, vulturistic real estate racket, and sinister high school classmate. Oh, and someone's been in my house, snoopin' in my office."

"You got my eyes poppin' like ping pong balls over here," Randy said, his gray eyes wide with shock. "What the hell are you sayin'?"

Hunter scanned the three screens. Everything looked good. "I'm thinkin' that a couple of these things might be related."

Randal said, "Let's see, the sinister high school classmate is having an affair with your wife while you were out of town, and he snooped in your office, while you—"

Hunter made a play buzzing sound. Then he imitated a game show host and said, "You're *wrong!*" And he hummed a game show melody.

"Okay, I'll take conspiracies for three hundred," Randal said, barely stifling his laughter. "A sinister real estate agent turned life settlement broker who's also Hunter's high school classmate is the son of a rich couple whose death puts Hunter's marriage—" Randy doubled over with laughter.

The plane bounced a little, up-down, up-down. The sudden turbulence made Randy stop laughing and say, "Sorry, Fly Boy. That is some crazy shit right there. However you string it together."

Hunter shook his head, wishing the image of Juan's eyes would erase from his thoughts. How fascinating that two light brown irises around two black pupils, and centered in white, could silently project such potent evil and violence. Hunter had only seen eyes like that on a dictator who had killed millions of his own people.

"This guy's eyes," Hunter said, "when I saw him today at the airport in Miami, his eyes were evil and mesmerizing and stunning all at once. Like a panther."

"What'd this guy have to do with all the other stuff?" Randy asked.

"Nothing, everything, I don't know," Hunter said. "But I do know, I saw him with Senator Boxley, you know the guy who's in on Carrie's Social Security plan? I saw them together at lunch yesterday."

"I suppose," Randy said with a joking tone, "they exchanged a secret envelope—"

"A big black suitcase, protected by a dog!" Hunter said.

"Get outta here!" Randy said.

"And I suppose you feel like you're being followed because they saw you."

"No fuckin' comment on that one, Randal."

Randy seemed to shrink back into his chair. No trace of humor lingered on his face. "You sure this guy wasn't just in a bad mood?"

"No, he changed. Did a 180 on me when I said I was down there to investigate a death claim. Oh, and he flies a Stealth Bomber disguised as a cute little red VLJ. Saw him flyin' on Friday. Shot away from me like somethin' outta the future."

Randy's round face twisted with bewilderment. "If I didn't know you better," Randy said, "I'd think—" he just shook his head. "You think somebody's after you?"

"If they are, they just decided to mess with the wrong guy."

89. New Orleans, Louisiana

Through his cell phone, Juan followed K's instruction on how to access a special area through the

Internet Portal to watch Hunter Knightly via satellite, from the comfort of his laptop computer.

"I put a tracking device on his plane," K said, "so not only can you physically watch him, but you can also use the Portal's GPS system to pinpoint exactly where he's flying at all times. So you'll know if he's close to you."

"You are one smart guy," Juan said.

"At your service, Mr. Panther. I've been watching all of this guy's electronic activity. He did punch in your tail number on flightaware.com."

"He likes planes," Juan said. "But before we take care of this, I need to find out who he's working for."

"Besides an insurance company," K said, "it looks like he's just a curious guy who's stumbled into a jungle that's much darker and thicker than he ever imagined."

"A good place to get lost," Juan said, watching the blue plane shoot through the skies over Kentucky.

90. Washington, D.C.

This meeting had two agendas: the official one that Russell was rambling about, and the secret one that was playing out in Carolyn's mind. It was all about Plan B.

"The deposits from the Social Security checks are streaming into the fund," Russell said, "with amazing speed and efficiency." Then he started talking about the security measures since the abduction threat.

That led Carolyn to worry that the clandestine aspects of her SOS Plan could be jeopardized by the increased military patrols in response to the terrorism threat. The President's ailing health also made her wonder, *What if Boxley got sick or died?* He was running the show; without him, she'd be all the way up the creek with no paddle. What if the only other two players involved were to suddenly meet an unexpected demise?

Thanks to those super-secret money transfers, things were going exactly as she'd planned. She would have access to as much of that as she ever needed.

Russell asked, "Did you see the editorial in the *Washington Times* about how the terrorist threat has actually boosted your ratings?"

"Amazing, isn't it," Carolyn said. Suddenly Plan B became clear as her momma's crystal. She would take that abduction threat and blast right back at 'em, if necessary.

91. Diamond Lagoon, Florida

Stella's stomach cramped with panic as she sat in the big leather pedicure chair as hot bubbles rumbled around her bare feet. With fingertips still wet with pink polish, she pinched the outer edges of this month's glossy *Retirement Magazine*. The pages rattled slightly; she was literally shaking with fear as she read the cover story under the headline, USE CAUTION: ACCIDENTAL DEATHS SPIKE AMONG SENIORS NATIONWIDE. The subtitle said, *You May Not Be As Young As You Feel.*

"Margie," she said to her friend in the next chair. Stella hated the cover design—a skull and crossbones—with the words ARE YOU SAFE? "Margie!" Stella said, as her friend focused on the magazine, her red fingernails also pinching the edges to preserve the fresh polish. "Earth to Margie!"

Her friend looked up. "What already? This article is horrifying. First I read about identity theft being on the rise and older people being the victims. Now this! Makes me want to run and hide."

"I feel a chill," Stella said over the chatter of ladies sitting in the 10 pedicure chairs around them. Classical music played as rows of pedicurists sat on little stools at the clients' feet, scrubbing, massaging, then polishing toenails.

Two young women—one peroxide blond, one Hispanic-looking—returned from kneeling over other ladies' feet here in the exclusive Diamond Lagoon Club Spa. Stella normally loved the nail salon, with its white walls backlit with neon blue, the fresh fragrant flowers everywhere, and these young girls who were always so nice.

One girl carried a tray of bottled water and crystal tumblers, with a bowl of fresh cut pineapple and strawberries. She set it on the small table between Stella and Margie.

"Are you ladies ready?" the blond asked, kneeling in front of Stella.

"Keep my feet in this hot water any longer," Margie said, "I won't have any skin left."

The Hispanic girl smiled. "The heat makes them soft."

"That's how you boil a potato, too," Margie said. "But my feet, I need these tootsies for walking."

Stella lowered the magazine. "Sweetheart, can you please pour our water? Our nails are wet."

"Of course," the blond said, standing to unscrew the caps and let the cold clear water clink the ice cubes in the glasses. "Anything else?"

"Thank you, sweetheart," Stella said as the blond lifted her soapy foot and scrubbed it with pumice stone. Stella felt so shaky; she wanted to call Ernie for reassurance. He'd told her to read this article last night. No wonder he'd looked so worried before they went to bed. She couldn't call him now, because her phone was in her purse, and her nails would ruin if she reached in. She'd tell him later, when the four of them got together for dinner at the Club. "Margie, did you read all these examples of how so many people died?"

"Well, first I can't get over the idea that we thought it was just a problem with people we know," Margie said, her eyes glowing with fear. "But it says there's a rise in deaths by accidents and natural causes all over the nation, and they're seemingly unrelated." Margie shook her head; her freshly coiffed auburn hair did not move. "I'm telling you, it's some kind of death cycle in the universe. The planet Uranus, it rules endings. Things come to an end—"

"Well they sure did for this Colorado woman," Stella exclaimed. Her voice sounded higher than usual. "Found dead on the toilet in an airplane!"

"Ew!" shrieked the blond girl, who looked up from scrubbing Stella's feet. "Poor lady. I heard that on GNN."

Margie continued reading: "...the Chicago man who choked on a hotdog at a Cubs game; the Baltimore man who fell from the balcony of a high rise office building; the two couples whose luxury sailboat sank during their cruise around the Greek Isles; and the woman found dead in her home sauna in California—"

The Hispanic girl said, "The Grim Reaper. Busy guy!"

The blond asked, "That kinda stuff happens, you know, all the time. Are they just reporting it more? Or, is it a situation where, you know, people are just adding it all up so it looks worse than, it really is? Like airplane accidents. You hear about every one of those. But flying is safer than driving."

Margie switched feet, dropping the scrubbed one back into the bubbling water.

"There's an accident statistics guy in the article," Margie said. "People are living longer, so anything that's already going on will have bigger numbers now. Which makes perfect sense. There are more people around to die."

The blond girl looked around at the bustling salon. "That's like so true. More people come for the season, you know, so we have more business. In the summer, in here, it's like a ghost town."

"They hired me," the Hispanic girl said, "just for the snowbirds."

"I want to know if these are truly accidental." Stella felt nauseous with fear. "Margie, you see the sidebar with safety tips? I wish Mark and Suzie had read this."

"Be careful," Margie read, "with everyday tasks that can be risky, such as changing a light bulb with damp hands, or placing a hair drier too close to the bathtub, or walking across an icy sidewalk."

"Is there more?" Stella turned the page and gasped. An icy bolt of terror shot through her. "Margie, go to the next article."

Margie's suntanned face looked gray. Because the headline said, OHIO LAWMAKER WARNS: SENIORS PUT THEMSELVES IN HARM'S WAY WITH 'DEATH BOND' LIFE SETTLEMENT POLICIES. A smaller headline said, *Politician Cites 1774 British Law Enacted to Stop Betting On Humans When Life Insurance Claims Pay Jackpots to Strangers.*

A blue box in the corner of the page described the law that Parliament enacted called the Life Assurance Act of 1774. Prior to that law, it had been perfectly legal for someone to take out a life insurance policy on a stranger, "guess" a date for that person's death, and literally gamble on cashing in if the person died before that predetermined date.

"Just like betting the marble will stop on a number on the Roulette wheel in Vegas," Stella said. The article listed the dates and times that a documentary would air on *History TV* about how this concept could apply to modern times.

"Look at this little box in the corner," Margie said, "about the exploding cell phone batteries."

The blond looked up from trimming Stella's toenails. "That happened to the woman my aunt nursed in Sebastian, Florida, rest her soul. She was 75 and you know, hated technology. But everybody was, you know, telling her she'd be safer alone, with a cell phone. So she got one, but like—" the girl closed her eyes, lined in a way that reminded Stella of Audrey Hepburn. A tear rolled down the girl's cheek.

"Is that what happened?" Margie asked. "The cell phone battery exploded?"

The girl nodded. "Just like that man at the golf course."

"We didn't know him," Stella said. "But our husbands were there."

Margie looked even more pale. That made Stella shiver with fear.

"I'm telling Ernest," Stella said, "to call our lawyer and get us out of this life settlement deal."

"You're already out," Margie said as the pedicurists chatted softly about the peach-scented exfoliate lotion. "Your two years, the television, what? It's done."

"That's what scares me," Stella whispered. "Somebody out there might be looking at me as a living, breathing lottery ticket for a 12-million dollar jackpot. The four of us, that's 48-million! But they can only cash it in if they kill us first."

92. Louisville, Kentucky

When the taxi stopped at the corner of Fourth and Broadway in downtown Louisville, Hunter stepped onto the sidewalk. The collar of his navy pea coat was turned up high, blocking his face. And he wore his gold aviation sunglasses with a navy blue cap. If someone were following him, or using technology for surveillance, there wasn't much he could do about it right now. What with satellites and all, a guy with the right connections could use the government's surveillance system to watch somebody's every move."

"Fly Boy," Randy said, looking up at the antique clock that was a historic landmark for The Brown Hotel, "you sure are spoilin' me. Jettin' off for lunch on a whim."

"I needed a change of scenery," Hunter said as they stepped into the opulent, two-story lobby of the 16-story building. Inside one of the most elegant hotels in the South, they passed a tour guide who was leading several families and saying, "Notice the ceilings. The plaster relief is hand-painted. The style is English Renaissance—"

"I just call it 'the high life,'" Randy said, wearing khakis with Rockports, a navy blue wool sweater that only partly obscured his thick middle, and a beige corduroy jacket. "Feel like I should be wearin' a tuxedo to come in here."

"You're fine," Hunter said as they strode past clusters of plush furniture beneath ornately carved archways over balconies with black and gold grillwork. "The English Grill does have a dress code—" Hunter looked down at his own navy slacks and slim-fitting white turtleneck under his coat. "We're just fahn."

In the restaurant, after they checked their coats, they were seated at a table by the polished paneled walls. Hunter took a dark blue and burgundy patterned armchair with his back to the wall, so he had a clear view of the restaurant.

"Now, Randal," Hunter said, "tell me what you came up with on the life settlement stuff."

"These insurance brokers are incredible," Randy said, "always thinkin' of some nebulous way to make a couple more million bucks."

Hunter laughed as a petite, brunette waitress approached.

"Welcome to The English Grill," she said, flashing a cute-as-a-button smile and an even cuter swath of cleavage inside her open white blouse. "We are a Triple-A, Four-Diamond restaurant and we are non-smoking throughout. May I offer you gentlemen something to drink? Perhaps a glass or bottle of wine from our list of more than 200 wines from around the world?"

"No thanks," Randy said with mock importance, "we cain't drink an' flah."

Hunter smiled at her baffled expression. "We'll take two iced teas, please."

"And we're ready to order," Randy said. "We'll each have one of your non-caloric Hot Browns, please."

She giggled. "Yawl are some characters! Two Hot Browns, comin' raht up. Yawl know the history of your lunch that's been featured on *The Today Show* among other media?"

"Wasn't there some big fancy party in the Roarin' Twenties?" Randy asked in a way that made Hunter smile. Randy B sure could play the humble pie routine to a tee, even though the guy was brilliant.

"Wait, wait," he said, holding his huge, plump hands to the sides of his straight brown hair like he was concentrating hard. "I remember hearin' the story when I was a kid. All the fancy-schmancy folks got hungry after dancin' the night away, and the chef tossed together some bread, turkey, sauce and cheese, with bacon on top?"

The girl giggled louder. "You better stop makin' me laugh before I sit down an' eat lunch with yawl."

Randy tapped an empty chair. "It's got your name—" he glanced past her cleavage to her nametag "—Janice, all over it."

"Thanks, but I gotta werk," she said, walking away.

"So do we," Hunter said, casting a let's-get-serious look at Randy.

"Okay, my crash course on life settlements, while you were workin' the Price case, came up with this." Randy leaned closer. "I think we're sailin' into the

Bermuda Triangle of the insurance industry. To some, it looks breathtakingly beautiful. But to others, something dangerous and unexplainable may, or may not, lurk beneath the surface." Randy shrugged. "All depends on how you look at it, and who you are when you look at it."

Hunter explained how his experience down in Florida proved that point on every level.

Randal responded: "Now, as you know, life settlements started when the AIDS epidemic struck. But after that, the insurance brokers started doing life settlements and selling existing policies on seniors. Then they figured out in a couple years that they could make a commission for sellin' a new policy. They go back to the client who they oversold at the end of two years. The client feels the policy's now too expensive. So the client sells those policies, and the insurance guy gets the commission, comin' and goin'."

The waitress delivered two iced teas.

"Then they figured out a couple years later," Randy continued, "that they could have a client sign up, borrow the money, have none of the client's money at risk, sell the policy in two years. Bam! The clients make money and the brokers make money, comin' and goin'. And they could increase the policy to incredible limits on OPM. Other People's Money. Ya follow me?"

"Oh yeah," Hunter said.

"Then these guys figured out they could borrow money for the client and the client could make their 50-thousand dollars up front."

"Meanwhile, the credit industry is goin' crazy," Hunter added. "These brokers borrow money from 20-plus lending firms in the U.S. and abroad that loan money for life insurance policies. Because heck, if a client dies, they automatically get paid back."

The waitress returned with their Hot Browns. Before each of them, she placed a steaming bowl of melted cheese garnished with strips of bacon and tomato slices, arranged in a star shape on top, sprinkled with parsley and grated Parmesan cheese. Tips of toast and morsels of turkey protruded from the melted cheese, forming little buttery puddles of indulgence.

"I think I've dahd and gone to that great dining room in the sky," Randal said to the waitress as he eyed his food. "Thank you, Janice."

"You'd think the market crash would've slowed all this down," Hunter said, reaching for his fork. He'd have to take an extra long run later, to make up for this. "But it hasn't, 'cause death benefits are guaranteed. Not from what I saw."

"Sssshhh," Randy said, aiming his fork at the sea of melted cheese. He pried up a perfect blend of meat, bread and cheese, all saturated with that mornay sauce. "Don't talk to me while I make love to my lunch."

Hunter chuckled.

After several minutes of eating, Randy said, "Fly Boy, my tastebuds are havin' a party on my tongue. Wasn't gonna tell 'ya, but I've been on a diet for a week. Hate it!" He grasped his thick middle and shook it. "Doc says 49 is no time to play around with my cholesterol. And this apple shape is the ideal breedin' ground for a heart attack."

"I sure hate to be a bad influence," Hunter said sincerely. "Come runnin' with me later."

"Got a personal trainer at the gym," Randy said, "a big Russian chick with guns like Popeye. She's gonna kick my ass tonight. Can't wait."

Hunter watched businessmen enter and leave.

"Back to the life settlements," Randy said, "from where I left off, it evolved even further. These brokers, they'd have the client come into the lunch seminars. The clients signed in, so they had a record of who was there."

Hunter shook his head. "Correction. They take a full financial history, on a little computer that looks like an Etch-A-Sketch. Or you can do it beforehand, online."

A disgusted expression took hold of Randy's face. "That's even worse. Because I found a few lawsuits where some really bodacious life insurance agents would use that information to commit fraud of the most brazen kind."

"How so?"

"They'd take the signature of the guy who attended the seminar, right? Didn't sign up for the life insurance life settlement. He signed nothing but the attendance sheet. He just went to the lunch to see what it was all about."

Hunter nodded. "Okay."

"The broker goes back to his office, draws up all the paperwork for a life insurance application, authorizes HIPAA, etcetera, and uses the guy's electronic signature to forge that signature onto the new life insurance application. Then he has someone else stand in for the client to do the insurance medical exam. They pull the guy's actual medical records from his doctors. Doctor's offices never report to the patient that records have been released, because the *client* authorized it in the first place."

Randal shook his head with disgust. "So the insurance broker gets all this information that's real and accurate. Then, after two years, the broker sells this 10-, 15-, 20- million dollar policy to one of those institutional funds."

Randy's eyes widened with the boldness of it all. "And the guy who attended the lunch, the guy whose signature and medical history and identity were used, he never knew the policy existed."

Hunter remembered that Ohio lawmaker on the news report saying, ""Whether abuse of these STOLIs occurs or not, they invite a rather macabre 'Guido factor' that should send a chill down the spine of every wealthy retiree in America."

Right now, the chill was going down Hunter's spine. Because he had just stumbled into something far more sinister than he'd ever imagined.

And this was no paranoid fiction. It was terrifying fact.

93. Naples, Florida

Stanley Goldstein had hated that aggressive insurance salesman from the minute he'd seen him at the lunch seminar last week at Luxury Suites. But the allure of 50- or 100-thousand dollars cash was so tempting, Stanley had agreed to the private meeting to learn more.

Plus, several of his friends had signed up for the life settlements, and received their money and other perks. Ron got a cruise that his wife loved, the Browns got that cute little sport scar, and Mildred got a television. But something about it just didn't feel right.

And now that he'd read that article in *Retirement Today*, Stanley didn't want anything to do with life settlements or Mr. Wuerthberg. His bowels rumbled again. He'd been so worried about the fact that he'd completed that financial profile for that pretty young girl, Shelley, was it?

And that article about identity theft against seniors in *Retirement Today* only cranked his worry up about 10 notches. "How could I have been so stupid?" He was a sophisticated businessman who'd been investing most of his life. Greed. It was greed. Anytime the idea of free money was put in somebody's face, it was like a naked woman, or a beautiful nurse. No man could help himself from getting excited. And Stanley was guilty of both.

The rumbling in his gut was urgent now. He'd go to the bathroom, then get on the phone with his lawyer. In fact, he'd call his lawyer from the bathroom. This level of worry had a laxative effect on him. And he certainly didn't need anything upsetting his body at this age.

He grabbed his phone and bounded toward the bathroom off the foyer. Alice, setting out cookies and tea for her social group this afternoon, walked past him with a china tray.

"You're going to the bathroom again?" she snapped. "Always so worried. I don't know why you cancelled the free medical exam. You're such the consummate cynic. Always thinking someone's out to get your money."

"They are, Alice," Stanley grumbled. "That's the American way. Even the Vice President is coming after us. She makes that announcement about her idea to save Social Security by making us pay, and the next thing you know, the President is signing off on it as law."

He hurried into the bathroom, shut the door and barely made it in time. Then he dialed his lawyer back in New York.

"The Martin Lewis Legal Group," the receptionist said. "How may I help you?"

"Hi Leona, this is Stanley Goldstein."

"Hello Dr. Goldstein. Enjoy that sunshine. We're getting quite a blizzard up here. Hold on, Mr. Lewis just returned from lunch."

Marty came on the line. "Stanley, I was just about to call you. The firm is trying out this new electronic security system that taps into data networks around the world. It's a safeguard we're using to protect our clients from identity theft."

Stanley's heart beat faster; his gut cramped. "What's that got to do with me?"

"Well I decided to use your name as a test run, strictly confidential, of course. And it looks like you applied for a 15-million dollar life insurance policy last week."

Stanley's head spun. He yelled, "I knew it! That bastard stole my identity."

Marty was silent, then exhaled. "I suspected foul play from the start. You won't believe, this company got access to your personal medical records in your name, and from what I see, you have signed off on all of it. After 40 years of working with you—"

"You know I want to sue the pants off everyone involved!" Stanley yelled. His deep voice echoed off the tiled floor. "I did not sign a thing!"

Stella knocked on the bathroom door. "Stanley, you okay in there?"

Everything was coming into clear focus now. He'd signed that electronic questionnaire at the seminar. That's how they got his signature in electronic form—easy to reproduce and stamp any- and everywhere.

"Stanley," his lawyer said. "We've got the names of the company involved, The Genuine Insurance Group, and pretty straightforward documentation on what they were doing."

"They got a whole lot of people down here hoodwinked!" Stanley said.

"I know," his lawyer said, "I did some checking in the legal community in South Florida. Turns out, the federal court there is handling an onslaught of lawsuits against insurance brokers and agents like this. Hell, they counter-sue as a defense and claim character assassination!"

"For fraud?"

"My associate just attended a conference where the general consensus was, these life settlements are a fancy get-rich-quick scheme for insurance agents," Marty said. "Part of me is like, who is allowing this to continue? Twelve states have already outlawed them."

"Money," Stanley griped. "Money is why. Pay off the right people, you can keep doin' whatever you want."

"Not once these lawsuits come to light," the lawyer said. "I can't imagine that the lobbyist groups for seniors, or the advocates for consumer safety, will let this go on much longer."

"Read the article in *Retirement Magazine*," Stanley said. "It calls these things STOLIs. Stranger Originated Life Insurance. That in itself should be cause for alarm. They never called it that at the fancy lunch at Luxury Suites!"

"I know," Marty said. "The latest legislation, in California, to ban these things, the bill was vetoed by the governor. But if enough voters get outraged—"

"Put me at the top of the list!" Stanley felt queasy. Every cell in his body was humming with fury that he had been duped. At least he'd listened to his intuition about beating the temptation to take 50-grand. Now they were trying to make money off of him and he wasn't even getting paid! Cramps sliced through his gut; he groaned.

"Stanley? You feel alright?" his lawyer asked.

"Not feelin' so good, Marty."

"Get some rest. We'll talk later. All I need is your approval to proceed with both a lawsuit as well as a petition to the federal prosecutor. This is classic fraud. And I'm wondering how widespread a problem this might be in the insurance industry as a whole."

Stanley thought of all the people who'd attended that luncheon. All the people he knew who had gotten life settlements. All the people who were attending those seminars across Florida and wherever else.

"I got a feeling," Stanley groaned, grasping his cramping gut, "it's mammoth."

94. Miami, Florida

Elijah Hanna had been trying to figure out how he could use that nitrogen gas technique to take care of an Order. But he needed just the right room that he could seal off long enough to pump in the gas, then let the room air out, without a trace of the killer fumes for anyone to find. Not in the air. Not on the walls, furniture or carpet. And not in the body.

Now, finally, he was making it happen. In the bathroom of a ritzy hotel. Thanks to one of his many surveillance gadgets, he'd learned that 83-year-old Alfred Burke would be attending a reunion for World War II veterans at the hotel. Since they were coming from all over the country, Alfred wanted to spend the whole weekend there to hang out with his war buddies.

Elijah had loved history class in high school. That was the one subject where he pulled Bs because he enjoyed it. So now, he felt a little guilty about knockin' off a man who'd defended America and the world from the likes of Hitler and the Japanese who bombed Pearl Harbor.

But the dude had lived a long life, got rich and would probably die soon anyway. Plus, he was a chance for Elijah to rake in some more dough. And saying no to Freddie over some tripped out patriotic shit or whatever, well, that just could never happen. A dude could get whacked for that.

But because Elijah did have a tiny soft spot for this WWII veteran, he waited until Sunday afternoon, after Alfred and his buddies had had a good time. Elijah decided to take him down as the man showered for the grand finale dinner.

How? Elijah and the Killing Crew had a huge network of people in the service industry: waiters and waitresses, bartenders, valets, concierges, maids, janitors. For a Benjamin or two, these folks were always ready to help a K.C. Team member get a uniform or enter through a back door or deliver a plate of food.

For Elijah, here at this hotel, his buddy on the maintenance staff had explained the ventilation system. He'd actually switched it off for the entire ninth floor for the 20 minutes that Elijah needed to fumigate the bathroom.

Wearing a gas mask, Elijah aimed a device that looked like a hand-held vacuum that blew out rather than sucked in. Thanks to a key to the adjoining room that the man thought was locked, Elijah snuck into the darkened room when the dude hit the shower. Then he left just as quickly.

That put him five grand closer to getting that new motorcycle.

Cha-ching!

95. Lexington, Kentucky

Framed by the huge open doorway into one of the horse barns, Hunter's father stood with his arms crossed, his blue eyes sharpening with disapproval. Suddenly Hunter felt five years old, cowering for the scolding that was coming. His father's glare was so intimidating, Hunter glanced away, toward the vast rolling hills of Knightly Farms. He couldn't wait to leave on his new Navy mission. Far, far away from this feeling that he could never be good enough. And that he wanted no part of being bossed around by his father every day.

The late afternoon wind whipped the bare branches of sourwoods, tulip trees and maples. Ice crusted the lake; snow dusted the training track. The rows of white horse fencing looked stark, almost eerie, against the browning grass.

"I wanted you to come and take a look at this, Son," handing over a large white envelope with The Genuine Insurance Group in metallic blue in the upper left corner.

Hunter's knees felt weak. He should have known that his father would find out and be pissed off. The fact that he wanted to have this conversation outside in the cold, by the barn, meant Dad viewed this as horseshit that Hunter needed to clean up, right away.

His father wore a plaid wool coat, jeans and mud-splattered boots. The tips of his salt-and-pepper waves peeked out from under an orange hunter's knit cap. The weathered ruddiness on his broad face made him look extra stern in the cold that pinkened the tip of his nose.

"I know you were just down in Florida and I'm wonderin' why you would use my name at a thing like this. You know I don't do any business with jokers I don't know. Got my team 'a folks I've had since b'fore you were born, and don't need any city slicksters tryin' to sell me some snake oil."

Hunter looked into his father's angry eyes. "The only way I could get into the seminar for my investigation was to say I was representing my parents. You had to be over 65—"

"Hell's bells, Son! You lied."

"I've told a lot of lies in my line of work, as a SEAL, for the greater good," Hunter said. His gut burned with worry that an unscrupulous insurance agent might use Dad's information to commit fraud. "A false identity is sometimes the only way to gain access—"

"Well you can keep your spy tactics to yourself," his father said. "I want you to call these people and tell 'em to take me off their mailin' list, and remove me from their system altogether."

His father stepped into the barn; Hunter followed.

"I just read about how they're usin' older people with assets to steal your identity and do all sorts a' things with electronics," his father said. "Don't want the name Knightly anywhere near any a' that."

His father stepped to a stall where Blue Ribbon Girl stuck her head out and blew a warm welcome. Dad patted the dark hair down her nose. Her giant black eyes glowed with gratitude for the affection. "We love 'ya, girl," Dad said.

A trainer came out of the next stall. "Mr. Knightly, I got Mister Champ's legs iced up and wrapped. Jezeblue, though, she's actin' like she won't eat a darn thing."

"I'll be there in a minute." He turned to Hunter. "You see all this? I worked my whole life so your mother, you and your sister could have a good future. I don't have to tell you, Son, how many vultures start to circle when a man reaches a certain age, or a certain income level. So I expect you to do your darndest, from here on out, to protect your daddy. Not toss him to the wolves."

Hunter nodded. "Dad, I need a little bait to trap those wolves."

96. Miami Beach, Florida

Bianca and Rosalee wore matching gold thongs and spike-heeled sandals—with nothing else. If the two old geezers didn't have cardiac arrest from these lap dances, then the white crystals that Bianca had sprinkled into their drinks would sure do the job. As for the third guy, the windshield of his BMW was getting an interior rub-down right now, with the magic crash gel.

Here in the cabana of this mansion on Biscayne Bay, the men had no idea that this little freak show was their final act.

"Work it, baby," said Order #1 as Bianca's bare ass jiggled over his lap. "I took some Viagra. If you want to make a 1,000-dollar tip, let's get private."

She smiled down into his wrinkled face. Good. They could blame his death on Viagra. Rosalee had just told her about a young guy who'd died of a heart attack after taking that stuff. Either because all his blood went to his dick, or it did something to constrict blood flow.

"We'll see, Sugar Daddy," Bianca grinned. Just a short time ago, before Freddie came along with his easy get-rich-quick scheme, Bianca would have thought this old dude's piddly 1,000 bucks was a fortune. And she would have done anything to get it. But now, she was a businesswoman, making far more than that chump change.

He could be her Sugar Daddy alright. Along with all the other dead geezers who'd fallen prey to her female wiles, never suspecting that the pretty Hispanic chick was truly a *femme fatale*.

97. Heavenly Mountain, North Carolina KMT1

Hunter stood on the landing strip at the top of the mountain, listening to the airport supervisor. Tiny drops of freezing rain assaulted his cheeks like so many needles. The wind sucked the breath right out of his mouth.

"Yep, them thar brakes decided to quit on 'em raht thar," the man pointed a gnarled, oil-stained finger toward the asphalt graveyard for two couples. "Saddest thing I ever seen up here. Them folks had everything in the world goin' for 'em. 'Cept the brakes on their spankin' new airplane, a' course."

Hunter squinted into the wind and focused on a huge tree that was snipped about 25 feet up; splinters of wood shot up like beige stalactites toward the dark gray sky. Bark peeled downward. A charred circle marked the ground.

"By the time they d'cided on a go 'round," the man said, "that little airplane was already givin' in to the pull a' gravity. *Ka-plunk.* That was all she wrote. All any of 'em wrote. Not much left of the aircraft, or the folks."

As the man turned and walked toward the one-story, cinder-block office next to the hangar, Hunter glanced over at his plane. Mother Nature was giving her quite a beating right now; he'd do best to wait until this storm passed before he tried to fly to his next investigation in Eastern Kentucky, then back home. And if anyone were watching him here in this remote mountain area, they'd have to be doing it by satellite. Chances of that, Hunter was sure, were quite small.

"Want some coffee?" the old man said, pointing to an ancient coffee maker and a pot of sludge.

"No thank you, sir," Hunter said, noticing that the office smelled like Ben Gay and cigarette smoke. On the desk, an ashtray brimmed with butts.

The man handed a folder to Hunter. "Raht here's all the paperwork we got on the flight an' the crash. They was regulars, seein' as they was always flyin' b'tween the houses over in Chattanooga and their winter places down in Diamond Lagoon."

"Florida?" Hunter asked. "My information said the two men owned a string of bed-and-breakfasts along the Outer Bank, with a winter place in Myrtle Beach."

"Florida, too," the man said. "Those two guys did everything together. Best friends, business partners, co-pilots. Even married a pair a' sisters. So 'course they got their warm-weather get-aways in the same place. You ever heard 'a Diamond Lagoon?"

Hunter was about to say, *Boy, have I ever...* when another man, wearing a business suit and dark overcoat, stepped into the office, calling, "Earl?"

"Eh, Mr. Stokes, see you're bravin' the elements in your fancy clothes. This here's—" he turned his tobacco-leathered face toward Hunter "—son, what's your name again?"

"I'm Hunter Knightly. Pleased to meet you." Hunter extended a hand to the 60-something man. An inch or two shorter than Hunter, he had a close-cropped silver beard and mustache and a humble look in his brown eyes. The man looked authentic, but if someone could break into Hunter's house and look through his things, then someone could certainly pose as a legitimate person just to get close—and inflict harm.

"I'm Ted Stokes," the man said, shaking his hand. "Lawyer for the estates of Mr. and Mrs. Meyers, and Mr. and Mrs. Hartley. I know you're investigating the insurance claim on the airplane. All the authorities have officially deemed this crash and the four deaths as purely accidental."

Hunter nodded, wondering why this guy was telling him what he already knew. The NTSB report had attributed the crash to brake failure. And the FAA had issued an A.D.—an airworthiness directive, requiring the inspection of equipment that involved any and all parts associated with braking—on all related aircraft before further flight. All that was pretty much an admission of equipment failure.

"Both my clients were meticulous about record-keeping and staying on top of their investments."

"Makes your job a little easier, doesn't it," Hunter said, glancing toward the window; a sheet of rain blew past. Standing around the mountains of North Carolina to indulge idle chit-chat was not on Hunter's agenda today. Hunter flipped open the victims' crash file; it contained a letter on stationary that said The Theodore Stokes Law Firm.

"Mr. Knightly, can we talk in confidence?"

"This is fine," Hunter said. "Earl, can we have some privacy, please?"

"Sure thing." The man headed into the attached garage.

"Mr. Knightly," the man said, "This is a little out of my range of duty, but I'm hitting brick walls in every direction."

Hunter watched his every gesture. Had any of the bizarre cast of characters he'd encountered over the past few days sent this man up here as an assassin or spy?

"Two things just aren't making sense about my clients' estates," Mr. Stokes said. "First, they and their wives signed up for some life insurance policies, I think about three years ago. But they gave up the policies about two years into the deal to some unknown fund."

The man ran a thick hand over his beard, making a bristly sound. "Now I'm no country bumpkin, but I've never heard of a deal like that. And my clients, for some gosh-darn reason, never informed me they were doing this while they were down in Florida."

Hunter's internal alarm rang ominously. Here, now, were three cases within two weeks, all involving couples who'd signed up for life insurance policies and, sometime after the two-year mark when they relinquished the policies, they were mysteriously dead. The policies were being paid to those blind investment funds that had so infuriated the Price's daughter. But in one such case—the 15-million dollars was not paid on the claim that Hunter had denied back in December, because the man had died two weeks before the mandatory two-year incontestability period. Plus, Hunter had discovered fraud, probably driven by an agent and settlement company.

"Now I'm not accusing anyone of foul play," the man said, "even though I am adamant that somebody messed with the brakes on my client's brand-new private jet." He cast a sad look out through the rain-splattered window at the landing strip.

"Hate to play devil's advocate, Mr. Stokes," Hunter said, "but last week the landing gear decided to play hide and seek on me as I approached my destination." He pointed to his plane. "My Baby Doll's as state of the art as they come. But even perfection has its moments."

Mr. Stokes turned a shade paler. He plunked into the creaky chair. "Something's just not right. The secrecy, the lack of information about these policies. So I drove all the way up that treacherous mountain road, when I heard you were comin' to town, to ask you as an insurance guy, what on God's good Earth is happening with these scams called viaticals?"

Before Hunter could respond, the man said, "Christ, I've called everybody and their brother to get some answers on why in the world my clients would give up 30-million dollars worth of life insurance. None of these companies I call—from customer service on up to the CEO's office—not a one of them will tell me where those policies went or who's collecting my clients' 30-million dollars now that they're dead!"

98. Heavenly Mountain, North Carolina KMT1

Still in the airport, Hunter listened as the lawyer talked fast and perspired.

"I've sent several threatening letters to the insurance company. No response whatsoever. And I got a buddy, former CIA type, he did some checking for me. Found out the policies went to some fund called LivesVest, but couldn't find anything about it, anywhere."

Hunter spoke in a calming tone: "Mr. Stokes, I want you to visit a couple websites for a crash course on these policies. Some folks call 'em viaticals, but the term I keep hearin' is life settlements or STOLI." He pulled his business card from his pocket with a small pen and wrote down his favorite insurance industry websites. "You can learn a lot from these sites."

Mr. Stokes put the card in his breast pocket. "I don't know. I just got a bad feeling. Like somebody's behind this and they know I'm onto their scheme. And their houses—"

"What about their houses?" Hunter asked. What the hell was the connection between life settlements, Diamond Lagoon real estate, and dead rich people in their seventies?

"This real estate agent called me about an auction," he said. "My clients had no children. I'm the only person who's authorized to make decisions about their estate. So their houses on the golf course, near West Palm—"

As the man removed his coat, rain pelted the window. Mother Nature needed to do her thing and clear things up so Hunter could fly the hell outta this eerie little airport.

"My clients and their wives, they were always joking about how they had the newest houses in the subdivision, and how the snowbirds from Jersey and New York and Chicago and Philly would 'kill' to get their hands on their waterfront real estate." The man ran his palm over his sweaty forehead. Was this man crazy all the time? Or was something making him insane with fear?

"Mr. Stokes," Hunter said, "has anyone threatened you?"

"Can't say that they have." The man stood and poured a cup of the sludge Earl had offered earlier.

"Well, Mr. Stokes, I know these life settlements sound strange. But from what I've seen and heard, the allure to wealthy people like your clients is that they get 'free money' just for signin' up."

The man sipped the coffee, then grimaced. "Free money! Is that like fire that doesn't burn? Sleeping with your eyes open?"

The guy had a point. His gaze darted out toward the storm. "In school, there was a word they taught us about things that contradict themselves. Free money, yeah, right. That's the biggest oxymoron I ever heard."

99. Washington, D.C.

Carolyn had a suitcase packed, just in case she needed to execute Plan B. How could she ever thank Sheik Sunami il Tabbul for providing this tremendous opportunity to cover her tracks, if necessary? The handgun—straight out of the hand of a dead Iraqi soldier over there in Baghdad—was in a box under the bed. Using that to off the Secret Service guys would make it look like a legitimate abduction, with the bullets traceable back to Sheik Sunami il Tabbul's turf. She would cut herself, wipe a little blood around the place, knock over some lamps to show signs of a struggle. Then she'd don her Angel outfit and fly away.

And if she had to do this, she would use it someday to her advantage, to win the Presidency. Now she had three ways there: President Anderson could die. Her SOS Plan could make her so popular that she'd get voted in on her own. Or, she would use the potential shock of Plan B to suck sympathy out of voters and get elected on a groundswell of patriotism.

For now, she was ready for any of the above.

For Plan B, she knew just where she'd go. It would be hot. Sunny. Secluded.

She stepped into her walk-in closet, opened and drawer, and grabbed her favorite bikini.

She thought about her passport, but smiled.

Won't need that for this trip. The Angel took care of everything...

100. Lexington, Kentucky KLEX

Hunter turned his phone back on as soon as the airport techie use a red "tug" to push his plane into his personal garage-like hangar. The screen flashed: 10 missed calls. Good, maybe returning phone calls would get his Dad's scolding voice out of his head. During the 15-minute flight back from an investigation in Eastern Kentucky, he had remembered what his Dad always said: *sometimes you wish you didn't know this minute what you didn't know an hour ago.*

It reminded him of Meredith's premarital pregnancy secret. And it had come to mind as Hunter had gone to interview some fellas who knew the man who had killed his wife and then himself. Classic murder-suicide, sparked by the wife's demand for a divorce, and subsequent shacking up with a new boyfriend. For Hunter, the death claim was small and incidental. Another methamphetamine death.

But it did make him ponder all afternoon why anybody would want to force their spouse to stay in a loveless marriage. Like his. What was keeping him with Meredith?

I'll be gone again soon enough. *Maybe for months or longer...*

He'd proven his point—albeit to himself—that because she failed his gold-digger test, he'd forever withhold the life of luxury that she'd sought by marrying him. No children were forcing him to stay, as so many men did, for the sake of the family. And while just a few days ago, he'd thought the perk of her domestic duties was reason enough to stay married, her bitch fits since he'd returned from Florida had stomped all over that idea.

Now, his missed calls included Meredith, his sister Heather, A-K, Randy and folks from the various insurance companies that he contracted for.

"Hunter, I need to talk with you," Meredith said angrily as the first message played. He held the phone to his ear as he walked through the airport lobby and waved at the girls behind the desk as Meredith's message continued, "Call me and—" he pushed DELETE.

"Hunter," his sister Heather said, "I'm out in Versailles and mah truck is stuck in the mud at my client's house. "Don't tell me you're up in the air someplace. Donnie's outta town, Mom took the kids out for pizza, and I don't wanna get chewed out by Dad about mah drahvin' skills—"

Hunter smiled and speed-dialed his sister. "Don't yawl have tow trucks 'round those parts?"

The female version of his voice spoke back: "Hunter, ah have imposed on these gracious clients long enough. Please tell me—"

"I just happen to be headin' in from the airport, on Versailles Road as we speak."

"Hunter Knightly saves my day," she gushed, then gave directions. As he drove, the phone buzzed with an incoming call. The screen said: UNKNOWN CALLER.

"Hunter Knightly," he said.

"Mr. Knightly, Detective Ray Gibbs with the Heavenly Mountain Police Department in North Carolina. Did you know an attorney named Ted Stokes?"

"*Did* I? Or *do* I?"

"I'm sorry, sir. Mr. Stokes' car skidded off a mountain pass in the storm. We found your business card in his pocket. If you have a minute, I'd like to ask you a few questions."

Hunter already knew what happened. Somebody killed that man. But who? And why?

101. Versailles, Kentucky

Heather's black Escalade was bumper-deep in mud. The tow truck guys were connecting their equipment to pull it out.

"We better haul her into the shop an' check for damage," the guy said.

"Mah big BRUH-ther," Heather exclaimed, sloshing over the muddy grass in her boots. The headlights from Hunter's Hummer shined on her shimmery pink coat. The fur-trimmed hood framed her face. Looking at Heather was like staring in the mirror at the feminine version of himself. Same sandy brown hair. Same blue eyes with dark lashes, somewhat pointed nose, full lips shaped like a figure eight, all set in a perfectly symmetrical rectangle of winter white skin. But the similarity ended there because she wore mascara, pink lip gloss and earrings.

They hugged and laughed.

"Don't tell me you're still doin' your massage therapy thing in strangers' houses."

"And if I am?" she sassed, framed by a white columned mansion overlooking a huge but now dark horse farm.

"Tell 'em your brother's gonna kick their ass if they get a hankerin' for anything more than your official services."

"Hunter!" she playfully hit his chest. "Get yer mind outta the gutter! Most of my clients are stressed-out professional women, housewives and athletes recovering from injuries. Besides, I am a happily married mother of two. Donnie's so busy with helpin' Dad on the farm, I need my own work."

"You sure got better luck in the domestic department than I do," he said.

As they drove down the long driveway back to the road, Heather said, "You look stressed. Meredith givin' you grief again?"

"I'm workin' on a real mind bender of a case," Hunter said, turning onto traffic-clogged Versailles Road.

Heather craned to see up the road that, during the day, looked like a huge black ribbon rolling over the Bluegrass hills lined with white horse fencing. "What's the occasion that all eight or nine lanes are bumper-to-bumper? Rush hour's over. Oooh, I know! Hurry and drive, Hunter!"

"I would if we were flyin'," he snapped, looking at the river of red taillights ahead of them. "But in a vehicle, you gotta wait your turn, girl."

She reached for the stereo. "Turn on the traffic station. I bet it's that king or prince, from Dubai. I bet he's movin' into Kentucky Castle with all his wives, and they shut down the whole road for his entourage!"

"You got a wild imagination, girl."

"And you don't?"

Traffic moved, then stopped again when they reached the front of Kentucky Castle. Lit from the ground, the 25,000 square foot medieval fortress made of gray stone looked ominous at the top of its 55-acre plot of frozen grass. Hunter had flown over the controversial structure many times, as it was just a quick dash from Blue Grass Airport. Tennis courts, pool and basketball courts, plus plenty of grass ringed the main castle at the center of an enormous square outer wall.

"That place looks as bizarre as all get-up here in the middle of horse country," Heather said. It'd been a source of speculation since a rich man built it for his bride in the late 60s, after she fell in love with castles during their honeymoon in Europe. But the marriage failed during the 70s, and the castle had sat empty ever since. Every now and then, rumor had it that a movie star was going to buy it.

And once, fire destroyed a good part of it, but it had been rebuilt and tossed back into the rumor mill. "Those four turrets look kinda creepy," Heather said.

"Almost as strange as the way we say Versailles," Hunter said, forcing himself to stop thinking about that North Carolina lawyer getting forced off the slippery mountain road.

Heather laughed. "Ah was drahvin' over on Vair-SAILS Road," she imitated playfully. "Gotta love our old Kentucky home, though. The place has boo-coo personality." She giggled. "My eighth grade French teacher used to have conniptions over our pronunciation. The French say *Vair-SIGH*. We say *Vair-SAILS*. All the kids said it as much as possible, just to get her goat."

She cast a concerned look at him. "Hunter, what's gettin' yours?"

102. Lexington, Kentucky

As Hunter drove home, A-K called.

"Stallion Six! I got a name for that company that owns your mysterious investment fund, but the faces on the owner's Bio are changing on us."

"Shoot," Hunter said.

"First, I found a whole slew of these blind institutional-size investment funds, all over the world, seemingly unrelated, that hold a shitload of life insurance contracts." A-K added, "An Arab sheik just sold one to an American company and bought the castle there in Lexington. Insurance for a castle. Nice trade."

"What about the fund that gets the policies for Serenity?"

"It was held by a German fund called LivesVest," A-K said, "which holds several hundred thousand different life policies. Wrap your mind around that one. You know how every star is a tiny blip in a galaxy? That's how these institutional funds are. Freakin' gigantic."

Hunter *was* trying to wrap his brain around all that. But it felt so nebulous, so intangible, despite his intelligence and financial savvy.

"You probably know this, but the richest man in America has invested more than 400-million dollars into one of the three funds in Germany."

"I just wanna know, who owns LivesVest now?"

"MagnaCorp used to own it," A-K said.

"The biggest bank in the world," Hunter said.

"Now I found out that a lot of policies for The Genuine Insurance Group, once they're relinquished after the two years, end up in the hands of a company called Chrisma Corporation," A-K said.

"I just denied a claim for Chrisma back in December," Hunter said. "A STOLI—"

Hunter froze. In that case, could the guy have been the target of some shady plot—as Lauren Price Miller had suggested—with a 15-million dollar price tag on his head? That documentary on *History TV* had talked about laws protecting people from being the victims of stranger originated life insurance policies in the 1700s in England. Back then, people were getting policies on complete strangers, then collecting the money when that person died.

Could a company or an investment fund be doing that right now, in twenty-first century America? Duping educated, successful people who had seven or eight decades worth of life experience and wisdom under their proverbial belts?

Now *that* was something Hunter could barely wrap his brain around. It seemed too huge. Too unwieldy. Too downright evil. Hunter knew of two types of individual investors: those motivated by greed; and those inspired by fear to make investment decisions. This world had plenty of both.

"A-K, tell me what you think of this theory," Hunter said. "What if—when a life settlement policyholder relinquished the policy after two years—then the insurance company sold it to one of these international institutional investment funds?"

"Tell me somethin' I don't know," A-K said.

"Here it is," Hunter said, "Then, someone would put out a hit on the former policy owner, the death would look like an accident, and the policy would be paid off. The institutional fund would get a 10- or 15-million dollar payoff!"

"I'm gonna open me one of these institutional funds," A-K said with his characteristic laugh. "I saw this sweet-ass Maybach in a magazine—"

"After the insurance agent collects the big commission, he may not have a clue what happens after the policy is sold," Hunter said.

"Hate to say it, Stallion Six, but it sounds like you got yourself quite a theory here. Probably a little too far out if you consider this is 2009."

"Then you figure, they're givin' away flatscreen TVs and cars," Hunter said. "Those are trinkets, and 50-grand is pocket change, compared to the 10- or 15-million dollar pay-off!"

A-K said, "Reminds me of when you took me to Keeneland last year. I bet a buck on that long shot, she won, and I took home a couple grand. Tiny bet, huge pay-off."

"I don't have solid answers yet," Hunter said, "but if my theory is true about these five couples—the two in North Carolina and now three in Florida—if some company or fund is havin' them killed, somebody just collected 45-million dollars."

"Forty-five mill, all in a day's work?" A-K said playfully. "The Maybach Fund. That's what I'll call it."

"A conspiracy," Hunter said. "That's what I'm calling this."

That's the word he'd heard on that *TheInsuranceGazette.com* report about life settlements. Ironically, the insurance broker had introduced the concept of conspiracy into the conversation. He was probably using reverse psychology, to deflect suspicion, because it sounded so damn outrageous.

"But if MagnaCorp no longer owns LivesVest," Hunter said, "then who owns it? And who owns Chrisma Corp?"

"Gets sucked into a black hole from there," A-K said. "Like it disappears. I got my guy doin' some super-sleuth work for me on that."

"Come again on who owns LivesVest now?" Hunter asked.

"That's the other million-dollar mystery," A-K said. "I still gotta find out who owns Chrisma. And who owns LivesVest. I'll holla back at 'cha."

103. Lexington, Kentucky

Hunter's investigation kept bringing to mind a conversation he'd had with his friend, Jake McAlistor, a horse trainer at Keeneland, back during the Fall meet this past October. Hunter had been as awed as every other year amidst the full glory of autumn leaves. Those red, orange and yellow explosions of trees against the bright green Bluegrass and the endless horse fencing were pretty enough to take anybody's breath away.

But that day, Hunter hadn't visited Keeneland to hang out amongst the sexy women in stilettos and mini skirts... or chat with the rich-looking owners in the stands.... or even place a bet or two, just for the fun of it.

No, Hunter remembered, Jake had asked him to explain
some serious questions.

"I just don't understand," Jake said as he rubbed a soothing balm on Miss Quick's shin splints after her morning jog around the track. "Why would they do an autopsy on my dad? The man was 82 years old. What's there to find out? He was just old!"

Hunter stood just outside the stall, one of many in rows and rows of white and gray stable buildings bustling with breeders, trainers, owners and stable guys. Jake, wearing boots and a down vest with his jeans, patted the black horse's side as she ripped into a bale of hay hanging beside the doorway.

"The insurance company has to cover all the bases," Hunter said. "Say a guy dies in a car crash. The company wants to know if someone other than the insured guy caused the death."

Jake wrapped white bandages around the horse's legs, from the knees down.

Hunter continued: "Okay, think about the guy who said he was a non-smoker on his life insurance application. Then three, four years later, he's driving in heavy traffic. Drops a lit cigarette in his lap, looks down to brush it off, swerves and hits a telephone pole. Did he die of an accident... or as a result of smoking! If he was smoking, and lied on the application about using tobacco, the insurance company could probably justify denying the claim as fraud."

Understanding sparked in Jake's eyes. "You gotta think too hard in your line a' work, Hunter. For me, all I keep thinkin' about, is how this relates to horses. You know, when we have to put one down for a broken leg."

Hunter's stomach soured as he remembered the first time he'd watched them "take down" a horse that broke its leg during a race. The track staff put up white sheet panels around the animal, right there on the track. Then the veterinarian came and euthanized it with a shot. A collective moan hummed through the packed stands.

"Why didn't they put down Molly?" Hunter asked, referring to the young horse abandoned by her owners when Katrina hit Louisiana. She was taken to an animal shelter, where a pit bull chewed up her leg. It became infected, and was amputated. She was all over the news when veterinarians fitted her with an equestrian prosthesis.

"It's all about the insurance," Jake said. "Molly's the equivalent of a stray dog. No money behind her."

"Insurance money," Hunter said.

"A prized race horse," Jake said, "gets put down if he can no longer race or stand at stud. The horse loses its entire future value. So the owner puts him or her down, and gets the insurance." Jake tightened the bandage on the horse's leg. She whimpered. "I know, honey, we're fixin' them nasty shin splints."

Hunter stepped in closer as several trainers led horses along the covered path leading past the stables.

"And the real value of a thoroughbred ain't even in race earnings. No better proof of that than Alydar."

"Who you tellin'?" Hunter exclaimed. "I will never, until my dyin' day, forget watchin' that Triple Crown finish at Belmont Stakes in New York. I was 13, watchin' from the stands with my Dad. The roar of the crowd, it was like thunder! Alydar sure gave Affirmed a run for the money."

"A close second, three times in a row," Jake said. "He went down in history that day. Sired 10 winners, too."

Hunter added, "That's why Calumet Farm won the Eclipse Award for Outstanding Breeder. Alydar was Proud Papa to Alysheba, winner of the Kentucky Derby."

"And," Jake said excitedly, "Blood-Horse magazine ranked him the 27th best among America's top 100 thoroughbred champs of the century. Of the century!"

Hunter looked into Miss Quick's gentle eyes. "It's a shame all that glory had to end in tragedy."

Hunter remembered the grim and suspicious expressions on faces all across horse country that day back in November 1990, as word spread that Alydar's leg had been shattered inside his stall at Calumet Farm, just a couple miles from Knightly Farms. Rumor had it that the owner of Calumet Farm was flirting with bankruptcy. And when emergency surgery on the chestnut colt failed to save the leg, they put him down.

"That horse had a price on his head," Jake said, "provin' my point about Molly. A stray with no value. Or a famous stallion with a huge insurance policy."

"It was $36 million, right?" Hunter asked.

"Yep, $36.5 million to be exact," Jake said. "Alydar earned purses just over $957,000 his entire career. Stud fees, 'a course, can add a couple more million. So you do the math. Which is more? Alive, earning a couple million bucks? Or dead, worth $36 million?"

Now, as the conversation replayed in Hunter's mind, it was the same dynamic as the life settlement puzzle he was piecing together.

Just like horses, those old people were worth a fortune when they died. A fortune for whomever now owned the life settlement policies. But who was that, exactly?

104. Kendall-Tamiami Executive Airport KTMB

Juan was striding through the airport lobby when he noticed a copy of *Retirement Magazine* on the coffee table. On the glossy cover, under a skull and crossbones, it said, ARE YOU SAFE? He picked it up, flipped through it, and saw the article warning senior citizens about the rise in accidental deaths.

Juan's heart pounded. He sat on the black leather couch and read the articles.

"Mr. Diablo, would you like some bottled water?" asked the girl behind the counter.

"No, Sarah," he said without looking up. Because he was reading the article about life how settlement policies were funding "death bonds." The report said the policies paid huge amounts of money—10- or 15- or 20-million—to an institutional fund after the former policyholder, who was usually elderly, has died.

"Aye, mamacita," he whispered as revelation rushed through his brain with so much force that he felt dizzy. Rage burned through him.

That's it.

They had him working as Eldorado, to orchestrate the Killing Crews across America, to knock off rich old people. Then the evil empire run by the Emperor, the Angel, Boxley, and whoever else was taking the insurance money.

If they had just one hit each state per day, that'd be 50 times 15-million dollars, or 750-million every day. But Juan had at least two Killing Crew Leaders in every state. And they each had up to two-dozen people working for them. And that was just what Juan knew about.

He calculated that Killing Crews of 50 assassins in 50 states... with just one hit each per day... equaled 2500 dead people. If he multiplied that by 15-million dollars on average, that totaled 37.5-billion dollars per day!

And I could be just one of several...

Now the Killing Crew members may not have been knocking off one person every day. But even if they did one hit per month, the leaders of Eldorado would be taking in that much money every 30 days.

Anger surged so violently through Juan's body that he was trembling. He was just a little pawn in the Emperor's deadly game.

I thought my 100K per hit was big time. But it's fuckin' peanuts to what they're raking in...

Who the hell was behind Boxley and his Angel? That blue-eyed blond nympho and that fancy black dude—there had to be a white man behind this. An international terrorist? Some high-powered CEO?

Juan's insides felt like the white-hot embers in the fires he liked to build on the beach and watch until he fell asleep in his hammock. His blood boiled with anxious rage; his muscles trembled with fury.

They're using me. Tossing me crumbs from the massive fortunes that they're earning from my work. Yeah this was far better than rotting away in that prison cell. But if they thought they had the perfect get-rich-quick-scheme, then it was time for Juan to beat them at their own game.

"Mr. Diablo?" Sarah called. "Are you alright? You know that nasty flu is goin' around. You look pale. You feel okay?"

"Never felt more like a winner in my life." He stood and strode out. He had business to handle.

105. South Beach, Florida

As Juan drove along Ocean Boulevard, past the pastel art deco hotels, the expensive sports cars and gorgeous people strutting along the sidewalks, the solution crystallized in his thoughts.

Somehow, all that insurance money was going somewhere. According to that article, it was going into an institutional fund. Juan never bothered to figure out all that stuff about Wall Street or mutual funds or stocks and bonds. He made pure profit, in this career and his previous one. The fewer records, the better. But now he wished he understood. Then again, perhaps a simple perspective was best.

They had an inconceivably huge bank account, fund, whatever, somewhere. The money was being poured into it every day. It happened every time Juan retrieved his list of Orders from the Portal, then delivered them to his K.C. Leaders, who handed them down to their street teams.

Now all Juan needed to do was tap into that fund, that had to be worth hundreds of billions of dollars, if not trillions!

All that money was being transferred in—from countless policies across the country, every day. So who would notice if a little money was transferred out?

Say, 10 measly, one-billion dollar wire transfers, into a secret account in the Cayman Islands.

Then *pouf!* Juan would disappear into the tropical sunset and live happily ever after.

I deserve to live like a king and will do anything to maintain my empire.

106. Miami, Florida

On the deck of his yacht, Juan logged into the Portal. He studied a recent list of Orders. He had to prove his theory. Was the money going into some government account? Or was it being funneled into a private company?

Whoever was masterminding this conspiracy of fortune would be smart enough to keep it all as private as possible. Away from watchdog groups or the IRS or lawmakers looking for a cause to exploit for re-election.

Juan remembered what Boxley had said at their latest lunch at Sailfish Marina: *"Juan, you should invest some of your earnings in a minority company. The government's trying to right the sins of the fathers by giving all sorts of perks to folks like you and me. People of color. People who've been left out of the game."*

When Juan had balked at the intensive application process and government regulations, Boxley had answered, *"So you get a holding company. It serves as a bureaucratic buffer between you and the business. Impossible for anyone to trace or connect you in any way. That's why it's a privately held minority company. I highly recommend it."*

"K," Juan said into the phone as he studied the list of recently executed Orders. I need you to do an electronic tail on a guy named Ernest Bloomfield, Diamond Lagoon, Florida. Tell me any insurance policies in his name, and the beneficiaries."

"At your service, Mr. Panther."

107. Lexington, Kentucky

Hunter had just taken a swim at the health club when Lauren Price Miller called.

"More bad news," she said with a tone that was both sad and angry. "My parents' neighbors, the ones you met in the kitchen? Dead. All four of them."

"Hell's bells," Hunter sighed.

"My lawyer filed a lawsuit against that insurance company for my parents. He said mine is the fifth one he's filed like this. And that the federal court down in Florida is getting bombarded with these lawsuits. Why is this legal? Why is this allowed to go on?"

"I'm trying to find that out myself," Hunter said.

"The lawyer told me that blind fund is called LivesVest. But it's like a phantom entity."

After that, Hunter called A-K. "I need you to trace two policies for me."

"At your service, Stallion Six. I think you're gonna owe me two airplane rides after all this."

"It's a deal."

"The names are Ernest Bloomfield and Herschel Goodman. I need to know who is the beneficiary for their life insurance policies that were handled through The Genuine Insurance Group."

"That'll be easier than you know, my friend. As always, right back at 'cha."

108. Washington, D.C.

Carolyn Snedegar Taylor beamed at her reflection in the mirror inside the luxurious hotel suite. This was workin' out even better than she expected. Not only was she rakin' in enough money to save Social Security and stash away the retirement fund of the century for herself, but she was trouncin' every one of these men who thought they were dominating her.

Starting with that gorgeous Master of the Universe over there on the plush canopy bed. He was waiting for her, after calling every day this week to whisper sweet nothings about their next tryst in their favorite suite. Thanks to that downright thrashin' by The Panther, her body was no longer screaming for satisfaction from this man here who could never deliver what she needed in bed.

But as far as her bank account was concerned, he was the ultimate Romeo.

"Carrie," Neal said, bare-chested with the burgundy blankets up to his toned waist. Even in the bed, without his expensive suits and starched white shirts and silk ties—he still emanated that look that announced "Harvard business school, East Coast Ivy League blue-blood, world-class banker." It was something about his super-clean look; the not-a-hair-out-of-place brown hair, the probing brown eyes, the pampered face and baby-soft, manicured hands.

As she sauntered toward the bed in a thigh-high black slip that hoisted her breasts up, out and on delicious display, she pulled a pin from her hair. His eyes danced all over her as her hair tumbled over her shoulders.

"Come here, beautiful," he said. "I need to show you how much I appreciate you."

She stood at the side of the bed. He pressed a fingertip to the thin black silk; her nipple hardened and made a point through the fabric. "I want you to know, I'm forever indebted to you for helping me bail out on that LivesVest fund."

"Oooh, I like it when you show me appreciation," she cooed. She couldn't wait to take off these damn high heels.

"You came along," he said, pressing his palm to her other breast, "at just the right time. Last summer, with the whole sub prime mortgage crisis, that's when panic struck."

She wanted to laugh. This was his foreplay; talking about a business deal. Then again, The Panther had had so many questions before they had gotten down to business in that limo. Money and power truly were the ultimate aphrodisiac. These bad boys were cut from the same ruthless cloth.

"I was just glad to help, Neal, you know that," she said with her most sultry drawl. "No better way to unload that underperforming fund than to have it get bought by a minority business. You better believe all those minority business assistance programs are helping my friend Boxley turn things around."

Neal smiled. His teeth looked especially bright in the dim light. She imagined that he was thinking: *"I couldn't wait to get rid of that freakin' fund. All those insurance policies, just sitting there. That portfolio gave new meaning to the term 'underperforming.' People are living longer than ever in retirement."*

Did he really think she was too stupid to know that he'd unloaded that specialty institutional fund just in time to shore up Magna's financial statement?

He thought he'd gotten over on her with the fancy finance talk. Telling her that bullshit sales pitch that uncorrelated assets like these were highly prized in the increasingly connected global financial world.

This bastard thinks I'm too ditzy to know that these returns are not dependent on how other financial markets do.

And since he thought she was such a bimbo—even though she was the Vice President of the United States of America—she'd darn well do her best acting job to let him think he was right. And she'd keep laughing all the way to the bank.

"Shame on you, Neal Worthington," she said playfully. "You should be glad modern medicine has folks livin' longer, healthier lives." Carolyn reached for a bottle of champagne in a silver ice bucket.

"I'm glad I got rid of that fund," he said. "Back when it started, good old fashioned cancer and heart disease meant people would actually die—"

"Oh hush your dirty little mouth," she teased, handing him a crystal flute of champagne. "Not another word about work. That deal is water that's way, way under the bridge. We're sailin' into much brighter seas. Now, cheers."

She clinked her glass with his, then smiled because, smart and successful as he was, this man didn't have a clue that by dumping his little fund on her and Boxley, he was literally handing over a diamond mine.

109. Washington, D.C.

Boxley found it hard to believe when Agent A told him that Hunter Knightly was working solo, or that no vindictive political enemies had put him up to investigating and denying death claims.

"I found nothing on this guy," Agent A said. "You are correct in your hypothesis that this Hunter Knightly fellow is simply a random monkey wrench who just happened to fall into the wrong machine."

"Time to extract him," Boxley said, "and toss him out."

110. Miami, Florida

As the sun rose over the Atlantic, Juan sat on deck with his laptop to retrieve the day's list of Orders. They included a profile that differed greatly from the others. This happened occasionally, such as the Order last week for the attorney in North Carolina. That guy had been only 64, with a net worth of only half million dollars.

But now, this name and profile practically jumped up and danced off Juan's laptop computer screen:

Hunter Knightly, 44, Lexington, Kentucky. Insurance Investigator, independent contractor for a dozen companies. Drives Hummer. Flies Maverick SoloJet. Married to Meredith, 39, marketing executive for nonprofit literacy group.

Juan was going to take care of this guy anyway, after he'd gathered enough information by observing Hunter to solve the "claim denied" and "death claim" mystery.

Juan followed the directions K had given him to watch Hunter through his computer, observe everything he was doing online, and track his airplane flights. Somehow his phone was blocked from even Juan's best eavesdropping devices, K had reported back. "It's probably," K had said, "some kind of blocker that Hunter had from his SEAL days or his current contacts."

His recent online activity focused on deaths in Diamond Lagoon, including Dr. and Mrs. Price, the botched robbery/murder of Stony Wilkerson, and the car crash of Ernest Bloomfield and Herschel Goodman. He was also all over the insurance industry websites, which Juan found boring, except that Hunter was focusing on any fresh material about policies being sold as "life settlements" or "viaticals" or "death bonds." Then Juan read the subject of Hunter's other recent online searches; *Juan Pantera Diablo. Episcopal High School. Pilot. Miami, Florida. Bogotá, Colombia.*

"You don't exist," Juan remembered his Angel saying so many times during their first meeting at the Chateau Frontenac. Juan felt confident that Hunter would find nothing on him online. Everything—and Juan had once tested this himself—showed that he disappeared after high school, consistent with his story that he went home to nurse his sick mother. All records were erased, including his federal conviction. The prison had no trace that Juan had ever been there; the federal courthouse records revealed nothing about anyone by that name.

But this Hunter Knightly guy, he was the type who could find disgruntled people from Juan's past, like the Ricky Perkins that Juan had refused to hire for a K.C. Team. That motherfucker had left a few phone calls saying he was coming down to Miami today to "convince" Juan to hire him to work for The Panther's most current enterprise. Making a threat on Juan's phone was like dialing 1-800-KILL-ME-NOW!

That made two motherfuckers who needed to be eliminated today.

Thanks to K's help, Juan saw that Hunter had gone online to various aviation websites. He had filed a flight plan and checked the weather to come down to Miami today, arriving at three this afternoon.

I'll let him come to me.

Suddenly the day's activities became as clear as the sunrise sky over the ocean: resolve two problems so that

Juan could get on to the business of deciphering his own mystery.

A Panther always acted quickly, using the element of surprise and a swift, deadly attack. It would be that much easier, as his prey walked right into the killer cat's deadly den.

111. Lexington, Kentucky

Hunter sliced through the water, his feet kicking, his arms pumping, and his brain clicking. All the pieces of this increasingly macabre puzzle had to fit together with perfect precision. Somehow.

Preston Mathers. Preston Mathers. A Diamond Lagoon resident. Dead. Apparent robbery victim. Owner of multiple homes… Colorado… Connecticut…

Hunter blew out a bubble of breath toward the blue tiled pool bottom, then turned his head. He glanced through his goggles at the wall by the deep end of the indoor pool here at the health club. A bright green poster said *Enjoy your life! Don't settle for anything than the best! 23 days until the Winter Fun Fest!*

The words joined the steady stream of ideas in his mind.

Life… settle… 23… Preston Mathers.

That was it! That name sounded so familiar because that was the claim Hunter had denied back in December. The beneficiary—that damn Chrisma Corp. that seemed to have a phantom owner—was trying to cash it in just 23 months into the incontestability period. But no insurance policy was "ripe" for the taking—if the person had lied and died before 24 months had passed.

Preston Mathers. On the paperwork, he was listed as Preston "Stony" Mathers Wilkerson, but Hunter had taken to shortening his name to Stony Wilkerson, the name on the cover letter when Hunter had received the assignment to investigate the case. And the claim had listed his home address in Greenwich, Connecticut.

No wonder a bell had not clanged in his head when he'd visited the Mediterranean style mansion down in Diamond Lagoon. Polly Chesterfield had called him Preston Mathers, and neither the nephew nor his partner Zack had said Stony or Wilkerson.

So, *that* was the death claim that Hunter had denied back in December. Had this man been a victim of the life settlement henchmen who were killing for profit?

And if so, what was the fallout at Chrisma Corp. when the 15-million dollar claim had been denied?

Hunter swam faster. Who was behind this? And where was the money going? His thoughts propelled him a whole length of the Olympic-sized pool without turning his head to breathe. It was the perfect muscle-burning exercise to top off his workout. At the end of the lane, he climbed out and pulled off his goggles.

"You swim like a torpedo," said an older gentleman who Hunter recognized as a retired developer for upscale homes in suburban Lexington. "At 76, I consider myself lucky to be swimmin' at all. Sure do wish I had your stamina, though."

"Why, thank you, sir." Wealthy men like this—and Hunter's father—were the perfect prey for the "death bond" killers. While Hunter knew of no such cases here in Lexington, it certainly was possible.

Plus, that slippery Wuerthberg down in Florida had Dad's information. Hunter's gut ached with guilt. What if some crooked insurance guy were committing fraud right now, using Dad's identity to get a life settlement arrangement, with a plan to kill Dad in two years? Hunter needed to figure it out—and put proof in the hands of the proper authorities.

I have to stop this. Now.

Later today, he would return to Diamond Lagoon, at Lauren Price Miller's request, to join a meeting with her lawyer. Hunter saw this an opportune time to learn more about Ernest Bloomfield and Herschel Goodman. If anyone proved the men were victims of murder, then the claims would not be paid. But the accident, as far as Hunter understood it, sounded like exactly that. An accident. Hunter knew it was no accident.

Dripping wet, he hurried to the locker room. He dried his hands enough to pull his phone out of his locker, then dialed A-K.

"Hey man, I need one more favor. Should be pretty simple."

"That'll be three plane rides now, buddy!" he said over his usual video game battle sounds. "To the Bahamas! Someplace hot. Water, boats, sun!" A-K's laughter shot into Hunter's ear. "OK, what 'cha need?"

"When you trace the claim for Ernest Bloomfield, I need you to look into what happened with a guy named Preston 'Stony' Mathers Wilkerson."

Laughter shot through the phone like A-K gun fire. "Holy guacamole, Batman! How many names does this buster have?"

Hunter smiled. "Enough to confuse a lot of people. I denied a claim on this guy awhile back. Just wanna see if there's anything more to it. I got a hunch there's a lot more."

"Hey, I found out who owns Chrisma Corp. It's a senator from Louisiana. Had more layers of holding companies and other bureaucratic bullshit than I cared to count. But—"

"Gerald Boxley?" Hunter asked, stunned. "The guy who's helpin' the Vice President with the new Social Security law?"

"You get the prize, smart guy! Just took ownership of it last year. Looked like a piece of shit fund that MagnaCorp couldn't wait to dump."

"Make that six plane rides," Hunter said, "and we'll fly to Hawaii."

"Always love a little seaside getaway. At your service, Stallion Six."

As he hung up, Hunter knew right away.

Carrie's behind this. She's using this insurance money to rebuild the Social Security Trust Fund. She'll make out like a hero, probably get elected President like she always wanted. And skim off a huge Fabergé nest egg of her own.

Now it made sense. She was puling it off with hidden companies, secret veils of bureaucracy and names, and electronic transfers. Nobody would ever know. The 20- million worth of policies that the dead dentist and his wife signed over to relinquish to a "blind" fund was LivesVest. And the face on that name was United States Vice President Carolyn Snedegar Taylor.

"Hells bells!" Hunter exclaimed. "I gotta stop her." But who could he call? With no proof, he'd sound like a lunatic. Even Commander Buck would think it sounded crazy.

Hunter needed more than a theory. And evidence to connect the killings all the way up from the streets to the White House. Who were the next layers down, after Boxley?

He remembered seeing Boxley at Sailfish Marina with Juan—and that mysterious suitcase. Was Juan a hit man? Was that a suitcase full of cash to pay for a killing? And if so, where was the cash coming from?

No one could get arrested or prosecuted based on a far-out theory like this. Without proof, Hunter would sound like one of those wacky conspiracy theorists who insisted that the government staged the moon landing.

Who would ever believe that the government—the beloved, beautiful Vice President—was killing innocent old people—to capitalize on their insurance money and bail out Social Security?

112. Miami, Florida

As seagulls flew and cawed around the yacht, Juan logged into the Portal, determined to find evidence to back up his theory. He kept thinking about Boxley saying "claim denied" and Hunter saying "investigating an insurance death claim."

A denied insurance claim would mean that no one got paid. And anyone who was expecting 15-million dollars and didn't get it, would be highly pissed off. No wonder Boxley had called a special meeting with Juan to reinforce the need for clean hits that looked like natural deaths and accidents only. This one had been "botched," Boxley had said, ordering Juan to remind all Killing Crew Leaders to reinforce the need for perfect jobs.

This had been the only such situation that Juan had experienced. And it happened with Freddie Buford's K.C. Team just after Thanksgiving. Looked like a robbery-murder for a guy in Diamond Lagoon.

Juan searched the files for that Order. In blue letters, the name Preston "Stony" Mathers Wilkerson popped onto the black screen. That was the same name that Hunter had been researching.

Meanwhile, Juan added to Freddie's Orders for the day two names: Hunter Knightly and Ricky Perkins. Their two-for-one carried special instructions: *at airport hangar at 3 p.m. today.* Juan knew the Orders would go to Lonnie, who would be working on Juan's car shortly after he would leave to fly South to handle some crucial business.

A Panther always had perfect timing.

Now, two seagulls landed on the starboard ledge between the deck and the water. Endless blue water and sky framed them.

"Get the fuck off!" Juan ordered. Those birds were such a nuisance, shitting all over the deck or dropping their germy feathers. "Go!" They screeched and flew off.

Now Juan needed to find out what company, person, fund or government agency was holding Preston Mathers' worthless life insurance policy.

And since Juan wasn't supposed to know anything about the insurance connection to his work, he needed to keep his hands clean. Couldn't go sleuthing around online. If the Emperor and Company were so ruthless, maybe they were monitoring his calls, his online activity and his meetings. Then again, they were probably so busy counting their money—and confident that the convicted drug lord would be so content with his freedom, women, cash and the high life—that they didn't ever have to worry about him.

How wrong they were. With every angle that Juan analyzed his situation—and the people who put him in it—he became more determined to skim his big fat cut from this conspiracy of fortune, and disappear into Bahamian island air.

Literally. He had already asked K to grant him access to the military's control of Google Earth. Said it was for surveillance for an assignment. But what Juan had really done was manipulate the lenses and Earth-mapping to make Casuarina Cay disappear from satellite pictures of the Bahamas. Anyone searching for his private island, his future place of refuge, would see a beautiful expanse of water. But no land. No runway. And no Juan.

"Leave me alone!" Juan shouted at four birds that had the balls to clench their claws on his yacht's railing. He glared at their beady eyes. He'd blast every one of them to bits if they didn't fly away.

Juan had to call K now. That guy knew how to handle business. He was available around the clock; seemed like he was always awake whether Juan called at three in the morning or high noon. His Angel—*that bitch!*—had said K was working for Juan and Juan only. Computer geeks like that knew better than to double cross someone as high ranking as his Angel. So, as Juan dialed him, he felt confident that what was exchanged between them, stayed between them. Juan said, "I need everything you can find on a guy named Preston 'Stony' Mathers Wilkerson. Including who owned insurance policies on him when he died last December."

"At your service, Mr. Panther."

For Juan, it was all making sense. An insurance claim had been denied because something had been wrong with the hit. The timing? The method? That article in *Retirement Magazine* said those life settlement policies could only be sold after two years. And it was at two years that the old people who got suckered into the "death bond" deals would sign them over. Within six months, they magically appeared as Orders in his Portal. Then, *bammo!* They slipped and fell, crashed into a tree, or had a sudden heart attack.

All courtesy of Eldorado and his Killing Crews across America. Perhaps the Emperor and the Angel had equipped Juan's plane with the Green Box because they were planning to expand their trillion-dollar enterprise overseas. Start with wealthy seniors in Latin America—it was ripe for the picking in places like Rio, Bogotá, Buenos Aires and countless other cities. Then—Europe, Africa, Australia, Asia. No wonder they gave him a little jet that was as fast as a rocket—so he could globe-hop to do maximum work in minimal time when the foreign orders appeared.

Maybe they weren't planning to toss him back into Hell. Maybe they were simply planning to work him to death. Rage shot through him so violently, he pulled his gun from his pocket. That fuckin' seagull was on the ledge of the yacht again. Suddenly, in Juan's mind, that bird was his Angel. Another bird landed beside it. A third one—

Pow! Pow! Pow!

His Angel—in the chest, tumbling backwards.

Boxley—blew the head off, sending the body airborne.

And whomever the fuck was giving orders to Boxley and the bitch. That motherfucker splattered—red feathers spraying up against the blue sky, blowing on the breeze.

All three... shark meat. Shot 'em all so fast, no chance to fly away. Didn't know what hit 'em.

Juan's every cell seethed with resentment that this was how "they" wanted him to serve his country. On a moral level, straight-up killing people ranked far worse than providing street pharmaceuticals to numb the pain of life and let people have a good time. Even if a few people did O.D. and die every once in awhile.

But this Angel, and Boxley, and whoever was behind them—they were the moral equivalent of Satan. And for using Juan as their head henchman, they deserved to pay.

Ten billion dollars, to be exact. They would never miss it.

113. Lexington, Kentucky

As Hunter packed his travel bag in the bedroom, Meredith was dressing for work. She had come home last night, apologizing for her accusations. He listened; none of it seemed to matter. Soon he'd be gone, serving his country, leaving Meredith and her drama behind. He didn't even bother to mention the upcoming assignment.

This marriage is over. I need to tell her...

She slipped into a baggy black sweater dress that she only wore at "that time of the month," always complaining that she was too bloated for her slim-waisted pants and skirts. So that was the culprit. Plus, she'd spent a long time in the bathroom, and her face looked puffy and pale.

"You feel okay today?" he asked.

With her back to him, she sat at her vanity and put on small diamond stud earrings. In the mirror, she her eyes glowed with anger.

"How 'bout I make us some breakfast before I go?" he offered.

"Uh," she groaned, brushing her silky yellow hair over her shoulders. "When you comin' back?"

"Don't know," he said, wishing he hadn't even tried to interact with her.

"That's quite a big deal of a case you got down there in Florida," she said. "She's really takin' center stage. All your other poor little cases are just sittin' there in your office, all sad and lonely."

Hunter put his running shoes in his bag. That swim this morning would do for today, but tomorrow he'd take a jog. Exercise always helped him think. And he couldn't wait to get away from this raging bitch who shared his bed. If she kept this up, they'd never sleep together again, though.

"Honey," he said. "I've been thinkin'. It's time that I help relieve your misery of bein' married to me. Clearly I'm not makin' you happy anymore."

She stood up, spun around, and threw the hairbrush at him.

"Bullseye," Hunter said calmly even though he wanted to punch the wall. "Right in the solar plexis. So I'll take that to mean you agree with me."

"No!" she screamed, clutching her stomach. "I'm pregnant!"

After shocking long moments, he hugged her. Kissed her. And her rage melted into passion. Passion that overwhelmed them both until they tumbled into an erotic tangle on the bed.

114. Near Aspen, Colorado

An icy fist of fear squeezed around his chest. The eerie blue light of the enormous projection screen—with its gun-toting aliens marching across an orange planet to face a two-headed beast—cast an ominous glow on the Sig semi-automatic. It always sat beside the game controller here in the big leather chair facing the screen.

I might as well swallow a bullet right now.

What had started as a seemingly innocent way to help an old SEAL buddy, had turned into what could look like the deception of the century. And any idiot knew that if you deceive a panther, *The Panther*, you got pounced. Of course, he wasn't supposed to know that the mysterious man he was working for was a convicted drug lord who'd been pulled out of prison to do work as dirty as any crimes committed by third world dictators.

But how could they have put him—a computer genius who once hacked into the Pentagon just for the fun of it—without expecting him to figure out who was calling him at all hours to do background checks on thugs across America. All races, all ages, all sexes. They were all working for The Panther. And the friggin' Vice President of the United States had masterminded it all, with a U.S. Senator as her pawn. He had her to thank for this great gig.

But like even the best of Halo 3 and Xbox 360, all good games had to come to an end. He would show his gratitude for all the fun with a secret email, warning her about the demise of Eldorado.

She's ready, thanks to me.

Meanwhile, on each side of him were computer keyboards and four large computer screens. They glowed with maps and databases and The Panther Portal, making it easy to help sort, organize and submit the information that the Panther fed into it every day.

Find out everything you can. Ernest Bloomfield. Herschel Goodman. Preston "Stony" Mathers Wilkerson.

For The Panther and for Stallion Six. Whatever they were trying to figure out, K already knew the answer. He'd known it back in December when it happened. But it wasn't his job to divulge information like that. A-K also knew that both Juan and Hunter were figuring it out like two race-horses running neck and neck. There would be a deadly photo finish to determine the winner.

Regardless, this was the swan song for K. A-K. Agent A. Daniel Monroe.

He always loved a good fight. But there was no way he could win this one. He smiled. What would happen if he crossed a Panther and a Stallion?

115. Kendall-Tamiami Executive Airport KTMB

Once he landed, Hunter had his plane pulled into the hangar to check the air pressure in the tires. He'd just read an article reporting that low air pressure could cause the "check landing gear" alarms to sound, as they had during his arrival in Florida last week. This hangar was about five stories high; its gray floor shined below a Lear, a King Air, two G-5s and a sleek black Navajo. Another aviation hangar that was so clean, a guy could eat off the floor.

I'm gonna be a Dad. Hunter still couldn't believe it, even though Meredith had shown him both the home pregnancy test and the paperwork from her doctor's office. It was still early, just a few weeks. But Meredith said she'd known since the night before his first Florida trip that magic had happened in her belly. Now she had the proof. Given her age, and the scarring in her womb, she would face some risks. But overall, she said the doctor gave her an optimistic outlook.

Then why don't I share that optimism? Part of him didn't even believe she was pregnant. Yet in those fleeting moments of belief, his heart pounded with excitement. But it slowed as he pondered the sad truth that their relationship was strained at best. Having a baby—and facing at least 18 more years of bickering—would only invite more tension into the marriage.

"We'll park her out on the tarmac when we're done," the mechanic said. "Should be ready soon, anyway, Mr. Knightly."

"Thank you," Hunter said. He had about 20 minutes before he'd take the Executive Flight courtesy car to meet with Lauren Price Miller. As Hunter stood in the hangar, something caught his eye. It was red, and parked all the way through the hangar, outside in the adjacent row of garage-style hangars.

A little red jet. Juan's plane.

Hunter positioned himself behind a stack of wooden cargo crates to watch unnoticed. A little black Jaguar pulled up. The license plate said PANTHER. Juan, wearing all black with dark glasses and his hair in a ponytail, stepped out. A guy hopped into his car and pulled away, while another guy used a tug to pull the plane out of the hangar and onto the tarmac.

Hunter went into the lobby and watched Juan take off. Man was that plane a beauty. But why was his tail number blocked? And where was he going? What did he do for a living?

"That guy's about the coolest pilot I've seen," Hunter said to the receptionist whose nametag said Sarah.

"Oh, yeah, Mr. Diablo," she gushed with a starry-eyed look. She nodded toward a glassed-in office where three women were having a meeting. "We all have a crush on him. But they shouldn't call him Panther. They should call him Playboy. The biggest one in town." She giggled. "And so nice, so polite."

"What's he do?" Hunter asked casually.

"Travels a lot, sometimes with his girlfriends. We just stand here—" she let her eyes get big and her jaw drop "—because it's like a beauty pageant when they strut through here. Every man just stops and stares!"

"Does he own a business?"

Sarah shrugged. "I get the feeling he's one of those rich guys with a trust fund. All he does is globe trot with beautiful women." The phone rang. "Must be nice," Sarah said. "He always pays in cash. And 100-dollar bills at that! Excuse me, sir." She answered the phone.

What in the world did Juan do to afford a plane like that? Hunter knew one thing: Juan wasn't a trust fund baby. Back at Episcopal, he frequently gave a speech as senior class president about how a scholarship from Colombian benefactors had paid his 20-thousand dollar annual tuition. He also tugged at everyone's heartstrings by embellishing how his single mom was raising him alone, because his father had died.

Carrie's eyes would always glaze with sympathy when she heard that story for the umpteenth time. "Love a guy who could break *down*, but breaks *out* instead," Carrie had said once. "He has every reason to be depressed about his dad. But he's our class leader. You gotta admire that."

But at the 25-year reunion last April, Carrie had kept her cool around Juan, like everyone else, as he explained that since graduation, he'd been down in his native country, nursing his sick mother, burying her, then working for an aviation company.

For Hunter, as he walked back through the hangar toward Juan's still open "garage," that story just didn't add up. A can rolling across the asphalt between the big hangar and the row of smaller ones caught Hunter's attention.

"Yo, hoss," the young guy in Juan's hangar called, "toss me that can."

Hunter, wearing gold aviator sunglasses and a beige baseball cap, picked up the can of Armor All. He stepped into the bright sunshine toward the guy in Juan's hangar, which had the same shiny gray floor and beige metal walls as the larger hangar. Lining the walls of the 50-foot-square space were a refrigerator, a red tool chest on wheels and a small black couch facing a huge, flat screen television.

At the center of the space sat Juan's black Jaguar; the guy was bending down, using a towel to polish the black rims. Hunter tossed him the can.

"Thanks, hoss," the guy said, standing slightly and looking at Hunter. He wore a blue jumpsuit.

"Sure thing, buddy." Hunter immediately recognized him as the electrician who'd been at the Price's house to investigate the fuse box that had allegedly killed Dr. Price. Then, as now, the guy's nametag was said JOHN. The first time around, after telling his story about being a country singer named Lonnie, the guy had registered in the shady zone on Hunter's B.S. meter. So what the hell was he doing in Juan's hangar?

"It's hot as blazes in here," Hunter said, noticing a large metal fan in the back corner. "Want me to turn on that fan for 'ya?"

The guy eyed him suspiciously, his gaze trailing down Hunter's white dress shirt and crisply creased khakis with loafers. "Sure, dude." The guy sprayed the tire and wiped it shiny. Then he lit a cigarette.

"Hey man, put that out. Unless you're tryin' to torch the place," Hunter said. "Smells like jet fuel in here."

The guy shrugged. "I used to work at a gas station. Smoked all the time. Nothin' ever happened. To me, anyway." The guy laughed.

Hunter didn't. "Man, you got the hook-up in here. Nice TV—" Hunter's voice stayed smooth and steady, but his insides were reeling with revelation. Because the television said in gold letters across the top "We appreciate your business. The Genuine Insurance Group."

Stolen. Hunter knew it right away. And that Mediterranean mansion in Diamond Lagoon, the one owned by the man who was killed during a robbery. "They stole a huge flat screen," Polly had said. And the victim had turned out to be Stony Wilkerson—the name on the death claim that Hunter had denied back in December.

Was Juan somehow connected? Was this the same TV? If so, how'd it get into Juan's hangar?

"Wow, where'd you get that sweet-ass flat screen?" Hunter asked.

"Everything around here is sweet," the guy said. "Open the fridge. Help yourself."

Hunter did; it was full of beer, champagne and soda.

"What's it like workin' on that jet?" Hunter asked. "I saw it take off from the other F.B.O."

"Same thing," the guy said without looking up. "Sweet. Sweet as hell. State of the art everything. That shit'll blow your mind. And my man always pays me—" he looked up at Hunter. "You ain't a fed, right?"

"Heck-ee-no," Hunter said playfully. "You couldn't pay me to work for the government."

"Anyway, hoss pays me in cash. It's cool. I don't ever have to pay taxes on that."

How the hell was Juan makin' so much money? And why was this life settlement perk in his hangar? And if the TV had been stolen from the Diamond Lagoon home of Preston 'Stony' Mathers Wilkerson, and if he were possibly the victim of a botched life settlement murder, was Juan somehow involved?

"His business must be boomin' if he can fly a two million dollar airplane," Hunter bluffed.

"Where you from? You got an accent."

"Grew up in the South. Live all over now."

"Sweet," the guy said, moving to the other side of the car. As he did, something black—the butt of a gun—protruded from his right front pocket. "This part of the country, for what The Panther does, it's a goldmine."

Hunter casually stepped back to the refrigerator. "Hey man, mind if I grab a water? They're workin' on my plane, should be done in a few."

The guy shrugged.

Hunter took a beer and cracked open the tab. The beer fizzed. "What's he do? Maybe I need to change my line a' work—"

A rough-sounding male voice interrupted: "Hey, I'm lookin' for The Panther." A white guy in sagging jeans, white gym shoes and a football jersey stood at the garage entrance with his arms crossed, one foot forward, his head cocked slightly to the side. With a brown goatee against pale skin, and oversized dark glasses, he wore silver hoop earrings in each ear.

John a.k.a Lonnie stood in a way that let the guy see he was strapped. So was Hunter, but neither of them needed to know about it.

"He ain't here," Lonnie John said, stepping toward the guy.

"We had a meeting," the visitor said. "When's he comin' back?"

Lonnie John shrugged. "What's your name? I'll tell 'im—"

"Call 'im now. Just say Ricky's here, like he asked, ready to work."

"I don't take orders," Lonnie John said, hands on hips.

"You will when you find out who I am."

"I don't give a fuck who—"

The visitor stepped forward with thuggish bravado.

Hunter stepped between them. He slipped an arm around the visitor and guided him out. He glanced back and winked at Lonnie John, who crossed his arms and nodded in a way that meant nothing but trouble.

"Maybe I can help you," Hunter said to the guy. "We'll find out when The Panther's coming back. You can talk with him then."

Meanwhile, this guy was about to give Hunter the inside scoop on why the hell Juan was known as The Panther.

116. The Cayman Islands

Juan stood in the shiny white, futuristic chamber. He faced a small, mirrored box. A tiny blue light flashed as the machine read his iris. No fingerprint, no I.D., no conversation. Just an iris scan.

And the doors slid open.

Juan walked into the sleek little room where a man in a dark suit said, "Welcome."

"I need to open a new account," Juan said. He already had accounts and money there, from his previous life. The Cayman Islands had proven to be the best place in the world to do banking.

But the deposits he was about to make would be mammoth in comparison. From here on out, everything would be electronic. Anonymous. Exhilarating.

As Juan left the bank, which was in a bustling strip of businesses and restaurants along the water, K phoned. Juan stepped to the edge of a white railing facing the endless expanse of ocean. The same ocean that he would soon be looking at, everyday for the rest of his life, from Panther's Peak. He kept remembering how his Angel said he and his work "didn't exist." Well, she would soon be saying that about him—for real.

"I found out everything you need," K said. "First, the policy for Stony Wilkerson didn't get paid. It was owned by a fund called LivesVest. LivesVest also owned the policy for your two old guys in Florida, Bloomfield and Goodman. Their policies did pay, 12-million apiece. Same for their wives. That makes 48-million."

"Who owns LivesVest?" Juan asked.

"There's a holding company. I had to peel back some layers. It's changed ownership over the past year. Now it's owned by Chrisma Corporation. And the principal for that is Senator Gerald Boxley."

Juan's body felt like a volcano was erupting at his core. Red-hot rage surged through his limbs like molten lava. He could almost feel steam shooting from his ears. He bit down hard, to stop an explosion of expletives from shooting out of his mouth.

"Anybody else?" Juan asked.

"No, Mr. Panther. Boxley is the only name anywhere to be found."

So all that money was going into the LivesVest fund. And Boxley was the gatekeeper. But there had to be someone behind him. He was the front man, the fall guy. And the only way to get more information now was to ask Boxley himself.

He's got his hand in the cookie jar and he's tossing me crumbs for doing the real work.

Juan breathed deeply several times to cool the flames of rage licking at his composure.

"K, before I let you go, one more thing. Authorize a wire transfer from the LivesVest fund, into a fiduciary account for a special project." Juan gave him the account number and routing number for his new account here in the Cayman Islands. Juan needed to space out the transfers, to avoid suspicion while he sought the Emperor.

"I need a transfer every 10 days," Juan told K.

The FBI techno-genius let out his peculiar laugh. "Mr. Panther, this is the easiest assignment you've ever given me. So damn easy. It's not like you're asking me to hack into something."

"Make each transfer for one, plus nine zeroes. One billion."

"Piece of cake," K said. "This is like a one-click kind of hook-up."

Ten clicks, actually.

117. Near Aspen, Colorado

Agent A for Boxley.
K for Juan.
A-K for Hunter.
And Daniel Monroe on his soon-to-be printed death certificate. He was all things to all people in this twisted triangle of deception and deceit. And to whom should he devote his final attention and intelligence? His videogame flashed purple and blue on the screen before him.

"I like it when the bad guy wins," K said. So he dialed The Panther and stared into his computer screen at the same time. He was about to set off an earthquake in Eldorado.

"Hello Mr. Panther," K said. "Your transfers are on schedule. The first one just cleared; you'll see another one every 10 days, as requested."

"*Gracias.*"

"*De nada, senor.* Mr. Panther, I've got some more info for you."

"Knew you would," Juan said.

K laughed his trademark laugh. "You know this has been the freakin' easiest assignment you've given me. Once I blasted through multiple firewalls and cracked the certificates of authenticity—"

"Don't confuse me with technical terms," Juan ordered. "Give me plain English about the money. Where it starts, where it ends."

K took a deep breath. He was totally betraying the smokin' hot Vice President; she and Boxley had made it clear from the start, back in February, that one whisper about this would mean immediate death.

I'll take really good care of her. He typed out that email, so it'd be ready to send to her at the right time. Then she could save her own brilliant ass with the Plan B that he'd helped her orchestrate, by getting the gun from a buddy in Iraq. Then she could flee Eldorado as its firewalls came tumbling down.

K's cleverness made him smile. "Okay, Mr. Panther, here's the deal. Every time your Crews handle an Order, and an old person dies, their huge life insurance policies drop into this ginormous fund— LivesVest. It's so huge, it's like the ocean, and every policy is like a drop of water."

"Why does the money go there?" Juan asked.

"It's a sneaky, but legal, insurance deal. The filthy rich grandmas and grandpas get cash for signing up. Then they sign over the policy in two years. You have to wait that long for any life insurance policy. They sign their policies over to a 'blind fund,' which is LivesVest."

"Who's behind it?"

"As I told you, LivesVest is owned by Chrisma Corp., which Boxley secretly owns under multiple Internet veils. When the money comes in, Boxley skims off his cut. Then somewhere along the line, thanks to EFTs with digital certificates in the SSL protocol—"

"English!" Juan's voice punched through the phone.

"I'm sorry, Mr. Panther. I just get such a kick out blasting right past all the new banking laws."

Juan's silent impatience shot through the phone.

K said, "What it boils down to is that LivesVest makes weekly money transfers into the Social Security Trust Fund. Holy smoke, I'm looking at it right now online. The transfers look like automatic EFTs, like a company paying payroll taxes. And the electronic tags make it look like the money's coming from block grants from LivesVest, as if it's a debt being paid."

K laughed and said under his breath, "She is brilliant."

"What?" The Panther demanded.

"This is brilliant," K said. "Because when the money pops into the Social Security Trust, it looks like it's coming from the U.S. Treasury, where all those Social Security 'donations' would be coming from the Vice President's new SOS Plan."

Juan groaned. *Carrie...*

"But the money's really coming from all the Orders that you're filling."

"Death bonds," Juan said as the whole operation clicked in his head.

"Well, this is a death bond conspiracy of magnificent proportions," K said. "I have to warn you, Mr. Panther. There's someone else who's figured this out. He's on a mission to expose Eldorado and bring it down. But I got a plan for The Panther to stop him in his tracks."

118. The Cayman Islands

Juan felt like a firestorm was howling through his brain as he listened to K's plan. His dream about his father warning him to get out before they used him up and tossed him out, played in his mind... going backward into Hell...

Paradiso! I deserve to live like a king and will do anything to maintain my empire.

He had to get to Boxley and extract more confirmation about the power structure behind Eldorado. Despite K's explanation, Juan still found it impossible that a woman–*Carrie!*–could be behind his Angel. There had to be a man, a powerful white man, calling the shots. Was it President Anderson? Someone in the Middle East? If Sheik Sunami il Tabbul was claiming to be the culprit for America's economic crisis, could he have masterminded Eldorado to reap the enormous fortune that K had just described?

Regardless, as Juan stood beside the Caribbean not far from his secret island escape, he had just put two and two together. "She's killing people," he whispered. "So I am."

119. Kendall-Tamiami Executive Airport KTMB

Hunter guided the angry guy into an open hangar garage that appeared unoccupied. No plane, no car, no items indicating that the space was being used by a pilot. It was the last hangar before the wide-open tarmac area leading into the airport lobby and the runways.

"Let's step in here to talk," Hunter said, guiding the guy out of the blazing hot sunshine and into the hangar. The huge garage door remained open.

"The Panther," the guy said, "he was a big-time drug lord back in the eighties. You never heard 'a him?

What kinda rock you been livin' under, man? Juan was the biggest drug dealer this side a' the moon."

"You worked for him?" Hunter asked as a tug pulled a black Navajo past them, onto the asphalt area where it stopped at the fuel pump. This guy's bad-ass posturing was failing to hide the fact that he was just a two-bit hustler whose "inside information" could get him killed.

"Hell yeah, I was rulin' from South Beach to Key West. We fell out though. He thought I was snitchin' on him. Got real paranoid before he went down. Started using blow all the time. They threw his ass under the prison." The guy laughed, taking a pack of cigarettes from his pocket.

"Don't smoke," Hunter said. "See that fuel pump right there?" The long cable was stretching from the white fuel pump—which had a red FLAMMABLE symbol on it—to the nozzle that was pumping gas into that black Navajo.

"Sorry, man," the guy said. "So now that he's back out, word on the street is, for anybody who wants to get *payyyyd,* Juan's the guy to call."

"What kinda work you lookin' for?" Hunter asked. He smelled jet fuel, but figured it was the breeze making it waft this way.

"Wait, who the hell are you?"

"Just an old high school buddy a' Juan's. I was down here on business," Hunter said, "thought I'd look him up. But I just missed him. Watched his plane take off just before you came."

The guy spat, "Fuckin' A, man!" He watched the Navajo pull away from the fuel pump and taxi toward the runways. "That's a sweet-ass plane. But I hear The Panther's got the shit."

"Seems like a good guy to work for," Hunter said. "Successful."

"I got three a' my homies workin' for him. One in Dallas. One in Jersey. One in my town, Phoenix. Easiest work you can get. Fat-ass cash, too."

Hunter smiled. "Sounds like somethin' I should get into. This economy, things are tight."

"Wouldn't know it if you're working for Juan. Not only are you takin' down crusty old bajillionaire motherfuckers, but I hear you get five K a pop."

Hunter felt dizzy.

The scent of jet fuel, the heat, and…

Juan is behind all of it.

But who the hell was behind Juan?

"So you're here for your job interview?" Hunter asked, forcing his voice to sound cool and calm. A static sound filled his ears. His blood was rushing as his heart pounded at the thought—

Juan uses his little red airplane to oversee murders across America. Old people. For insurance money.

"Woulda been," the guy said, glancing back at Juan's hangar, where the garage door was coming down. "Looks like I just missed him."

Hunter heard a trickling sound.

The ground was shiny. Wet. But it wasn't raining.

Hunter looked toward the fuel pump.

A wave of Jet A fuel was surging across the asphalt toward them. The pump was on the ground, gushing out gold liquid.

Whoosh!

120. Washington, D.C.

Juan was waiting in Boxley's office when the senator returned from his session on the Hill. Boxley's caramel complexion turned as pale as oatmeal when he saw Juan sitting on the couch, petting Kat.

"Close the door," Juan said, handing biscuits to the dog, who remained next to Juan despite his beloved owner's arrival.

"Where's my staff?" Boxley asked.

"Anthrax scare," Juan said. "Some powdery white stuff came in the mail. They all breathed it in. You just missed the paramedics. Hazmat suits and everything."

Boxley's eyes grew huge and scared. He reached for the phone.

"Close the door and sit down."

Boxley crossed his arms. "I don't appreciate your tone of voice."

"Close the door and sit down."

Boxley did as told.

"What is LivesVest," Juan demanded. "Tell me what am I being paid to do. Sit down and answer me."

"You've got a lot of gumption coming in here," Boxley said, standing by his desk. "What you're being paid to do is highly classified government—"

"Cut the bullshit," Juan said. "Tell me the truth."

Boxley's lower lip trembled.

"Sit the fuck down," Juan said. "If you're gonna play silent, I'll tell you what's going on. We're knocking off people who have huge life insurance policies and the beneficiary is your company."

Boxley sat on the leather wing-back chair facing the couch. He crossed his leg and laced his fingers together, resting them on his upper leg, halfway between his knee and his hip. "I'm going to chalk this extremely inappropriate outburst up to the mental anguish you must have endured in 23 hours a day of solitude."

Boxley's words only ratcheted Juan's determination up a notch.

"Solitude that you can easily revisit if you decide you are unhappy with this assignment and the extremely privileged lifestyle that you're enjoying as a result," Boxley said.

"Tell me the truth," Juan said, petting the dog's head. "Tell me that I'm getting paid to kill rich old people so that their life insurance proceeds flow right into your company."

Boxley tilted his head back and laughed in his upper crust way. Deep, controlled, egotistical.

"I'm afraid you are sadly confused, Juan. That is not at all what you're doing. Your mission is simple. There are these people who have no reason to live. People who've been privileged all their lives. And they need to go away."

"You're bullshittin' the wrong guy," Juan said flatly.

Boxley reached for the crystal decanter of scotch on the coffee table, just like Juan knew he would. He took a tumbler, used silver tongs to drop ice cubes from the ice holder into the glass, then poured a generous drink. He took two extended sips.

"Juan, this conversation is over," Boxley said.

"Who's calling the shots for you?" Juan asked.

"I said this conversation is over." Boxley took two more sips.

"I have proof that two of the most recent hits in Diamond Lagoon paid 12-million apiece into your company."

"I'm afraid that you are sadly misinformed," Boxley said. The ice cubes clinked as he raised the glass. That motherfucker was so nervous, he was shaking. He took another gulp.

"Who's calling the shots for you?" Juan asked.

Juan removed a clear glass vial, the size of a woman's pinky-finger, from his pocket. It held bright blue liquid.

"I poisoned your scotch," Juan said. "You've got two minutes to live." He held up the vial. "Tell me what I want to know, and I'll give you this serum. You'll live."

Boxley turned gray-beige.

"Tell me," Juan said, "and this conversation never happened. We'll all leave as friends. Working together. Prospering together."

Boxley eyed the serum. "You're bluffing." He coughed. And coughed harder.

"Carolyn," Boxley said, loosening his tie.

"Carolyn what?"

"She's the mastermind. It was all her idea. She calls the shots."

"Who's telling her what to do?"

"Nobody."

"The President?"

"No, no, he has no idea. He believes her SOS Plan—"

"So it's all about that?"

"Yes, to save Social Security."

"By killing people?"

Boxley nodded.

Juan held the serum close to the Senator. "Let's go talk to Miss V.P. right now. So she can tell me what's going on, and who's the boss. Get up."

"She's in New York," Boxley gasped. "At the Waldorf—"

Juan offered the serum to Boxley, who lunged for it. Juan snatched it away. Boxley fell to the floor, holding himself up by the coffee table.

"Oh, there's one more thing," Juan said. "There's no need for you anymore. You built a pretty nice company for us. But you've just been replaced." Juan opened the vial.

"Give it to me!" Boxley groaned.

Juan drank it, tilting his head back. "Ahh. Gatorade. Drink of champions."

Boxley groaned. Collapsed to the floor.

"C'mon Katrina," Juan said, tapping his thigh. "Let's go. We got one more stop to make."

121. Kendall-Tamiami Executive Airport KTMB

The flash of flame... the silvery wave of heat in the air... it all made Hunter think of the Greek God Mercury... sprinting so fast that he was flying.

That's how Hunter felt as he ran, then dove into an open hangar garage.

The flames *whooshed* in front of him.

And a gun cocked behind him.

122. New York City

The thrill of standing before a thousand financial types here on this stage in Manhattan was even more thrilling than the night she'd announced her SOS Plan on global television. Because here in this hotel ballroom, she was standing behind this podium on a lighted stage, facing the brightest of the bright on Wall Street and all the financial giants headquartered here in the center of the universe.

To her right, on the dais, sat the man who was helping her make it all happen. Neal Worthington, CEO of Magna Corporation, the world's largest financial institution. But even its holdings would someday look paltry compared to the massive fortune that Carrie was masterminding right under the noses of all these arrogant, Ivy League pricks. Those stockbrokers and hedge fund managers and money managers—they called themselves

Masters of the Universe. They were now all humbled by the economy.

And she was beating them all! She was sure some of her high school classmates were in this audience, guys who'd told her in statistics class that the female brain wasn't hardwired to handle complicated numerical formulas.

Ha! Those pricks could eat cake right now. Because she was having hers and licking her fingers, it was so good.

"Right now, as I'm sure your clients have informed you, the ultra rich across America are receiving in the mail their instructions to contribute their Social Security back into the fund," she spoke like she owned the place. Her voice was strong, her confidence high, and her exuberance made every word pop. "Some enthusiastic supporters have already contributed their checks to the fund."

She smiled, making eye contact with several men in the audience. She was sure that even the most professional and respectful among them still viewed her, on some level, as T & A. Sure, she was second in command of the most powerful country in the world. But these men—the heterosexual ones, anyway—would bone her if they had the chance. That fueled her ambition even further; someday, as President, she would prove to all of these men just what a woman could achieve.

And the only man among them that she wanted was the one with the most money—Neal, sitting to her right. And she secretly had the one with the libido that wouldn't quit—The Panther. Neither of them would ever know just she was getting over on them, and building her golden Eldorado as a result. She was outsmarting them both, and would keep it that way. Forever.

Having the brains and the beauty to get what she wanted, well, a girl couldn't be happier. Some girls married rich to secure their life of luxury. Other girls worked their asses off to earn it—like the blue-suited women in this audience—still making 73-cents for every dollar a man earned. But Carrie had every gold-digging bitch out there beat by the biggest long shot in history. And nobody would ever know.

"Ladies and gentlemen," she continued. "The tremendous outpouring of support for my SOS Plan across America exemplifies the amazing spirit of good will that our ultra rich are exhibiting toward less fortunate people."

When Carrie finished her speech, the audience shot to its feet with a thundering ovation. Neal was taking her to dinner at the exclusive new Opaque restaurant, for a custom-cooked meal by the world-class chef, in a private room.

She just had to dash up to her room to freshen up, and slip on a dress over some sexy undergarments. And top it off with her black mink. It was so cold and gray here. Her four Secret Service guards walked her to her hotel suite. As they arrived, an agent came out with a bomb-sniffing German Shepherd and said, "It's all clear."

The men stood outside in the hallway as she entered and closed the door. She kicked off her shoes, then unbuttoned her jacket. The lights and classical music were already on; a gas fire glowed in the fireplace. She strode through the living room toward the double French doors leading to the dark bedroom.

Standing by the window, in the eerie glow of city lights—

She gasped.

He knows.

Juan Pantera Diablo focused those Panther eyes at her. She gasped again. Because this time he was not casting that seductive make-a-girl-melt look down on her.

His eyes burned with enraged lust for power. She stood, frozen, staring into his eyes, stunned. What now? In every other encounter with him, she had had all the power. All the control. All the knowledge.

Now, he knows. This wasn't part of Plan B. She'd only considered if something happened to Juan; she'd never thought about him having the balls to turn on *her*. Now, if she screamed or ran—

I'm dead.

Her breath felt like it was caught sideways in her throat. Her chest was still. But her heart was banging.

What the hell should I do?

Sugarcoat it. Play dumb. And win.

"Juan, darlin'." Her attempt at a sultry whisper sounded squeaky. She noticed movement, on the dim floor, something wagging. A dog. She gasped as it trotted toward her. It rubbed its nose against her leg. The blue eyes of a spotted gray-brown dog stared up at her.

"Katrina, how'd you—"

Carrie went numb.

Boxley's dead. Now Juan's here to kill me, too.

123. Naples, Florida

In his sun-splashed, modern kitchen, Stanley Goldstein opened the metallic bag of Kenyan coffee beans. This was the best brand; he had to order it online. And like clockwork, his weekly supply had arrived by delivery yesterday afternoon.

It was only eight o'clock in the morning; he had plenty of time to sip his coffee on the back terrace, read the paper and relax before the meeting with his lawyer. Marty was coming down here to get more information about Stanley's clear-cut case of fraud against that Wuerthberg slickster and The Genuine Insurance Group. And Marty said, he was planning to file a class action lawsuit on behalf of the families of other seniors who had mysteriously died shortly after relinquishing their life settlement policies.

"God, I love this place," Stanley said, looking through the kitchen windows as the sun sliced through the humid air over the golf course and moist vapors rising from the green. He stood at the counter, watching two flamingos strut across the golf course and splash at the edge of the pond by the sixth hole. At the same time, Stanley held the coffee bag up to his nose. He glanced down at the shiny brown beans, then inhaled their delightful scent. "God, I love my life."

He had worked hard to earn this life of leisure and luxury for himself and Alice. They were good people, not perfect, but they deserved this. And Stanley wasn't going to let anybody jeopardize it.

His gut cramped. He didn't need this coffee. It would just have him going to the bathroom even more. But the soothing sensation of that hot liquid on his tongue, with just the right amount of cream and sugar, would calm him before the meeting.

"Just one cup," he said. Then, hopefully, after Marty took care of this, Stanley could get back to the business of enjoying himself here in the closest thing to paradise he'd ever experience.

The beans pinged into the grinder; he pushed the button and it roared. Then he poured the beans into a filter, which he set it inside the coffee maker. Poured in the water, pushed a button, and voilà.

Just a few minutes later, he was standing on the terrace, gulping down the last drop of his first cup. It was so delicious, and the warmth in his belly soothed him all over.

"Oh, forget it," he said, making a beeline back inside for the steaming pot. "One more cup isn't gonna kill me."

124. New York City

Carrie would fake it 'til she made it. No matter what. She was not going to let this rogue killer steal her glory.

It was all my idea. And I'll be damned if I let him take it!

She stroked Katrina's head. "You a jet-setter now?" she cooed, her confidence returning.

"I got a deal for you, Carrie."

"No," she said sweetly, "I'm afraid you're mistaken. I make the deals here. I'm in charge of you. And if you forget that, there's a nice little cell in solitary confinement with your name still on it. They're holdin' it for you, Juan, just in case things didn't work out."

Juan smiled. "Carrie, I got a deal for you."

"You bastard," she spat. "I don't know what the fuck you think you've figured out. You can't cross me. You won't get away with it. And believe me, there's a half dozen other convicted felons I can yank outta prison to do what we need done."

"Who is we?" Those Panther eyes were like a damn stun-gun. When he looked a certain way, she just felt paralyzed. She loved that in the bed, but not now.

She glared back, crossing her arms. "What do you want?"

"I'll take care of everything," Juan said. "Don't replace Boxley."

"I have to have someone at that level," Carrie said.

"No you don't," Juan said, stepping close. "Your secret is safe with me, Carolyn Snedegar Taylor. I'm here to help. The Panther and his Angel. Silent partners. Nobody needs to know anything. Give me my space, I continue my work, you continue being the toast of the town. I want nothing but success for you, Carrie. Just answer one question: where is the cash coming from?"

He stepped closer. She backed against a wall.

"Did the money come from Saddam's palaces?" he asked, leaning close. "Uncle Sam wouldn't just deposit all that loot back into the Treasury. Tell me, Carrie."

Her chest rose and fell, not with lust, but with fear. Her own perfume rose with the scent of nervous sweat from her panting chest. His cologne and his natural raw man pheromones made her head spin. Between those eyes and his machismo, this man had supernatural powers.

"I'm in charge!" Carrie shouted up at him. His face was inches above hers; his hair was loose, like a dark cape.

"Keep it down, Carrie," he whispered with his deep guttural rasp. "You don't want your Secret Service men to tell the President you've been a very bad girl."

"They'd come in here and shoot you dead," she spat up him.

"And you'd have a lot of explaining to do," he said. "If anything happens to me, I've made arrangements for the President and the world media to receive a detailed explanation of just where you're getting the real money for your SOS Plan."

"You brilliant bastard." Her right hand rose; she would smack his beautiful cheek—

He caught her wrist, squeezing hard.

"You're quite the brilliant bitch yourself," he said. "If you're really working alone, you've masterminded the most brazen, lucrative conspiracy ever. Calling on my services, well, you knew we'd make perfect partners. In bed. And in crime."

"I don't need a partner," she snarled, yanking her wrist out of his grip. "I hate you!"

125. New York City

Juan knew it now. Brown-haired, brown-eyed Carrie had the same sassy expression in her eyes, and defiance in her voice, as the blond-haired, blue-eyed vixen who'd welcomed him out of prison.
Carrie is the Angel.
A wig, contacts and a spray-on suntan, plus a different way of talking, had fooled him. Or had it? He loved Carrie, always had. He hated the Angel, for using him. But they were one and the same.
And The Panther had to look out for himself, and keep this pretty little pussy cat purring under his control.

126. Kendall-Tamiami Executive Airport   KTMB

The metal pressing against the back of Hunter's head could only be one thing: the barrel of a gun.
"Time's up, Columbo," Lonnie John said behind him as sirens roared and black smoke plumed from a wall of flames just outside the garage. "This way."
The guy pulled Hunter's arm, turning him around, marching him to a door at the back of the hangar. At the first opportunity, Hunter would overpower him and get away.
The gun pressed harder into his head as the guy said, "Go through that door. Get in the truck."
The metal-on-scalp sensation continued as Hunter stepped into the hot sun onto a gravel lot behind the hangar. To the right was a dark green Dumpster; to the left, empty brown boxes. The black SUV had dark windows and its engine was running.
The door behind the driver opened.
"Get in," Lonnie John said, pushing him and getting in behind him. Heavy metal music blasted from the stereo;

the air conditioning was ice cold. A thin, brown-haired guy with pockmarks and dark glasses was already in the back seat. Hunter squeezed in the middle between him and his abductor.

As the SUV sped off, the tip of Lonnie John's gun now found its home at Hunter's temple.

Hunter's brain ticked at warp speed. He had to bust out of this car. They'd already tried to kill him with fire. He never would have escaped if he hadn't been super-fit and fast. Chances were, the other guy, a smoker at that, was probably dead. A smoking corpse.

"To the boat?" the driver asked with a husky voice.

"Yeah," Lonnie John said. "The Panther wants to do this himself."

"Always love a good fight!" the driver exclaimed. He laughed loud—like a machine gun. The sting of betrayal, the metallic taste of danger on his tongue, and the shock of it all, made Hunter feel numb.

A-K turned around. Pale, scrawny, malnourished, hair in greasy clumps under a black Xbox cap. He was half the man, literally, that Hunter had known as a SEAL.

"Stallion Six!" A-K said, "looks like we're takin' a ride on a boat instead of your plane. Hope you don't mind."

127. New York City

Juan's evil eyes mesmerized Carolyn as she struggled to outsmart him.

"I'm your partner now," he whispered.

"No! I'm in charge. You take orders from me!" She tried to twist away.

He pinned her against the wall. "You'll have everything you want," he said close enough to kiss her. "I'll take care of business. And I'll take care of you." He pressed his mouth to her parted lips. Then he whispered, "Yeah, I'll take care of everything."

"I hate you!"

He smashed his lips into hers. Why had she chosen such a sexy man to do her dirty work? Why had she mixed business with pleasure? Why had she ignored what she knew about herself—that she loved bad boys—and let it come to this? Because she had seen it as foolproof. She thought Juan would be so happy to be a free man again—with every high tech toy, a bevy of women, a yacht—

And me! The man gets to fuck the Vice President of the United States of America! Now he wants more?!

The rage burning through Carrie's limbs only blazed hotter as Juan kissed her. He pressed his long, lean body against hers, ran his fingers up through her hair in that dominating way that made her cream her panties every time.

She loved and hated everything about him, all at once. The domination in his eyes. His potent sexuality that made her absolutely defenseless. His brilliantly criminal mind. His fearlessness. His win-at-all-costs attitude.

He's everything that I want to be.

And when she yielded her body to him, letting him inside, she was, in a way, sucking up his essence to literally become part of hers. She needed the power now, to figure out how to beat him back into submission.

Because she hated this feeling of being tricked. Overpowered. Controlled.

But she had no choice. She would never become President of the United States if anyone besides Juan ever discovered Eldorado. Without Boxley, and without Juan, what would she have? Juan was in charge of the rank and file crusaders of death all across America. Without Juan, who would do the work? And now that they were doubling the Orders to get as many paid before that stupid estate tax black hole in 2010—when the government would really get screwed—she had to comply.

Juan picked her up and laid her on the bed. Yes, she would let him in, one more time. She'd let him think he was winning. Then she'd strike when he least expected it.

128. The Ocean near Miami, Florida

With AK-47s strapped over their bulky shoulders, two hawk-eyed men sat facing Hunter on the deck of this enormous yacht called *The Black Panther*. They'd been sitting here for hours, since the SUV had stopped in a field by a waiting helicopter. Lonnie John had forced Hunter inside at gunpoint. And they'd flown to this boat about a mile out from the sparkling lights of South Beach, which reflected off the black water. A soft drizzle danced atop the water, visible only in the yellow glow from the yacht's lights.

"You got it all figured out now, Stallion Six?" A-K asked, laughing, then biting into a huge sandwich exploding with meat, cheese, lettuce and tomato. Hunter hadn't eaten all day and his metabolism was especially revved by that swim this morning and the adrenaline of fear. What if he never lived to see his own baby? What if Juan continued killing senior citizens and stealing their money with the crooked Senator Boxley and Vice President Taylor? What if nobody ever found out?

"You always were too smart for your own good," A-K said. He came close and whispered: "I do owe you an apology, though. I was too stupid to know you were workin' against my boss. Remember I said, if I told 'ya what I was workin' on, I'd have to kill 'ya?"

A-K let out his characteristic laugh. "I'm afraid that was more prophetic than either of us would like to believe.

When I realized the idiotic shit I was doin', I knew my days would be numbered, too. Sorry, Stallion."

Four beautiful women in bikinis strutted past again. For the third time, they looked at Hunter like he was some caged bird, sitting here with two armed guards for their viewing pleasure.

"He's gorgeous," said one chick with long black hair.

Another, with a British accent, said, "Get your bloody mind out of the gutter."

They turned on a TV built into a wall panel near the guards.

"Find the weather," a girl said. "It has to stop raining for the party tomorrow."

"...the Vice President gets a rousing applause," a reporter said, "when she addressed the financial industry in New York today. She tells GNN that she's building momentum for a summit with federal lawmakers tomorrow morning in Washington, to talk about her SOS Rescue Plan for Social Security."

One of the women on the boat exclaimed, "She's hot!"

"Turn it!" another one screeched. "Find the freakin' weather report."

The deep beat of helicopter blades drew their attention to the sky. The women cheered.

"Love a good fight!" A-K exclaimed. "A Panther and a Stallion—fight to the death!"

Hunter's heart pounded. He could leap into the black water and swim away. But the bodyguards, who had tossed his gun, wallet and phone into the ocean, never looked away from him. Nor did they loosen their grips on their assault rifles. The roar became deafening as the helicopter landed on the roof of the yacht.

"Reunion number three," Juan said, strutting in wearing all-black and a ponytail. His eyes shimmered with intrigue and evil as he walked toward Hunter. "Welcome to my humble boat, my friend."

Hunter said nothing.

A dog followed Juan from the outer staircase leading to the helicopter pad.

"What a pretty dog!" the women shrieked, rushing in from the sliding glass doors opening onto an opulent living room with couches, chairs and a long gleaming bar with stools.

"Go inside," Juan ordered; the women scattered like so many ants.

That dog looked familiar. The guard dog, the suitcase. From Sailfish. That was Boxley's dog.

Juan killed him.

Juan stood in front of Hunter and glared down with those big, mesmerizing eyes. His voice was hard, almost scratchy, as he demanded, "Who told you to spy on me?"

"Our good friend from high school," Hunter lied. "She wanted to see just how good you were. Obviously not good enough."

"You're bluffing," Juan said. "And flirting with a shark swim."

"She put me on your tail as a test," Hunter said, glancing at A-K, "to find leaks in the system."

"Liar." Juan handed a phone to Hunter. "Ask her yourself."

The phone rang once. "Ooohh, I knew you'd call, darlin'," Carrie drawled. "After a thrashin' like that, you got a girl feelin' all languid. Even if I am still pissed off, 'ya brilliant bastard."

So Juan and Carrie were literally in bed together. Hunter felt sick to his stomach. He couldn't get through to her, but she was cavorting with this murderer!

I have to get off this boat—alive—and have them both locked up. Or a lot more people are gonna die.

129. The Ocean Near Miami, Florida

Juan's only question: How should he kill this Southern rich boy who'd just sniffed up the wrong tree? A money tree, guarded by The Panther.

Execution style? Strangulation? Or make shark meat out of the high school swim champ turned Navy SEAL?

"I don't like interference," Juan said, glaring down at this all-American boy whose father and mother would visit him at Episcopal and treat him like a little prince. Juan hated this guy's wholesome look and the humble façade over his cockiness. "Interference. That's what you are."

The doors to the cabin burst open. Gigi came running out, giggling. Cheyenne was chasing her, followed by Josette and the rest of them.

"Give us the bottle!" Josette shrieked. Gigi, gripping the champagne bottle, ran in circles around the bodyguards.

Juan pulled his gun from his pocket. Gigi stood between the guards and Hunter, holding up the bottle, teasing them.

"Go inside!" Juan shouted.

They giggled, lunging at Gigi and the bottle.

And Hunter Knightly dove overboard.

130. The Ocean Near Miami, Florida

Gunshots popped and boomed around him as he dove three stories, from the upper deck to the ocean. He punched through the surface, plunging deep into the water. Bullets rained on the surface all around him. His hands pierced the inky blackness. Holding his breath, he dove deeper. Then he'd swim parallel to the shore, head toward land, and go straight to Washington. He would go to the Attorney General himself and ask him to arrest the Vice President.

131. Kendall-Tamiami Executive Airport KTMB

Carolyn sure appreciated Agent K's kindness, letting her know that all hell was breaking loose between them boys. That gave her plenty of time to execute Plan B. Now here she was, in her Angel disguise—the blond wig, the blue contacts, the spray-on suntan—getting out of a rental car at Juan's favorite little airport down here in Florida. Now all she had to do was climb on that adorable jet she gave him, and wait for The Panther to whisk her away to *paradiso*.

Who knew such a small plane could have such a comfortable cabin? Plenty of space to stretch out and watch the world news explode in the palm of her hand:

"United States Vice President Carolyn Snedegar Taylor now believed... abducted by Sheik Sunami il Tabbul from her luxurious penthouse condo in Washington, D.C." Video on her BlackBerry Storm showed the exterior of her building, then poor Russell. He'd be in a panic about this, and the authorities would come looking for him if anybody ever discovered Eldorado and the Killing Crews.

The anchor said, "Her chief of staff discovered the bodies of four Secret Service agents, shot dead with a gun traced to the battlefields of Iraq—" The report showed pictures of those poor men who died in the line of duty inside her foyer.

Then Carolyn's picture flashed across the screen. She smiled. Just about everybody in the world was looking at her picture, talking about her and wondering when the hell she'd show up. And if they'd ever see her alive.

Maybe someday. For now though, it was time to disappear.

132. The Ocean Near Miami, Florida

This was Juan's cue to exit stage right from this high-stakes drama. Now. Hunter was a champion swimmer. It would be a waste of precious time to drive the boat up and down the coast looking for him. He could go to the police, or to Carrie or to whomever else. And he would take Juan only one place: down. *Hell no!* Juan was about to go up, up and away, and disappear on Panther's Peak. He turned to K. "Did you handle that second transaction today?"

K stood. "Of course I did, sir. There should be one automatic transfer every 10 days now."

"Good work," Juan said. Then he blew a bullet in the center of K's pale forehead.

133. Miami, Florida

Hunter crawled onto a dark spot on the beach. His heart felt like it would explode and his lungs were on the verge of bursting. So he sat there, panting, for just a minute. Then he ran to the street, caught a cab to the airport.

"Had an emergency," he told the mechanic, borrowing 20 dollars to pay the cab driver.

"Tires are ready," the mechanic said. "Careful, though, we couldn't fill up the tank. Accident earlier today blew up our fuel station."

Hunter sprinted to his airplane. As he was programming a flight to Washington, D.C., he was glad that the midnight hour meant air traffic would be light.

He'd be there in no time—
Something red blurred past him.
Juan!
Hunter fired up the plane and shot off behind him.
Never knew he'd be using his 8,000-feet-per-minute features on this plane to chase the baddest of bad guys. But here he was.

Juan's thugs had taken his phone, but his address book was downloaded into his plane's verbal command telephone system. He had to call Commander Buck—

"Shit the bed!" Hunter exclaimed. "Only got half a tank a gas!"

The sultry computerized voice soon reminded him of that. But all other systems were ready to ride. How much fuel did Juan have? Where was he going? And if he took off at laser speed, as he had that morning over Florida, Juan would leave Hunter in the dust.

"Commander Joseph Buck," Hunter ordered. A dialing sound filled his headset.

"Stallion Six!" Commander Buck shouted over a siren in the background. But the line disconnected.

No, he had to tell somebody what was going on. He had to tell authorities to arrest the Vice President for murder!

"Commander Joseph Buck," Hunter ordered. A dialing sound filled his headset.

The red lights on Juan's plane glowed in the dark sky. He was getting farther away.

Phone static crackled; the line disconnected again. Juan's scrambler had to be the culprit.

Hunter was going to catch him, report him and Carrie. *Or die tryin'.*

134. The Sky Over the Atlantic Ocean

Two billion dollars. A private island invisible to satellite surveillance. And his two favorite bitches in his private jet. In his headset, he could not hear them in the cabin, but when he'd picked Gigi and Cheyenne over the other girls, they'd shrieked like they'd won the lottery. They didn't know they'd be gone forever.

The Panther rules! Nothing, no one, could stop him now. Not even that country bumpkin motherfucker trying to chase him in an airplane right now. A VLJ, sure. But nobody could beat Juan's military-grade machinery.

Even if Hunter had a full tank of gas, he could never outlast Juan's long range, triple tanks.

And Juan was quite sure, that ole Kentucky boy didn't have a Green Box. While Juan could fly right across the ADIZ, anybody else would get shot down by the U.S. Air Force. Even a death-defying swim champ named Hunter Knightly.

135. The Sky Over the Atlantic Ocean

Hunter hoped he could make it to Bimini—just 53 miles east of Miami—to refuel and somehow catch back up with Juan. But he had not filed a flight plan to obtain clearance to fly over the international border. Any unidentified aircraft buzzing over the ADIZ was asking for a hail of bullets from an F-17—or at least an interception and an escort back to the States for a heavy-duty interrogation. Especially since the latest terrorist threat and the President's beefed up patrols. Patrols that Commander Buck was overseeing.

Hunter couldn't just fly to the Bahamas. Unless he got clearance from Commander Buck. But the phone still wasn't working.

Besides, Juan was zig-zagging through the clouds like a drunk driver. He flew west, then north, then south again.

Hunter pulled out his laptop and with trembling fingers typed an email: "S.O.S. Navy SEAL Hunter Knightly 137 ... approaching ADIZ... low fuel... ARREST Vice President, LivesVest, ChrismaCorp, Senator Boxley for Death Bond Conspiracy..."

"All systems malfunctioning," the computerized voice warned. The three avionics screens turned to snow. Just like that day when Hunter had first seen Juan. It was him. He had activated the scrambler on his plane, like Air Force One, to scramble all avionics within a certain distance around his jet. "All systems malfunctioning."

Hunter addressed the email to Commander Buck, Randal, and his contacts in the FBI, the CIA and the White House. Then he pushed SEND.

"All systems malfunctioning."

Then, suddenly, Hunter's three avionics screens turned to normal.

Did my message even go through?

"All systems go," the voice said. "Warning, low fuel. Warning, low fuel. You now have 100 pounds remaining. Refuel now."

"He's fuckin' with me," Hunter said, his stomach cramping as he watched the Fuel graphic on the Garmin dip below an eighth of a tank.

Plus, Juan was flying through thick clouds. So Hunter activated the synthetic vision. He was sure that Juan had the same.

But how much farther could he fly?

If he actually ran out of gas, his all-plane parachute would save him. But even that would be treacherous swim number two for the day. As a SEAL, they'd simulated plane crashes in the water. The key was to stay calm, and to navigate out of the plane in a way that didn't allow the water to gush with such force that it knocked him out. Also, he had to get out of the craft before it sunk too deep into crushing pressure or a distance too far to hold one's breath on the way up.

He'd also have to swim away from the airplane. Otherwise it could snag him and drag him down, or suck him down with the force of its sinking. And he'd have to get away from the parachute and its cords, lest he'd get tangled and pulled down with the plane. At least, since his fuel tanks were empty, they would act as floatation devices for a few extra seconds.

"No!" Hunter had to survive. He had to save himself and all the innocent people who would keep dying if he died. Because no one else on the planet knew exactly what was going on. "Only me."

Suddenly Juan turned southeast again. And he was heading straight for the ADIZ.

136. The Sky Over the Atlantic Ocean

Operation Vanish was in full effect. Juan smiled. He was about to shoot over the ADIZ. By now, Hunter would be out of gas, plummeting into the ocean to join the eerie lore of the Bermuda Triangle. And Juan would be lovin' life on his island paradise.

"Aye, mamacita," he groaned. "The Panther rules."

A female scent, and hot breath on his cheek, made him freeze. The headset lifted from his right ear and he heard: "Juan, darlin', I sure do love this little airplane I got for you." A blond curl fell over his shoulder.

He slowly turned in disbelief. His Angel—with Carrie's smoldering brown eyes—winked back. "I cannot wait to see your little island. The girls have been tellin' me all about it back here. We're all gonna lay on the beach and just *relax*!"

137. The Sky Over the Atlantic Ocean

Hunter was flyin' on fumes. And staring in shock that Juan had just flown his pretty red jet over the military-patrolled ADIZ. No F-17s yet, but...

There... lights showed up on both sides of the plane. Two F-17s flanked Hunter's plane.

He would have to turn around and go back to Florida.

But he couldn't.

"Refuel immediately!" the computerized voice warned. All three screens flashed red. "Refuel immediately!"

"United States Air Force to Tail Number 137 Hotel Kilo. Please return to Miami, Florida, and proceed to United States Customs."

"Danger. Zero pounds of fuel. Danger." The Garmin screens blinked red.

Then Hunter heard what every pilot dreaded: silence.

The engine died. No gas.

His altitude dropped from 5,332 feet to 5,001 feet.

Hunter trimmed the airplane stall speed. He reached up. Yanked the handle on his parachute. His stomach flipped as he continued to plummet. With a sudden jerk, the plane stopped falling. Then it floated down, down, down.

"F-17. I am Hunter Knightly. Navy SEAL Number 137 Hotel Kilo. Access my Private Navy SEAL File CST489. Have the Vice President arrested for murder."

The battery continued to power the electronics. The outer lights, red, green and flashing white, provided the only light over the churning black ocean.

Hunter's heart hammered with terror.

He was about 25 feet above the water, as far as he could tell. Would he survive? Would he ever see his wife or his parents or his unborn child? Would Juan and the Vice President get away with murder? And would old people continue to die at the hands of this wicked conspiracy?

He remembered a saying that Commander Buck repeated often in Spanish: "Lo Que Sea, Cuando Sea, Donde Sea." It meant, Anything, Anytime, Anywhere.

Hunter opened the door. The wet wind slapped his face.

He thought of his family... his child... all those innocent old people. Hunter Knightly had to save every last one of them. And himself, first.

So he dove into the ocean and swam for his life.

THE END